A C R O S S   F I V E
VALLEYS

AN HISTORICAL NOVEL OF THE
AMERICAN CIVIL WAR

ACROSS FIVE
VALLEYS

AN HISTORICAL NOVEL OF THE
AMERICAN CIVIL WAR

WAYNE E. TAYLOR

Word Association Publishers
www.wordassociation.com

Printed in the United States of America.

ISBN: 978-1-59571-425-1
Library of Congress Control Number: 2009930970

Word Association Publishers
205 Fifth Avenue
Tarentum, Pennsylvania 15084
www.wordassociation.com

Cover Design and Painting by Linda Kay Whitesel

DEDICATED
TO ALL THE
MEN AND WOMEN
WHO CONTRIBUTED
TO THE EXTREME
EFFORT TO KEEP
OUR NATION UNIFIED
1861-1865

INTRODUCTION

The little village of Academia of mid-western Juniata County, Pennsylvania, and its surrounding region abounds in history. About two miles southwest of Academia in a field bordering the Tuscarora Creek just north of Bryner's Bridge on SR 3019 is situated Book's Indian Mound. In 1929 an excavation at this site uncovered the remains of twenty-six Native Americans, which were believed to be three to four thousands years old.

More than a mile downstream from this burial ground is an area known as Half Moon. Half Moon received its name because the Tuscarora Creek makes a huge loop to the south and then meanders northward. For several hundreds of years, Half Moon was the location of Native American habitation, the last known in the mid-eighteenth century as Lackens or Lacken.

Below the Half Moon area, an early settler, John Patterson, constructed a dam for a gristmill. The dam was reconstructed several times, but nature finally removed all but a few traces of the impoundment. A few yards below the dam, a covered bridge was constructed in 1902, replacing an earlier bridge. The Pomeroy-Academia Covered Bridge has withstood the ravages of time and flood, and in 2008-09 it has undergone a complete refurbishment due to the outstanding leadership of the Juniata County Historical Society. This bridge is the longest remaining single-span covered bridge in the state at 271 feet and 6 inches. It is listed on the National Register of Historic Places.

The village of Academia is situated north of Half Moon and since the 1760s has been graced by the Lower Tuscarora Presbyterian Church. In 1837, the Tuscarora Academy was established under the auspices of this Presbyterian church. The Tuscarora Female Seminary was chartered in 1857 and joined the church and the academy on the hill. The female seminary and the academy are the opening setting for this endeavor, just prior to the outbreak of the American Civil War.

For most of my life, I have been intrigued by the Academia, Pennsylvania, area. The area known as Beaver's Meadows of the Pomeroy Dam on the Tuscarora Creek above the covered bridge was one of my family's favorite picnic spots. I have pictures of my brother Wib and me swimming in the Tuscarora Creek in that area. We spent many Sunday afternoons in the early 1950s with relatives and friends enjoying fishing, swimming, picnicking, playing ball, pitching horseshoes, playing badminton, boating, floating on inner tubes, just plain having fun.

I remember quite vividly sitting on the middle pier of the covered bridge tempting rock bass, sunfish, pickerel, or black bass with an assortment of lures, although I have to admit I don't remember catching anything worth bragging about.

More times than I can possibly remember or count, I have floated this section of the Tuscarora Creek either in my old Ouachita aluminum canoe or in various kayaks. In more recent years, I have helped to introduce the Tuscarora Creek to numerous fellow kayakers. If you have never experienced the beauty and solitude of this usually tranquil creek, it's time for you to get off the couch and do so.

During my teenage years, my high school classmate Jim Barton, my cousin Glen "Skip" Kepner, and I camped on the banks of the Tuscarora in the area known as Devil's Kitchen. My grandfather, Norm Taylor, introduced me to Devil's Kitchen, one of his favorite fishing holes when he was a boy living in the Academia area during the 1890s.

After I turned twelve, I remember hunting woodcock, ring-necked pheasants, quail, and grouse in the Beaver's Meadows and Half Moon area. However, it was the ridge west of the Lower Presbyterian Church that held the biggest challenge. In the honeysuckle and briar patches west and north of the female seminary was found the best cover for our state bird, the ruffed grouse, and its imported colorful companion, the ring-necked pheasant.

We often trudged past the ruins of the female seminary, always regarding the massive building as a relic from a time long forgotten. It was an intriguing area and as I grew older, the building slowly deteriorated. I read stories about the school and heard legends regarding what occurred within its walls. The same was true with its stone counterpart to the southeast of the church, but the boys' academy was not nearly as intriguing. Even with its plastered stone walls the boys' academy, still standing much as it had since the 1850s, didn't measure up to the allure of its female counterpart to the west.

In the 1980s, my cousin Florence Boyer Henry and her husband, Brad, from New Jersey, purchased a large parcel of land to the west of the seminary. This led to many walks to the structure and as the Henry and Taylor kids grew older, it was impossible to curtail their curiosity about the ruins. They, like many kids from the area, explored what was left of the school despite concern that the delicate walls, a piece of roofing, or one of the remaining doors or window frames would fall on them. Then, too, there was always the possibility that a dozing copperhead snake might be startled or stepped upon and strike out in defense. Luckily, none of the above-mentioned calamities ever occurred and our children moved on with their lives.

In the mid-1990s I enrolled in a series of classes on historic preservation. One of the projects that I undertook was entitled "What Should Be Preserved in Mid-Western Juniata County." Of course, both the boys' academy and the female seminary were included in my study. By that time, it was far too late for anything to be done about the deplorable condition of the girls' school, and my professor and fellow students were appalled that such a noble building had been allowed to slip into such a state of disrepair.

As the class observed slides of the roofless walls and paneless windows, we shook our heads in disbelief. If only someone had truly cared, this once magnificent building could still be with us.

I often have speculated about the impact the two schools could have had on the social, financial, and academic conditions of midwestern Juniata County had the two schools survived into the mid-twentieth century. Today's Academia might have become the home of Tuscarora College or University. How many local students would have matriculated to this institution instead of traveling to similar institutions of higher learning? When one looks at the meager beginnings of many of Pennsylvania's fine colleges and universities, it would not be too far-fetched to imagine the emergence of a fine institution on the slopes of Academia Ridge that might have gained a position of prominence in today's academic world. Remember, Pennsylvania State University began as a farmers' high school in 1859.

Interestingly, the institution of higher learning from which I was awarded my bachelor's degree was at one time separate male and female institutions, located on a hill and separated by a church. Later the two schools were joined as Carson-Newman College.

This, of course, was not to be; instead, the female seminary's existence was of short duration, while the boys' academy was able to continue for almost a half-century longer. Nevertheless, we are concerned about the impact the two schools actually had on the area, the state, and the nation during the mid-nineteenth century.

While I was involved in research for my historical novels, *Hope on the Tuscarora* and *Hope Rekindled,* I was pleasantly surprised to learn that the land upon which the two Academia institutions were located was at one time claimed or owned by one of my Taylor ancestors. It appears that a Robert Taylor (my fifth great-grandfather) sold the land in this area to one John Waddel in June 1754 prior to the Albany Purchase of July 1754. At this time, the government of Pennsylvania purchased the land north of the Blue Mountains from the Iroquois who didn't own the land in the first place.

I have always had an interest in this area, its schools, its bridge, its dam and mill, its fabulous hunting, fishing, and boating possibilities, its church, and most of all, its unique history.

My keen interest in the Shenandoah Valley began when I traveled to Jefferson City, Tennessee, to attend Carson-Newman College. I had studied and read about Stonewall Jackson and the Gray Ghost, John Mosby, and the Shenandoah Valley campaigns of the Civil War, but the valley never caught my fancy until I began to travel the length of it on old U.S. Route 11 on my way to and from school.

My wife, Lucy, shares my interest in the Shenandoah, and usually we make at least two trips each year to enjoy its enchantment, beauty, and history. When we travel to Virginia, we usually take the same route I took as a student, out of the Tuscarora Valley into Path Valley, the Conococheague Valley, the Potomac Valley, and finally the Shenandoah.

In this endeavor, I will take you back to the 1850s, a time of America's intrigue with Manifest Destiny, intertwined with the impact of the Industrial Revolution, the attempt to maintain the Union while peacefully solving the slavery issue, the early quest for Women's Rights, and the movement to provide an education for all Americans.

We will examine the events culminating in the 1860 election of Abraham Lincoln, the secession of the Confederate States, the firing on Fort Sumter, and the advent of the Civil War. We will follow the activities of the Forty-Ninth Pennsylvania Volunteers from the late fall of 1863 when David Evans, the hero of this story, enlists in the unit at Warrenton, Virginia, to the dissolution of the regiment in July 1865.

Unlike my previous endeavors, the two major characters and their families in this novel are fictional, although the majority of the other figures are historical.

CHAPTER 1

FALL 1857

David Evans had been climbing this ridge behind the church that he and his family had attended since he was about six years old. The first time that he had struggled up the steep incline had been with the companionship of his cousin James, when they had stolen away after church services in the early spring of 1850. Unfortunately, two years ago, James's family had moved west to Iowa, and David had not felt close enough to anyone else to consider sharing this unique viewing location.

Today the sun shone brilliantly on the steep slope of what was referred to as Academia Ridge. It was late April, and the buds on the variety of deciduous trees were just beginning to exhibit their desire to burst forth into their springtime ritual of producing a huge green canopy that would camouflage not only this precipitous vantage point, but the entire Tuscarora Valley.

The valley in which David had been born was named after the nation of Native Americans who had emigrated from North Carolina in the early 1700s after they had been nearly exterminated in a series of wars against the white settlers. These wars were referred to as the Tuscarora Wars. The Tuscaroras had sought permission to migrate north through the Shenandoah Valley of Virginia, Path Valley, the Tuscarora Valley, and the Susquehanna Valley of Pennsylvania, and continued into New York where they joined the Five Nations, the Iroquois, and expanded that confederation to become the Six Nations.

The impact of the name Tuscaroras was evident throughout the placid valley, which extends from eight to twelve miles in width and over fifty miles in length.

Directly south of his viewpoint is the Tuscarora Mountain, which serves as the southern boundary of Juniata County, extending from the Franklin County and Huntingdon County lines for about thirty-five miles eastward to the Juniata River. When he looked southwestward towards the village of East Waterford and the gap that allowed the early settlers of the valley passage into the valley on the Trader's or New Path, he saw the pronounced humps of the Conococheague Mountain rising above the Tuscarora. To the north the Black Log, Blue Ridge, and Shade Mountains bound the valley.

Looking either right or left from his vantage point, he could observe irregular ridges and smaller intervening valleys that break the interior of the Tuscarora Valley. The diversity of the topography creates a beautiful panorama offset by the rugged surrounding mountains. The mountains, ridges, and interspersed valleys provide the inhabitants with a variety of lumber products, outstanding hunting grounds, excellent soils for diverse agricultural products, as well as unsurpassed mountain scenery.

Up until about a hundred years ago, near the location of the Evans farm had been the site of a large Native American village known as Lackens. Lackens was located on the northern bank of the creek that also bears the name of Tuscarora. At this unique position, the Tuscarora Creek makes a huge incursion to the south in its meandering to join the Juniata River and creates a geographic oddity that the local citizens call Half Moon.

David loved the Half Moon region dearly. Disappointment had seized him the first time that he had climbed to his current vantage point because a moderately sized ridge located to the north of Half Moon was directly between him and the huge bend in the creek. The slight ridge obscured his view of flat bottomland, which contained the Half Moon area, and impeded his ability to observe his family's farm and the two-story farmhouse in which his family resided.

At this point in his young life, not too much was expected of David Evans. He spent many hours exploring the creek and its surrounding bottomland, as well as the ridge to the north of the Half Moon region. His formal schooling was the realm of his mother, but he knew that this would soon change and he would be attending the boys' academy next door to the Lower Tuscarora Presbyterian Church that his family attended every Sunday.

Suddenly, there was an explosion of beating wings and feathers as a brace of ruffed grouse flushed out of an entangled tree covered with honeysuckle and briars about ten feet in front of him. As always, when this occurred, David was startled and drew back in surprise, but he quickly recovered and marveled at the grace and beauty of the brown-speckled airborne creatures as they gathered speed and height. The grouse's wings are short and broad, designed for maximum flight control in tight situations. It always amazed him that after launching themselves out of dense thickets, briars, or honeysuckles, they could perform lightning-fast corrections in their flight path and avoid collisions with seemingly impenetrable canopies of trees and shrubs.

After achieving an altitude of about twenty-five feet, they leveled off, set their wings, and glided about two hundred yards where he could no longer view them, but he could hear them landing in the small hollow located to the west, seemingly safe for the moment.

He hoped that this was a mating pair so that soon the female would be constructing a nest and propagating their species to continue the life cycle of the beautiful birds. Earlier in the spring, David had heard a male grouse drumming in this area. The drumming is usually performed on a fallen log, which gives the male a vantage point above the forest floor. The male bird braces his stance on the log with his tail and begins to beat the air in short, powerful, forward strokes of his wings. The air movement of the wings produces a sound like low, rolling thunder that can be heard for several hundred yards.

The drumming is a ritual that ushers in the breeding season but can be heard at just about any time of the year. The muffled drumming roar not only challenges other male grouse in the area but also attracts females that are ready to mate. The pairing lasts just long enough for the breeding process to be performed; then the female leaves to begin the solo task of nesting, hatching, and rearing the young. The male moves on to attract another female and performs the breeding process again.

The young grouse are hatched in a nest usually located on the forest floor. The grouse chicks are precocial, meaning they are independent at birth. They are born with a protective downy coat which enables the chicks to get around on their own almost immediately, and they follow along behind their mother and feed on their own.

David moved away from where the grouse had flown and began to climb farther up the ridge in a northward direction. Within two hundred yards he spotted a deer bed pressed into the decaying leaves and freshly emerging foliage. Its occupant had apparently just fled a few minutes before, indicating to him that he was not moving as stealthily as he should be.

He changed his direction northeastward, hoping to gain a better view of the ridge and the hollow below. Sure enough, on the game path to his west a reddish-gray deer was cautiously picking its way below him. The deer moved at a constant pace, constantly scanning the terrain, glancing left and right in a random pattern. It continually flicked its ears, probably attempting to rid its head of harassing mites that plagued the deer throughout their lives.

David noiselessly moved behind a fallen tree covered with honeysuckle, then froze and held his breath, hoping not to divulge any sign or sound that would frighten the deer in a different direction. His diligence paid off as the deer continued to amble on the path right past him. The deer's tail flicked from side to side, usually an indication that all was well within its sight and sound surroundings.

The deer slowly sauntered on the path, continuing its cautious surveillance of its surroundings, and David observed its movements until the game path made a sharp turn to the left, which took the deer farther up the ridge and out of sight.

This was the type of discovery that endeared this ridge to him, and he hoped he could enjoy its beauty and solitude forever. Someday he would like to share this splendor with someone else. Who knows, maybe even a member of the opposite sex?

Reluctantly he turned and headed east, back towards the church and his awaiting parents and sister. Soon he was able to view the steeple of the Lower Presbyterian Church and the cemetery that was located to the west of the church. A church structure had graced this ridge since right after the first white settlers had moved into this section of the Tuscarora Valley.

The church services had been over for quite some time, but David knew he had time to do some exploring of the ridge, because it was the custom of the older Evanses to spend a great deal of time socializing after the church services. Within a few more minutes, he knew from experience that his family would be ready to head home, and he knew that he'd better be on the scene and ready to ride home with them.

As they rode past the boys' academy he realized that in the beginning of November this cluster of buildings would become the focal point of his education, and that his life was about to undergo an abrupt transformation. Was he prepared for this? He was not quite sure, but he knew all too well that November first would arrive sooner than he wanted it to.

CHAPTER 2
HISTORY OF THE SCHOOL

The Tuscarora Academy was the brainchild of the Reverend McKnight Williamson who became the pastor of the Lower Tuscarora Presbyterian Church when he answered the call in the spring of 1835. At his previous charge, Williamson had been involved in teaching the classics. In his first year he taught higher mathematics and the elements of the classics and Latin language to young men in the vicinity of the small village in the confines of his own home.

In 1837, Reverend Williamson moved his efforts into a house owned by Andrew Patterson and attracted fifteen students to profit from his endeavors. Williamson's commitment to teaching and the large void in educational opportunities in the Tuscarora Valley inspired the pastor to conceive the concept of establishing an institution of secondary education. In that same year, he approached the merchant John Patterson with the idea of incorporating an institution in the village of Academia.

John Patterson generously and enthusiastically donated two thousand dollars and several acres of land for the creation of a school. Many other residents of the valley also saw the tremendous need and possibilities for a school and gave liberally towards the school.

The mission of the Tuscarora Academy was to prepare young men of the Presbyterian faith for eventual entrance into the ministry and to provide the model for the public schools of the region.

In 1837, through an act of the Legislature of Pennsylvania, the new Presbyterian institution in Academia became the first secondary education institution in the newly created Juniata County. The legislative act provided for the creation of a board of trustees that would control the operation of the new institution. The act also appropriated two thousand dollars for the maintenance of the school. The legislative action gave the new institution credibility and permanence.

The school welcomed its first formal class in 1839 under the capable tutorship and leadership of Professor David Wilson as principal. Professor Wilson proved to be a very capable leader and continued as principal and teacher until he left the Tuscarora Academy in 1852 and joined the staff of the newly created Airy View Academy in Perrysville.

Unfortunately, during the years from 1849 to 1852, three successive fires destroyed the original buildings that had been constructed beginning in 1839. These fires necessitated the suspension of the school and for a short time it was thought that the school would not recover from this severe series of blows. Undoubtedly, the fires were highly instrumental in Professor David Wilson's decision to move five miles east to the town of Perrysville and the new institution of Airy View Academy.

The staunch Presbyterian leadership accepted the challenge of resurrecting the school from the ashes and rebuilt the institution on a grander and more expensive scale than had existed previously. The buildings were ready for occupancy at the opening of the new school year on November 1, 1853. The major building, a four-story brick structure that measured eighty feet long and forty feet wide, boasted the latest improvement in heating, a hot air furnace. The first floor served both as a boarding hall for students and as a residence for the new principal, Dr. G. W. Thompson, and later, the Reverend G. W. Gartewaite.

In 1816, the "Old Stone Church" had been erected, measuring sixty feet long and forty feet wide, but had been abandoned in 1849 when the new brick church was constructed on the hill above the old church. Due to the series of fires from 1849-1852, the one-story Old Stone Church was remodeled for educational purposes. A second floor was attached to the original floor and the stone walls were plastered.

The first floor of the Old Stone Church was arranged for chapel and school exercises, with two society rooms attached. The second floor contained twelve dormitory rooms for students who could not be housed in the main dormitory of the new brick building. As the student body increased, it became necessary for some students to find board and lodging among private homes in the small village.

The dormitory rooms in both buildings were neither extravagant nor Spartan in décor, but certainly were limited in comfort and coziness. The only furnishings were the beds or bunks, a simple desk, a washbasin with table, and a closet. Any other comforts of home were the responsibility of the student.

Food served family-style in the large dining hall was plentiful, but lacked the refinement to which most of the young men had been accustomed in their affluent homes, Not that the food was flavorless, but it was somewhat bland.

CHAPTER 3
DAVID ATTENDS THE ACADEMY

David Evans began his formal schooling at the academy in November of 1855 when he was eleven years of age, and he was one of the youngest students in attendance. Since his family's farm was located less than two miles from the village of Academia, he was not enrolled as a boarding student. Instead, he rode his own horse, Tuscarora Chief, each day to the school, escorted by two older cousins, Jim Patterson and David Stewart, who lived on farms on the south side of the creek in the direction of the Tuscarora Mountain.

Since their farms were located on the other side of the creek, the cousins utilized the ford that connected the road leading to Ebenezer Methodist Church and the village of Pleasant View, or the one off the Tuscarora Valley Path, known in earlier days as the Tuscarora Path. During inclement weather or when the creek rose too high, the trio would spend the evening at the home of their fathers' younger sister, Elizabeth, who lived about a half-mile from the school.

David proved to be an outstanding student and a promising candidate for the law or medical profession, although teaching and the clergy were not ruled out, but that was a decision to be made later. He became involved in numerous extracurricular activities, many of which were religious in nature. Singing in choirs and glee clubs were of major significance, as well as involvement in debating societies.

Although he was deeply involved in his studies and school activities, he spent much of his free time fishing, hunting, and canoeing on the Tuscarora Creek. He still had responsibilities involving the farm. From the time he entered the academy in November of 1855 until May of 1857, he did not attend the school during the summer term that ran from May until September. During those formative summers, he was expected to perform the duties of a regular farm laborer. He learned to plow, harrow, and disk with a team of horses and was very much involved with the oats, wheat, and rye harvests.

The labor he performed during those long hot summers enabled him to appreciate where the money originated for him to attend the academy. His body also underwent a tremendous evolution during those sun-up to sundown hard labor activities, as his muscles and overall body growth increased to pre-manhood proportions.

Early in November 1856, David came home from school all excited. "Mother, Father, I've been invited to join the Philomathian Society. The society's name means 'lovers of learning,' and its primary objective is to further the intellectual and social needs of the student body.

"I will be given a Philomathian Society badge to wear on the left chest pocket of my waistcoat. The badge is deep blue and sky blue in color, and it has a wreath with our motto, 'Knowledge and Virtue,' embodied on it. It should dress up my coat splendidly.

"Currently the society has eighteen members, but with my membership and David Stewart's, the society will contain its full complement of twenty members.

"The Philomathians meet each Monday evening to participate in oratory, debating, book reviews, impromptu speaking, and parliamentary practice. They also hold social events such as dinners, picnics, and ice cream socials throughout the school year."

Mrs. Evans smiled at her exuberant son. "David, it sounds exciting. Just don't get so involved in activities that you neglect your studies."

CHAPTER 4
LEARNING ABOUT LOCAL FLORA

Mr. Evans insisted that his children develop an aptitude for a consummate knowledge of horticulture. While engaged on long leisurely hikes around the farm, along the creek, or up on the ridge, he would quiz them about the type of flora they were observing. If they didn't remember the flowers and plants by their botanical names, the children would be assigned to look them up and learn their spellings.

Mr. Evans would emphasize repeatedly, "You need to learn which species of mushrooms, plants, and berries are edible, just like our ancestors did in this valley. That will enable you to pick wild foods to upgrade your meals when you are out in the wilds, or even at home. You can never anticipate when you might find yourself in a situation where food is not easily accessible, and if you feel confident about identifying the edible species, you might be able to survive indefinitely until other foodstuffs become available.

"It is my desire to prepare you for an emergency so that lack of food will never cost you your life. You should never suffer from lack of nourishment, because there are all kinds of wild foods just free for the eating.

"There are hundreds of edible wild plants in our state and the eastern United States. Don't be concerned about possible poisoning, because with a little practice at identification you should not make any mistakes. We will try to avoid any borderline plants that cause confusion.

"We'll start with several edible wild greens and fruits and each time we go on one of these jaunts, we'll add a few more. Instead of attempting to have you learn all the wild delicacies located on the farm and its surrounding area at one time, I will add a few more edible wild plants each season of the year. In this manner, both of you should soon feel quite confident about identifying various edible, wild-growing plants, berries, and mushrooms. You will be amazed to learn just how delicious many of these can be.

"In a few years you'll be able to readily identify hundreds of wild edibles. For instance, I remember that both of you have enjoyed reading about the Lewis and Clark Expedition. Remember, there was a time on their homeward journey when their food supply was almost exhausted, and they were reduced to consuming just one biscuit a day. To survive they relied on the sweet yellow fruit of the papaw.

"Let's walk down along the creek. We should see several papaw trees in this vicinity. Look for a tree with large drooping leaves, from six to twelve inches long on short stems. The leaves are dark green on top and a paler green underneath. Their fruits look like short bananas, up to about five inches long. They have a bright yellow pulp which, after you acquire a taste for them, has a mellow sweetness."

Shortly, Julie exclaimed, "There's one just on the left. The tree has leaves just like you described. Look, David, there's some fruit just like Father said there would be."

"Now don't be too disappointed if you find the fruit quite bitter at first," explained Mr. Evans. "You really have to try them several times before you begin to acquire a taste for them. Also, it depends on how hungry you might be, but at least you know one good fruit that you can depend upon for food in an emergency."

As the lessons continued, the Evans children were introduced to the numerous common cherries, plums and grapes, crab apples, and the little wintergreens. The berrylike fruit of the wintergreen can be an important emergency food, even in the winter, Mr. Evans told them. He also taught them how to prepare a drink out of the red berries of the staghorn sumac that tastes somewhat like lemonade.

Then there were the common gooseberries, cranberries, chokecherries, and blueberries. The Evans children were amazed at the versatility of the rose family, such as the raspberries, strawberries, and blackberries. Although the ripened berries were the obvious food, the children found that the young stems and stalks were tasty and the leaves could be steeped for tea.

When Mr. Evans pointed out some serviceberries or June berries, he told them that the raw fruit would be better either dried or cooked. The opened umbrellas of the May apples were easily identified. Mr. Evans cautioned them that the roots, leaves, and stems could be poisonous, so they were only to eat the lemon-yellow fruits, which are delectable when ripe.

As time went on, the Evanses learned to gather all types of wild greens. The best known was the ordinary dandelion whose tender young leaves became an instant favorite. Other wild greens added to their growing list of edibles were lamb's quarter, plantain, sow thistle, scurvy grass, roseroot, glasswort, wild cucumber, clover, mustard, watercress, miner's lettuce, wild celery, fiddleheads, fireweed, wild rice, and common chickweed.

"There will be times when potatoes, carrots, beets, or turnips won't be available; therefore, you need to learn the wild roots and tubers. The Natives introduced all sassafras roots, arrowhead roots, Jerusalem artichokes, groundnuts, and the young roots of the cattail to our early settlers here. The toothwort, evening primrose, and spring beauty are also roots you should learn.

"If you learn to drink coffee, you best learn about the roots of chicory, because it can easily be used as a substitute for coffee. Dandelion roots and beechnuts are also good coffee substitutes. Other wild beverages besides all those wild fruit juices I previously mentioned are spearmint, Oswega tea, wild coffee, sweet fern, sassafras, spicebush, birch, sumac, and hemlock.

At the mention of hemlock, the children gasped.

"Now don't get excited about me mentioning hemlock," Mr. Evans exclaimed. "I know that both of you have read about Socrates and the poison hemlock, but those deadly brews of the ancients were entirely different plants extracted from members of the parsley family. Hemlock tea is drunk hot and black, and its taste is reminiscent of the familiar aroma of the hemlock trees we bring into our house at Christmas. Actually, any members of the pine family will provide an aromatic and beneficial tea.

"The numerous pines, firs, spruces, and balsams provide some life-saving features too. One is that you can eat the bright green young tips raw in the springtime. Another is that the inner bark can be cut off and consumed, either broiled or raw, and give enough nourishment to sustain your life."

Suddenly David came upon some mushrooms and asked his father, "Can we eat these?"

Mr. Evans shook his head. "Let's talk about mushrooms when you are older. I don't want you to make a mistake in identification and end up quite ill."

Instead, he talked about the obvious wild edibles in their area. "I think you already can recognize the butternuts, black walnuts, hazelnuts, hickories, and beechnuts. From the time I was a youngster we've gathered these. It just makes sense to gather the edible wild nuts that are so abundant in our valley. All we have to do is keep them in a cool, dry place, and they'll last from one year to another. I know you're not too keen on removing the husks from the walnuts because you end up with stained hands and it takes several weeks of scrubbing to remove the stains. But those sweet kernels are always a treat."

Although the lessons that David learned in those outings with his father seemed rather trivial during those pre-teen and teenage years, they would prove to be invaluable during the dark days of 1863 to 1865. Without them, David might not have survived.

One of the jobs that David enjoyed thoroughly was taking items to be fixed or orders for manufacturing new iron or steel products to the local blacksmith, John Taylor. John Taylor lived beyond Pleasant View, and that meant that David would have to pass the Laird and Barton Store located in the village of Pleasant View where he would buy several pieces of candy or a sarsaparilla drink.

A similar chore was to take messages to Jonathon Packard, who worked as a teamster for valley farmers, delivering seeds, fertilizer, and farm equipment. Mr. Packard seemed to take a liking to David and filled him with a myriad of information about people and events in the valley. David was never in a hurry to return home, and when he did, he was full of stories and new ideas.

CHAPTER 5
DAVID'S INTRODUCTION TO BASEBALL

In May of 1856, David was introduced to the new game of baseball that was sweeping the nation. He began to spend every off-hour from school and farming attempting to increase his skills in the fundamentals of this sport. He was often caught tossing a homemade baseball against the side of one of the sheds or tossing stones into the air and hitting them with a homemade bat. He saw pictures in a copy of *Harper's New Monthly Magazine* of a type of uniform that some baseball players were wearing, and he attempted to sew one for himself. Although it was of inferior quality, he was not deterred in wearing it and of attempting to improve its design and style.

From time to time, the summer students at the academy would play some of the local baseball teams that sprang up in the local villages, including Johnstown, Bealetown, Spruce Hill, Academia, East Waterford, Perrysville, Doyles Mills, and Pleasant View. Whenever possible, David would ride his horse to watch these games unfold, arriving well before the appointed game time, and to participate in the pre-game practice sessions.

He gained appreciable skill from his involvement in the practice sessions and observing the players. Later he would mimic any new skills displayed by the players. His desire to improve and become a member of one of the local teams did not go unnoticed, and finally his perseverance paid off in late July 1857, when the team from Bealetown arrived at Academia without enough players.

No one expected anything from a thirteen-year-old kid, but when he displayed his batting skills by driving three balls into open spaces for hits out of five attempts, the older members of the academy's squad took notice. His amazing fielding abilities saved the day for the Bealetown nine by spearing a line drive with two men in scoring position in the last inning and ending a rally for the scholars. After the game, one of the older academy boys approached him. "We're really impressed with your batting and fielding skills. Would you be interested in joining our team for the remainder of the term?"

He couldn't believe his ears, a senior classman asking him to play for the academy. "Would I? It's a dream come true. When is the next game?"

"Next Saturday at four o'clock at the Pleasant View field."

"I'll have to ask my father, to see if I can be excused from my farm chores that early in the day. I'm sure he will understand and allow me to play. If I can't come, I'll send you a message."

With his father's blessings, David began contributing to the academy's team on a regular basis. By the time he reached seventeen, he was considered the best player on the team, and by some, the best player in the valley. As he grew in strength and stature, the opposition began to respect his increasing power and skill as a batter.

Whenever David had any free time he honed his baseball skills. Hour after hour he would toss a homemade ball against the side of a shed. The ball would rebound off the shed, and David would either attempt to catch it before it struck the ground, or he would allow it to bounce once or twice before snagging the ball.

He made a homemade bat out of a piece of maple and then spent many hours tossing stones into the air and driving them towards the creek. Drawing from an endless supply of stones, he would practice this skill-builder until he could barely lift his arms. Both activities turned David into an outstanding baseball player. God, how he loved to play that game of baseball. It became a complete passion for him.

The baseball players of the Tuscarora Valley faced the same problem that plagued players throughout the nation: a lack of uniformity in the rules of the game. Every section of the country had its own rules and customs for the fast-spreading game.

In the Philadelphia region, the game was played with eleven men on a side for either two or eleven innings. When the game lasted only two innings, all the players on one side batted in each inning. One out would retire a side when the game lasted eleven or more innings. At least seventy-five runs were scored in a typical game. Often stakes were driven into the ground to serve as bases.

The Yankee or Massachusetts version usually matched teams of eight to fifteen players on a square field with bases or stakes at each corner of the field. The hitter or batter stood halfway between first and fourth (meaning, home) base and attempted to hit the ball. The ball was made out of yarn tightly wound around a piece of cork or rubber and covered with quartered calfskin sewn with snug, even seams.

In some variations of the game, the ball was delivered by the pitcher underhanded with no chicanery to allow the batter to hit the ball. The version adopted by the academy boys and their rivals allowed the pitcher to throw the ball swiftly overhand with as much speed as he could generate. The poor receiver (catcher) stood well back and attempted to catch the ball in his bare hands. He wore no mask or protective devices; he was simply at the mercy of his own skills to protect his body by catching the ball before it struck him.

In some areas the bat was a paddle with a blade about two inches thick and four inches wide. In other areas the bat was round, measured thirty-six to forty-two inches in length, and could have served as a rake or pitchfork handle.

The batter could hit the ball in any direction because there was no foul territory. He could be retired if the catcher successfully caught three missed balls, or if he hit a ball that was caught on the fly. (Some rules held that a ball caught on one bounce also was an out.) After hitting the ball, the batter ran around the bases until he reached a base or was put out, or if the batter or any runner was struck by a thrown ball while running the bases.

During the summer of 1857 the Tuscarora Valley teams adopted most of the rules created by the New York Knickerbocker Club of the 1840s. These rules called for a diamond instead of the square with bases and had the batter standing at home plate or the fourth base. The major deviation was that the pitcher was allowed to throw overhand instead of underhand. Under the Knickerbocker rules, a ball hit outside the range of first or third base was considered a foul ball. The batter was out if a struck ball was caught on a fly or first bounce, or if a fielder held the ball on a base before the runner arrived.

Another rule was that the team that scored the most runs after nine innings was the victor. A year later a rule was adopted that permitted the umpire to call a strike if a batter refused to swing at an otherwise good pitch.

The one rule that most players were hoping would be changed was the elimination of the one bounce for an out. They wanted it replaced with a fly game rule only. To David and the better players, the bounce rule was unmanly and required less skill. Unfortunately, this rule was not adopted until 1864.

Before each game it had to be decided whether a runner could be retired by the soaking- or burning-a-runner rule. This controversial rule allowed a runner to be called out if he was struck by a thrown ball while running the bases. Due to the amount of injuries inflicted this way, the rule was eventually changed to disallow soaking, but a runner could still be called out if a fielder who had the ball in his hands touched him.

The length of innings and the duration of the game were also major concerns due to a variety of rules governing these two items. The Tuscarora boys finally agreed to two new rules: three outs would retire the side, and twenty-one runs or aces would decide the game. The latter rule led to some undecided games when the loss of daylight prevented either team from reaching the designated number of runs. Eventually the issue of the length of games was dependent upon the amount of daylight remaining when the game began. Finally, the Tuscarora boys borrowed the rule allowing so many rounds of batting or innings to determine the length of the game.

Before long baseball became the most predominant form of athleticism and amusement in the Tuscarora Valley with large crowds attending many of the games. The female population became enthusiastic supporters of the sport, and the games soon took on a holiday atmosphere with picnics becoming a mainstay of the events. Often after the games, the two teams would share good conversation, food, and drink.

Health, exercise, good fellowship, good sportsmanship, and the desire for competition aided in spreading the game throughout the nation prior to the 1860s. One negative outgrowth of these very competitive games was that some of the observers or fans found a different form of amusement by placing bets on the outcome of the sporting events.

Even in the Tuscarora Valley heavy betting became commonplace, and was the theme of several lengthy sermons from the pulpit of the Lower Presbyterian Church in the late 1850s. Pastor Thompson addressed the situation one Sunday morning after a hotly contested game ensued the previous afternoon:

No one enjoys the thrill of competition more than I do, but what has been transpiring at some of the baseball contests this summer goes against the very grain of the teachings of this church. Several members of this community, some members of this congregation, and even some of the very souls that occupy these pews this morning are engaged in an activity that some people may scoff at as indulging in mere childish amusement, but to me in the eyes of our Lord they are involved in degrading themselves and rendering disreputable the surroundings of these healthy, athletic, and competitive contests that are being held among the youthful enthusiasts of this valley.

In the very name of decency, I employ you to resolve this form of deceitfulness and debauchery in your own way before a little additional decadence reduces the attendance at our valley ball matches or games to the level we usually associate with the intimidating manner of the prize-fighting rings and the race courses. Let us return to the purity and innocence of a grand exhibition of athletic excellence and competition and put away our change purses, wallets, and moneybags.

Those of you that seemingly have enough money to wittingly and purposely place it in jeopardy of being lost and depriving your families of the fruits of your monetary labors, I suggest that instead of passing these monetary surpluses on to one of your neighbors or acquaintances who will probably place these ill-begotten gains up for grabs at the next baseball contest, you simply deposit those gains in the collection plates as they are passed among us this morning. The Lord could do wonders with this amount of monetary sustenance. I can assure you the rewards that he will reap upon you for your generosity, will be much greater than what you could ever enjoy here even in our beautiful valley.

David was amused as he observed several husbands receiving some scathing looks from their incensed wives. He thought to himself, "I certainly wouldn't want to be in those fellows' shoes on the ride home from church and especially once they arrived at home. They will not know any peace of mind for a long time to come. I bet some of them won't be attending many ball games the rest of the summer."

CHAPTER 6
THE FEMALE SEMINARY IS BUILT

In March of 1857 the young men of the Tuscarora Academy were daydreaming of an early spring and all its usual dalliances—the new game of baseball that was sweeping rural America, the always-popular pastime of fishing, and now to many of these immature men folk, the introduction of young women into their mundane lives.

To the west of the academy, beyond the cemetery that served as the border to the Presbyterian Church, construction had been underway for over a year. An impressive three-story stone edifice had risen upon the flat area of the hill that overlooks the academy and its outbuildings.

During the early phase of the construction period, the students of the academy had speculated about what the new building would house. Finally, it was official: the new stone structure was to be the new home of a female education institution, a sister institution to the academy.

The new structure became a source of fascination and anticipation for the young scholars as the furniture and appliances were delivered in a timely manner. All that was needed was the arrival of the young female students, undoubtedly the same age as the boys just down the hill.

The structure was constructed of native stone found in the valley, and it was situated in such a manner that it entertained a commanding, enchanting southern view into the Tuscarora Valley with the mountain of that same name framed in the windows that faced in the southerly direction.

The female seminary was one of the most impressive edifices in the entire Tuscarora Valley. People traveled great distances to marvel at its dominance of the ridge on which it was located. With its beauty and quiet dignity, it truly was one of the main attractions of the region, and it easily became the pride of the Tuscarora Valley.

A wing of equal height on each side enjoined the three-story center hall. The upper region of the structure was elegantly presented with six large gables. Five huge chimneys protruded above the skyline of the roof, connecting fireplaces or ornate stoves located in each room, in an attempt to keep these southern belles warm and comfortable during the cold Yankee winters. The center or main gable was topped off with a gleaming white cupola. Anyone brave enough to climb the rickety ladder to gain entrance to this vantage point would be rewarded with a breathtaking vista of most of the Tuscarora Valley.

Some claimed that it was possible to see beyond the Juniata River to the east and observe the gap in the Tuscarora Mountain which led to Path Valley. Perhaps this is an exaggeration, but the viewing platform of the cupola acquainted one with the vastness of the valley and its varied geographical projections.

The magnificent stonework of the walls was interspersed with the wooden framework of sixty-seven windows and ten large outside doors, many of which were extra-wide, to accommodate the large hoop-skirts which fashionably adorned the young, maturing female scholars. Five windows were located on each end of the main hall on the first three floors, while the wings contained two windows on each side.

The interior of the structure entertained fifty-five rooms. Two large bake ovens and kitchen facilities were located in the basement. The aroma of the bread, cakes, or any food being prepared in the lower regions easily wafted upward and throughout the building, tantalizing the belles to find their way to the spacious dining room.

The main entrance, which was located in the center of the huge edifice under the main gable upon which the cupola was positioned, was reached from the south by ascending one flight of steps to a center landing, then making a right turn and continuing up a second flight to a spacious porch that extended the length of the center or main section of the mansion.

Upon passing through the wide door of the main entrance one

entered an elegant hallway or foyer, its center graced with an ornate open grand stairway that presented an impressive entranceway into the seminary. The intricate wood moldings added to the charm and gracefulness of the entire building. Fine, tasteful furniture embellished the interior of each room, while the walls were adorned with colonial and present-day pieces and prints.

The huge formal dining room dominated the middle of the first floor, which was separated from the large living rooms by the open stairway. The second floor was devoted mostly to classrooms. The third floor contained most of the living quarters for the young women, but it also contained a large room that was utilized for the immensely emphasized music program of the school. A piano and harp graced this functional room, and numerous encased instruments were stored within. This region of the school was reached from the ground floor or basement by several stairways.

The true spirit of the school was exhibited in the large room set aside as the library. Although not extravagantly stocked, the shelves were filled with many famous books of the period. An observer would find several of Longfellow's works, such as *Tales of a Wayside Inn*, Herman Melville's *Typee* and *Omoo*, Nathaniel Hawthorne's *Evangeline* and *The Song of Hiawatha*, as well as numerous works by Ralph Waldo Emerson and Edgar Allen Poe.

The majority of the dormitory rooms were decorated in a subdued but still elegant style, with wallpaper adorning the four walls. Each room had its own identity, with the wallpaper pattern varying from room to room. Beds, desks, and a marble-topped washstand were provided in each room, although the girls were encouraged to ship personal furnishings in order to give them a touch of home and allow for the comfort and convenience of the individual.

Each student was responsible for providing a silver fork and spoon and several table napkins for dining room use. The girls were also accountable for personal items such as bath towels, toothbrushes, hairbrushes, combs, umbrellas, India-rubber shoes, and kerosene lamps or candles.

The table napkins, towels, and any clothing that needed to be washed by the washwomen hired by the school were required to be distinctly marked for easy identification. Cleaning of clothing was a constant concern of the majority of these style-conscious young ladies and was an additional drain on their budgets, or really their parents' pocketbooks.

Books, paper, writing stationery, ink, and writing utensils were available for purchase on the premises or could be obtained at Pomeroy's Store in Academia if transportation was available.

The grounds of the stone mansion were in the process of being meticulously landscaped. A spirit of perfectionism and tasteful knowledge of landscape design was evident throughout the surrounding acreage, as the planting and pruning of every tree, shrub, and flower progressed and greatly enhanced the property.

One newspaper account reported that the new girls' school was not as grand as a glorious French chateau or as elegant as Henry Knox's Montpelier or Thomas Jefferson's Monticello, but it was "as handsome a building as money could build in this region in 1857."

CHAPTER 7
THE ROLE OF THE SEMINARY

Prior to the arrival of the female population, the boys were summoned to the church for what they figured would be the usual obligatory chapel program. Instead, the boys were introduced to the educators who would be in charge of the female education institution.

Alexander Patterson was the first to be introduced. Being a local man, he was fairly well known to the boys. Mr. Patterson had two daughters, Nancy and Margaret, whom the Pattersons had begun educating in 1848. Since that time, the Pattersons had expanded their educational endeavors to include several other local girls.

It was through the efforts of the Pattersons and a few other progressives that the school had become a reality. On this special day, Mr. Patterson's role was to introduce the new principal of the female institution, the Reverend William S. Garthwait, who also was involved in the administration of the male academy. Reverend Garthwait was a Presbyterian minister, which was only fitting since the church and male academy were Presbyterian-sponsored and -administered.

Reverend Garthwait thanked Mr. Patterson for his kind introduction and then began to outline the mission of the new school:

> You young men will be somewhat amazed at what we are going to accomplish next door to you. We will be engaged in developing a respectable academy or seminary with a highly rigorous environment of education for women, which might be unusual for most female institutions. Perhaps some of you young men have sisters, female friends, or cousins who attend female institutions, and you

might have heard them complain that they are not challenged academically or being truly prepared for the real world.

Gentlemen, that will not be the case next door; we will not be just another finishing school. Our objective is not to produce an atmosphere where our scholars will only gain a suitable husband from the population of your institution, nor to prepare for the propagation of a large family. Neither do we relish producing a female whose only role is to be accomplished in the art of managing servants and the entertainment of guests.

There is no doubt that we will prepare our girls for home duties, and we will cultivate a formal gentility and grace for social value. However, we will construct a curriculum that will foster the discipline of the mental endowments. Our female students will utilize many of the courses and books used by you young men.

We do not believe that women are intellectually inferior to you. We are raising the standards and expectations by providing a substantial portion of the liberal studies provided at your institution. In addition, there will be an emphasis on the sciences and mathematics, which many female institutions are just beginning to accentuate. Therefore, our students will be prepared for a variety of professional opportunities.

Since we have a strong religious affiliation with the Presbyterian Church, there will be a constant affirmation of religious and Christian purpose. Students will be required to attend church services, prayer meetings, chapel talks, and Bible study groups. Twice a day teachers and students will dedicate time to private devotions.

After a few closing remarks, the program was turned over to the headmistress or principal teacher, Miss Lizzie C. McGinnes, who addressed the male audience:

Young men, it is somewhat rare that an institution of learning is established to offer an education to young women. The people of this community, the leaders of the Presbyterian Church of Pennsylvania, the congregation of the Lower Presbyterian Church of Academia, the leaders of your institution, and the leaders of this Commonwealth, have had the foresight to take this progressive movement, making it possible to offer a foremost education to any young women that desire to take advantage of this unique opportunity.

You young men will fulfill a significant role in the development of this new sister institution. Many activities offered by your institution and this church will be made available to the young women of this new school. Therefore, there will be many opportunities for cooperation and sharing between the populations of the two schools.

With that stated, I must caution you young men—and your professors will reiterate my cautionary mode—we will not encourage complete fraternization between the populations of the two schools. From time to time, we will schedule ample social activities between the two schools, but on most occasions we will not tolerate unscheduled visits from you young men.

I know this might sound harsh and demeaning, but we have the responsibilities of protecting the reputations of our female students. We are simply requesting your cooperation with our policies, and we do not anticipate the need for stricter rules and the enforcement of "no fraternization" regulations.

We will welcome you to visit our institution in the near future. We plan to hold a tea on a Saturday afternoon at which time we will offer a brief tour of our new facility and acquaint you with our female population.

I thank you young men for your time and cooperation in welcoming our first class for the next semester. Just remember, you are welcome as invited guests. Please try not to undermine the cooperative effort that we desire in order to survive as neighboring institutions.

When the boys were dismissed from the chapel meeting for the day, they were all aflutter with more speculation and anticipation about the opportunities and obstacles that surely would await them when the girls finally arrived.

Many of the boys were shaking their heads in disbelief as they scrambled down the steps of the church. Charlie Young complained the loudest. "I just can't believe our dumb luck in having a building full of giggling girls for neighbors. You wait and see, we'll have all kinds of new rules and regulations. They probably won't let us explore the ridge and countryside like we used to."

"Yeah, they'll be afraid we might see an ankle or even worse, a thigh," chimed in James Medford.

"What I'm afraid of is that we'll be expected to attend all kinds of social events. We'll have to always be on our best behavior, watching what we say, and making sure we follow all the social graces of our society," offered David. "Life is not going to be the same."

After classes, several of the older boys proposed a search for local flora on the ridge behind the church, but what they really were seeking was the opportunity to select advantageous viewing positions from which they could catch a glimpse of the girls once they occupied the building.

One of the boys suggested constructing blinds similar to those used in hunting ducks and geese. Not only would the boys then have an unobstructed view, but there would be little chance of the girls having any idea that they were under scrutiny. This proposal did not receive much enthusiasm because most of the boys were afraid of the type of punishment they would receive if such an enterprise were to be discovered by either school's authority.

Soon the upper classmen developed a schedule whereby someone on watch duty would inform the rest of the males when the first females arrived. The boy on watch was expected to report back on the approximate age, color of hair, color of eyes, and amount of luggage of each female. The latter was regarded as a telltale sign of the alleged wealth of the young woman.

With the buggy-watch on duty, the news spread like wildfire throughout the school when the initial buggy arrived with the first of the female students. After several days, it was generally assumed that the first class of females was settled in. Therefore, it was with great anticipation that the boys down the hill awaited the first co-ed church services and the invitation to the tea that had been mentioned in chapel.

The first Sunday that the female student body attended church, they did so en masse, and never broke their ranks while strolling to and from the church. The two student bodies were segregated on opposite sides of the church. There was no giggling, gawking, or stealing glances toward the other side of the church, and no attempts whatsoever to make contact with the other school. The movement and demeanor of the female student body was almost military in its procedure.

Most of the boys were quite disappointed; all they were able to observe were several rows of bonnets and bodices, and the permeating of the church's interior with the pleasant aroma of numerous new fragrances. Finally, several days later, the invitation to the tea arrived and it was read at chapel.

The invitation came with a stern warning about the type of behavior expected of those who opted to attend. Everyone was encouraged to attend the affair, and classes were conducted as to proper attire, behavior, and etiquette for those who chose to attend.

David discussed the situation with his mother, and she encouraged him to follow through and attend, even if the tea was conducted on a Saturday, normally a day of labor on the farm for him. Unfortunately, David knew very little of the opposite sex prior to this social event. Sure, he had to exist in the same house with his older sister, Julie, but he had learned at an early stage of life that the less he knew of her activities and moods, the better. There had been occasional encounters with female cousins and friends at various family and church functions, but those were of the frivolous teasing happenstances.

He remembered quite vividly his first physical romantic contact that he considered to be a kiss. One of his good friends, John Patterson, who lived on a farm on Ebenezer Church Road, invited David to go on a hayride with the younger members of the Ebenezer Methodist Church. As the evening progressed, like teenagers everywhere, the boys and girls paired up. David was not amused by the development, but went along with sitting alongside Amy Barton of Pleasant View. Before long, Amy had cuddled up to David; she took his right arm and placed it around her neck. David knew what was coming next and braced himself for it. Amy took his chin in her right hand, turned his head toward her, and proceeded to kiss David, who offered no resistance at first. Then she kissed him fully on the lips; to his consternation, his mouth suddenly appeared to be on fire, and the aroma of chewing tobacco filled his nostrils.

David grabbed Amy by the shoulders, pushed her backward, and screamed, "Ugh! My God, you're chewing tobacco. That's disgusting. Get away from me. I can't tolerate the smell or taste of that offensive weed."

The rest of the teenagers began to yell teasing remarks at David. "You just don't know the fun you're missing," yelled one. "Just relax and let Amy teach you a few things," giggled another.

Eventually David settled back in the hay beside Amy, but he tried to keep her at arm's length. This first kiss was one of those experiences that he and his friends had fantasized about for years, but for David it was an utter disappointment. Strangely, it did make him feel good throughout his body, except that he couldn't overcome the sensation inside his mouth.

David did not want to offend Amy, because he did enjoy her company. Finally he said, "I'm sorry, it's not that I find you unattractive; it's just that I can't tolerate tobacco."

Amy smiled at him. "Don't worry, I'll just throw it out," she said, then spit it over the side of the wagon. Thereupon, she snuggled up to David just as if nothing had happened.

At school on Monday, several of his friends who had been on

the hayride strode up to him and punched him on the shoulder. "You dummy, that was what we've been talking and dreaming about for years and you messed it up. "

David replied, "I know it was a good opportunity, but the burning sensation and smell did me in. I learned one good thing about this encounter: from now on, when I meet a girl, one of the first things I will take note of will be her mouth and teeth. I'll be looking for any telltale signs that she is a tobacco user. You don't realize how disgusting it is to kiss a girl with a wad of tobacco in her cheek."

Charlie chimed in, "I did it all evening, and I enjoyed it. So did several of the other guys."

David regarded his friend with amusement. "I guess I'll look at a girl the way you look for a good horse, and I'll check her teeth first."

Harry couldn't keep from laughing, "Well, you can look at their teeth first, but I can tell you that will be one of the last places I'll be looking at. If teeth are the first criteria, you're going to end up with some awfully homely women."

The others nodded in agreement. They said in unison, "Teeth will be way down the list for us."

CHAPTER 8
THE FORMAL TEA

When the big day arrived, David's Sunday-going suit had been thoroughly washed and pressed, and his boots shined, and David even took a bath without being told to do so. His mother gave him his last instructions, which ended with, "No matter what, be the perfect gentleman. This is a good experience for you and your friends, and you should be able to learn a great deal about the opposite sex by attending functions like this. Who knows, maybe you'll even find a girl to your liking."

Like all the boys, David approached the new stone building with apprehension. The majority of the boys walked en masse from the dormitory to the girls' school, but David rode right up to the school on Tuscarora Chief.

At the front entrance of the stone mansion, a loading-unloading area was designed for easy entrance and exit for buggies and traps. To avoid congestion the driveway continued in a circle turnaround. The inside of the circle turnaround was enhanced with various species of flowers and shrubs, with a small eastern hemlock planted as a centerpiece.

At the eastern end of the building was a hitching post area where visitors could tie up their individual steeds or teams. During weekends, holidays, and special formal events such as this tea, this became a congested area that certainly would need a thorough cleaning after so many horses were stationed there for several hours.

Since the area was already crowded, David guided Tuscarora Chief around the circle and found a sturdy branch on a tree in the fencerow to tie his horse. Therefore, David stood out as perhaps being something special in that he arrived on his own transportation. This did not go unnoticed by some of the girls.

As David and his classmates entered the wide doors of the main entrance into the foyer, they were introduced to several of the older girls who were functioning as greeters and guides. The girls eagerly extended their gloved hands and curtsied, while the boys accepted the female hands briefly and bowed slightly.

They were ushered into the formal dining room, where they were greeted by a roomful of very fashionably attired teenage females. Introductions were made, and then the boys were served tea and small cakes. Although tea was not David's favorite beverage, he did manage to sip one cup. On the other hand, all the boys ate more than their shares of the tasty little cakes and cookies.

The females were all fluff, powder, perfume, makeup, smiles, giggles, charm, and grace. Luckily, David had an older sister and knew what to expect of a female of this age. This was not his world; he simply wasn't impressed with what he observed. He wanted to bolt for the door, but he realized what was expected of him, so he calmed down and tried to make the most of it. He could hardly wait for the ordeal to end.

He hung out with three of his classmates, and as the young women were either introduced to the boys, or as they paraded by in their silk, hooped dresses, the boys made sly comments about each girl among themselves. "Too Fat, Too Skinny, Too Short, or Too Tall." Those were the nicest remarks. Most referred to the girls' anatomy. "Buck Teeth, Hawk-Nosed, Slant-eyed" and many other unkind descriptions flowed from their mouths, which would have been washed out with soap if their mothers had heard such nonsense.

It was difficult for the boys to judge the size of hips, thighs, ankles, or even the maturing bust lines of the young girls, due to the style of dress that they were wearing. None of the girls had chosen a dress with a plunging neckline because they were warned about wearing such a garment. There was no revelation of which young woman might be more endowed than another.

The boys handled the questions posed by the girls with very little difficulty. The most frequently asked were: "Where is your home located?" "What year of school are you?" "How old are you?" "Do you enjoy school?"

Some were more inquisitive. "What do you do for fun around

here?" "Would you like to correspond with me?"

The boys answered the questions rather vaguely, but they did shed some insight about their social lives. They rattled off about playing baseball and shinny, which was a form of lacrosse. They mentioned horseback riding, buggy rides, fishing, hunting, sleigh rides, ice skating, spelling bees, debates—and if a fellow were sly enough he could sneak off to a barn dance.

A girl with strawberry blonde hair who appeared more forward than the others did step forward and cooed, "All those activities sound like fun. Hopefully we'll be able to enjoy some of them with you all."

David's arrival on Tuscarora Chief had not gone unnoticed by several of the girls, and they were quite curious about his unique situation. One young brunette, probably about fifteen, approached David and purred in a low southern drawl, "I just love horses. I have a bay of my own back home; her name is Queenie. What's your horse's name? I would just love to go for a ride some Sunday afternoon."

David wasn't too keen on answering the questions but reluctantly and patiently responded to the cute southern belle. "My horse's name is Tuscarora Chief, and I'm allowed to ride him to school because I'm not a boarding student. I live less than two miles from the school, and when the weather permits, I ride to and from school each day with two of my neighbors. Normally it takes about thirty-five to forty-five minutes for the trip. My aunt lives just two houses from the school so it's convenient for me to stable my horse in her barn while I attend school. During inclement weather I stay at my aunt's house in a small room off the kitchen, not because of the lack of funds, but because all the other rooms are rented out to other students."

The girls appeared to be satisfied with the responses; they smiled and gracefully withdrew. One turned and smiled flirtatiously at David. "See you all later," she said with a wink.

From time to time, several of the older girls escorted small groups of the boys on a tour throughout the school. In the music room and in the dining room, girls were performing on a variety of musical instruments. The girls were extremely friendly and engaged the boys in normal teenage conversations. Several of the girls took the initiative and boldly suggested that it would be nice if the boys would write to them, and didn't hesitate in exchanging names with the boys.

In the short period since the first girls had arrived at the school, it had been drilled into them that nice young ladies did not encourage the young men from down the hill, or any local young men, to venture up the hill to visit the school, unless they were invited for some special occasion. The young women had been lectured repeatedly that it was very unladylike for them to show any interest in the opposite sex.

Any young woman who knowingly enticed one of the young men would be subject to stern punishment, mostly in being assessed demerits that would curtail much of the young lady's freedom of movement. Nevertheless, as time went on, there were occasions when a young lady would throw caution to the wind and create a situation where a lucky young man would be the recipient of her budding young charms.

When the social concluded, the boys made their exit while thanking their hosts for an enjoyable afternoon. As the boys bounded down the stone mansion's steps, they immediately began to compare notes as to what they had learned of their female neighbors. Harry blurted within the girls' hearing distance, "There are certainly some stunning girls living in this building. I hope we'll be invited back again."

"Well, Dave, did you find any with the perfect set of teeth and the sweet-smelling breath?"

"I really wasn't looking that closely, but I can't imagine girls of this breeding indulging in such a distasteful habit. However, you are correct; there are some nice-looking girls here. Wait, I need to get Chief, and then I'll walk down the hill with you."

John Duncan chimed in, "Did you ever smell anything so fragrant, so enticing? Did anyone get any names?"

Everyone shook his head. David confessed sheepishly, "I think some of the lads did, but getting names didn't even enter my mind.

I guess none of them appealed to me that much. Besides, I was so concerned about dropping a cup or saucer, or spilling something. I just wanted to get through the function without making a fool of myself. Names can be an objective the next time."

"If you noticed, it was the older boys that were exchanging names," observed Harry. "Those girls weren't interested in us younger ones. Guess we just have to remember that in a few years when we'll be the older ones. Then look out."

"Look out for what?" joked John. "How much do you think we'll change in two or three years?"

David smiled, "My mother and sister keep telling me that in another year or so I'll probably be interested in girls. I don't know, after what happened on the hayride, I'm not too anxious to get involved with females."

When David returned home, his mother and sister were full of questions, but he didn't offer much information. "To tell you the truth, all of us were very nervous. I think we all were thankful that we apparently didn't say anything or do anything foolish. I doubt if most of us made very good impressions on the girls; maybe we'll do better the next time."

His mother and sister just smiled and let it go at that. It seemed that girls always handle social situations like teas much better than young men do. To David boys were fish out of water and doomed from the start.

CHAPTER 9

THE SUMMER OF 1857 AND THE
ENLIGHTENMENT ABOUT SLAVERY

Now that David was older, it was more urgent that he acquire as much knowledge as possible. Thus, he attended the summer session, which began in May and ran through September. School was not very enjoyable during the hot, sultry summer of 1857. Non-school hours were spent working in the fields, fishing, or playing baseball.

The students of the academy were blessed with several progressive educators who, in their desire to keep their students abreast of national and international events, arranged for the school to receive a subscription to the *New York Times*. In most cases the newspaper arrived nearly a week after it was published, but even a week-old prestigious paper was better than hearsay and rumors.

David was not aware, nor was anyone else, that the world outside his placid valley was about to erupt into a gigantic struggle that would split his nation apart and alter his life. He was an adept history student, and he had studied how the institution of slavery had influenced the construction of the Constitution with the embodiment of the Three-Fifths Compromise, and how the document had specified an end to the slave trade.

His Presbyterian instructors had enlightened him about the outlawing of slavery in the Northwest Territory in 1787 and the maintaining of the slave state/free-state balance under the Missouri Compromise of 1820. It was difficult for a teenager to comprehend how such concepts as a protective tariff, nullification, states' rights, and emancipation would ever affect him.

The summer students were introduced to the doctrine of popular sovereignty which had been advanced by political leaders after the acquisition of the Mexican Territory in the Mexican War. This doctrine advocated that when a territory wrote its constitution and applied for statehood, the people of the territory would vote to be slave or free. This doctrine did not apply to California in 1850, but it was to apply to all other territory acquired in the war.

The students learned that four years later, when the territories of Kansas and Nebraska applied for statehood, the provisions of the Missouri Compromise were augmented, and the doctrine of popular sovereignty was extended beyond the territory acquired in the Mexican War, thus eliminating the 1820 slave/free line.

This Kansas-Nebraska Act applied a match to an explosive fuse. There was no problem in Nebraska, which voted to be a free state, but in Kansas a chronic state of civil warfare led to the development of pro-slavery and antislavery factions. The situation became known as "Bleeding Kansas."

Harriet Beecher Stowe's *Uncle Tom's Cabin* was optional reading; any students from below the Mason-Dixon who considered the book offensive would not be obligated to read it. The young men who read it were deeply moved by the humanity of the slaves and were horrified by the depiction of slave life.

They learned that many northern Presbyterians supported a secret network known as the Underground Railroad, which smuggled slaves out of the South and into the free states of the North and sometimes into Canada. And they heard rumors that certain homes and buildings in the Tuscarora Valley were being utilized as way stations. David was also introduced to the abolitionist periodical *The Liberator* published by William Lloyd Garrison since 1831. It declared that slavery was no less than an abomination in the sight of God and called for the immediate emancipation of all slaves.

The summer session of 1857 was a period of enlightenment, enrichment, and inspiration for David and his fellow northern students. The reading of Garrison's and Stowe's works left a lasting impression on his young, fertile mind. By the end of September, he had been transformed from a lukewarm disapprover of slavery into an ardent abolitionist.

When the students returned to the academy on November first, they learned that the Supreme Court of the United States had made slavery a Fifth Amendment issue when the high court heard the appeal of Dred Scott, a fugitive slave. The chief justice of the Supreme Court, Roger B. Taney, declared the Missouri Compromise unconstitutional, a violation of the Fifth Amendment in that it barred the government from depriving an individual of "life, liberty, or property" without due process of law. If slaves were property, no state had the right to liberate them by simply taking them from their owners.

The southern students were elated over the ruling, but the decision drove a bigger wedge between the students from the two sections of the country, just as it was doing throughout the whole nation. Even these young men began to realize that there was no middle course anymore. If the constitutional rights of slave holders were to be upheld throughout the nation as long as the institution of slavery existed, slavery would have to be universally accepted. Otherwise it would have to be abolished.

David cringed when he thought about those lovely young ladies attending the sister institution up on the hill. Slavery made it possible for many of them to attend that educational institution. It became more and more difficult to look them in the face and act civil to them, but then he realized it wasn't their fault that their families might own slaves and use the profits from their labor to better their lives.

The new year of 1858 brought little change in the tense atmosphere as the gap widened between the North and the South. A major event occurred that year in Illinois when Stephen A. Douglas, the Democratic Senator from that state and champion of popular sovereignty, sought reelection. Douglas was challenged by a former Whig congressman and a rising figure in the newly created Republican Party, Abraham Lincoln. In June Lincoln accepted the Republican senatorial nomination with a ringing speech at Springfield. Lincoln stated, "A house divided against itself cannot stand. I believe this government cannot endure permanently half slave and half free."

Lincoln and Douglas did something quite unusual in that they appeared on the same platform seven times. The highlight of the debates occurred at Freeport on August 27. Lincoln requested that

Douglas reconcile popular sovereignty with the Dred Scott decision. Douglas asserted that it didn't matter what the Supreme Court decided because "slavery cannot exist a day or an hour anywhere, unless it is supported by local police regulations.'

This statement became known as the Freeport Doctrine and carried Douglas to victory in November and back to his seat in the Senate in Washington. Out of these debates, Abraham Lincoln became a towering political figure to be reckoned with in the next presidential election.

CHAPTER 10
THE JOHN BROWN INCIDENT

Nearly a year later, Mother Nature was showing off her dazzling brilliance on the morning of November 1, 1859, as the boys filed into the classroom of Professor Stone and took their assigned seats. The professor greeted the boys with his usual, "Good morning, gentlemen," and the boys responded in turn, "Good morning professor."

Professor Stone glanced around the room. "Gentlemen, we are going to dispense with today's scheduled assignment on Athenian Democracy. Instead we are going to examine in depth a situation that has developed in the last four days. "Does anyone know where the town of Harpers Ferry is located?"

David Sutter, who lived in Hancock, Maryland, raised his hand. "Sir, it is located in Virginia where the Shenandoah River flows into the Potomac River."

"That is correct, Mr. Sutter. Does anyone know what is located in that town that could be of strategic importance to the welfare of our nation?"

George Thompson quickly raised his hand in response.

"Go right ahead, Mr. Thompson."

"The sleepy little town houses a federal armory and arsenal, and there is a rifle works nearby."

"Very good, Mr. Thompson. Has anyone heard of a man by the name of John Brown?"

Several students nodded.

"Mr. Curtis, what do you know of John Brown?" asked the professor.

"John Brown was born in Torrington, Connecticut, and grew up in Ohio. Most recently, he has gained fame as an ardent advocate for action to end slavery, and in 1855 he moved to Kansas to retaliate against pro-slavery actions in Lawrence. Since then Kansas has become known as 'Bleeding Kansas' because of the bloodshed in that state.

"Last year he proposed to establish a mountain stronghold in Maryland for escaping slaves that would be financed by abolitionists. I'm sorry I don't have any knowledge of his activities since then."

"That's fine, Curtis. You almost brought us up to date. In February 1857, Brown returned to his native state and ordered one thousand pikes made from long-bladed Bowie knives to be attached to six-foot poles. These pikes were to be used by slaves to kill their masters and anyone else who got in their way.

"In December of last year Brown led a practice raid into Missouri and freed eleven slaves who then escaped to Canada. This was all a dress rehearsal for what he attempted just four days ago.

"On October 16 John Brown seized control of the federal arsenal and armory in Harpers Ferry and then waited for a slave uprising where the escaping slaves would join his 'army of emancipation.' Instead, a federal force led by Col. Robert E. Lee overpowered Brown's men, killing ten of them and capturing the others. Brown was wounded and captured and faces three capital offenses: conspiracy with slaves, murder, and treason. If found guilty of these charges, he undoubtedly will face execution by hanging.

"Gentlemen, I would like you to discuss your observations regarding Brown's activities. Try not to raise your voices and control your ardor in this discussion."

James Brooks was the first to claim the floor. "I believe this incredible raid was long overdue. Slavery is completely wrong and what John Brown attempted is wholly right. I hope that in the near future all slaves either run away from their masters or are freed by actions similar to Brown's."

William Plumer reacted immediately. "I believe you go too far in your methods of freeing the slaves. I agree that slavery is immoral, but taking lives to free these people goes directly against the Ten Commandments. There are other methods to be employed in this endeavor other than the use of force and bloodshed."

David Sutter bounced to his feet. "Neither of you has any idea how important slavery is to some parts of the South. Economically, slavery has been forced upon many plantation owners in their struggle for existence. The South is dominated by agriculture, and Eli Whitney's invention of the cotton gin in 1793 altered the South's economy and its attitude towards slavery. The textile mills of the North have gobbled up the cotton production, and at the same time, the demand for slaves to work the crop has escalated. Cotton has become king, not so much in the South anymore, but instead in the western states.

"Recently, I read a magazine article which stated that of the six million whites living in the South in 1850, only about 350,000 owned slaves. Of that number, only 37, 662 owned twenty or more slaves."

"I think that what you are saying," interrupted John Harper from the back of the room, "is that cotton has saddled the South with a labor system that is uneconomical and outdated. Isn't it possible to cultivate cotton with free laborers? The South has foolishly invested its capital in human muscle and not in machinery. I believe that white day-labor would be cheaper."

Sutter retorted, "Where would you find this abundance of white workers? Would any of you in this room dirty your hands in picking cotton? I think not. Our only hope would be to attract a profusion of immigrants to the South, and at the moment that does not seem to be a possibility."

"It appears to me that John Brown was simply an enthusiast who envisioned himself commissioned by Heaven to liberate the slaves," stated Robert Rooney. "What he created was not a slave insurrection as he had devised. I believe it was an attempt to stir up a revolt among the slaves, in which the slaves refused to participate. Even in the slaves' limited knowledge, some may call it ignorance, they saw it could not succeed and therefore did not join in."

Professor Stone finally spoke. "Many of you have strong views regarding what occurred in Harpers Ferry and you are entitled to them. I would like to caution you in how you approach the subject when you are in the company of our female neighbors up on the hill. The majority of the girls reside below the Mason-Dixon Line, and most assuredly, their viewpoints would not coincide with those held by most of you. If the subject of John Brown arises, remember, they are our guests here in this valley, and they also are the alleged weaker sex, so don't be too opinionated and cause hard feelings.

"As the case goes to trial, we will follow the proceedings and examine how the outcome will affect the relations between the northern and southern states. I hope that the hotheads on both sides will not cause the bitter feelings to escalate. Class dismissed, but continue to contemplate the situation."

CHAPTER 11
ABBEY COMES INTO DAVID'S LIFE

On November 1, as David and his schoolmates returned to the academy for the winter session of school, a new session of the female seminary also commenced. The first Sunday of the new session began just like any other fall Sabbath with the Evans family traveling to church for worship. David ordinarily sat with his classmates, but for some reason he just sat down with his family on this morning.

He had completely forgotten that this Sunday would be the first worship service in which the returning female students would be in attendance. He observed his schoolmates turning and stretching their necks to have a good view of the female school population. He would have realized the moment the girls entered even if he hadn't heard the boys twisting in their pews to view the girls. The sudden change in the aroma in the church as well as the swirl and bustle of the materials of the hooped skirts told him the female entourage had arrived.

His family's pew didn't allow him to see the girls as they politely took their seats in the back on the right side of the church. It wasn't until the services had concluded that he was able to observe that section of the church. By that time, it was too late to view any of their faces; all he saw was the back of many fashionably attired females. He watched as the girls paraded down the church's driveway, their bonnets bobbing in unison, and turned right into the school's driveway.

When he caught up to his classmates after church, all they could talk about were the attractive faces they had seen that morning. He had to admit to them that he had seen nothing. "Too bad, too bad," they all chimed in. "Better luck next Sunday."

The following Sundays didn't provide any better opportunities to view the female students. Bonnets and bodices of various colors and hair of a variety of shades were all that the boys were able to observe with any clarity. They were never in a position to clearly identify facial features and the color of eyes even though some of the returning females who had had previous contact with some of the returning males sent signals that they recognized the young men and were ready to resume their previous arrangements.

In the meantime, David Evans celebrated his sixteenth birthday on November 22. Reaching this milestone was a special event in the Evans family. He was now looked upon as a man, although he didn't feel any different.

It wasn't until the first Saturday evening in December that the boys were finally able to make face-to-face contact with the female students. On this evening, a spelling bee was held between the neighboring schools at the boys' academy. This was the first attempt at creating a healthy competitive atmosphere between the two schools. Prior to this evening, each school had held its own spelling competition in order to ascertain the top ten spellers in each school.

Promptly at seven o'clock, the female delegation entered the dining hall of the academy, and the twenty scholars took their places on chairs arranged in the front of the hall. David was one of the participants and he nervously took his place on the right side of the hall with the rest of the male team. The girls sat on the left side of the front of the hall on chairs arranged just like the boys.

Reverend Thompson was the moderator of the contest and he asked each student to stand and introduce himself or herself prior to the pronunciation of the first word. David was concentrating on the task at hand when one young woman introduced herself as Abigail Volkner. He was completely spellbound.

Abigail had the flaxen hair and azure blue eyes of some far-back German ancestors. Her complexion was clear and wholesome, with maybe a few freckles around the nose. The aspect of the freckles would take a much closer examination to determine if they did exist as David suspected. He surmised that she often wore a wide-brimmed straw hat to protect her rather delicate complexion.

The very fact that she attended the female seminary indicated that her family was propertied, perhaps well endowed. David hoped she wasn't one of those girls born with a silver spoon in her mouth, so privileged that she was accustomed to being waited upon, hand and foot. He didn't want to become associated with a girl of great substance. He would never feel comfortable around such a female.

Suddenly aware that he was too deeply involved in speculation about this alluring young female, he shifted back to reality. He observed that the alluring one moved with the easy grace of a young woman who has been trained to walk and stand correctly. Her body was straight and erect, and her arms hung close to her sides.

After strolling purposefully across the room, she sank gracefully into her chair and spread her wide silk skirt to allow only the tips of her satin slippers to show; the insteps must always be covered. He continued to cautiously keep her under surveillance. He didn't want to be caught gazing in her direction; that would be extremely embarrassing and would spoil his whole approach to the subject.

The contest was conducted slowly, and as it continued, the words became much more difficult. Eventually there were only two boys and two girls left, and finally the spell down was reduced to David and the girl with the flaxen hair and blue eyes. The first three words given to the two finalists were spelled quite easily. Then once again, it was David's turn to go first. The word was "obstreperous," and he thought he knew it, but somehow in the pressure of the moment, he inverted the "r" and "e." He had spelled it incorrectly. A huge smile of triumph spread across the attractive young woman's face, and she exhibited a set of perfect teeth.

David was transfixed, barely hearing her spell the word correctly and Reverend Thompson proclaiming her as the winner. Dumbfounded, he crossed the floor and congratulated her. She graciously accepted his handshake, and later he couldn't remember anything that he had said to her.

He was very confused. He couldn't believe that he had let his school down and, worse yet, to a female. On the other hand, he couldn't believe that she was so beautiful; at least he drew some consolation from knowing that the most beguiling female he had ever observed had beaten him.

His classmates approached him and offered their congratulations that he had been a finalist, and offered condolences over his loss. Harry was at his best. "Well, one thing for sure, you finally found one with good teeth. I've never seen such a smile. One of us should get to know her better."

As the food was laid out on the tables, food was the last thing that David wanted. All he wanted was to go home and suffer in solitude. David sat by himself well back away from the social activities that followed the spelling bee. He felt utterly miserable, completely depressed. How could he have made such a silly mistake? Under normal circumstances, he would never have committed such an error.

He sat with his head slightly bowed, his eyes cast upon an irregular pattern in the wood floor. He was aroused from his reverie by the bustling of silk, a sweet-smelling fragrance, and a slight southern drawl enunciating his name.

"David, David Evans. I want you to know that you handled your disappointment like a true gentleman. I realize it's always difficult to suffer defeat, but in your situation I assume it's even more demoralizing since it was at the hands of a wretched female."

His eyes lifted to behold the enchanting possessor of the melodious drawl. She was absolutely breath-taking. He jumped to his feet with a start and once again observed those azure blue eyes and sparkling white teeth less than two feet from his face.

She continued in a non-condescending manner, appearing quite sincere. "David, I imagine that you probably don't have very good thoughts about me at the moment, but I hope you will put those conceptions aside so that we can be friends."

At first, he had a very difficult time comprehending what this goddess was disclosing. Many of the females from the seminary were quite attractive, but he never anticipated entertaining any feelings towards them. What he was experiencing now was beyond his wildest dreams. This young woman was completely enchanting.

Somehow, he finally responded to her seemingly heartfelt, compassionate assertion. "I certainly have no ill feelings toward you. You simply proved to be the better speller. I made a mistake, and you took advantage of it, and that is the way it should be. I certainly want to thank you for approaching me and offering your kind words; that took a special person with an inner spirit filled with kindness and understanding, which I deeply admire. Once again, I want to offer my congratulations on your triumph; you appear to be a remarkable young woman."

She smiled. "David Evans, if you would be so inclined, I would desire for you to call upon me." She continued beguilingly, "We are permitted gentlemen callers on Saturday evenings and Sunday afternoons. You may correspond at your convenience regarding this matter." With that, she turned on her heel and withdrew with a semblance of graciousness and preeminence.

David shook his head in disbelief. He was completely flabbergasted. What a turn of events, from utter disillusionment and defeat to unreserved ecstasy and euphoria! How would he ever sleep tonight?

During the next day's church service, David couldn't take his eyes off the young maiden who had turned his life upside down the evening before. At the conclusion of the service, David moved quickly to find Abigail before the girls were swiftly escorted back to their school.

"Good morning, Miss Volkner," David said. "Would you please do me the honor of allowing me to call upon you Saturday evening?"

Her blue eyes sparkled as she stood in front of him. "I would be most honored for you to call upon me Saturday evening. Shall we make it seven o'clock? I'll place your name on the list of expected guests for the evening. Do have a good week. I'll be waiting for you in the parlor."

CHAPTER 12
THEIR FIRST RENDEZVOUS

That week was the longest week of his life; he thought Saturday would never arrive. When it finally did, he was of little help to his father throughout the day, as his concentration was elsewhere. His mother didn't need to urge him to bathe and put on his best suit. It was all he could do to constrain himself from spurring Tuscarora Chief into a full canter on the road to the academy and then up the lane to the seminary.

Even though David was attracted to this beguiling young woman, he was bothered by the likelihood that her family owned slaves. This would be in direct conflict with his ardent anti-slavery sentiments which had emerged while reading *The Liberator* and *Uncle Tom's Cabin*. His heart and his conscience might not agree on his choice of female company.

There was only one way to find out, and that was to meet her on Saturday evening. Wild horses couldn't drag him away from this rendezvous with this enchanting southern belle.

On his way to the seminary, it hit him. "I know nothing about this young woman. What am I going to say to her? Please, oh please, don't let me make a fool of myself." He quickly hitched Tuscarora Chief to the rail and bounded up the two flights of steps. He stopped in front of the double door, wiped the dust from his shoes on the back of his pant legs, straightened his waistcoat, took a deep breath, and struck the knocker.

A young female student with a huge smile opened the door, curtsied, and inquired in a rehearsed fashion, "Good evening, sir. I am Miss Gallatin. Whom shall I announce is calling, and for whom are you calling?"

David was taken aback by the formality of the greeting, and after a brief hesitation, he stated as firmly and positively as possible, "I'm David Evans, and I'm here to call upon Miss Abigail

Volkner."

"Do come right in, Mr. Evans. Miss Volkner is expecting you. Please follow me and I'll announce your presence."

David felt like a little boy about to be punished as he followed Miss Gallatin into the great hallway. After she disappeared through the double door to the right, he could hear her announcing that Mr. Evans was here to call upon Miss Volkner.

When Miss Gallatin reappeared in the grand hallway, she urged him to enter. "Miss Volkner awaits you, Mr. Evans. Do have a good evening." She curtsied once again and retreated out of the doorway and back across the hallway to her chair by the front entrance.

"Thank you, Miss Gallatin, and may you have a pleasant evening as well."

David entered the parlor and was completely spellbound. He knew that she was absolutely beautiful, but in this atmosphere of candlelight and shadows, she was beyond description. He experienced tightness in his chest, and at first he found it difficult to speak. He approached her slowly and deliberately and bowed slightly, while extending his right hand. "I'm so delighted to be here; thank you so much for inviting me to share this evening with you. You look so radiant and beautiful." He could hardly believe that he had uttered those last words.

She arose and walked lightly and erectly toward him, every movement smooth and graceful with a hint of sensuousness. She halted, curtsied, and lifted her right hand fashionably to accept his. A joyous light leaped into her blue eyes, and a happy smile curved her red lips. "Thank you so much for accepting my invitation. I've been looking forward to this evening all week. Please come and sit; we should have much to discuss."

"I guess you are correct about having much to discuss. I hardly know anything about you, and I doubt if you know much about me. Miss Volkner, why don't you tell me about yourself first?"

"Please, if we are going to get to know one another better, we can't continue to be so formal when we are alone together...well, somewhat alone," correcting herself as she observed the presence of several other couples engaged in conversation in the parlor as well as Miss Everett, the chaperone. Please call me Abbey and I'll call you David, unless you want to be called Dave."

"Abbey it is, and you can call me anything that you want."

"My full name is Abigail Louisa Volkner—all good German names. My ancestors originated in the town of Strasburg in the Rhine River Valley of Germany. When my family arrived in America, some of them migrated through Pennsylvania and the German town of Ephrata where many of the inhabitants belonged to the Sabbatarian or Dunker faith. Eventually, many of these Germans moved through the Cumberland Valley and into the lower Shenandoah Valley.

"Some of the main leaders of the movement to the Shenandoah Valley were brothers or monks of the Dunker faith. About three miles from my hometown of Strasburg, Virginia, which was named after the town in the Rhine Valley, the monks established a monastery nestled in against the mountain on the eastern bank of the North Fork of the Shenandoah River.

"The clays and soils located on the banks of the river proved to be ideal for the outstanding production of pottery. The monks quickly learned the pottery trade and taught many of the other German settlers the pottery business. Now, nearly a hundred years after the founding of the town of Strasburg in 1761, the pottery trade continues to flourish. The town is known throughout the Shenandoah Valley and surrounding region as 'Pot Town.'

"Strasburg is nestled along the North Fork of the Shenandoah River ten miles west of Front Royal, where the two branches of the Shenandoah River join. Winchester is situated eighteen miles to the north and the nation's capital is about eighty-one miles to the east.

"To the east of our quaint little town we enjoy beautiful vistas of the Massanutten Mountain, while our western view is blessed with the Allegheny foothills. Three Top Mountain lies to the south and east, and Little North Mountain to the north and west.

"The Valley Turnpike connects travel north and south in the Shenandoah Valley. The Winchester and Potomac Railroad and the Manassas Gap Railroad intersect in our little town, and this enables our pottery and agricultural products to be distributed to other parts of Virginia and beyond. The railroads make it quite easy for me to travel north to the Tuscarora Valley to school.

"Some people refer to our section of the Valley as the 'Garden Spot of Virginia.' It's really a beautiful location. I hope you can visit it soon and find out why we feel so strongly about our valley.

"Our fork of the Shenandoah River reminds me a great deal of your Tuscarora Creek. Both streams are a combination of quiet lengthy pools and short riffles that add to the beauty of the flora found on their banks.

"When you come to visit, I want to row you across the river and climb up on Three Top Mountain to my favorite viewing spot. You can see for miles and miles. The Indians used to send smoke signals from atop the mountain. Someday I would love to have a cabin built up there where I can view the seven curves of the river and see up north to Cedar Creek and Winchester. I know you'll love it just like I do."

David looked inquisitively at the young beauty. Things were happening too fast. She talked as if it were settled that he would be seeing her often. "You mentioned the Dunkers as being some of the first settlers in your region of the valley. I'm not real familiar with that faith; someday you will have to explain their basic beliefs."

"But what about your family?" Abbey asked. "I've done all the talking so far. I'd like to know more about you."

David shrugged. "There's really not much to tell. Our family farm lies just beyond the ridge in front of your school. We've been on that piece of land since the turn of the century, so we are the second generation to live there.

"My mother grew up on a farm about five miles up the valley, and we're pretty close to her family and my father's. Besides farming, my father sells seeds and fertilizer to augment our income. We attended the church next door ever since my family moved here. I have one older sister, so I know a little about teenage girls.

"I guess I'm somewhat odd in that I enjoy school and all its activities. I also fancy hunting, fishing, boating on the creek, riding my horse Tuscarora Chief, and most of all, I'm crazy about baseball."

Abbey shook her head. "This baseball, I've heard of it, but I know nothing about it. You'll have to tell me about it. It sounds like you enjoy the outdoors. I do too, although at my age, many of the things I used to do are no longer considered ladylike and I'm discouraged from participating in them. Maybe you can help me overcome the obstacles to my enjoying the outdoors."

Long before they were ready to conclude the evening, the chaperone rang a melodic bell to signal that it was time for the male guests to say goodnight and be on their way home.

David stood and looked longingly into Abbey's twinkling blue eyes. "I've enjoyed visiting you immensely, and I hope I'm not overstepping my bounds, but I would desire to call upon you again in the near future."

"David, it has been a splendid evening. I would have been very disappointed if you had not asked to call again. With the Christmas season upon us, the next two Saturday evenings are filled with church activities, but I feel sure that there will be opportunities for us to spend some time together at those. If not, sadly for me, I won't be traveling home for the holidays, so perhaps we can meet during this festive season."

"I don't want to put a damper on our budding relationship, but I have one question I really need to ask you. I hope you won't be offended by this prying question, but I have very strong feelings about one particular subject." After an awkward pause, David blurted, "Does your family own slaves?"

A look of dismay flooded her pretty face, and then she smiled knowingly. "No, my father is staunchly against slavery and war. It's all part of his Dunker background, although my mother's family is Presbyterian. When we have more time, I'll explain the Dunker beliefs concerning those two bedeviling problems. There is no offense taken in regards to that question. I really was concerned it was centered on a more intimate subject."

She escorted him to the door, but with the chaperone standing at the door it was difficult to say goodnight with any fondness. He simply stated, "Thank you for a lovely evening, Miss Volkner, and I look forward to seeing you in church tomorrow."

Abbey felt equally hindered by the chaperone's presence. "Thank you, Mr. Evans. Have a safe ride home."

Their first evening together went as well as either of them could have anticipated. Both of them were disappointed that the time had been so short, and so few subjects had been broached. However, there would be many more evenings to come, and their relationship would slowly grow and mature.

Abbey and her dorm mates practiced the art of seductiveness without ever anticipating the actual seduction of a young man. It was all a game that they had been introduced to before the age of ten. They practiced their southern drawls continually, although the womenfolk of northern Virginia where Abbey resided did not naturally utilize such a dialect in everyday life.

Much of their experimentation was a façade, a ruse to gain the attention of these young Yankee men and to tantalize them with their charms. They followed the guidelines that had been drilled into one southern female generation after another. Keep your feet quiet, with your skirts spread to cover your insteps, and never, ever cross your legs. Keep your knees together, with your hands at ease on your lap. Always look people straight in the eye when you speak to them or when they speak to you; most people of character and standing can't abide a sliding, shifty eye.

It was enforced in the young belles that it was very unladylike to lounge in a chair, and one should never hold a glass at arm's length, like the posture of a man drinking in a tavern. Seminary females walked with their shoulders back and moved with grace and fluidity. All of this had the right effect on the young men of the academy and the surrounding region. In most situations the females were treated like princesses, and in the eyes of many young suitors, they could do no wrong.

CHAPTER 13

The pre-Christmas season went by in a whirl, with no real opportunities for the young couple to continue their discussions and learn more about each other. Like so many of the couples attending the two schools, they corresponded by depositing letters or notes on, beside, or under designated tombstones in the cemetery. Other couples found hiding places for their billets-doux in fence posts that lined the lane to the seminary.

David knew that Abbey was going to be quite lonely and homesick over the Christmas holidays. While most of the young women of the seminary and the young men of the academy returned home for a short holiday visit, about a dozen women remained on the hill.

David knew he might be jumping the gun, but he apprehensively approached his mother. "Mother do you think it would be inappropriate for me to ask Abbey for lunch on Sunday after church?"

Mother Evans smiled perceptively at her son. "That young woman is welcome in our home anytime that you desire. I understand that she and many of her classmates will be spending the holidays at the school. Perhaps you would like to entertain some of them in our home during that time."

Sunday lunch was a huge success, as Abbey joined the Evans family in their traditional Sunday chicken dinner. She and David spent the rest of the pleasant afternoon going for a long walk down along the Tuscarora Creek.

When the young couple returned and entered the living room, Mrs. Evans observed that their cheeks were rosy from the cold. "Could I interest you two in a cup of hot chocolate?" she teasingly inquired. Of course she quickly received an affirmative reply.

As David and Abbey donned adequate clothing to ward off the cold on their ride back to the school, Mrs. Evans extended an invitation to Abbey. "Abbey, I would like to open my home to you and any of your classmates during the holiday season. I know that several of you will be unable to return home for Christmas, and it is going to be quite lonely, so I would like for you and your schoolmates to feel that our home is your home away from home."

Abbey glowed with happiness at Mrs. Evans's invitation. "Why, thank you so much, Mrs. Evans. We girls plan to attend church on Christmas Eve and morning, and the staff at school is preparing a Christmas dinner for us. We also are going to exchange some small gifts, but beyond that the days will probably be uneventful and lonely. So, on behalf of the girls on the hill, we happily accept your gracious invitation."

"Unfortunately, we don't have enough room in our house to accommodate all of you," Mrs. Evans said, "but I know that David will be very happy to shuttle you back and forth so that you can spend as much time on the farm as you like. If it snows, you youngsters can sled ride on our ridge or on the hill at school or take a long sleigh ride in the valley. I'm sure that you'll be able to find plenty to do around here during the holidays."

Two days before Christmas the valley was greeted with the first substantial snowfall of the winter. Some of the southern belles were introduced to two more Yankee traditions, sleighing and sledding. The school and church were located on a distinct slope that provided a challenging sled run when snow-covered.

When Christmas day dawned, the snow that had fallen two days before still covered the ground, and the temperature was cold enough for the snow not to melt for several more days. After the Evans family had celebrated their Christmas traditions and had enjoyed their traditional dinner, David hitched the sleigh to the horse and went to retrieve the girls. Since he expected eight girls to be coming from the school, he had asked for volunteers from among his cousins and friends to help transport and entertain the lonely female students. Not to his surprise, he was overwhelmed by the enthusiastic response from the young men and eventually he had more boys than girls, but his cousin Laura quickly solved his problem by agreeing to join the group.

That afternoon and every afternoon and evening until the end of the year were filled with social activities, mostly outdoors-related. On New Year's Eve a special party was held at Robert Brackbill's across the creek from the Evans farm. The female students were given special permission to observe the arrival of the new year, but they had to return to school shortly after the stroke of twelve.

The social whirl of the holidays left little time for David and Abbey to be alone, but on one occasion, he was able to question her more about her background. "Why did you decide to leave the Shenandoah Valley and come north to school?"

She looked away from him for a moment, as if she was trying to gather her thoughts. "It's a little complex. It was a combination of a lot of things: geography, religion, social standing, wealth, the slavery issue, and politics. Mostly, it was my mother's insistence. She had received a good formal education in the North, and her family was Presbyterian. Once she learned that this school was sponsored by the Presbyterian Church and was not too far from our home, she persuaded my father to send me north to school. He doesn't believe it's necessary for a woman to be educated, but my mother won, and here I am."

David had always wondered why so many of the female students from Virginia did not travel home during school breaks in April and October, and especially during the Christmas and New Year's holidays. "What makes it so difficult for you to travel home by rail? Isn't there a rail connection between Harrisburg and the Shenandoah Valley?"

"It's complicated to explain, but I'll do my best to answer your question. I've listened to my father and his neighbors discuss this subject at length, so I believe I know something about the subject.

"In Virginia, for economic reasons most of our railroads are located east of the Blue Ridge and are designed to connect the Piedmont region to the port cities in eastern Virginia, mostly Alexandria or Richmond. For a railroad to be constructed to cross the Blue Ridge Mountains would be a major engineering challenge.

"The lower Shenandoah Valley got its first railroad in 1834

when the Baltimore and Ohio, better known as the B & O, reached Harpers Ferry where the Shenandoah River flows into the Potomac. Two years later the Winchester and Potomac Railroad connected Winchester to the B & O, but unfortunately no connection has been constructed up the valley south towards my home of Strasburg and farther south towards Harrisonburg.

"My father has always maintained that the heavy freight traffic moving along the Valley Pike should have justified extending the railroad southward up the Shenandoah Valley. The sole authority to issue railroad charters in Virginia is held by the Virginia General Assembly, which is controlled by Piedmont and Tidewater regions of the state.

"The controlling interests in the general assembly did not want Shenandoah Valley products being shipped by the B & O Railroad to Baltimore. The merchants in Alexandria and Richmond have traditionally benefited from the Shenandoah Valley trade, and so far they have been able to deter construction of a railroad system that would shift the Shenandoah trade north to Baltimore.

"What it comes down to is that Eastern Virginia has politically dominated Virginia politics and the Board of Public Works, which is the government body that controls the construction of railroads, turnpikes, and canals. So far, the Eastern Virginia investors and merchants have been able to restrict the economic outlets for products produced in the Shenandoah Valley.

"The Shenandoah Valley is without a north-south railroad. My father argued for the construction of connections to the Virginia Central Railroad that was proposed back in 1852. The Virginia Central was originally planned to connect Harrisonburg with Richmond, but it was redirected to Charlottesville.

"The last time I was home I read in the Winchester newspaper that a tunnel is being constructed at Rockfish Gap, which will enable the Virginia Central to reach Staunton. We simply have an inefficient transportation system for the farmers and industries in the Shenandoah Valley. The path of the old Wilderness Road, with the easiest route from the Shenandoah Valley to a port capable of handling ocean-going ships, has been ignored.

David was impressed. "I'm sorry to interrupt you," he cut in, "but I just want to compliment you. I'm willing to bet a hundred dollars that there is no other female at the seminary or probably any girl your age in Pennsylvania or Virginia with the amount of knowledge that you have about geography, travel, or railroads, and probably politics. You are an absolute marvel. I admire you so much; you are one of a kind."

Abbey was quietly pleased. "You should know me well enough by now to know that I want to gain as much knowledge about my world as I possibly can. I want my man, my husband, to be proud of my background and knowledge. Hopefully, he and I will be able to travel extensively throughout this great nation of ours, and who knows, perhaps we can explore the whole world together."

Then she looked him straight in his eyes and point-blank asked him, "Are you that kind of a man?" She smiled a smile of triumph because she knew he was.

"Now to return to my extended answer to your question. For me to get to Academia, I boarded the train in my hometown of Strasburg because the Manassas Gap Railroad reached our town in 1854 and extended southward to Mount Jackson in 1859. This railroad was never extended south or up the valley beyond Mount Jackson, so as I said before there is no complete north-south railroad.

"The Manassas Gap runs eastward to Front Royal, where a one-mile spur was constructed from Front Royal Junction into downtown Front Royal. It then passes through Manassas Gap, Linden, the Plains, through Thoroughfare Gap, Gainsville, and finally to Tudor Hall or Manassas Junction.

"At Manassas Junction I transferred to the Orange and Alexandria Railroad. This railroad extends southward to Gordonsville where a link with the Virginia Central provides a through route to Richmond.

"I of course did not travel south but northward to Alexandria to a point along the Potomac River waterfront. The Orange and Alexandria was the first railroad constructed on the south side of the Potomac River near the nation's capital. There is no bridge across the Potomac River that can maintain the weight of rail traffic; thus, I had to transfer to a coach that would carry me across the river on a road bridge.

"Once I crossed the bridge, at the foot of the bridge I was transferred to the Alexandria and Washington Railroad which was just completed in 1858, and then it transported me the six miles to Washington.

"From Washington I was transported to Baltimore, then to Bridgeport and Harrisburg, and finally to Perrysville. Someday, maybe you can travel to Virginia to visit me and gain firsthand knowledge of the chaotic railroad system."

CHAPTER 14
FUN ON THE ICE

Although Abbey detested the cold Yankee winter at first, she quickly learned that these winters could be fun. When the first cold snap descended upon the Tuscarora Valley and the slower-moving or stagnant bodies of the creek froze over, she was introduced to the beauty, skill, and athleticism of ice skating.

About a mile or so from the school just above the crossing of the Tuscarora Creek was a dam built to supply waterpower to Patterson's gristmill. After about five days and nights of well-below-freezing temperatures, the huge pond above the dam froze solid enough to allow ice skating without the fear of breaking through the ice.

Most of the southern girls were quite timid at first, but after several spills and falls upon their delicate derrieres, they learned to struggle to keep their feet. With the enthusiastic help of some of the fine young students at the boys' academy, the girls managed to stay on their feet and finally gained enough confidence and skill to glide from one side of the creek to the other.

Soon they were swooshing and gliding without any fear, just as if they had done this all their lives. Once they lost the fear of losing their balance and falling abruptly, they took part in the daring game of "crack the whip" in which everyone held hands in a long chain with the girls at one end. The boys delighted in building up speed and momentum before suddenly releasing the girls into a swirl of petticoats across the ice. It was great fun and no one was injured, although the potential for serious injury did exist.

After church and lunch on the second Sunday of the new year, a huge crowd ascended on Pomeroy's Dam just above the ford at Academia. The earlier snowfall had almost disappeared, and the boys from the academy joined the local boys in removing the remaining snow by utilizing their shovels, brooms, and stable scrapers.

Soon a game known as hockey, which had recently been introduced to the area, commenced among most of the young men. As the afternoon progressed, so did the number of participants on each side or team.

As Reverend Thompson skated down the ice towards the throng of young men involved in the fray, a slight tussle erupted, and a few oaths were exchanged. The preacher could not ignore the expletives flowing from the mouths of the disruptive skaters.

"Now, boys, I shouldn't need to remind you that this is the Lord's Day. But no matter what day it is, that type of language should not be used or tolerated, especially in the presence of young ladies."

Jimmy Davis attempted an explanation. "Sorry, Reverend, but you see, we're losing to the Ebenezer Methodists 5-3, and we're trying to give an all-out effort to even the score, and we just got carried away. We're without our best skater, David Evans. It appears he's on up the creek entertaining some of the young ladies from the seminary, but we sure could use his skills. Perhaps, Reverend, you could skate up there and persuade David to come down here and help us out."

"I'll be glad to do just that," agreed the preacher, "but in the meantime, let's watch our language. Just because you're behind isn't a valid excuse to use the Lord's name in vain. On the other hand, we can't have those arrogant Methodists getting the best of us. If you boys lose, we'll never hear the end of their boasting all winter. I'll be right back with David."

The pastor skated up the ice until he found David and Abbey gliding across the creek arm in arm, although she didn't need any help. "Excuse me, David, but your chums are in dire need of your skating skills down by the dam. The Methodists are up two goals on us. We certainly can't have them beating us, can we? Your church, your school, your chums, all need you." Then he added, "I'm quite sure Miss Volkner is capable of skating without your assistance. Perhaps she and the other young ladies would be happy to skate down the creek and urge the boys from the academy on to victory."

Abbey gave David her smile of approval, and he hurled himself down the ice at a rapid rate to join his teammates amid their cheers of welcome. As the intensity of the match increased dramatically, it probably wasn't a scene that proper young ladies should have been witnessing. But the slashing of sticks, the crashing of body into body, and the propelling of skaters at breakneck speeds didn't deter the girls from watching and loudly cheering the academy boys. The girls seemed to enjoy the speedy and physical sport.

Soon the female academy supporters had competition, as a huge number of young girls from the valley discontinued their skating and arrived on the banks of the creek to cheer their boys on. A large fire was built on the bank of the creek in an attempt to allow the spectators a means of warming their bodies if they became chilled.

One of the Virginia belles queried the pastor, "Reverend, we've never seen such a spectacle before. Where in the world did these boys learn to play such a violent sport?"

The pastor seemed pleased to explain the origins of the sport. "Our Irish, Scottish, and Dutch ancestors brought various versions of hockey-like games to the New World. Versions of hurling, shinty or shinny, and field hockey seemingly have all been adapted for icy conditions.

He went on to explain the etymology of the word hockey. The French word for a shepherd's crook is *hoquet*. The Dutch word *hokkie* means shack or doghouse, and in the vernacular, goal. The Micmac Indians had a game called *dehuntshigwa'es*, while the Chippewas and Sauks called it *baggatiway*, which the Canadians termed *le jeu de la crosse*, or simply lacrosse.

"What you see being played before you is a combination of these ancient sports," he continued. "The games have simply been moved to the ice, which definitely speeds up the competition.

"I read that the ball or piece of wood that is being propelled across the ice with those sticks is derived from the Irish word *poc* which means to poke or deliver with a blow. Our Scottish and Gaelic ancestors had the word *puc* for the same object. We simply call it a puck."

The pastor had a warning about the game. "As you can see, hockey is a full-contact sport with numerous body checks being allowed. It is a very dangerous game, and we always have some casualties. Sooner or later, there will be blood on the ice, and someone will need to be patched up. Luckily, we never have had any major breakage of bones; usually it's just a few gashes or scrapes.

"Just don't be too appalled if someone comes out of a scramble with blood running down his face. Normally, they just apply ice or snow to the wound until it stops bleeding, and then they return to the ice. Hockey has become a rite of passage here in our valley."

Another interested female spectator inquired, "How do they determine a winner? It appears that this violence could continue all afternoon."

"Normally they determine a set number of goals before they start to play," the pastor explained. "Today the winner will be the first team to score ten goals. Right now, the score is Methodists–6 and the Academy boys–5, but that could change anytime. Anyway, I hope it ends in our favor, and you better too. Losing puts our boys in a terrible mood."

Just then, a chorus of triumph rang out as the academy boys thrust the puck against the log serving as a goal and tied the game. The struggle continued for almost another hour, and then with the score tied at eight apiece, both teams agreed to a short respite in order to reorganize and partake of a few refreshments to shore up their strength for the remainder of the fray.

No sooner had they resumed play than a lucky shot ricocheted off an academy boy's shin and against the goal or log he was defending. This stroke of bad luck seemed to incense the boys from the ridge, and they went into a complete attack mode. There was no thought of playing defense; every academy player attacked like hornets defending their nest against an intruder.

The newfound energy and offensive assault paid off, as within a few ferocious minutes of nonstop harassment, the solid "thump" of a puck against the log-goal announced that the match had been tied.

When play resumed after the face-off, in which two opposing players while facing each other at the center of the ice whacked their sticks three times while hovering over the puck, on the third whack the quickest player won the puck and attempted to pass it to a teammate.

In this case, the Methodist player won control of the puck and passed it to a teammate who streaked down the ice on the right side of the creek, only to be abruptly parted from his stick and the puck by a vicious collision, causing the direction of the puck to be reversed.

The intensity of the action heightened considerably, and the air became thick with foul language, which caused the spectators great uneasiness. For a moment it looked like skating was a forgotten art; then somehow David ferreted the puck out of the mass of humanity and broke for the goal. Two Methodists and one of his teammates mirrored his movements, and the race towards the poor, defenseless defender of the goal accelerated.

The two Methodists caught up to David and thwarted his onrush towards the goal by shoving him well off to the right, but neither chose to abandon David and defend the other academy attacker who continued down the middle of the ice towards the goal. David's first attempt to pass the puck to his teammate was frustrated by blows from two slashing sticks.

Suddenly David spun backwards from right to left, and for just a split second he was uncovered. The puck left David's stick and slid across the ice for what seemed like an eternity to David, but it finally arrived at its destination. His teammate Philip caressed the puck against his stick, faked a shot to the left, withdrew the stick, and rammed it home against the log for the victory.

Shouts of jubilation and agony reverberated across the ice at the same time as Philip became the hero of the afternoon. Every player was exhausted. Each boy or man had given his all, but there could only be one winning side, and this time it was the boys from up on the ridge. The same two sides would meet several more times throughout the winter, but no match would ever enjoy the same intensity as this one, the first Sunday of 1860.

That night, and for several more to come, every competitor would feel the effects of that glorious afternoon on the ice on Pomeroy's Dam. Different remedies would be employed throughout the valley to gain relief from all the cuts, bruises, and strains that were sustained during the afternoon. The southern belles who witnessed their first hockey match would forever be impressed with the competitive spirit displayed by all these Yankee males.

CHAPTER 15
THE TAFFY PULL PARTY

Not all of David's social life was centered on his fellow students at the academy or the young women of the seminary. He also had a considerable amount of social interaction with his cousins, friends who didn't attend the two schools, and neighbors in the valley.

During the winter of 1860, David was allowed more freedom of movement in his social life, and therefore more responsibilities. Some of his younger cousins would occasionally take advantage of David's independence by asking him to provide transportation to social events, either by buggy or, during snow, by sleigh.

One frigid and quiet night in the middle of January, David's mother approached him. "David, do you have any plans for this Saturday afternoon and evening?"

"Nothing of great importance. I was considering taking a rabbit hunt up along the creek, but if there is something you need me to do, I can go some other time."

"Your Aunt Sarah was wondering if you could take Laura and some of her friends to a taffy pull at Sally Fisher's near Doyles Mills on late Saturday afternoon and evening. You and Laura have always been such good friends, and it would give you the opportunity to reacquaint yourself with some of the young people of the valley that you haven't seen for awhile due to all your school activities."

"Yes, and I know Laura, she's always trying to get me interested in one of her friends, especially Michelle Kelley. Michelle is a nice enough young lady, but she's too opinionated. Also, she talks too much."

"But, David, you have to admit that she's very pretty. Your Aunt Sarah says that she's extremely bright, and probably will become a teacher."

"That's all well and good; I just don't like people trying to arrange my social life. Oh well, I do enjoy Laura's company, and it will be fun to take the sleigh for a ride up the valley. What time do I have to pick them up, and how many are going?"

"I told your aunt that you would be over around twelve o'clock, and I think there will be three other passengers."

"Three it will be. I just hope it's cold enough that Michelle will have to keep her mouth closed, and then she won't talk so much."

On Saturday afternoon David arrived at his aunt and uncle's promptly at noon. He attempted to load all four young females in the back seat of the carriage, but was promptly informed that they didn't want to be that crowded and that Michelle would occupy the front bench seat with him.

David protested, "I placed the charcoal heater on the floor in the back of the carriage just for you, and I also packed two extra robes in the backseat to ensure that you girls won't get cold."

Michelle smiled demurely from under the hood of her bright-blue cloak. "I never have minded the cold, and I assure you that I am dressed appropriately for this frigid weather. I always like to ride in the front seat so that I can have a better view of the countryside. It certainly is a beautiful afternoon, and I want to enjoy every moment of it by sitting next to you, David."

David received the message loud and clear. It was exactly as he had feared; his dear little cousin and this maneuvering female had planned the seating arrangement to the delight of Michelle. David thought to himself, "Just sit back and enjoy the ride to Doyles Mills. Who knows, maybe she won't talk the whole trip. Maybe she's maturing and doesn't need to express herself as often."

All went well as David guided the horse and sleigh out of the confines of Half Moon, past the dam, millrace, and mill, and then up the hill to join the valley road in front of the store. Michelle talked sparingly, quizzing him about school, skating, and even hunting. They soon glided past the road that leads to the academy, church, seminary, and the main center of the village of Academia.

Then from the backseat Laura cried out, "There's a horse and sleigh catching up with us, and the driver's not slowing down. It looks like he intends to pass you going up the hill before we enter into the turn."

David glanced over his shoulder. Just a few yards behind him was a dashing horse propelling a bright-red sleigh at breakneck speed, far too fast for good control. It was Will Laird; the darn fool was going to try to pass. David clucked to the horse, Trotter, and gently slapped the reins across the horse's back as an incentive to pick up the pace. Trotter reacted instinctively and increased his rate of picking up and laying down his hooves.

The race was on up the hill. The hill made it a little more difficult for the approaching horse and sleigh to overtake David. The occupants of David's sleigh suddenly realized that the other sleigh was not going to be able to overtake them before sliding into the sharp left-hand turn that within twenty yards was complemented by another sharp turn in the other direction.

David gritted his teeth and hung tightly onto the reins; the last thing he wanted to do was wreck the sleigh with his trusting passengers. He guided Trotter into the sharp turn, and the horse responded as they had been doing this maneuver for years. The girls were now squealing with delight and cheering him on to maintain his lead. David wasn't about to be outdone; he yelled encouragement to Trotter, and the horse took up the challenge.

The other horse had now pulled up to within the padding on the back of the backseat, and David could hear the horse breathing deeply in order to answer the urgings of this driver. Slowly, David pulled away, and just in time, because suddenly there was a terrible screeching noise and the sound of metal striking a solid stone formation, followed by a huge thud, and then the sound of wood and metal being dragged behind David's sleigh.

The shrill scream of a frightened horse, and even worse, the terrified shrieking and then the cries of humans in peril interrupted these sounds. David looked around and saw that the other horse had suddenly broken its gallop and was attempting to pull a load that no longer was in balance nor sliding on its runners. The sleigh was on its right side, and four human forms were being scattered along and across the snow- and ice-covered road.

David expertly guided his horse and sleigh through the second sharp turn, slowed down, and finally came to a stop with the sleigh well off the road and partially in a huge snowdrift. Just as he came to a stop, Will Laird slid by, white with fear and tugging frantically at his horse's reins while attempting to remain in the seat of his overturned sleigh.

The upended sleigh slid erratically down the road at a diminishing pace. David jumped out of his seat and ran after the out-of-control sleigh, finally catching up with it within fifty yards. Will still held the reins tightly clenched in his gloved hands, but his hands were now numb with pain and useless to him.

David slipped the reins from Will's unresponsive hands and unhitched the horse from the damaged, tipped-over sleigh. Then he called back to Laura. "Laura, I know you have a way with horses. Could you please come here and take control of this poor animal? I've seen you handle skittish horses before, and I know you can talk this one back to a degree of normalcy. Have the other girls come here and look after Will. I'm going back to see how the others fared."

Will's passengers were quite lucky. What could have been a total disaster turned out to just be a few cuts and bruises, with no broken bones or twisted knees or ankles, except for George McDonald who developed a large goose egg above his right eye.

Still somewhat shaken, the boys worked in unison to flip the sleigh off its side and back onto its runners. The sleigh didn't fare as well as its passengers. The tops of both seats were badly scraped, and the padding had been ripped in two different locations. The left runner had received the brunt of the damage. The runner was badly twisted and bent. The boys did their best to straighten the runner so that they could continue to their destination, the same taffy pull that David and the girls were attending.

Then David turned to Will. "Just what did you think you were doing? You could have killed one or both of the horses—or us. If you had caused injury of one of these girls, I wouldn't have wanted to be in your shoes once her father caught up with you. As it is, I hope these girls have learned a lesson and won't risk their necks riding with you in the future."

"I know what I did was dumb," Will said sheepishly. "I just wanted to show these girls how well I can drive, and all I did was scare them half to death. That isn't the worst of it; my dad is going to tan my hide when I get home. This sleigh is his pride and joy; it's been in the family for years."

"The sleigh can be fixed, and none of you were harmed that much," David emphasized. "At least maybe you'll think twice before you try something like this again. Maybe it was a good learning experience for all of us."

Laura yelled from the Evanses' sleigh, "Come on, we're getting cold and we're going to be late for the taffy pull. You boys can discuss the accident when we get to the pull."

"Yes," chimed in Michelle, "I'm not only cold, but now I'm getting hungry. Let's get these horses moving."

Looking up ahead and seeing snowdrifts blocking the road, David decided to take the path through the snow that turned into the field and went cross-country, creating a short cut to the Fishers' house on the outskirts of the village of Doyles Mills.

As soon as David and his passengers arrived at the Fishers' door, they were greeted with the tantalizing smell of molasses cooking in two big heavy iron skillets on the wood cook stove. The molasses would be used not only to make the taffy, but the teenagers would also prepare popcorn balls.

The mixture of molasses, sugar, butter, and vinegar was cooked slowly while it was constantly being stirred until the mixture began to boil. After it was brought to a slow boil, a small quantity was dropped into a cup of cold water. If a hard ball was formed, it was ready to be removed from the stove and poured into an open greased pan for cooling. Some people like to add lemon extract once it is removed from the heat. Lemon extract was not always available, but tonight it was added to the cooling recipe.

Also located on the top of the wood cook stove was a huge kettle of venison stew, which the teenagers would consume before and during the taffy pull. The boys headed for the stew immediately; all that good cold air had expanded their appetites.

After the boys had eaten their fill of stew came the part of the evening that most of the boys dreaded, being paired up with a pulling partner. The girls apparently did the arranging of partners while the boys were filling up on stew. Strangely, there were always the same number of boys and girls at these affairs.

David knew there was no mystery or suspense as to who his pulling partner would be. He realized from the moment his mother approached him about driving Laura and her friends to the party that he would be matched up with Michelle. It wasn't a fate worse than death, but let's face it, he would much rather be down the road in Academia with Abbey. Oh well, the things you do for your kin!

Not all the boys were pleased with the match-ups and they showed their dismay by displaying forlorn and despondent expressions on their faces. David knew there was little use in objecting; he was just a pawn in a female scheme.

On a given signal, the young women approached their designated pulling partners. Laura eagerly sought out Scott Jefferies, while David surveyed the room, hoping that perhaps he had been traded off to some other female. It wasn't to be; bouncing up to him, perky as ever, was Michelle. He had to admit she was a little beauty. Her light brown hair was perfectly arranged and flowed onto her shoulders and down her back. Her dark brown eyes danced with anticipation, and her cheeks were pink with excitement.

Maybe he was a complete fool but he decided he might as well enjoy the company of this radiant young stunner; there was no rule that you had to be infatuated with a member of the opposite sex to play games with them. It wasn't that he was leading her on; he just didn't want to take advantage of her feelings for him.

Michelle was one of those girls who took delight in anything that she was undertaking, and the taffy pull was certainly no exception. Her whole body seemed to tremble with anticipation, and when he gazed into her eyes, he sensed a deep but immature desire for him. He cautioned himself to be careful with this girl.

She reached out and grabbed him by the hands. "Come on, let's get started." She directed him to the table where the recipe was cooling in an open pan. "Here, we have to grease our hands first, so that the taffy won't stick to our fingers. Some people use flour instead of grease, but we think grease or butter works better and gives the candy a better taste."

Mrs. Fisher stood beside the table, warning the couples, "You'd better wait a few more minutes for the recipe to cool. It's almost ready for me to cut into smaller portions for pulling. If you try to start before it's cool, you could end up with blistered fingers where the candy will stick fast to your skin."

Finally, the recipe was cool enough. Michelle directed David to a portion of the cooling mass, and she placed one end of the piece of taffy in his hands, allowing just enough intimate contact to send him a tingling message. She faced him, grinning sensually and moving with a supple, refined gracefulness. Pulling on her end of the taffy, she slowly moved away from him but never took her eyes off him. When the taffy became stretched into a thin string, she returned to him, lapping her end of the string into his hands, just making the right amount of contact to gain his undivided attention.

The loose end of the string was taken in her hands, and the pulling or stringing effort was reenacted. This time when the taffy was stretched thin, she returned her end to his hands, then began to braid the string elaborately; this enabled intermittent touching of their hands.

A smile never left her radiant face; she was thoroughly enjoying this process. He went along with the endeavor; it was a unique pleasure just to observe this young female in pursuit of her prey, because that was exactly as he envisioned himself. Finally, after braiding their string into an elaborate design, she returned it to the kitchen table and efficiently cut it into bite-size pieces. She gave him one to test, and much to her delight, he nodded his approval. When he reached for a second piece, she playfully slapped his hand away. Instead, she took the piece and tantalizingly placed the candy in his mouth herself, while gently brushing his lips with her sweet-tasting fingers.

She tittered merrily and busied herself with the remaining pieces of taffy. David peered over her shoulder to see what was occupying her, and immediately wished he hadn't. On each piece of taffy, she had taken the sharp point of a knife to inscribe their initials. She turned around with one of the pieces between her right thumb and index finger to show him her handiwork and probably, he figured, hoping to seek his approval.

It was difficult for him to mask his dismay at this display of affection, but he smiled meekly and accepted the offered piece of taffy. He knew he should have shown his disapproval, but how could he dampen the spirits of this beguiling creature!

She quickly wrapped the initialed pieces in wax paper and placed them in her purse. Then she picked up another lump of taffy, and they began the same process as before. Her flirtation never diminished; she appeared to enjoy every moment she was near him, but he simply did not share the same feelings.

When he had time, he observed the other couples. Several appeared to be genuinely interested in each other, and their flirtations amused David. On the other hand, he could tell that some couples were not a good match. Things were getting out of control with one couple. A boy by the name of Earl, whom David did not know, purposely stuck molasses in his partner's long braided hair. This was going to be one very unhappy girl when she began to prepare for bed that night and attempted to unbraid her hair.

As the evening wore on, the taffy began to harden, and it was much harder to pull. The facial expressions of the couples became more strained, and the pulling process took more concentration and effort. Some couples pulled so strenuously that blisters developed on their hands and fingers.

After all the taffy was pulled, the iron skillets were cleaned, grease was reapplied, and popcorn was placed in the skillets with lids to contain the popping corn. Some of the teenagers ate the popcorn with salt and butter; some returned to the molasses pots and poured the sweet syrup on the popcorn, producing popcorn balls.

Another treat enjoyed that evening was the creation of snowbank taffy. The taffy recipe would be poured in a thin stream into a snow bank. The recipe would become hard and brittle immediately, ready to eat or to pull.

The all-afternoon event would not be complete without a snowball fight and a few sled rides down the hill towards the small creek known as Doyles Run. The snowball fight turned into a free-for-all, as the girls decided to take on the boys. In the end, quite a few female faces were washed with snow.

Most of the girls opted not to go sled riding once they saw the steepness of the hill they would have to descend. They also knew that the sleds, which were homemade of wood, were almost impossible to steer. The boys gamely took a few rides and then returned to the warmth of the kitchen and parlor.

The winter sun began to sink behind the Herringbone Ridge, signaling that a very entertaining afternoon was coming to a close. The teenagers thanked their hosts for their hospitality and boarded the sleighs after the drivers had removed the horses from the protection of the stable and hitched them to the sleighs.

Once again, Michelle claimed her position in the front seat beside David for the return trip back to Half Moon. She moved closer than what she had sat before, so close that David could feel her silky hair, which protruded from under the hood of her cloak brushing gently against his cheek. It wasn't long until she felt heavier against his side and he realized that she had fallen asleep. He looked down at her angelic face; she was truly a captivating young maiden. Undoubtedly, she would someday become an attractive and willing lifetime partner for a lucky young man, but it would not be David.

He could not, nor did he want to, forget his feelings for Abbey. It would be grossly unfair for him to lead Michelle on any further. When they arrived at his aunt and uncle's, he helped the girls alight from the sleight. As he helped Laura step down, he whispered to her, "Laura, you and I need to talk—and soon."

She smiled knowingly at him. "And I have a good idea what we will be talking about."

"You're exactly on target. Michelle has to be informed that I have no designs on her. She needs to accept the fact that I am quite interested in a young lady from the seminary."

"Oh, she knows all about your relationship with Abbey," Laura said quickly. "She feels that if she just bides her time, your relationship will falter, because she is here all year round, and Abbey goes home to Virginia for part of the year. She adheres to the concept that absence makes the heart grow fonder, but for somebody else."

David spoke more sternly. "In the future, as my cousin, you should not maneuver me into such predicaments as I endured today. You should protect me. Please try to keep that girl away from me. She's too young to be having the thoughts that I think she's having. She could be dangerous to me."

"David, Michelle is my best friend, and you are my favorite cousin and neighbor; you make a great combination."

David ignored his cousin's remarks. "Furthermore, I'm too old for her; she's just a child."

Laura exploded with laughter. "Yes, you're such an old man. You did a great job of babysitting this afternoon. According to my calculations, you're not even two years older than she is. Age is not a relative factor in this situation. Let's face it, big cousin, the girl is smitten with you; she has been for several years. You are her hero, her ideal man, her dream man."

"All right, I've heard enough. I'm just sorry I'm involved in this situation. I guess I should be thankful that she's not a Presbyterian, for if she were, I would have to see her every Sunday morning."

CHAPTER 16
THE ISSUE OF SLAVERY

One gloomy Thursday morning in February, out of the blue Peter Reese posed a question to Professor Campbell that intrigued all the members of the class and would become the subject of discussion and debate for many days to come.

"Professor, I know we are supposed to deal with facts and logic in your class, but recently there have been rumors that slave catchers are operating in the valley because it is alleged that stations for the Underground Railroad are operating in the Academia area. Several are supposed to be located very near to our school, perhaps even outbuildings of this institution. Could you please explain this institution's viewpoint concerning the concept of the underground railroad?"

"The Underground Railroad?"

"Yes, sir. You know, the secret organization that provides a method for slaves to escape to the states north of the Mason-Dixon Line or even across the border to Canada and complete freedom. These activities are contrary to our federal fugitive slave laws."

"I'm not sure the administration or the faculty of this academy has ever considered adopting an official policy regarding this alleged organization or activity. Knowing that you reside below the Mason-Dixon, you undoubtedly have a compelling opinion regarding this practice that probably is in opposition to the majority of most of our students."

Peter retorted, "Sir, I don't believe that is a fair or accurate assumption for you to undertake. Just because I reside in the South doesn't mean that I can't express liberal views concerning the peculiar institution. Many white farmers and plantation owners in my native state do not engage in the use of slave labor, because it is not morally or financially expedient. Because of the geographic diversity of my state, there is a difference of opinions between the eastern and western sections of the state regarding the promotion and practice of slavery. This can be illustrated in a number of ways."

Professor Campbell interjected, "I believe that we should reserve our thoughts and opinions on the subject until we are able to research the subject and find some concrete evidence regarding the matter. I propose that we divide the class into three committees and each committee will be responsible for researching one aspect of the issue and informing the class concerning its findings.

"One of the committees will study the origins of slavery in the United States, and in this state in particular. Another committee will research the abolitionist movement and the Underground Railroad. The third committee will examine Presbyterian theory and policy regarding slavery in the United States. The most difficult assignment will be to uncover reliable information regarding the Underground Railroad, because most people in Central Pennsylvania are privy only to rumors and hearsay. Nevertheless, whatever you are able to find will enable the class to understand the practice employed to move slaves to freedom.

"Several other committees could be utilized, but if we were to include existing constitutional concepts, laws, and ordinances, as well as Supreme Court decisions, we would become so deeply involved that it might be impossible to really examine Mr. Reese's original question.

"So that there is no bias involved, I am going to write a number on a slip of paper that corresponds to the manner in which I announced the committees. The number you draw from my hat will be your committee. If anyone feels very strongly against serving on a particular committee and you can find someone to swap committees, that will be acceptable to me.

"Tomorrow's class will meet in committees, either here in the classroom or in the library. Your committee findings are due one week from Monday; that gives you over a week to prepare for your presentations. It will take you several days to complete the assignment. Besides being prepared, bring an open mind to class; some of you just might change your minds concerning the issue. We will proceed in the order that I established the committees. Good luck, gentlemen."

When the following Monday's class came to order, everyone appeared quite anxious in completing their assigned roles in the committee system. Professor Campbell didn't hesitate in commencing the process and turned the class over to the first committee, whose objective was to enhance the class's knowledge of the background of slavery. Each committee had chosen a de facto chairman to introduce his findings and to facilitate each member's contribution.

Philip Shuman, who headed the Origins of Slavery Committee, stepped to the front of the class and introduced their findings. "We are going to attempt to make our findings quite brief, because we assumed that all of you were well aware that Virginia tobacco farmers purchased twenty slaves from Dutch traders in August 1619 and began the slave trade in the English colonies. Prior to this, Spanish and Portuguese slavers had introduced more than a million bondage Africans to their South American and Caribbean colonies.

"Indentured servants became a far more common source of cheap labor in the English colonies, but by the end of the seventeenth century, the price of slaves fell while the wealth of the planters increased. Planters were now able to make an investment in a slave who could possibly produce one generation after another of slaves; thus, slavery became an eternal bargain.

"In the northern colonies slavery didn't gain much of a foothold because farms were typically small and were worked by the families who lived on and owned them. In the South, where there were usually vast plantations, slavery became essential, especially after the invention of the cotton gin by Eli Whitney.

"Cotton exports soon came to exceed the value of all other American exports combined. Whitney's invention made cotton king in the South and the nation's leading product. A completely new economy enveloped the South and dramatically increased the demand for slave labor to keep up with every aspect of cotton production.

"Even though many white southerners were small farmers and

owned few or no slaves at all, the institution of slavery influenced every aspect of life in the South. In the first census taken in the United States in 1790, there were 697,897 slaves counted. The third census, taken in 1810, showed a 70 percent increase or 1,191,354 slaves. The last census, taken in 1850, showed over three million slaves.

Fred Wright took over. "We are not going to elaborate on the whole perspective of slavery, but we will concentrate on how it affected Pennsylvania. By the end of the eighteenth century, slavery had been well established in the Commonwealth; especially in the southern counties just across the border from Maryland where the farms differed little on either side of the Mason-Dixon Line.

"On February 29, 1780, Pennsylvania's state legislature, greatly influenced by the Quakers, passed the Gradual Abolition of Slavery Act. This legislation was designed to eliminate slavery over a period, beginning with the provision that no child born in the state would be a slave. One of the few exceptions was that children born to mulatto or black slave mothers would be freed automatically when they reached twenty-one years of age.

"Because of this legislation, the 1790 census of Pennsylvania listed 6,500 free blacks and 3,737 as slaves. In the last census, Pennsylvania had no blacks listed as slaves and over 50,000 counted as free blacks.

Fred then yielded the floor to Alex Igram. "Our neighboring county of Franklin is one of the best examples to examine as it is home to a large number of free African Americans. The census of 1850 maintains that 80 percent of the black residents of the county had been born in Franklin County. The others had apparently migrated from Virginia and Maryland. These blacks had probably not run away from their masters because if they had, the close proximity to these two slave states would have left them vulnerable to the activities of bounty hunters or slave catchers who would have eagerly tracked them down and returned them to their masters for substantial rewards.

"In examining Juniata County's censuses from 1790 to 1850— keeping in mind that Juniata didn't become a separate county until

1831—we were to identify numerous individuals of African American heritage who reside in this county, some of whom were listed as slaves in the first census. Most of these people held jobs similar to other blacks throughout the North, which unfortunately gave them little of value to show for their endeavors. Many in this county worked as farmhands and unskilled laborers. There are few exceptions to this, but there were and are those who somehow managed to obtain valuable property and the prestige that is attained with ownership of property.

"It is highly feasible that wherever you find a black population there are people that would serve as allies to escaping slaves and offer refuge to these runaways and help to move them into the mountains of central Pennsylvania and along secret paths to freedom. Along with these free blacks, there are numerous white people who are filled with the zeal to aid runaways on the road to freedom in Canada.

"Since another committee will examine the role of religious groups involved in the slavery issue, we will not pursue this matter at this time."

After a few brief questions, the time for the class had expired, and the class was dismissed until the next day. Professor Campbell commented, "I want to thank the committee for their commitment to the subject today. You enabled us to begin our examination on a positive note; hopefully, this type of effort will continue throughout our investigation of the Underground Railroad."

CHAPTER 17
THE UNDERGROUND RAILROAD
IN CENTRAL PENNSYLVANIA

When the class resumed its discussion on Tuesday, the committee to uncover information on the Underground Railroad began its presentation, with Keith Wells as chairperson speaking first. "The anti-slavery movement began in 1693 when George Keith, a Quaker, wrote a pamphlet condemning slavery. In 1754, the Quakers denounced slavery because they believe that God does not want people to have slaves.

"As pointed out yesterday, Pennsylvania became the first state to abolish slavery when the legislature passed the Gradual Abolition of Slavery Act on February 29, 1780, which abolished slavery over a period of time.

"An organized system to assist slaves in running away appears to have been in existence since George Washington's time, because in 1786 Washington complained that one of his slaves had been assisted by a society of Quakers. Since that time, the effort to help slaves has grown tremendously and by 1831, it became known as the Underground Railroad.

Thomas Kidd explained the format of the organization. "The Underground Railroad is an overlapping network of escape routes and safe havens from the southern slave states to the North or on to Canada where slavery does not exist. There can be no recorded or published paths or trails, and the majority of the routes are cloaked in secrecy, because the federal Fugitive Slaves Law of 1850 enables slave owners to recover their escapees.

"The Underground Railroad appears to have no central structure or chain of command. It is made up of small, independent groups who have knowledge of connection stations along a given route, but possess few details of the immediate area. The "conductors," or guides, include free-blacks, white abolitionists, Native

Americans, former slaves, and members of churches such as the Quakers, Methodists, Mennonites, German Reformed, Congregationalists, Presbyterians, and Baptists.

"The people involved in the care, transportation, and relocation of these fugitives come from widely divergent backgrounds, and they do so at considerable personal and financial risk. In most cases, they simply hide and feed the escaped slaves and then pass them on to the next station or hiding place."

"Along the route to freedom there are men, bounty hunters, who make it a business to arrest runaways and return them in order to gather the rewards offered for them," reported James Barr. "The county is filled with rumors of many places that are used as hiding stations and men and women who support the movement, but we were hard pressed to find anyone who would actually admit to harboring runaways or aiding them in their escape.

"We were able to obtain limited information that one of the main routes comes through Central Pennsylvania. Towns and cities such as York, Columbia, Lancaster, Gettysburg, Philadelphia, and Harrisburg are said to be located along the main escape routes. Closer to home, Carlisle, Shippensburg, Chambersburg, and Mercersburg are believed to be important stops on the railroad.

"The Juniata River and its canal system and the newly constructed Pennsylvania Railroad offer easy access through the heart of this state. Harrisburg appears to be the hub of escape in our part of the state, with Hollidaysburg and Bellefonte as the next major way station. Perrysville and Mifflintown are way stations utilizing the canal and railroad along the Juniata River.

"Additionally, our area is said to be served by a secondary route that comes through Perry County and Ickesburg, and also a route from Path Valley via Mercersburg. It is thought that the key conductor in the Perrysville-Mifflintown area is Samuel Imes. Imes guides the fugitives up the Juniata River to Lewistown to an itinerant black preacher and conductor, Reverend William Grimes. Grimes's circuit ends in Milroy where Reverend James Nourse, the pastor of the Milroy Presbyterian Church, takes the runaways into his home. Members of the Milroy Anti-Slavery Society who aid

Nourse include John Taylor, who attended this institution, Samuel Thompson, and Dr. Samuel Maclay.

"After successfully avoiding detection in Mifflin County, the fugitives are escorted across the Seven Mountains to Bellefonte. From Bellefonte the route leads westward to Punxsutawney.

"You must realize that the information we are imparting to you in this classroom is all hearsay. There is no evidence to back up our conjectures. We are merely repeating rumors, speculation, unconfirmed reports, and gossip."

CHAPTER 18
PRESBYTERIANS AND THE SLAVERY ISSUE

On Wednesday, the committee to which David Evans was assigned reported on the role of the Presbyterian Church in the anti-slavery movement. David spoke first. "I would like to remind the class of our basic Presbyterians beliefs. We believe in original sin and that man was given a free will by God. Along with free will is the concept of Providence. Man has the ability to make any decision he chooses, although nothing can occur that has not been previously ordained by God. We adhere to the unique philosophy of predestination, the concept that God has chosen certain people to receive eternal life.

"Our Church is founded on the reformed thinking and writings of John Calvin. Our most important standards are found in the *Westminster Confession of Faith and Catechisms* of 1627. Our Presbyterian ancestors were some of the earliest immigrants in America. In 1684, the first Presbyterian congregation was formed in Maryland. The first American Presbytery was organized in Philadelphia in 1705 and was called the Philadelphia Presbytery. Shortly after this, what became central Pennsylvania had a huge influx of Scotch-Irish on the frontier. In 1766, Charles Beatty and George Duffield traveled throughout the Pennsylvania frontier, stopped here on this spot in the summer of 1766, and helped to establish what became the Lower Presbyterian Church of Academia.

"Eventually, the Presbyterian Church was involved in a struggle between traditionalist and revivalists, and discontent began to arise in the spiritual realm. The opposing sides became known as the Old School and the New School.

"It didn't take long for the Presbyterian Church to develop anti-slavery sentiments. In 1787, the Synod of New York and Philadelphia proposed a resolution in favor of "universal liberty," condemning the institution of slavery, and supported efforts to promote the abolition of slavery.

"The Church's General Assembly of 1793 confirmed its support for the abolition of slavery. However, in 1795 it refused to consider discipline of slaveholders in the Church and advised the Church's membership to 'live in charity and peace according to the doctrine and the practice of the Apostles.'

"The Presbyterian Church of Pennsylvania in 1808 ruled that slave ownership was a sin and the practice of slavery was unjustifiable and morally evil. Ten years later the General Assembly of the Church made a stronger statement, calling slavery a sin that was utterly inconsistent with the laws of God, a gross violation of the sacred rights of nature, and totally irreconcilable with the spirit and principles of the Gospel. The General Assembly proclaimed that it was the duty of all Christians to obtain the complete abolition of slavery."

George Hodgdon continued the presentation. "Southern Presbyterians believed that the Church should not comment on slavery because it was a secular issue, not a religious one. On the other hand, most Northern Presbyterians believed Christians had a moral obligation to prevent social injustices. Therefore, by 1837 a division had occurred within the church.

"The Church's assembly also advised against harsh censures and uncharitable statements concerning slavery, and reaffirmed its decision not to discipline slaveholding members of the church. In 1859, the General Assembly condemned slavery once again, and many southern ministers withdrew from the jurisdiction of the assembly. So it is today in 1860, we now have four Presbyterian denominations in the United States.

"The South defends its position by pointing to Abraham's slaveholding and his covenant with God not to free them but to circumcise them. Southern theologians maintain that Moses did not abolish slavery but rather regulated it, and that is what should be continued in the United States. To justify their stance on runaway slaves, they cite the examples of Hagar in the Old Testament and Onesimus in the New Testament who as runaway slaves were commanded to return and submit to their masters.

"The Presbyterian churches of Pennsylvania are not fully united in their efforts to oppose slavery. Many congregations and their ministers are quite active in their opposition to slavery by providing shelter and financial aid to runaways, and promoting conductors and guides in their geographic regions.

"A few Presbyterians, mostly located in the western section of the state, are ardently opposed to the Church's support of the Underground Railroad, and some churches have even split over this very controversial issue."

Professor Campbell thanked the speakers for their presentations and then posed a challenge to the class. "Well, gentlemen, I know we have not explored all the underlying issues involved in this tremendous controversy. The research that you have presented certainly should provoke some soul searching as you leave this classroom today.

"I want us to attempt something rather unorthodox in the analysis of this dilemma. Normally, I would encourage you to interact and discuss our findings at length, but I don't want you to utter one single word about what we have uncovered. Instead, I want you to think and analyze the subject for twenty-four hours. When we return to class tomorrow, you are to write your reaction to our endeavor. Still, I don't want you to enter into discussion. After writing your reactions, every class member will in turn read each other's papers. Then we will develop a formal position that this institution will promote concerning the question of supporting or opposing the Underground Railroad."

The following day, after all the papers had been read, the class took a vote and then authored its stance on the Underground Railroad. It was unanimous that the Tuscarora Academy promote physical and financial support for the movement to guide fugitive slaves to the "Promised Land" of Canada or to aid them in hiding in the free states of the North. To the professor's utter amazement, the students took an oath of silence that they would not divulge their findings to anyone outside their class, which would otherwise jeopardize the routes, stations, and conductors in Perry, Juniata, and Mifflin counties.

CHAPTER 19

NOMINATIONS FOR THE ELECTION OF 1860

While Academia's two institutions of learning were abandoned by their student populations in April 1860 for spring vacation, the two major political parties of the nation began preparing for the presidential election of 1860. This was to become the most fateful presidential election in American history; on its results hung the issue of peace or war.

The Dred Scott decision proved to be a major catastrophe for the Democrats as it divided the party into a northern and southern wing. The divided Democrats gathered in Charleston, South Carolina, in April, with both groups concluding that the schism in their party was irreconcilable. After ten unsuccessful days of balloting, the convention broke up when the delegates of seven southern states walked out, and they reconvened at Baltimore on June 18.

The issues dividing the delegates could not be compromised, and within a few days the Democrats held two separate conventions. The conservatives or northerners, following a platform of popular sovereignty, nominated Stephen Douglas, the "Little Giant" of Illinois for president and Herschel V. Johnson of Georgia for vice-president.

The southern wing reaffirmed its demand for federal protection of slavery in the territories and nominated John C. Breckinridge of Kentucky for president and Joseph Lane of Oregon as his running mate.

Meanwhile in May, also convening in Baltimore, the representatives of the defunct Whig and American Parties nominated John Bell of Tennessee for president and Edward Everett of Massachusetts for vice-president. Their platform recognized no political principles other than the Constitution, the Union of the States, and the enforcement of the laws.

Later the Republicans met in Chicago, where they attempted

to draw up a platform that appealed to every major interest in the free states. They condemned popular sovereignty and threats of disunion and denied Congress territorial legislature, or any individuals, the authority to sanction slavery in any territory of the United States.

Abraham Lincoln of Illinois was nominated for the presidency on the third ballot, and the vice-presidential spot was given to Hannibal Hamlin of Maine.

CHAPTER 20
THE SUMMER 1860

When school reconvened in the tiny hamlet of Academia in May 1860 and throughout the summer months until the anniversary exercises were held on the last Wednesday of September, the theme appeared to be business as usual. From time to time serious discussions concerning the impact of the election were entertained in several of the classes, but all too often the impression was that the students and the professors desired to avoid thinking about the unthinkable.

This was especially true of the young lovers. During the month of separation in May, they had the opportunity to develop their writing skills and to utilize the federal government's postal service, as one letter after another found its way between Strasburg, Virginia, and Academia, Pennsylvania.

Once they were reunited back on the hill in Beale Township, they sought every possible opportunity to spend time together. Rides throughout the countryside, fishing and boating on the Tuscarora, picnicking, baseball games, and dances were the highlights of the off-school hours. They ignored the growing schism in their nation and simply went ahead with their plans and dreams as if nothing of importance was occurring in their outside world.

One of the exercises advocated by the seminary for the preservation of health was horseback riding. Under seminary rules, the young ladies were required to ride sidesaddle. This meant that they had to be attired in a proper riding habit. Riding habits of this period had skirts that were five feet long from waist to hem, in order for the skirt to drape gracefully over the side of the horse. Under the skirts, the girls wore pantaloons or pants. In the summer, the skirt was made of lightweight, light-colored material and the girls wore a lightweight straw hat to protect their fair faces.

The academy men had been taught the proper procedure for

accompanying a young woman for a ride. David's first duty was to provide a gentle horse that was properly caparisoned. (A caparison was an ornamental covering for a horse's harness.) He made sure the girths were tight, and then he led the horse to Abbey. The next part became a little uncertain and took considerable practice. With her back to the horse, Abbey took hold of the horn of the saddle, grasped the reins in her right hand, placed her left foot upon David's shoulder as he stooped before her, and made a stirrup of his clasped hands. David raised himself gently and placed Abbey in the saddle. Then he put her foot in the stirrup, adjusted her dress, mounted his own horse, and took his position on Abbey's right. When it came time to dismount, Abbey lifted her foot from the stirrup and adjusted her dress from the saddle. David would then receive Abbey into his arms and safely lift her to the ground.

Abbey detested riding sidesaddle. As they rode, she would complain about having to ride in this manner. "It's so uncomfortable. None of these saddles was constructed to accommodate young bodies. Back home I rode like a man, and if I have the chance I will here too."

Therefore, on most occasions, David would call for her in the carriage; then they would drive to the Evans farm and ride the way she wanted to. Usually they rode down along the creek and forded it away from the prying eyes of the school.

During these rides, David would acquaint her with many of the features of the valley and the people who inhabited it. Abbey was fascinated by the Amish population that had begun moving into the valley, because they reminded her of the Dunkers and Mennonites of the Shenandoah. She became familiar with the David Esh farm just across the creek and John Esh's farm on the hill overlooking the Methodist church. Half Moon also had several Yoder families living on farms as David's neighbors. These plain people had moved from Lancaster and Mifflin Counties, and more families would soon follow.

In early July, a fancy envelope arrived via the U.S. mail at the Academia post office. It was addressed to David, and written in a familiar exquisite, but delicate, script; of course, it was Abbey's distinct handwriting.

It was highly unusual to receive such a formal communiqué from his Virginia belle, and he opened it hurriedly. He chuckled as he quickly scanned the invitation, thinking, "Those southern girls are at it again, always looking for an excuse to entertain the academy boys."

The contents were simple and to the point:

Dear Mr. Evans,

You are cordially invited to the first annual croquet social of the Tuscarora Seminary for Females, to be held Saturday afternoon the twentieth of July 1860. The first genteel game will commence promptly at 4:00 p.m. If you desire a comprehensive review of the rules and a preview of the setup of the fields of competition, please arrive one half-hour early.

An appetizing buffet including non-alcoholic beverages will be served on the lawn following the first round of matches. The standard double diamond pattern will be employed as the setup for the field of play. If time allows, after the buffet all participants are encouraged to compete in the Poison or Cut-Throat competition. This does not involve team play, only individual players. The final player or victor will receive a special prize for his or her playing skills. Please RSVP by July the thirteenth.

That night David responded that he would attend. When the invitees began to compare notes on the function to which they had been invited, the first question posed was, "What are the rules for croquet?"

Finally, after many queries, William Cyrus, who had lived in Philadelphia for a period of time and had been introduced to the game, attempted to explain the concept of croquet. By the end of the week, the academy boys had produced some rather crude mallets, balls, and wickets with which to practice. There was no way these boys were going to be outdone by the girls on the hill.

July the twentieth arrived bright and clear, but also quite humid and hot. By mid-afternoon the stiff collars and waistcoats required to be worn by the young men rivaled the long-skirted and high-necked dresses worn by the young ladies. David and his friends took the advantage of arriving early and listened intently to the description of the rules before walking over to the three fields to examine the gradation of the various terrains, and to look for depressions, bumps, or other abnormalities.

The boys couldn't believe their good fortune in being able to participate in a mixed-sex sport, and soon were pushing social boundaries. The girls were no different; they instantly became involved in all manner of flirtations, giggling at opportune times, and matching the boys for remarking about the physical attributes of their opponents or teammates.

Just about every player, at one time or the other, attempted to take advantage of the bushes and trees surrounding the fields of play. Knocking an opponent's ball out of bounds into the shrubbery or trees meant that one had to be a good sport and follow one's opponent out of bounds to help him or her retrieve the ball. The young scholars fell in love with croquet that hot July afternoon.

The boys soon discovered that the girls routinely cheated by using their attire to their advantage. Repeatedly, the girls disguised or camouflaged a subtle kick of the ball that either directed their opponent's ball away from the wicket or moved their ball into a more advantageous position. At first, the boys took exception to this ploy and cried foul, but eventually they ignored the girls' behavior and immensely enjoyed the company of their alluring hostesses.

Most of the boys had been in similar situations and were now wise and mature enough to accept this leveling of the playing field and weren't about to judge the girls' competitive morality according to the sporting codes they exacted of themselves.

When it came time for the dinner break and the consumption of the scrumptious buffet, the girls resorted to their former elegance and grace, and the competitive measures were no longer in evidence. Refinement, daintiness, and demureness were now in vogue, but it did not deter the innocent flirtations and amicable camaraderie exhibited previously. In most cases, the girls paired off with the young men they had invited and sought a solitary area of the lawn to share their food and drink. Most of the boys thought they were in heaven.

After most of the food had been consumed and the leftover food returned to the kitchen, April Baldwin stood up to explain the later segment of the social event. "We are now forgoing the genteel game of croquet that has been exhibited thus far, and embarking on what could become a fiercely competitive game of skill and strategy.

"Each of us will draw from a hat a slip of paper with a 1, 2, or 3 on it . The number represents which field you will compete on for this final round. Field one is in front of the school, two behind the school, and three to the east towards the church. The winner from each field will meet to determine the overall victor.

The phase of the game that we are entering is known as Poison or Cut-throat. It's quite simple. Once a player completes the course, he becomes 'poison.' When he hits another ball, that ball is dead and taken out of play. When all the players except one are eliminated, that player is the winner. The three winners will then meet to determine the overall champion. Good luck to all the players, and may the best man or woman win."

David pulled a one, while Abbey drew a three, so the only way they would compete against each other again would be in the finals. This was not to be, because Abbey was the next to last to be knocked out of her field, and David, by the luck of a bad bounce for April, represented the ones.

The eastern field was chosen for the final round of play because the sun was sinking behind the ridge, and this field would have sunlight for a few minutes longer than the others would. The cheering, ridiculing, and teasing was monumental throughout the competition, and with very little sunlight remaining, Fred Demsey stroked a fortuitous shot that struck David's ball dead center and ended the fun and competition for the day, a day that all the participants would remember the rest of their lives.

David took the lucky shot all in stride and enthusiastically congratulated the ecstatic winner. Fred's trophy was a fitting one, a croquet ball signed by all the girls. Not to be outdone, the boys signed it as well.

David and Abbey strolled back to the school, allowing their hands to touch as they watched the final rays of the sun disappear from the valley.

"I certainly thank you for inviting me to partake of this delightful afternoon and evening," David said. "I'm sorry I didn't win the ball for you, but since this was the first annual croquet event, we should have at least one more chance to win it."

"Thank you so much for coming and making this event so enjoyable," Abbey replied. "It means so much to be with you, even though we can't enjoy much physical contact. I just enjoy sharing with you."

"I'd better saddle Chief and ride home. Hope to see you tomorrow in church. I'll try to walk you back to school if I'm permitted. I know I'll dream of you."

"And I will dream of you. Be careful on your ride home. Goodnight."

With the last days of the summer session looming and vacation awaiting them in the last week of September, the inseparable couple concocted a scheme that would allow them to spend several weeks of the October vacation together.

David's aunt, his father's older sister, lived in Winchester, Virginia, just a few miles from Strasburg. The plan developed that David would visit his aunt for at least two weeks during October, so that he would be able to ride on a daily basis to visit Abbey and her family on the outskirts of Strasburg. Amazingly, his mother went along with the scheme and soon obtained her sister-in-law's agreement to the plan. He would have to decide whether to travel by railroad or simply to ride on horseback to Virginia.

Soon Abbey had drawn up an agenda of activities that they could enjoy together while David visited northern Virginia. One journey that was especially important to her was a day's trek to the top of Three Top Mountain, located just across the North Fork of the Shenandoah River.

"You think you have some beautiful vistas here in the Tuscarora Valley," she gushed. "Well, you haven't seen anything yet. We'll be able to see for miles and miles once we reach the zenith of that mountain. It's a real challenge to climb to the lookout, but I assure you it will be worth the struggle. We'll wait for the weather to be just right. We want to have the clearest day possible. I want you to fall in love with my section of Virginia, just as I have fallen in love with your Tuscarora Valley."

CHAPTER 21
THE FAIR AT PERRYSVILLE

One event in early October which David did not want to miss was the agricultural fair held in Perrysville by the Juniata County Agricultural Society. The agricultural society had been organized in 1852, and the first fair was held in October of 1853.

Between 1853 and 1858, the exhibition had been held alternately between Mifflintown and Perrysville on grounds rented by the agricultural society. In 1859 the Juniata County Agricultural Society took the initial measure to ensure a permanent location for the fair by purchasing three acres of ground near Perrysville along the Tuscarora Creek just below the bridge and ford between St. Tammany's Town and Perrysville.

(AUTHOR'S NOTE: About 1833 a post office was established in St. Tammany's Town called Port Royal. In 1847 the post office was moved to Perrysville, but the name of the post office remained Port Royal. Finally in 1874 the name of Perrysville was dropped and the borough took the name of the post office, Port Royal. St. Tammany's Town then became known as Old Port.)

Several exhibition buildings were constructed on the site for the local people to display their agricultural products, handcrafted wares, and baked goods, as well as the latest devices and inventions on the market. Most of the devices involved modern labor -saving conveniences for the women to purchase. Farm equipment, new seeds and fertilizers, and new breeds of animals usually attracted the men.

Traveling theatre groups and shows also attracted a great deal of attention at the fair. Minstrel shows had become the rage in some areas of the country and eventually found their way to Perrysville via the Pennsylvania Canal or the newly constructed Pennsylvania Railroad, which had stops in the little town of Perrysville.

The Juniata County fair was held at a convenient time of the year for most local farmers. By this time of year, the only major crop that had not yet been harvested was corn, but most valley farmers were picking it by this week.

For many residents of the Tuscarora Valley, the fair at Perrysville had become one of the major highlights of the year. People of all ages looked forward to this special week. Their entire work schedule was rearranged so that the whole family could enjoy the festivities.

Early October was an ideal time for David because the summer school term had concluded in the last week of September, so there was no concern about missing school. This year the fair held a special meaning: for the first time, his parents had given him permission to enter Chief in the horse races.

As soon as the frost had left the ground, he had begun working with Chief to build speed and endurance in preparation for the races held at the end of the fair session on Friday and Saturday. David had paid particular attention to the type of feed that he fed his horse. Chief was a willing participant in the training process, and now he looked stronger and swifter than ever.

On Friday morning of the fair the Evans family packed a picnic lunch, some homemade lemonade, two blankets, and a few folding chairs in the family buggy. David did not mount Tuscarora Chief; instead, he hitched the horse to the back of the buggy. He didn't want to tire the horse by having to carry David's weight the five miles between Half Moon and Perrysville.

It was a beautiful fall day; a few clouds decorated the blue sky, and the sun was shining brightly, promising temperatures in the high seventies' range. The trees on the Limestone Ridge and Herringbone Ridge, which paralleled the valley road and the Tuscarora Creek, were displaying a wide range of oranges, reds, and yellows. It was one of those days that made one realize just how magnificent the works of Our Creator really are.

As the Evans family proceeded down the valley, they observed little puffs of dust rising from the road at uneven intervals. These little wisps of dust indicated that many of their valley neighbors were headed for the fair also. That was one of the most attractive aspects of the fair, the socializing that went on among neighbors, friends, acquaintances, and even relatives whom you might not see from one fair to the next.

The fair at Perrysville, like any fair, was a special gathering of young people where they could encounter new acquaintances, especially of the opposite sex. Many married couples attributed their romantic origins to the fair.

In about a half-hour after beginning their journey, the Evans horse and buggy trotted between the two impressive Groninger homes located on opposite sides of the road just before the Groninger ford on the Tuscarora Creek. Both Groninger buggies were missing from their usual parking spot, so it was assumed that the Groninger clan was already at the fair.

The Groninger ford was not that great a challenge, but one did have to be careful. The water was not deep or swift at this time of year, but one never knew where a submerged rock might give a good jolt to the wheel of the buggy as it made contact. David was concerned about Chief becoming spooked at the crossing of the creek, so he unhitched the horse and walked it to the other bank. After Mr. Evans had urged his horse up the east bank of the creek, he halted and David reattached Chief to the buggy.

In another ten to fifteen minutes, the Evans buggy turned left onto what was the old Tuscarora Path, which most people referred to as the Tuscarora Valley Road or Pike. Just before they arrived at this intersection, if they looked eastward, they could view the race-track and fairgrounds located south of Perrysville near the Tuscarora Creek. Now they were descending Hertzler's Hill and soon crossed Hunter's Creek that was dammed just above the road. The dam provided power to Hertzler's Mill located downstream of the dam and now on the buggy's left.

After crossing the stream and observing the dam, the road made a sharp turn to the left, while another road intersected from the right. On the left side of the road at this intersection stood Hertzler's store, which was established in 1838. Beside the store was a nondescript stone house built in 1842. Across from the store was an impressive brick building, nearly a mansion, also owned by the Hertzler family.

Just ahead stood one of the treats of the trip, a covered bridge crossing the Tuscarora Creek. Mr. Evans had a question for his family. "Before we cross the bridge, I want to pick your brains about your knowledge of your county. From what county was Juniata County formed and in what year?"

Julie piped up immediately, "Originally we were part of Cumberland County, which was formed in 1750, and later we were part of Mifflin County until Juniata County was created in 1831."

Mr. Evans was impressed. "That's good to know so that you can understand the background of a tragic tale regarding the ford located below the site of the bridge we are about to cross.

"In November 1813 Thomas Gilson, a resident of Spruce Hill Township, was summoned to serve as a juror in the Mifflin County court located in the county seat of Lewistown. Mr. Gilson was engaged in the operation of successful flouring mills, saw mills, and fulling mills, so after spending much of the week away from home he was anxious to return to his business and family, especially since he had ten children, the youngest an infant of only six months.

"It had rained heavily throughout the week, and when Mr. Gilson arrived on horseback from Lewistown on Saturday, the Tuscarora Creek was full to its banks. Nevertheless, he was desirous to cross the swollen creek via ferry operated by Thomas Henderson, since no bridge existed at this time. The ferry boatman advised Gilson not to attempt the crossing, but Gilson insisted that the crossing be made.

"Against his better judgment, Henderson allowed his two rowers to attempt the crossing. It was a cold day with a very high wind, and Gilson was dressed in a heavy overcoat, his hat drawn down tightly over his forehead to ward off the cold wind. About midstream, the boat capsized and all three occupants and Gilson's horse were thrown overboard.

"The two rowers were not as heavily dressed as Gilson, nor too far out in the creek so they were able to make it back to shore. Thomas Gilson was not so fortunate, and he was swiftly carried downstream and drowned. The Tuscarora Creek, Juniata River, and

Susquehanna River froze over shortly after this tragic incident, and the body of Mr. Gilson was not recovered until the following March near Shelley's Island in the Susquehanna River, nearly sixty miles away from the scene of the terrible accident.

"So, just think how fortunate we are to have a bridge right here. Even though the creek is low and tranquil at this time of year, it can be a challenge to cross during high water. If you look downstream, you can see the ford which is still used by cattle drivers and wagons too heavy for the bridge. It also is a good place for the locals to come and wash their dusty and muddy wagons and buggies.

"The floor of the bridge was constructed across the creek in 1818. It was a huge improvement because the eastern creek bank was steep and some wagons and buggies probably lost their loads prior to the bridge's placement. The sides and roof were erected later to preserve the bridge's floor."

The Evans kids enjoyed whooping and hollering inside the bridge's interior but not enough to spook the horses. Even in their advanced teenage years, Julie and David reverted back to earlier childhood and gave a few whoops while crossing the bridge.

Just beyond the bridge, the road turned to the right, and the excitement and anticipation increased, because there in the field was their objective, the fairgrounds. The entrance to the Juniata Valley Fairgrounds was at the intersection of Sixth and Middle (Main Street today) Streets.

The fairgrounds were enclosed by a perpendicular board fence, with a gate at the entrance, which was accessed from Sixth Street. An oval dirt racetrack was the pride and joy of the grounds, and in the center of the oval was a long hitching post for the competing horses. A few trees graced the grounds and offered some shade on hot, sunny days of autumn.

The horses from the buggies were hitched along the interior of the southern and western sections of the fence. The buggies were parked either at the far corners of the fence or near the hitching posts and the horses.

In the last few years, several permanent buildings had been erected on the grounds to serve as exhibition halls. At the middle of the homestretch, which was on the north side of the track, an elevated observation booth had been built. From this slightly up-raised, enclosed deck, the race officials could monitor the start and finish of the races as well as scrutinize any irregularities that might occur during the running of the race.

Although betting on the races was illegal in this locale, it didn't stop the male citizens from placing good, hard-earned money on their favorites. The constable, sheriff, and police who had sworn to enforce the local and state statutes simply looked the other way when it came to betting on the horses, and no one was ever ushered away or fined for this activity.

The races weren't slated to start until two o'clock, but David had to check in by eleven, so he went to perform that duty immediately. He made sure Chief was hitched securely and had plenty of water and oats before rejoining his parents. By that time, his sister had met some of her friends, and went off with them to see the sights. He told his parents he was going to find some of his friends from school and that he would see them before checking on Chief at one o'clock.

He no more than left his parents when he came upon his cousin Laura and her friends, including Michelle Kelley. The girls were bubbling with excitement and Laura asked, "Would you like to join us in seeing the sights?"

"No, thank you, Laura. I'm supposed to be meeting George and Charlie from school, before I have to report in with the race officials again at one o'clock. Have fun, I'll see you after the races."

Disappointment flashed across Michelle's face, but she managed a forced smile. "Good luck in the races. We hope you win the big race and take the grand prize."

"Thank you," David replied cheerfully, and took his leave to find his friends.

Each year the fair had grown and improved. The food stands were operated by the borough's three churches—Presbyterian, Lutheran, and Methodist. Their food was served family-style, all you could eat, and was quite appetizing.

David soon met Charlie and George, and they made the

rounds together. David's anxiety finally motivated him to return to Chief's hitching area well before one o'clock. He checked and rechecked the saddle and the reins, and all was in order. The saddle's weight had been reduced by eliminating some of the leather and padding, giving them the advantage of less carrying weight than many of the horses and riders.

There were five heats; the winner of each heat would be eligible for the final race, and the grand cup would go to its winner. David was scheduled to run in the second race, which he won by two lengths. After the race, David walked and exercised Chief, and then rubbed him down well.

When the first call for the championship race was announced, David's family walked into the infield of the track and wished him good luck. Laura and her entourage yelled good luck from the other side of the track, but David was concentrating so much on his preparations that he hardly noticed. He then walked Chief to the starting gate, and made his final adjustments on the cinch and reins.

Before long, the moment of truth arrived, and he was astride Chief awaiting the dropping of the starter's flag. When the flag dropped, the five horses broke into a frenzied gallop. David held Chief back at first, getting the feel of the track and the pace of the other horses. Midway through the backstretch, he let Chief have his head, and the horse responded magnificently, increasing the length and timing of its stride.

Coming out of the third turn, they were in second place, just as he had planned. He yelled encouragement in the horse's ear and applied additional pressure with his knees and heels. David could sense Chief's reaction and maneuvered the reins to pass the leading horse on the outside.

The lead was easily within David's grasp, and then the unthinkable occurred. From out of the crowd lined along the beginning yards of the homestretch, a bonnet was blown by a sudden gust of wind into the track. Chief bolted, broke stride, and stumbled. David was launched from his saddle headlong towards the fence. He hit the ground with a terrible crunching sound, and then rolled head over heels, coming to a rest face down in the dirt.

A gasp erupted from the crowd, as David lay motionless on the turf while the other four horses galloped to the finish line. David's father vaulted the fence and raced to his fallen son, anticipating the worst possible scenario. Race officials and fans also sprinted to David's side.

Very cautiously, Mr. Evans turned over his unresponsive son. Mr. Evans laid his son's head on his lap as he kneeled on the track; he leaned over to check for a pulse, and David reacted in pain to the pressure of his father's grasp. Mr. Evans let out a cry of relief when David opened his eyes. He hugged his son, who managed to whisper, "I'm fine, Father, I just had the wind knocked out of me. Just give me a minute to regain my wits, and I'll get off this track." By now, Mrs. Evans and Julie had arrived and began to cry tears of joy upon seeing that David appeared to be on the way to recovering his senses.

After a short time, David stood and tested his extremities to make sure nothing was broken. Everything seemed to be in good working condition, except for his left wrist. Dr. John P. Sterrett, who happened to be in attendance, made his way down to the track to examine the wrist for a possible fracture. Dr. Sterrett had been born in Milford Township and studied with Dr. Joseph Kelly of Spruce Hill. In the fall of 1849, he had opened his own office in Johnstown (Walnut), and then the following spring he moved to Academia.

Before he would allow the doctor to examine him, David insisted that he see Chief and examine the horse thoroughly. Chief had bolted and bucked down the homestretch and finally was brought under control by several race officials. Now they walked the nervous animal back to its owner, who ran his hands over Chief's withers, legs, stocking, and hooves. Once it was apparent that the horse had not suffered any broken bones or pulled muscles, David allowed the doctor to examine him.

Dr. Sterrett tested his clavicle, his left elbow, wrist, the hand bones, and the fingers and thumb. Finally, he made his analysis. "I don't think anything is broken, but your left wrist is badly sprained.

I think it will be best if we immobilize it for a week or so. I'm going to splint it and place it in a sling. It's going to be uncomfortable for a period, and you won't have your normal strength for a month or so. You're very fortunate that you didn't break your neck, legs, or arms. That's the nastiest racing spill I've ever observed."

With every part of his body hurting, David walked Chief over to the infield, gathered his equipment and clothing, and painfully walked over to the Evans buggy. His fair visit was over; all he wanted to do was lie down in the back of the buggy, which he did.

He told his parents, "Don't worry about me. I'm just going to rest for a while; you three continue enjoying the fair, and I'll join you eventually."

David didn't get much rest as well-wishers dropped by the Evans buggy and expressed their concern. Whenever the subject of the outcome of the race was brought up, he simply said, "I don't want to discuss the accident. What happened is just one of the risks you take when you enter a race. I'll be back next year, and Chief will win the big one going away."

Strangely, Laura and her troupe of females were not among the well-wishers. No one ever told him the truth about the origin of the wayward bonnet that caused the accident. It belonged to one of Laura's group, but everyone felt it was best that David never know from whose head it escaped. David failed to notice that his former most ardent admirer, Michelle, had not approached him as aggressively as she had in the past. David thought it strange that Laura didn't come to inquire about his welfare, but it soon passed from David's thoughts. There was still plenty of fair to see before it closed that night for another year.

While David was recuperating, his parents visited the booths that contained new farm machinery, new household items, and the food displays. They also visited old acquaintances. George and Charlie talked David into leaving his perch on the buggy and making the rounds of the fair. Everyone he saw was glad to see that he was up and moving about; he had given all the fair-attendees quite a scare.

Since Perrysville was on the mainline of the Pennsylvania Railroad between Harrisburg and Pittsburgh, the fair was easily accessible for all types of new shows and acts from the big cities of the east coast. One of those new attractions was a minstrel show. Minstrel shows had grown in popularity over the past ten years, and it was only natural that one would find its way to Perrysville.

The Moore Minstrels were scheduled to perform at seven o'clock. This troupe of white entertainers, who appeared in blackface, portrayed and lampooned blacks in stereotypical and disparaging ways.

The troupe pranced onto the makeshift stage doing a dance called the walkaround and then exchanged wisecracks and sang songs. One of the endmen related a nonsense riddle: "The difference between a schoolmaster and an engineer is that one trains the mind and the other minds the train."

David was offended by the lazy, buffoonish, and ignorant portrayal of slaves. The greatly romanticized and exaggerated projection of blacks as cheerful, simple slaves always ready to sing and dance to please their masters did not sit well with him. He simply did not agree with the theme that masters need not worry about the slaves because they were happy with their lot in life.

The phase of the show that was more of a variety show appeared to be a big hit. Again, the performers danced and played instruments, but they also performed acrobatics and juggling.

The final act consisted of a slapstick musical plantation skit loosely based on *Uncle Tom's Cabin*, but Uncle Tom was portrayed as a harmless bootlicker to be scorned. Here again, David took offense at the interpretation.

On the way home, David mentioned to his parents, "I'm glad I was able to see a minstrel show, but that will be my last. I just don't agree with the message they send regarding racial stereotypes and pro-plantation attitudes. On the other hand, maybe observing this portrayal will prepare me for my travels below the Mason-Dixon Line next week."

CHAPTER 22
DAVID VISITS VIRGINIA

Monday, October the fifteenth, dawned bright and brilliant. David Evans and his cousin George Patterson loaded their carpetbags into the Evans buggy, and Mr. Evans drove the two boys down the valley to catch the seven o'clock Pennsylvania Railroad train at Perrysville. The cousins were full of excitement as they boarded the train to embark on the first phase of the journey that would take them to Harrisburg.

The train chugged and built up steam as it crossed the Tuscarora Creek and swung along the ridge south of Perrysville, passing the villages of Mexico and Tuscarora before stopping at the Thompsontown station. Millerstown and Newport were next, and soon they arrived at the Rockville Bridge at Marysville, which traverses the wide Susquehanna River, and arrived at the station in Harrisburg. From there they traveled south along the eastern bank of the Susquehanna to Columbia. Columbia had been the western terminus of the Philadelphia and Columbia Railroad, which became part of the Pennsylvania Railroad in 1846.

At Columbia, they switched to the Northern Central Railway, and the tracks crossed the Susquehanna River on the Columbia-Wrightsville Bridge. From Wrightsville they passed York and headed to Baltimore.

Because railway companies were connecting the Shenandoah Valley of Virginia to Baltimore and Pennsylvania rather than Richmond or Alexandria and Washington, the route the boys would follow would be that of the Baltimore and Ohio Railroad.

The lower, or northern, portion of the Shenandoah Valley had received its first railroad connection in 1834 when the B & O Railroad extended westward to Harpers Ferry, Virginia. In 1836, the Winchester and Potomac Railroad connected Winchester, Virginia, to the Baltimore and Ohio Railroad, but it would be several years until a connection was constructed up the Shenandoah to Strasburg and Harrisonburg. The boys were traveling to Winchester on the first leg of their journey, and it would only be David's need to arrive in Strasburg to visit Abbey later.

If they had been going directly to Strasburg, they would have taken the Orange and Alexandria Railroad out of Alexandria, Virginia, across the Potomac River from Washington, D.C., to Manassas Junction. At the junction they would have used the Manassas Gap Railroad to Front Royal and then to Strasburg.

When the boys arrived in Baltimore, they disembarked at Bolton Station and decided to save money by walking the nearly two miles to Camden Station of the B & O Railroad. The B & O transported them through the nation's capital westward along the Potomac River to the town of Harpers Ferry where the Shenandoah River empties into the Potomac River.

At Harpers Ferry, they transferred to the Winchester and Potomac Railroad for the final stage of their journey to Winchester, Virginia, the home of David's aunt and uncle. His aunt was his father's sister, Sarah, who had married a native Virginian, a successful banker and businessman in Winchester.

The boys spent Tuesday and Wednesday exploring Winchester and meeting his Aunt Sarah's numerous friends. Then Aunt Sarah suggested, "Boys, I know you didn't come all this way just to visit your old aunt and uncle. I've been told that David's real interest lies just a few miles down the road in Strasburg. She must be some kind of young lady to inspire you to make this lengthy trip."

"She's a true southern beauty, Aunt Sarah," David declared. "I want you to meet her and see if you agree."

"It doesn't really matter what I think, but knowing you, I would imagine what you say is true."

George spoke up. "I hate to admit it, but for once David is right. Abbey is one of a kind; she's really special. I hope she has a friend just like her waiting for me."

"Young men, I suggest that you don't keep Abbey and her friend waiting any longer," Aunt Sarah said. "Tomorrow you may borrow the horse and surrey and drive down to Strasburg. I'll pack you some sandwiches and cookies to sustain you on your short journey. I certainly don't want you to arrive famished. Do you plan to stay overnight?"

David looked puzzled. "We hadn't discussed any details, and therefore we'll return tomorrow evening. If all goes well, I would imagine we would be returning to Strasburg the next day, perhaps for several days. We didn't make any definite plans; we were just excited about the prospect of visiting the Shenandoah Valley."

The boys were up bright and early on the eleventh day of October 1860, and quickly headed south on the Valley Pike. They passed several wagons headed in both directions, causing clouds of dust to form and cover the horse-drawn vehicle and its passengers.

Abbey's directions to her home were easy to follow, and they soon left the Valley Pike and passed through the small town of Strasburg. About three-quarters of a mile out of town they turned towards the river on a tree-lined lane which led to an impressive brick home that resembled a parallelogram with bows on the north and east sides.

Abbey was excited to see the two Yankees, and greeted them enthusiastically but within certain boundaries, although she did plant a generous kiss on David. "I've been anticipating your arrival ever since I returned home from school. There are so many people I want you to meet and so many places to show you, I don't know how I'll be able to accomplish it all in such a short time."

David's eyes quickly perceived the interior of the brick home as a charming picture of elegance. The front double doors from the porch entered into a wide, cool paneled hall. One side of the hall led into an impressive dining room, while the other side housed a drawing room with a huge marble-mantled fireplace. The end of the hallway led to an open stairway and a second-floor landing lighted by a triple window. The hall, dining room, and drawing room all were graced with an elaborate chandelier.

David's scrutiny was interrupted by Abbey who had noticed a look of anguish or distress on George's face. "George, don't look so mournful," she told him. "Just you wait until you see my friend, who has agreed to entertain you. You won't be disappointed, and you might not want to return to Pennsylvania. She's a real flower of the Shenandoah Valley. Her name is Anna Mason, and she lives just two farms down the road. After we meet my family and make sure you've had plenty to eat, we'll ride over to meet her."

Abbey introduced the boys to her family. Within an hour, they were back on the road, with George in the driver's seat, and Abbey and David in the backseat getting reacquainted. Once they picked up Anna, the seating arrangement would be reversed.

Abbey was true to her word; Anna proved to be more attractive and affable than George had dreamed. George was all smiles, thinking Abbey might be correct, that he might just stay here in the Shenandoah Valley. It was love at first sight for George, but with Anna, the jury was still out. Anna apparently found George charming, but unknown to George, there was a boy who attended VMI and he had set her heart aflutter this summer.

At least it appeared that George was going to have a good time while he visited Virginia; no one had promised him anything else. Abbey directed David to follow the road towards the river, and eventually they crossed the slow-moving and water-deficient stream. Soon they came to a grassy opening among some huge sycamores and water maples.

Abbey exclaimed, "This is it, my favorite spot on the river. I come here often by myself, and I've been hoping to share it with you ever since I met you. There's a basket of food and two blankets in the back." That was all she needed to say. The next two hours were spent making up for the absence of several weeks, while the new couple simply began to get to know each other.

The spectacular autumn afternoon sped by all too swiftly, and soon they had to head back to the Mason farm, where they said their goodbyes to Anna with the promise that on Saturday they would pick her up early and spend the day at the look-out on the extreme northern end of the mountain.

When they arrived at Abbey's home, plans were made for Abbey and her brother Joseph to pick the boys up in Winchester at noon the following day. The boys were invited to spend the weekend and into Tuesday in Strasburg.

The boys returned to Aunt Sarah's worn out but happy about the day's events. It didn't take any urging for them to leave their beds on Friday morning, and they were anxiously waiting for Joseph and Abbey long before noon. Joseph and George sat in the front seat, and Joseph encouraged the horse to maintain a steady gait down the pike to Strasburg and then onto the farm.

As they rode down the Valley Pike, Abbey asked, "How do you boys like Virginia?"

The boys looked at each other, and then George answered. "It's a beautiful state. The Shenandoah Valley is just like the Cumberland Valley—wide valleys with rich farmland surrounded by picturesque mountains."

"Do either of you know the origins of the name Shenandoah?" Abbey then asked.

David shrugged. "I imagine it's an Indian name, but I have no idea what it means."

"It's a Senedos tribal name that means 'Daughter of the Stars.'

David smiled. "That's a beautiful name…really quite fitting for you."

Abbey allowed his comment to slide by. "During my time at the seminary I've been fortunate to learn a lot of history of the origins of the Tuscarora Valley, but David never has had time to learn much about my valley. If you will indulge me, I'd like to acquaint you with what I know of my home region."

David nudged George to encourage him to react enthusiastically, which he did. "Oh, I'd love to learn all about your valley."

Delighted by the boy's response, Abbey launched into a discourse on the history and geography of the Shenandoah. "This valley is very similar to your Tuscarora Valley. Just remember that north of the Potomac River, the valley continues into Maryland and Pennsylvania, but it is called the Cumberland Valley. Both of them extend on a southwest-to-northeast bearing, but the Shenandoah is much longer. From the headwaters of the two branches of the river just north of Lexington to the Potomac River is a distance of nearly 140 miles.

"The mountain you see to our right, the northwest, is North

Mountain, the first range of the Allegheny Mountains. To the left, the southeast, is the Blue Ridge. At its widest, the valley is nearly twenty-five miles across.

"The Shenandoah Valley has a unique dividing feature, the Massanutten Mountain, which extends through the middle of the valley from Strasburg southwest to Harrisonburg. We live on the banks of the North Fork of the Shenandoah River, which arises from Shenandoah and North Mountain. Smith Creek, Stony Creek, and Narrow Passage Creek are main tributaries that join the river before Woodstock. Between my home and Woodstock the river meanders northeast through a series of abrupt twists and turns that are known as the 'Seven Bends.'

"Near my home, the North Fork curves sharply east across the head of the Massanutten Mountain, where Cedar Creek joins it. East of here, the South Fork, which is formed by the North and Middle Rivers, merges with the South River at Port Republic. It flows down the Luray Valley and conjoins with the North Fork at Front Royal. From Front Royal the Shenandoah flows northeast and empties into the Potomac River at Harpers Ferry.

"The road we are riding on is one of the oldest and most historic routes in North America. This major northeast-southeast road is now known as the Valley Pike. The Native Americans referred to it as the Warrior Trace. Later it became part of a road system that ran from Philadelphia into the backcountry of the Carolinas and the Cumberland Gap known as the Great Wagon Road.

"The area that Winchester occupies has been a vital transportation hub for over a hundred years and probably will increase in importance with the advent of railroads." Abbey paused for a moment and surveyed the valley. "You see, I love this valley, and it will be very difficult for me to leave it permanently."

She looked at David, allowing the last clause of her sentence to sink in. "Maybe, just maybe, you will be enough of a man to remove me from the valley, and replace my love of it with a more intense and lasting love."

No one said anything for a short period of time; then David

took her in his arms and, ignoring his audience, declared, "I accept the challenge of making you forget this valley, and I pledge to you and these two witnesses that in due time we will both love each other more than our home valleys, and we will make it possible to make our home elsewhere and raise a family."

Soon they turned off the Valley Pike and made the short drive through the streets of Strasburg back into the countryside and up the lane to Abbey's home. David and George were reintroduced to the members of the family and the Yankee boys were soon feeling right at home.

That evening Anna and two of her female friends, Leah and Jessica, and Anna's brother, Jacob, along with Leah's beau, Thomas, called at Abbey's home, much to the delight of George. These young couples all decided to make the journey to the mountain the next day, so the chance of David and Abbey having any time alone was rather remote.

Due to the roughness of the terrain, all the adventurers were mounted on horseback. The females shunned the sidesaddle-riding habit and instead wore riding breeches under their crinoline skirts, which were lightweight and light-colored. The girls also wore fashionable straw hats. Baskets containing food, drinks, and blankets were secured behind the saddles of the young men.

The five couples rode up the mountain until they had to begin the toughest part of the trek on foot. The females excused themselves for about ten minutes. When they returned, all five girls had exchanged their lacy blouses for shirts that were similar to those worn by the males, and had shed their skirts to reveal their riding breeches.

David looked at Abbey in awe and admiration. The breeches showed off all the curves of her beautiful young body, and the shirt enhanced her bosom, which almost set him afire with desire. Perhaps it was just as well that they were not alone; had they been, one can imagine what it might have led to.

All ten young people were soon confronted by the steepness of the barely visible path, and for nearly three-quarters of a mile they aided each other in clambering over the rocks and bushes, sometimes on all fours, to reach the crest of the mountain.

David surveyed the mountain in awe. The face of the mountain was dotted with bushes and short, stunted trees. For hundreds of yards there were rocks and boulders piled one against the other.

The group rested frequently, as even the strongest males found their endurance and strength severely challenged. The boys cast admiring glances at the resolve and tenacity of their female counterparts. These females were not typical of the young women of Virginia; they represented the epitome of cultivated elegance, yet displayed an almost masculine simplicity.

After scrambling like raccoons, they arrived at a narrow ridge, which led them to the look-out on the extreme northern edge of Three Top Mountain. Here a tremendous pile of overhanging rock created a huge precipice. David and the others simply stood and marveled at the scene before them.

Abbey slid up beside David and took him by the left arm. "Isn't it spectacular? You have to admit that you don't have anything this magnificent in your valley, do you?

David just shook his head. "My, oh my, it's breathtaking. It reminds me of the first time that I saw you."

She looked at him in wonder, a huge smile on her face, and then she pecked him on the cheek. "My father and uncles brought Joseph and me and some of our cousins up here in April of 1858, and I always wanted to return. However, it's really special to be able to share it with you."

Joseph began to explain some of the landmarks that were easily visible to the naked eye. "That white ribbon out there in the center is the Valley Pike. If you follow it northward, you can make out Winchester in the distance. As you move south, you can identify Newton, Middletown, and just below us, Strasburg. Our elevation makes it misleading; the whole view is like a large natural map or picture of three counties of Virginia. If we had a good glass, we probably could see the streets of Winchester and those other towns.

"The Blue Ridge Mountains are on the right and the Alleghenies are on the left. That narrow ditch that meanders with one bend after another is the North Branch of the Shenandoah River, and if you look close enough, you can see Cedar Creek flowing into the Shenandoah.

The five couples slowly dispersed among the trees and bushes, taking with them a basket filled with food and drink and a blanket. After eating their fill, they spent the rest of the early afternoon observing the patchwork of woods and fields in the valley below them, and resting comfortably in each other's arms. All too soon, the sun began to sink towards the Alleghenies in the west and Joseph led the exhilarated nature observers and lovers back down the precipitous route to the little glade where the horses were tethered.

By the time they had returned to their respective farms and homes, the Three Top Mountain adventurers were practically exhausted and ready for more food and a good night's rest.

The two weeks journey to Virginia ended too swiftly for the boys from Central Pennsylvania. The boys and Abbey returned to the Tuscarora Valley via the railroads that took them to Virginia. The winter session of 1860-61 of their respective schools opened three days after their return.

CHAPTER 23

THE ELECTION OF NOVEMBER 1860 AND SOUTH CAROLINA'S REACTION

On November 6, 1860, the American people went to the polls and elected Abraham Lincoln as the sixteenth president of the United States. Lincoln carried all of the free states except New Jersey and received 180 electoral votes and about 40 percent of the popular vote. John Breckinridge secured 72 electoral votes, all from the slave states, but only 18 percent of the popular vote. Stephen Douglas polled more than 29 per cent of the popular vote, which translated to only 12 electoral votes. John Bell obtained 39 electoral votes but less than 13 percent of the popular vote.

In the end, 123 electoral votes were divided among the Democratic candidates, while Lincoln garnered 180. Although clearly victorious in the electoral vote, Lincoln only won a plurality of the popular vote, receiving 1,866,452 out of 2,815,617 votes cast for all his opponents.

With the results of the election, the *Charleston Mercury,* which had championed nullification since 1832, became the foremost newspaper to advocate secession. The paper urged, "The political policy of the South demands that we should not hesitate, but rise up with a single voice and proclaim to the world that we will be subservient to the North no longer, but that we will be a free and an independent people. All admit that an ultimate dissolution of the Union is inevitable, and we believe the crisis is not far off. Then let it come now; the better for the South that it should be today; she cannot afford to wait."

On November 9, a New Orleans newspaper carried this statement: "The Northern people, in electing Mr. Lincoln, have perpetrated a deliberate, cold-blooded insult and outrage upon the people of the slave-holding states."

The remainder of November sped by swiftly, but at every opportunity David and Abbey enjoyed each other's company. In some cases, it was simply a matter of David joining Abbey when she was going for a stroll with her roommate Katie along the perimeter of the seminary's expansive lawn and adjoining woodlands.

Due to a message deposited at a prearranged gravestone in the graveyard, David knew the exact time and location to intercept the two girls, and in most instances brought George along to keep Katie company. While the young lovers reveled in each other's arms, the political situation deteriorated in the United States.

In the opinion of many southerners, the election of Lincoln to the presidency was the last straw. The *Richmond Examiner* stated, "With Lincoln comes something worse than slang, rowdy-ism, brutality, and all moral filth; something worse than all the rag and tag of western grog-shops and Yankee factories…With all those comes the daring and reckless leader of abolitionists."

A South Carolina convention met on December 20, 1860, and began the secessionist parade by formally repealing the state's ratification of the United States Constitution and all its amendments, and adopting an ordinance of secession from the United States government by a unanimous vote of 169 to 0.

The news of South Carolina's secession reached the Tuscarora Valley between Christmas and New Year's, bringing a mood of depression and despair to the Evans farm and dampening the festive spirits of the young couple who were falling deeper and deeper in love.

A northern newspaper quoted one observer: "South Carolina is too small for a republic and too big for a lunatic asylum."

David and Abbey viewed the political events with a stoic attitude. "There is nothing we can do to alter the events in Columbia. We have each other for the moment, and we're going to make the most of it. We can't allow politicians to spoil our holiday."

The political atmosphere in December 1860 and the deepening relationship between Abbey and David led to the decision that Abbey should spend the Christmas and New Year's holidays on the Evans farm on Half Moon. In addition, train travel from Perrysville to Strasburg was slow and unpredictable, and over half of her short holiday break would have been spent on the train. It was a major decision for the young Virginian woman, because she had spent all but the last two Christmas holidays of her life with her family on the banks of the Shenandoah River.

This would be her second Christmas away from home, because she had spent most of the previous Christmas at the female seminary. She recognized that not only was she going to miss her family immensely, but she also expected to undergo some culture shock, assuming that the inhabitants of the Tuscarora Valley would engage in traditions and celebrations that were different from those of her family, friends, and neighbors in Strasburg, an area rich in German heritage.

Nervous chatter and laughter greeted David as he jauntily ascended the front steps of the seminary to escort Abbey to their farm on Half Moon. The main drawing room in the seminary was congested as the young ladies scrambled to assure that all their luggage was assembled and marked for their journey home for the holidays.

Abbey was busily involved in wishing many of her friends a happy holiday and safe passage when David entered the huge hall between the living and dining room on the first floor. She broke into a huge smile when she saw him, and he instantly reciprocated, but motioned for her to continue her farewells. David waited patiently off to the side of the wide doorway until she had completed her send-offs, and could turn her undivided attention to him.

They had a tremendous urge to leap into each other's arms in a warm embrace, but that was definitely against the rules and could lead to further complications. They restrained their impulses and merely continued to smile at each other in anticipation of spending almost a week together.

Abbey gestured to the right of the stairway leading from the second floor. "Those are my bags over there. I hope you're feeling good and strong today; they're quite heavy."

That proved to be an understatement. Not only were the bags heavy and overloaded, there were five of them. He immediately realized that he would have to make two trips down the front stairs to their awaiting transportation. This proved to be no problem, but he did decide to tease her about the amount of luggage.

"Had I known you would have such an accompaniment of travel cases and valises I would have borrowed a barouche or landau or brought our phaeton instead of our trap. I don't know if I can arrange all this in the trap, let alone have one lone horse pull this load."

"That isn't the least bit funny. A lady has to have all her accoutrements and necessities, besides her refinements, when she is attempting to impress a special someone's family. I just want to make you proud of me over the holidays."

"There is no need to worry about me being proud of you and the way you look and dress. I would be impressed if you were dressed in the plainest calico or gingham work dress. You are and would be beautiful in anything—or nothing at all."

"Now, David Evans, you'd better watch your tongue. That last statement will get you and us in big trouble. No more thoughts like that—for the moment at least."

As he took the reins of the single horse and turned the trap around in the driveway and headed down the lane past the church, David mentioned, "I was so hoping there would be more snow on the road so that we could have used the sleigh. Father says there is snow in the air, so maybe over the holidays we will be able to go for a good long ride in the snow."

He turned right onto the main road and cracked his whip

above the horse, and they lurched ahead quickly. They soon crossed the main valley road and approached the ford to the Tuscarora Creek, which they did not need to cross. Instead, the road to the farm turned right up the creek and into the area known as Half Moon.

The young horseman allowed the horse to follow its own lead because the horse had made this same journey hundreds of times and needed no coaxing to cover the distance to the warmth and security of its own stall where an abundance of hay and oats awaited it. Now that they were well out of sight of prying eyes of busybodies who might inform the authorities at the academy or seminary, the two exuberant lovers pursued the warmth, stimulation, and sensuality of a long-awaited embrace. They eagerly sought each other's mouths and engaged in a protracted caress that left both of them fervently desiring more.

David reached up and gathered the reins in his hands again and pulled them backwards, indicating to the steed that it was to halt its progress, and the horse immediately obeyed. They sat at the zenith of a small rise and engaged in fondling and groping beneath Abbey's heavy winter garments until they both realized that to continue was inviting disaster. Reluctantly, David collected the reins in his hands and gently urged the horse to head for home.

The Evans farmhouse was not the most impressive dwelling in the valley, but it was comfortable and spacious. It was a two-story clapboard house with a porch that surrounded three sides; the side towards the barn was left uncovered by a porch roof. Chimneys jutted above the roofline at both ends of the house, into which four fireplaces discharged their waste.

The entryway at the center of the front porch opened into a foyer with a large staircase descending from a balcony-encased open hallway on the second floor. To the right of the foyer was a door that opened into a commodious living room, while the door to the left shut off the airy dining room. The back portion of the house contained a voluminous kitchen and a rather cramped study.

The second floor encompassed three ample bedrooms and one master bedroom. During the course of Abbey's visit, Abbey would sleep in the room at the end of the hall. Julie would continue to occupy her own room, although she had offered it to Abbey.

Since it was the Christmas season, a huge, twelve-foot, eastern hemlock had been firmly secured in a stand located to the left of the staircase in the foyer. It was not decorated with candles because the onrush of cold air every time the front door was opened would be a fire hazard. Instead, it was generously adorned with brightly colored Christmas balls, figurines, strands of beads, and strung popcorn.

The mantels and mirrors of each fireplace were lavishly festooned with pine boughs, holly, and ribbons. Candles and figurines were positioned on the mantels in the living and dining rooms. A wreath with its bright red bow hung in every window of the house. The wall opposite the huge fireplace awaited a second Christmas tree, which traditionally was decorated by the Evans family on Christmas Eve.

To the right of the fireplace in the living room was a Nativity scene that had been skillfully hand-carved by David's grandfather over a period of years at the beginning of the century and had grown to include over thirty pieces. The scene immediately attracted Abbey's attention. All she could think was, "And I was worried that I would miss my family's traditional Christmas customs! The Evans family is almost a duplication of my family! I'm going to feel right at home here on the Tuscarora Creek."

It was still four days until the celebration of our Savior's birth, but there was much to be accomplished in the Evans household before that special day. Again, Abbey felt right at home as she aided Mrs. Evans in the preparation of the food for the holiday. Much of the food was the same as she experienced in the Shenandoah Valley. She had been unaware of the German influence in this valley until she realized, "This part of the valley is called Groninger Valley, and Groninger is about as German as you can get."

She tried not to think of her family but instead concentrated on having as much fun with David as possible. When she wasn't helping Mrs. Evans and David wasn't aiding his father, they spent every moment together. She could feel herself falling deeper and deeper in love with this young man, and she could sense that he was doing the same with her.

CHAPTER 25
CHRISTMAS EVE 1860

When she awoke the day before Christmas Eve, Abbey was thrilled to observe that the valley had become a winter wonderland. At least eight inches had fallen overnight, and it continued to snow. They were going to have a white Christmas, something that rarely occurred, if ever, in her section of Virginia. She often observed snow clinging to the slopes of Three Top Mountain, but never covering the valley floor.

This would be a Christmas she would never forget. Now she and David could go for the long-anticipated sleigh ride in the moonlight, that is, if the moon cooperated.

Before dinner on Christmas Eve, David approached her with a mischievous grin on his face.

"David, just what put such an unusual grin on your handsome face?" Abbey wanted to know.

He reached in his coat pocket and removed a small box. "I'm sorry this is not worth more monetarily and doesn't have the same meaning as a diamond to the rest of the world, but I want you to have this as a token of our relationship."

She hurriedly eliminated the wrapping and removed the small package. Her eyes opened wide with excitement when she beheld an emerald ring. She gazed at the ring, not moving; then after a short time David took it from her and slipped it on the third finger of her left hand where it glowed in its dark beauty.

"It's an absolutely beautiful ring," Abbey gushed. "It's a true symbol of our love. I'll wear it forever." Tears came to her eyes; she truly did love him. If only they weren't so young and had to control their emotions! She flung herself at him and gave him a passionate kiss, and he reciprocated.

"It's a rather impressive ring, one of very special meaning in our family," David told her. "It was my grandmother's, given to her by my grandfather on Christmas Eve in 1824. Then my father gave it to my mother on Christmas Eve 1842. So the tradition continues. Let's hope we have as much love in our relationship as they had and have in theirs. I know we are several years away from jumping over the broomstick."

Abbey cut him off. "I don't want you to refer to our relationship in such a manner. I don't want us to make any reference to the institution of slavery. We agreed that politics would be banned as a subject over the holidays. No mention was to be made of the election of Lincoln, the probable secession of South Carolina and the other states, and slavery."

"I'm sorry. You are right. Please allow me to retract that statement; I don't want anything to upset our holiday."

"I'm sorry also. I shouldn't have reacted in such a manner. Let's forget that the incident took place. You've made me so happy with the ring. It's so beautiful and full of tradition and heritage. As I said, I'll wear it forever. God, I love you!"

"And I love you. Let's go to the dining room and see how soon we can eat. All of this excitement makes me hungry."

As they stepped into the foyer, they noticed that someone had hung a sprig of mistletoe and a kissing bell over the doorway. They certainly couldn't ignore tradition. One kiss led to several others, as they enjoyed honoring this tradition immensely.

Eventually Abbey pulled away. "Now, I have to hurry upstairs and dress for the Christmas Eve services. Just remember how good those kisses tasted. If you're a good boy, Santa will make sure that you receive some more during this festive season."

A half hour later, David was back in the foyer impatiently waiting for her to descend the stairway in preparation for the sleigh ride to the church. A tightness swept across his chest as he heard her gently close the bedroom door and walk softly to the stairway.

As Abbey descended the open staircase, David was in awe, almost stupefied. He had never seen her look so magnificent; she was absolutely stunning, completely beguiling. Her green velvet evening gown clung in an appropriate, figure-hugging, unpretentious fashion. The low-cut neckline, although not plunging, left little to the imagination that she truly was the pride of southern womanhood, a real flower of the Shenandoah.

A slight sigh of relief shuddered through his body when he noticed that a bright red cloak clung to her shoulders that would prevent any onlookers from enjoying the very sight that he was appreciating at this moment. He knew she would be very discreet and clasp the opening, thus preventing any prying eyes from delighting in her dazzling beauty.

The candelabrum lighting the foyer highlighted the flaxen ringlets that dangled from her bouffant and aided in accentuating her flashing blue eyes. Her coquettish smile made him feel like a lust-intoxicated dolt. It was all he could do to contain himself from hurdling the remaining steps and snatching her in his arms, but he remained the gentleman. He maintained his poise and waited until she completed her descent.

"You look like Christmas. In that red cloak and green dress, you are holly and lighted candles, and sugar candy all together in one beautiful package. I just never imagined that anyone could look so ravishing. You are exquisite, a delight to behold."

He was enraptured or bewitched; he was living a fantastic fairytale. David regained his composure and hastened to grasp her left hand as she alighted from the last step. An intense, irresistible force overwhelmed the infatuated young lovers, their arms swiftly entwined, and they enjoyed a passionate embrace.

"Oh dear, now you've smudged my lip makeup," she remarked teasingly. "I'll have to refresh it before we go."

David laughed, "You make it sound like it was all my doing. You certainly seemed a willing participant."

"Yes, I was, and I'm going to be again," she said as she pulled him to her with even more passion and desire, pressed her voluptuous body against him and kissed him fervently. She culminated the ardent embrace with a slight flick of her succulent tongue inside his mouth, which left him weak-kneed and aroused.

Abbey whirled on her heels and headed for the mirror at the end of the foyer to repair the damage to her makeup, but she halted abruptly and returned to him. With a mischievous, demure smile radiating on her exquisite face, she embraced him just as passionately. Then she took his bewildered face in her soft, sensual hands, looked alluringly into his eyes, and in a honeyed, melodious voice, murmured, "I hope you are beginning to realize how much I love you and how much I want to be your wife."

He nodded. "And I love you too, and certainly want you to be my wife. In this atmosphere of good will to all, I rather selfishly want to keep you all to myself."

She withdrew from him once again, glancing over her left shoulder as she walked the length of the foyer and then blew him a kiss before she turned her full attention to the mirror and the task of repairing her makeup and replacing a few strands of hair.

Finally, his mother appeared in the foyer in search of her cape, and the magical spell was broken.

The Christmas Eve service was a showcase of hymns that she had enjoyed since childhood, and she was elated to share them with the Evans family. On the return sleigh ride to the farmhouse, David and Abbey snuggled in the backseat and enjoyed the beautiful moonlight scene that unfolded before them.

Once inside the gaily decorated farmhouse, everyone said goodnight, except for David and Abbey who lingered before the fireplace in the drawing room. It was all so magical, but knowing that next Christmas could entertain a completely different scenario, they were going to make the most of this one.

Early the next morning, David and his father quickly completed the chores, while the three women prepared a special Christmas breakfast. Upon completion of the meal, they retired to the living room to open the presents under the tree.

The presents were exchanged and opened to squeals of delight and laughter, and the next hour was spent in a very festive mood. At last Mr. Evans announced, "It's time we get warmly dressed for the sleigh ride to the Andrews farm."

David explained quickly, "I guess I forgot to tell you that we go to my mother's home for Christmas dinner. It's a family tradition that began when my parents first got married."

The trip to and from the grandparents' farm just west of

Doyles Mills was delightful, and Abbey was greeted enthusiastically by the members of the family. She fit into the family very well.

CHAPTER 26

THE BEGINNING OF 1861

The vacation from school was going by too quickly, and before they knew it, it was New Year's Eve. Just before dusk, Jonathan Hood pulled up in a sleigh. Jonathan had attended the academy and now lived near Chambersburg, but during his days at the school, he had become Julie's suitor.

The young couple had corresponded constantly, and on special occasions, Jonathan made the lengthy journey to see Julie. David had a feeling this visit was special, because soon after the young man arrived he accompanied Julie's father into the drawing room, and the doors were closed.

The two men emerged soon afterwards with big smiles. Jonathan announced to the others, "I've just asked Mr. Evans for Julie's hand in marriage and he has given his approval."

Mrs. Evans gasped, but quickly regained her composure and exclaimed, "Congratulations, I knew it would happen sometime, but as a mother, I cannot bear the thought of losing my only daughter. How much time do we have to prepare for the ceremony?"

Julie glanced nervously at Jonathan. "We'd like to have the wedding on the lawn of the farmhouse on the fourteenth of June. If it rains, we can always have it here in the parlor. We don't want anything elaborate, but since both are families are large, there will be a rather large guest list."

Abbey and David bestowed congratulations upon the ecstatic couple. Jonathan thanked them and said, "Some of my friends are having a small congratulatory party for us over in Jonestown, and we'd like you two to attend with us."

David glanced at Abbey, who bobbed her blond curls in agreement. Julie whispered, "We're going to break a few rules tonight, we're even going to dance." She laughed merrily as she glided up the stairs. "Come on, we girls have to bedazzle these two handsome devils tonight."

It was an enchanting evening, full of dancing, merriment, and tenderness. After the second dance, Abbey pulled away from David and gave him a hardy slap on the left cheek, and she laughed teasingly when she saw his reaction. She kissed hin quickly, and merrily ran from the room, with David in hot pursuit.

"What was that slap for?" he inquired in a confused manner. "What did I do wrong?"

"Wrong? You silly damn Yankee. How did you ever learn to dance so well?" she purred. "Come to think of it, you kiss pretty well too. You had to learn from some Yankee female." Then she kissed him on the right cheek, but only for an instant; then she moved her lips from his cheek to his lips.

David drew her close to him. She became motionless in his arms, but her lips were soft, warm, and sweet when he kissed her. Just then, one of the older men walked into the room and observed, "It's a full moon, so why don't you young people go up into the cupola? It will be quite a view in the moonlight."

"That's a wonderful idea," blurted Abbey, and she began to lead the way. As David shouldered by the older man, the man said with a twinkle in his eye, "As a man who has observed feminine tricks all these many years, I would say that young lady wants you as a bedfellow."

David's face turned bright red, and he spun around to confront the man.

"Don't be a fool," the man said. "I meant that as a compliment. Everyone here can see the feelings you two have for each other."

Up in the cupola there was no thought of the moon as it cast shadows on the lawn below them; their only concern was each other. Her face turned to catch the rising moon; strands of her glorious blond hair, loosened by the wind, blew across her exquisite face. She was such a charming creature, especially at this moment when her blue eyes took on a dreamy look.

David thought he would explode with desire, and he could sense she was fighting the same emotions. He noticed the agitation of her bosom, he left the impulse to touch her breasts, he conquered the impulse for a moment; then she urged him to caress them, and he did.

Eventually they disengaged; she struggled to regain her composure and breath, and he did likewise. She looked at him longingly. "I know I am old enough to understand one thing, and that is, I am going to be your wife."

"And I want you to be my wife. Oh. Abbey, I know most people think we are too young to be thinking of marriage, but I certainly want to marry you when the time is right. When I've finished my schooling and have a chance to establish myself, then we can be married. You will wait for me, won't you?"

She hesitated and then smiled teasingly. "You know my father will be upset, you being a Yankee, a damn Yankee according to my cousin Donald. But I must say, the offer intrigues me." She laughed wholeheartedly. "I do rather like you as my actions must tell you when you hold me and kiss me. Fact is, I adore you. Of course, you silly Yankee, I'll marry you. I just wish we didn't have to wait so long, but I guess you are worth the wait." Then she kissed him long and seductively.

Suddenly they observed couples beginning to leave. The new year, 1861, had officially begun, but they had been too preoccupied to notice. Abbey gazed into David's eyes. "Don't you wish this night would last forever? It's been so enchanting. Tomorrow I have to return to school, and it may be a long, long time until we enjoy a time like this again."

David smiled. "You're right. If ever there was the opportunity to make time stand still, tonight would be it. I dread to think of what the days ahead will bring. Nevertheless, no matter what occurs, we have each other's love and commitment; in the end we will be together".

When school reconvened, the January weather allowed few opportunities for outdoor activities; therefore, the two institutions cooperated in debates, taffy pulls, spelling bees, charades, and chess tournaments. But no matter how much time or under what conditions the young lovers were able to be together, they would never be able to duplicate the special joy of this holiday vacation, especially the short time they spent together in the cupola on New Year's Eve.

CHAPTER 27
THE FIGHT, LATE FEBRUARY 1861

David was the last to enter the classroom, just in time to hear the last of the searing, sarcastic words of John Turner. "I tell you, we ought to go up there and drag out every one of those secessionist bitches and teach them a good lesson, just like their slave-owning daddies treat their slaves. Anyone who associates with those southern whores should be horse-whipped too." When John saw David, he paled and halted his tirade against the females from up on the hill.

"Don't stop on my account, John," retorted David. "Continue, I want to hear what else you're going to do to defenseless females. I'm also quite interested in what you're going to do to the likes of me, for I certainly enjoy fraternizing with your alleged enemy. Come on! Let me have it!"

"I'll let you have it. If you're man enough to meet me down at the barn after lights out, I'll show you what I think of your kind. I'm going to make you wish you had never gone near that white trash from Virginia."

"I'll be there with bells on," David said coolly. "I'm going to make you eat those offensive words. I'll see you tonight!"

Throughout the remainder of the day, David worked on a plan of attack against the much bigger and more muscular John. There would be no backing out; he would have to face the bully, he would have to beat him, and he would have to win an apology from him. It was the least he could do for his beloved Abbey and her fellow students. It wasn't their fault that many of them lived below the Mason-Dixon Line.

David wasn't very hungry at supper. He excused himself, saying that he had forgotten an assignment and needed to return to the school for a few hours. Luckily, there was ample light from a three-quarter moon so that he didn't need to carry a torch.

He arrived at the barn well in advance of lights out, but already a small crowd had begun to form. The word of the fight had spread throughout the school, and before long most of the upperclassmen had arrived to watch the spectacle. Many of the students began to place bets on the outcome of the fray. David was amazed that anyone would bet his money on him. Maybe he wasn't as bad off as he thought.

George and Harry volunteered to serve as his seconds, and were full of advice in how to survive the ordeal. David didn't want to just survive; he wanted to win and teach John Turner a lesson.

John arrived with his entourage, who jeered and cheered as they stepped into the crowded confines of the barn. If the school authorities discovered the fight, there would be the devil to pay. Demerits would be handed out, maybe even suspension from school.

All those thoughts left David's mind as he concentrated on fighting the good fight and winning. Jeff Hassinger acted as the referee and brought the two fighters to the center of the makeshift ring and issued instructions. George Irvin was designated as the timekeeper, with each round to be of two-minute duration. George struck a gong with a hammer to signal the beginning of the first round.

John Turner charged across the ring and struck David with a short, straight, jabbing blow to the chest. David failed to sidestep the next attack, and received a blow to his uplifted right arm, which did no real damage but filled his arm with severe pain.

Turner managed to jab a fist into David's face, which brought a rush of blood from his nose. David weaved, jerked, and tried to strike his opponent in the face, but the blow rolled off the side of the head. He followed with another quick jab, but crowded too close and his face pushed over Turner's shoulder.

The bully pushed David away towards a corner and immediately followed him there, raining blow after blow on his upper body. David absorbed the punishment by holding his hands high in front of his face. Mercifully, the first round ended, and David sought refuge in his corner, where a piece of cotton was stuffed into his right nostril to halt the flow of blood.

The second round began much like the first, with David attempting to defend himself from a barrage of ringing blows to his body. These blows did little damage to David, who felt refreshed and invigorated and aware that the blows didn't have the thrust of the first series. Maybe Turner was tiring—that was his only real chance.

David balanced himself like a dancer, and jabbed at Turner's face, then quickly landed a blow to the midsection, followed by a lightning-fast, heavy blow to his nose. The blow snapped Turner's head back, his face became contorted, and for a split second, his arms dropped and hung loose.

When David noticed this, he must have become overconfident, but this loss of concentration cost him dearly. A fist slammed into his stomach and brought vomit to his throat, causing him to give ground. He absorbed a solid shot above the right eye, which caused blood to partially blind him. Somehow, he kept his feet and backed away until the terrible taste dissipated and he could breathe freely. He wiped at his right eye so that he could observe his opponent's next move.

Turner charged in for the kill and swung wildly but missed his mark. David ducked under the wild swing and hit John in the face with all his force, causing David's hand and arm to tingle.

The belligerent John fell forward, his body as loose as a sack of ground meal. David, dizzy and half-blind, stepped forward, stared John straight in the face, and planted a thudding blow below the left ear. Then the right fist came down into the face and the left fist gave him one last jolt.

The next thing David saw was John attempting to rise from the floor, one hand on the ground and one knee up. David strode forward. "Have you had enough, John Turner? Will you apologize to all those girls you insulted this morning?"

"Yes, yes, I've had enough. I'll gladly apologize to every girl on the hill, in person and by letter. I've learned a good lesson tonight."

David reached out with his battered right hand and shook John Turner's equally damaged right hand. "I just want you to know that most of the young women you insulted do not reside in states that have seceded from the Union; therefore, they are not 'secessionist bitches.' We will say no more of this incident. As far as I'm concerned, it never took place."

Everything began to seem distant and bright around David, and the shouting of the small crowd of onlookers seemed muffled. He had taken a severe beating, but he had persisted, he had endured, he had fought more than a good fight.

As George and Harry attended to his cuts and swollen face, Harry enthused, "You really showed him. I witnessed it, but I still don't believe it. You're going to be a legend in your own time. How we're ever going to keep this from the professors and the minister is beyond me. The way your face is battered, it will take weeks for it to heal."

David ran his fingers over his face, exploring the gash above his right eye and the acute swelling of his nose. "I'll be lucky to be able to see out of this eye by tomorrow morning. My mother is going to have a fit. I probably won't be allowed off the farm for the next month. There's no use me fretting over my face. It had to be done, and I guess I must have done it well."

"'Well'? You were fantastic," George exclaimed. "Wait until the rest of the school hears about what you did to John Turner. Better yet, wait until the girls hear about you defending their honor. You'll be their knight in shining armor. Who says chivalry is dead? They just haven't met David Evans."

When he returned home, it took him a long time to give Chief a rub-down and feed him because he was stiff and sore.

His mother had been waiting up for him. "It certainly took long enough for you to bed Chief down for the night. Is something wrong?"

"No, there is nothing wrong," he lied. "I'm fine, I'm just tired. It's been a long day." He kept his back to her, hoping she would simply head for bed and allow him to slip up the steps to his bedroom.

Her motherly instincts told her something was amiss. "David, look at me. I know something is wrong."

He obeyed and turned to face her. She gasped in shock and fright when she saw his battered face. "Oh, David, David! What in the world happened to you? You look like someone took a club to your handsome face. Are you hurt badly?"

Again he lied. "No, I'll be fine. It was just a little misunderstanding at school that had to be straightened out."

His mother called to his father and sister to come downstairs and help her in treating David's wounds. Haltingly David explained what had transpired that day and evening.

"It was for the goodness of a cause—Abbey's cause. John Turner had no right to insult the girls in such an uncouth and vile manner. Sure, many of them reside below the Mason-Dixon Line, but most of them are not from families who are slaveholders. Even though I feel and look this way now, I'd do it all over again."

"Just how badly are you hurt? Do you hurt internally? Do you feel that anything is broken?"

"It just like I told Mother, I'm fine. I'll probably feel and look worse in the morning, but I'll heal. It's good Chief knows the road from home to school, I'm afraid I wasn't much help in getting home tonight, and the morning won't be any better."

"Maybe you ought to stay home from school tomorrow and rest."

"No, that would be the worst thing I could do. Besides, if the school authorities find out about the fight, I could be in big trouble, and the sooner I face the consequences the better it will be."

His father said thoughtfully, "I have a feeling that the administration isn't going to get involved in this matter. Sometimes it's better if the boys sort these things out for themselves. Now let's get you up to bed and some much needed rest."

For all David's insistence that he was fine, his father had to help him navigate the steps and into bed. David's whole body ached, but his head was the worst, as it throbbed and smarted from the beating he had absorbed.

When he awoke in the morning, the joy that he had felt in defending Abbey and the other girls gave way to guilt. Fighting was against the basic principles of the school and David's own guidelines. But where do you draw the line and push those principles and guidelines aside and defend what you feel is right? It was ironic. Here he was, an ardent abolitionist defending women of a slave-owning background. David and his fellow students would soon be facing an even greater moral dilemma, regarding taking the life of another human.

It just so happened that on this very day the two schools were holding a joint chapel program. When he saw Abbey across the expanse of the church during chapel, he could tell that the news of the fight had spread up the hill to the seminary. She looked at him and mouthed, "Are you hurt?"

He lifted his hand to touch the places on his face where the bruises and cuts were located. He had forgotten them when he had seen her. He mouthed in response, "No, I'm just fine. It is nothing."

At the conclusion of chapel, she maneuvered so that they could be close to each other as they left the church. "I heard about the trouble," she said. "It's all over both schools. Some of the boys told us about it as we entered the church. Why did you fight a bully like John Turner?"

"It was just a little misunderstanding. A man thing...you wouldn't understand."

She looked at him curiously, with a smile that bespoke more wisdom than the lips could convey. He felt extremely ill at ease and he wanted to wait for her to say something, but he plowed ahead. "I fought on impulse. I'm not sorry that I did it. I'd do it again if I had to. If Mr. Campbell finds out about it, I'll be in very serious trouble, but it was worth it."

"You can't fool me, David Evans. I know exactly why you fought and I love you for it. I'm extremely proud of you for standing up for me and the other girls. I'll have to keep my eye on you. I'm afraid some of the girls might attempt to reward you for your chivalrous act. I wish I could embrace you and kiss you right here on the spot."

Then he saw that she was smiling at him in a way that told him a kiss might not suffice.

CHAPTER 28

MORE STATES SECEDE

By February 1, 1861, six more states had followed South Carolina's initiative. Mississippi followed on January 9, 1861, then Florida on January 10, Alabama on January 11, Georgia on January 19, Louisiana on January 26, and Texas on February 1.

Of the remaining eight slave states, four—Virginia, North Carolina, Tennessee, and Arkansas—with fewer slaves and a larger non-slaveholding population than the lower South, delayed their secession until after the bombardment of Fort Sumter and Lincoln's call for troops. Virginia would secede on April 17, Arkansas on May 6, North Carolina on May 20, and a deeply divided Tennessee on June 8.

A congress of delegates from the six cotton-producing states met at Montgomery, Alabama, on February 4, 1861, to organize the Confederate States of America. Jefferson Davis, a U. S. senator from Mississippi, was elected its president and Alexander Stephens of Georgia was named vice-president.

The secessionist leaders agreed that inasmuch as the southern states had entered the Union voluntarily under the "constitutional compact," they were now at liberty to leave it. The constitution adopted in Montgomery was similar to the United States Constitution except that it guaranteed the protection of slavery.

The four remaining slave states—Delaware, Maryland, Kentucky, and Missouri—remained in the Union despite powerful secessionist factions. When Virginia voted to secede, the mountainous counties of northwestern Virginia, which were inhabited by mostly non-slaveholding people of Scotch-Irish and German ancestry, supported the federal government and seceded from Virginia. *Montani semper liberi* (Mountaineers are always free) would express the attitude of backwoods western Virginia towards the relatively prosperous Tidewater Virginia.

When Virginia finally seceded on April 17, 1861, the United States seat of government, Washington D. C., was facing a hostile new nation just across the Potomac River.

CHAPTER 29
TWO PRESIDENTS ARE INAUGURATED

On February 18, on the steps of the capitol of the Confederacy in Montgomery, Alabama, Jefferson Davis was inaugurated as the Confederate president with Alexander Stephens as vice-president and the other officials were sworn in as well. Davis and Stephens were elected for six-year terms.

In his inaugural address, Jefferson Davis stated that the Confederacy "illustrates the American idea that governments rest on the consent of the governed, and that it is the right of the governed, and that it is the right of the people, to alter or abolish them at will whenever they become destructive of the ends for which they were established."

In accordance with the Constitution of the United States, Abraham Lincoln was sworn in as the sixteenth president of the United States on March 4, 1861, after Hannibal Hamlin of Maine was sworn in as vice-president. Lincoln, while resolving to be president of the whole Union, issued a grave warning. "In your hands, my fellow countrymen, and not in mine, is the momentous issue of civil war. The government will not assail you. You can have no conflict, without being yourselves the aggressors. You have no oath registered in Heaven to destroy the government, while I shall have the most solemn one to 'preserve, protect and defend.'"

The next day, three Confederate commissioners arrived in Washington, D.C., and their request to present their credentials was rejected by the new secretary of state, William Seward. The day following this, the Confederate government established the Provisional Army of the Confederate States. The Confederate Congress formally adopted the Constitution of the Confederate States of America on March 11.

The aged United States Army general-in-chief, Winfield Scott, advised the newly inaugurated president to inform the "wayward sisters to depart in peace." Secretary of State Seward advised similarly, "Let the erring sisters go."

The "wayward sisters" or "erring sisters" were references by the press to the Seven Sisters of Atlas and Pleione of Greek mythology. According to myth, these seven sisters were transformed into the stars of the constellation Pleiades, which served as the inspiration for the configuration of seven stars, representing the seven secessionist states, on the new Confederate flag.

Lincoln had also stated in his inaugural address that he would do all in his power to "hold, occupy, and possess" the property and places belonging to the federal government in the seceded states. The key property that Lincoln was referring to was Fort Sumter, a pentagonal brick stronghold located on an island near the mouth of the harbor of Charleston, South Carolina. Sumter was one of four forts located in Confederate territory still flying the Union flag.

The sight of the Stars and Stripes was considered an offense to South Carolinians who could not countenance the existence of a foreign fort in the middle of one of its most important harbors. Confederate delegates attempted to persuade Lincoln to evacuate the fort.

CHAPTER 30
PARTING IN EARLY APRIL 1861

The winter session of school culminated in the last week of March, which normally meant that all the students would leave Academia and return either in May for the summer session or in November for the winter session. In the spring of 1861, this was all conjectural since the secession of the seven southern states left open all forms of speculation as to what action would occur next.

David and Abbey discussed the situation at length because their world had been completely shattered. The young lovers were astounded by the events of the last five months. Even though her beloved Virginia had not seceded, it was only a matter of time until it did so. The pressure for Virginia to secede was overwhelming; with the failure of the peace convention followed by Lincoln's inauguration on March 4, 1861, the die was cast; there would be no last-minute peace-patching compromise.

Abbey decided to delay her departure from Juniata County for a week. She and David would attempt to squeeze a lifetime of togetherness and intimacy into that week, sleeping only enough time to refresh their bodies. They agreed that there would be no timidity or hesitancy in their relationship. There would be no consideration of what other people thought or what they saw. This could be the last time that they would ever be together; for them the world held no tomorrows.

They discussed their religious beliefs concerning chastity; no matter how deeply they loved each other or how much they wanted each other, they agreed that they would not submit to improper sexual activities, and would remain undefiled and unblemished sexually.

The work, eating, and sleeping schedules of the Evans family were rearranged throughout this special week to focus all activities around the young couple, who came and went as they pleased. At times they would walk or ride down to the banks of the creek, skipping stones across the water or just sitting and watching the movement of fallen leaves or sticks through the riffles. Inevitably, they would end up entwined in each other's arms, enjoying the full contact of their eager bodies.

On the last night, he said to her, "On New Year's Eve in the cupola, we wished that the night would last forever. I wish *this* night would last forever and a day."

"Yes," she sighed, "but only if you are with me."

"Ah, you say that now, but we are so young, and you are just beginning to become a woman. Suppose another man comes along who is more exciting to you than me?"

"You will never have to worry about that. I find you irresistible, so tantalizing."

He drew her close to him and kissed her. As she pressed her breasts against his chest, he whispered, "My darling, please promise me that you will not kiss anyone like that while we are apart."

"You know only too well that no man will ever kiss me like you kiss me. But will you still let me kiss you when we meet again when this is all over? If there is a war, we will be on opposite sides, remember."

He laughed, "There is no way that you and I could ever be enemies. Even though we are not yet married, I consider you my lifelong mate. I wish we were older, and we could stay together, that we could go up to the church and be married tomorrow, and you would not have to return to Virginia."

That was too much for Abbey, who broke into sobs. The subject of remaining together was never brought up again. They spent most of the night sitting on the front porch, just enjoying being entwined in each other's arms. All too soon the sun began to peek over the horizon, and the day they both dreaded became a reality.

The Evans family and Abbey ate breakfast in silence, and Abbey said her goodbyes to the family while David hitched up the buggy for the ride to Perrysville and the train station. David allowed the horse to plod down the valley as he sat with his right arm around Abbey's waist. She laid her head on his shoulder and from time to time their lips would meet.

All too soon they were crossing the bridge over the Tuscarora Creek approaching Perrysville, and then down Market Street to the rail station. The stationmaster informed them that the train would arrive in about a half-hour. They walked across the tracks and down along the river, holding hands and stopping from time to time to embrace.

Well before they were ready, the locomotive's whistle signaled the arrival of the train at Casner's crossing between Patterson and Perrysville, and they hurried back to the station. In a few minutes, the train huffed and puffed into the station and shuddered to a stop.

As they stood on the station's platform, they had time for one last kiss. Tears were gathering in Abbey's eyes, but she made no sound of weeping. Finally the tears spilled over and ran down her cheeks, but she made no effort to wipe them away. He noticed anew the freckles on her cheeks and the tiny ones over the bridge of her nose.

Their kiss was interrupted by the conductor warning Abbey to get aboard or she would miss the train. She quickly found a seat next to a window where she could wave her last goodbye as the train approached the slight turn east of town just before the tracks crossed the Tuscarora Creek.

Major Robert Anderson, a Regular Army officer, was in command of Fort Sumter and the sixty-eight-man force within its walls. On April 6, President Lincoln announced that he was sending provisions to the beleaguered fort but that he would not reinforce or re-arm it unless it was attacked.

Confederate Secretary of State Robert A. Tombs cautioned President Davis about an attack on Fort Sumter. "Mr. President, at this time it is suicide, murder, and you will lose us every friend in the North. You will wantonly strike a hornet's nest that extends from mountains to ocean. Legions now quiet will swarm out and sting us to death. It is unnecessary. It puts us in the wrong. It is fatal."

Nevertheless, on April 10 the Confederate commander at Charleston, General Pierre Gustave Toutant Beauregard, was ordered to take Fort Sumter. The next day Beauregard sent an official demand for surrender to Major Anderson. Anderson refused to surrender but added that he would vacate the fort on April 15 if the Confederates did not attack and no further orders were received from Washington. Anderson concluded, "Gentlemen, if you do not batter us to pieces, we shall be starved out in a few days."

Word came from the capital at Montgomery to "reduce the fort." At dawn on April 12, Beauregard began the bombardment of Fort Sumter. Anderson and his force held out for 34 hours, but at 7 p.m. on April 13, the flag was lowered and the U. S. forces boarded a steamer from a relief expedition that was sent to observe rather than fight.

CHAPTER 32
DAVID'S DECISION

When the message of Fort Sumter's surrender reached Washington by telegraph on Sunday, the message was also sent across the rest of the nation by wire. The message arrived at the telegraph office in Perrysville, and when the stage left there on Monday morning, the stirring message was sent throughout the Tuscarora Valley. Mr. Evans was down at the mill and heard the news. He knew there was no use in attempting to delay in informing David about the attack.

As soon as he arrived home, he called the family into the parlor and told them what he knew about the surrender of the fort. Then he said to the women, "Would you please excuse us? David and I need to have a man-to-man talk." The women left the room, and the men went out on the front porch.

"David, I know all too well your first reaction to this news. I know also that you are going to be facing a great deal of peer pressure based on elated patriotism. I went through the same thing back in 1846 when the Mexican War broke out.

"A group of my fellow students and friends and I were so sure that we were going to do the right thing by joining up right away when war was declared in May. Luckily, my parents intervened, and we eventually reached an agreement that I finish school first and then I would be free to make my choice if my fervent patriotism still motivated me.

"I was seventeen at the time, about a year older than you. Three of us left for the recruiting station the Monday after we finished school in September 1846. At first, it was a great lark. We ended up in Philadelphia, and then we were shipped to a staging area at the mouth of the Rio Grande River in Texas in February 1847. Fevers and dysentery hit many of the 12,000 troops quite alarmingly.

"We were transported by sea to a beach south of Vera Cruz

and landed on March 10-11. The city was surrounded by combined naval and land forces, and surrendered on March 28. Almost immediately, we began marching inland to attack Mexico City. We met only sporadic resistance until we reached the village of Cerro Gordo.

"The weather was terribly hot; water and adequate food were in short supply. We had heard and read stories about the terrain of Mexico, but until you observe it firsthand, you'll never appreciate the harshness of the desert.

"We complained about the weather, the scarcity of food and water, the dust, the wind, and of course, how sore our feet became due to the constant marching over the rough terrain. All this was a walk in the park compared to what we actually endured once we encountered Santa Anna's troops.

"William Worth led the attack on April 18, but it was the engineers, including officers Robert E. Lee, George B. McClellan, Joseph E. Johnston, and P.G.T. Beauregard, who found a trail that enabled us to rout Santa Anna's forces. We had only 64 killed and 353 wounded, but our advance had to halt for a month because the army had over 1,000 bedridden in Vera Cruz and another 1,000 sick at Jalapa.

"On May 14-15 we moved into Puebla where the citizens opened the town to us and we routed Santa Anna's cavalry. Unfortunately, another 1,000 of our soldiers felt sick, apparently from the local water supply. By July 15, we had an army of about 14,000, of which 3,000 were ill or convalescing, and the sickness rate did not subside.

"Finally on August 7, we moved towards Mexico City. Extreme temperatures took their toll on us as we followed a route across lava beds and very difficult terrain. Heavy fighting broke on August 19-20 near Contreras and at Churubusco; we suffered losses slightly more than 1,000. More fighting took place at Molino Del Rey. The final battle for Mexico City occurred at the fortified hill of Chapultepec, with an American artillery bombardment being followed by an infantry assault on September 12. On the afternoon of the thirteenth, we entered the city, and Santa Anna evacuated his troops.

"Santa Anna resigned the Mexican presidency on September 16, and his army command on October 7. Then he fled the country. Pedro Maria Anaya became the acting president, and entered into negotiations with American peace commissioner Nicholas Trist.

"I'm sure you have fanaticized about all the fanfare and the glory of massed marching troops, but that's only for the troops before they engage the enemy, and for those who survive and are still able to march when they return from the war. Instead, you will face shot and steel, and storm battlements with a fixed bayonet, suffer deprivations, and worse, have to take the life of another human in order to survive, while your friends and comrades are being killed and wounded all around you.

"What takes place during a battle and immediately afterwards is something I wish to spare you or anyone else. You will never, ever, be the same after you have experienced the gore, carnage, and extreme suffering of warfare. What the young men of this upcoming war will encounter will be worse than what I experienced. New and deadlier weapons have been developed since 1848.

"The armies that probably will be engaged in this coming conflict will be ill-trained, poorly equipped, inadequately led, and much larger in numbers. Therefore, casualties will be in much larger numbers. It will undoubtedly be a catastrophe the likes of which humankind has never witnessed.

"Your mother and I will not permit you to enter the army at such a young, formative age. We do not believe that you are socially or psychologically capable of withstanding the many temptations of army camp life. The gambling, profanity, drinking, womanizing, stealing—the overall coarseness of the type of men who will be serving in the ranks—will appall you.

"If you still desire to be a soldier when you reach eighteen and have completed your studies at the academy, your mother and I will give you our reluctant blessing to join the ranks."

"Eighteen and have finished my studies?" David retorted angrily.

"That will be September of 1863. The war will never last that long. I'll miss the greatest adventure of my generation. If you had waited another year before joining the Mexican War, it would have been over. That's what is going to happen to me. It's just not fair. All my friends will be going, and I'll be here at home being accused of being a slacker or even worse."

Mr. Evans nodded. "You can exhibit all the support you can generate for your classmates and friends if their parents allow them to volunteer. Somehow, after the first wave of patriotism wears away, I believe that the majority of most parents will be instilling some general guidelines for their sons. Your friends will exhibit a great deal of bravado and spout forth exemplary patriotism, but when it comes down to the nitty-gritty, common sense will prevail.

"I have a good hunch that this war is going to last longer than the Washingtonian politicians are boasting. Neither side has a trained nor equipped army to put into the field, and from my meager military experience that in itself requires a great deal of time and money.

"Have you considered the dilemma it will be for you if you have to face some of those young men from Virginia that you met last fall when you visited your aunt and Abbey? Or, even worse, if you have to face some of your fellow students from the academy who reside south of the Mason-Dixon and choose to fight for the South?

"So, show your support and enthusiasm for the northern cause and those young men who go off to war, but please temper your desire to volunteer at this time. The choice to fight is never as simple as first thought. Just remember, we love you and want you to live a long, productive, and enjoyable life." The discussion about David's immediate volunteering ended on that note.

When school resumed at the beginning of May, David found that several of his classmates had not returned to school. Three had chosen to follow the course of their native states and joined the Confederate cause. Two had persuaded their parents to allow them to join local regiments and were now in the vicinity of Washington, D.C. after being mustered into their units at Camp Curtin at Harrisburg.

After lengthy discussions David found that the majority of his classmates had encountered parental guidance similar to his own. All the parents apparently desired for their sons to perform their patriotic duty, but at a time in their lives when they might be mature enough to cope with the horrors of warfare.

CHAPTER 33
JULIE GETS MARRIED

With all the excitement about the attack, the planning for the June wedding on the farmhouse lawn was forgotten. It hadn't really sunk in to Julie that her future husband might be considering enlisting, until he showed up at the front door late Monday afternoon. As soon as Julie emerged on the front porch, it struck her that there was a degree of urgency to Jonathan's impromptu visit.

The smile vanished from her beautiful face, and she began to murmur, "No, Jonathan, no. This visit can't mean what I think it does." She began to cry uncontrollably, and he took her in his arms and tried to soothe her. He kissed away her tears, and stroked her long, silky hair. Eventually, she regained her composure and whispered, "How soon are you going? Do we have time to get married?"

"That's the main reason I'm here. Tonight I'll go talk to Reverend Thompson to see about the arrangements for the ceremony. Tomorrow we'll drive to Mifflintown and fill out whatever certificates are necessary, and we'll be married on Wednesday."

"I believe I've changed my mind about the location for the ceremony," Julie said. "I'd like it to be in the church at seven o'clock in the evening instead of here on the lawn. The suddenness of the marriage means that many of our friends, neighbors, and family will be unable to attend. Therefore, I would like for us to replicate the ceremony and our vows when you return from performing your duty for our nation."

He smiled and kissed her gently on the cheek. "That sounds like a fine idea to me. I know it would be a major imposition for your parents to prepare for a large ceremony with only two days' notice. Besides, as you pointed out, most people would be unavailable during the middle of the week.

"I need to ride to Perrysville immediately to send a telegraph to my parents informing them that the wedding will be performed on Wednesday, in order for my family and friends to arrive at the church on time."

In the background, Mrs. Evans began to fret. "How in the world will we ever be able to prepare for a wedding in two days' time? We have no food prepared or any flowers to decorate the church. Come to think of it, Julie doesn't even have her dress finished."

Mr. Evans spoke in a calm voice, "David can ride to the neighbors and begin to spread the word about the wedding and ask each family to bring whatever food they have available. The people of this valley will pitch in, and everything will work out just fine. As for a dress, I remember the one you wore was just about the prettiest dress I ever saw. Surely, you can adjust it to fit Julie; she's about the same size you were when we got married."

At seven o'clock on Wednesday evening the wedding was performed without any hitches. Afterwards all the guests found their way to Half Moon and consumed the sumptuous array of food set up on tables on the lantern-lighted lawn. The moon rose over the Tuscarora Mountain shortly before ten o'clock and added to the magic and beauty of the night.

The couple spent two days in a remote cabin beside the creek overlooking the popular fishing spot known as Devil's Kitchen. Unbeknownst to the newlyweds, David and two of his cousins maintained a vigil a safe distance from the cabin so that the happy couple would not be disturbed by any intruders.

CHAPTER 34
BOTH SIDES MOBILIZE

The attack on Fort Sumter changed from the talk of war to an actual affront to the flag, uniform, and a military installation of the federal government. Fort Sumter became the nation's call to arms, a sudden need to confront those rebel offenders and to raise troops to meet the crisis.

On the day that the attack on Fort Sumter ended, President Lincoln assembled his cabinet, and announced to the nation that he was calling on the states for 75,000 militia to serve for ninety days commencing on April 15 against "combinations too powerful to be suppressed by the ordinary course of judicial proceedings."

Immediately after Fort Sumter, a tremendous surge of patriotism spread throughout the North. Patriots arose from every walk of life, all ages, classes, both sexes, and from all manner of employment. Later, Oliver Wendell Holmes would write, "The first gun that spat its iron insult at Fort Sumter smote every loyal American full in the face."

Lincoln's call to arms was met with tremendous support, as one northern state after another oversubscribed its quotas, although the president's request for troops backfired in the South.

On April 4, 1861, prior to the bombardment of Fort Sumter, the Virginia Secession Convention had met in Richmond and voted against secession. This became null after President Lincoln requested the creation of a 75,000-man army to invade the states in rebellion against the authority of the United States. The Virginia Secession Convention reconvened on April 17 and, by a vote of 85-55, passed the Virginia Ordinance of Secession to provisionally secede on the condition of ratification by a statewide referendum.

On May 23, the Commonwealth of Virginia conducted its popular vote, and secession was formally pronounced. Arkansas

Governor Rector on May 6 stated, "And they will defend to the last extremity their honor, lives, and property against northern mendacity and usurpation." On May 20, Governor Ellis of North Carolina announced that his state would "be no party to this wicked violation of the laws of the country and this war upon the liberties of a free people." The Confederacy reached its final number of eleven on June 8 when Tennessee's Governor Harris sent a message to President Lincoln. "Tennessee will furnish not a single man for the purpose of coercion, but fifty thousand if necessary for the defense of our rights and those of our southern brothers."

Tennessee was the last state to secede from the Union, because the four other slave states, or border states, chose not to leave the Union, even though sentiment in these states was evenly divided. Maryland voted on April 29 not to secede, but passed another resolution on May 10 not to take part in the war. Kentucky had a secessionist governor and a Unionist legislature and therefore, on June 8, proclaimed its neutrality. Delaware's Governor Burton announced that since his state had no militia, he could not comply with the call for troops, but the state did not secede. Missouri also refused to secede, but during the course of the war, the state was the scene of virulent partisan warfare.

Four days after the fall of Fort Sumter, President Lincoln offered the command of the United States Army to Robert E. Lee of Virginia. Lee bided his time in making his decision, waiting to see if Virginia would secede. Once it did, Lee resigned and took command of Virginia's military forces. He stated quite simply, "I cannot raise my hand against my birthplace, my home, and my children."

A total of 270 officers, active or retired, resigned to fight against the United States, instead of spending the war incarcerated in federal prisons.

In a move to honor the State of Virginia, the Confederacy moved its capital from Montgomery, Alabama, to Richmond, Virginia. This move placed the two capitals about a hundred miles from each other and eventually prompted both sides to mass large forces to protect their respective capitals.

At the age of seventy-five, Winfield Scott, known as "Old Fuss and Feathers," was the leader of the Union army. Pained by gout and much too fat to mount a horse, he had been named general-in-chief of the United States Army in 1841.

Although unfit for active physical duty, General Scott had a plan designed to benefit from the economic, population, and industrial advantages the North enjoyed over the South. He knew that his tiny Regular Army and undisciplined and disorganized state and local militias were not prepared to fight an offensive war. Scott decided that he needed time to prepare a Union army that could take the offensive to attack and invade the South.

General Scott advocated a two-pronged blockade of the Confederate states. The plan was designed to cut off the Atlantic and Gulf seaports, while simultaneously sending troops and a flotilla of gunboats down the Mississippi to capture New Orleans. If successful, the South would be cut off economically from Europe and cut in two geographically. This was intended to slowly constrict or strangle the Confederacy, while his army gained the necessary size, discipline, and organization to propel assaults and offensives against the rebel forces. President Lincoln announced the Union's plan for victory on April 19, calling it the Anaconda Plan.

With the advent of war the United States found that the Regular Army was ill-prepared and lacked sufficient manpower to conduct a war to subdue the rebellion of the seceding eleven states. The Regular Army had about 16,000 troops in its ranks. The existing regiments were scattered across the country, mostly in the West facing hostile Native American tribes, and they would not be readily available.

To expand the undermanned Regular Army, President Lincoln requested that the governors of the states that remained loyal to the Union provide 75,000 militiamen to serve for a term of three months, the maximum time allowed under existing laws.

It appeared that the population of the Commonwealth of Pennsylvania was reluctant to believe that the formal secession by the first southern states beginning with South Carolina could lead to civil war. On the morning of April 12, Governor Curtin of

Pennsylvania had received a telegram with these startling words, "The war is commenced. The batteries began firing at four o'clock this morning. Major Anderson replied, and a brisk cannonading commenced...."

The contents of this disconcerting message flashed across the Commonwealth. Its message was undeniable: the nation was being torn asunder and war was a certain reality.

Simon Cameron, a fellow Pennsylvanian, was Lincoln's secretary of war, and on the afternoon of the fifteenth, the secretary telegraphed Governor Curtin that Pennsylvania's quota would be sixteen regiments. The urgency was so dire that two regiments were needed within three days to prevent a sudden thrust by the rebels to the capital.

Lincoln was rightly worried about a virtually undefended Washington, which was surrounded by slave territory. In these early dark days of the war, the defense of Washington was in the hands of six companies of regulars, fifteen companies of volunteers, and a small contingent of marines stationed at the navy yard.

At night, the president could observe the flickering campfires of the enemy on the south side of the Potomac River. Lincoln could look out of his second-floor window in the White House with the aid of his spyglass and see a Confederate flag waving in the breeze over Arlington Heights, Virginia.

On Washington's side of the river, the city was surrounded by the State of Maryland. The state's governor remained loyal to the Union, but he was intimidated and harassed by a secession-minded legislature. The security of the railroad and telegraph lines through Maryland was in doubt. Basically, the capital of the United States was isolated.

CHAPTER 35

THE LEWISTOWN LOGAN GUARDS—
THE FIRST DEFENDERS

Pennsylvania did not disappoint the president and the secretary of war. The president's urgent request was telegraphed by the governor to every section of the Commonwealth, urging men to answer the call and serve their nation in its darkest moment. To compound the problem, few of the militia companies were fully manned, armed, or equipped.

As the appeal for manpower spread throughout the counties and cities, the officers of the few organized companies rallied their men to muster. Five militia companies answered the urgent request to report immediately to Washington.

The first five companies to respond were the Ringgold Light Artillery of Reading under Captain McKnight; Washington Artillery of Pottsville with Captain Wren in command; National Light Infantry, also of Pottsville, commanded by Captain McDonald; Allen Rifles of Allentown lead by Captain Yeager; and from Central Pennsylvania, the Logan Guards of Lewistown, Mifflin County, under the leadership of Captain Selheimer.

As of January, the Ringgold Light Artillery had been in a state of readiness. When the company received its marching orders on April 16 from Governor Curtin, the 102 fully armed and equipped men were transported to Harrisburg by the Reading Railroad by eight o'clock that evening.

The two Pottsville companies, the National Light Infantry and the Washington Artillery, received their marching orders on April 17 and arrived in Harrisburg that same evening at eight o'clock. The well-drilled Allen Guard also arrived from Allentown at the same time.

Farther to the west in Lewistown, the Logan Guard, which had been organized in July 1858 when they were armed with thirty-four Springfield muskets, also received their marching orders from the governor on the sixteenth. In 1857, Pennsylvania's legislature had passed a law that encouraged the formation of volunteer military units. The act provided generous provisions for both officers and men. With state provisions and local contributions, the Logan Guards had been organized in the summer of 1858. John B. Selheimer, the Guards' captain, received his commission on August 7.

The main promoter of the Logan Guards was Major Daniel Eisenbise, who was the inspector of the Second Brigade, Fourteenth Division, Pennsylvania Militia. Eisenbise was the proprietor of the Red Lion Hotel in Lewistown and proved to be an enthusiastic supporter of the company.

This unit had been meeting for parades and drill about once a month. They had participated in encampments since their formation. Dressed in their United States Regulars uniforms they had participated in Governor Curtin's inauguration in January 1861 and in the reception of President-elect Lincoln on February 22.

Unfortunately, they could only muster twenty-six members when they first received the urgent message. Captain Selheimer opened a recruiting office in the National Hotel, and the drum call was sounded in the streets of this town, which served as Mifflin County's county seat. Within an hour, a full company of Mifflin countians answered their nation's call and signed on to augment the company's numbers, swelling the unit's size to 106 men, which included the original twenty-six members.

The new enlistees and original members made hurried preparations to depart. The word of the Guard's departure spread throughout the countryside. By nightfall, scores of men, women, and children massed in front of the Red Lion Hotel and the courthouse. Soul-inspiring martial music provided by the fife and drum corps flooded the air, as everyone, with great excitement and anticipation, wished the Logan Guards well.

At ten o'clock the night of the sixteenth, the company formed ranks in front of the Red Lion Hotel and marched to the tune of "The Girl I Left Behind" across the Juniata River to the Pennsylvania Railroad station to await transportation to Harrisburg. A great many of the well-wishers followed the citizen soldiers along the parade route to the station.

The Guards' arrival at the station was met with word of a slight setback: a train would not be available until the next morning. Most of the company remained at the depot with their followers throughout the night, although a few did return to their homes and loved ones for just one more night.

Early on the morning of the seventeenth, the company boarded an eastbound passenger train and arrived in Harrisburg in less than two hours. Word had spread beyond Mifflin County that the Logan Guards were on their way to Washington to defend the nation's capital, and scores of well-wishers thronged the small railroad stations all along the route.

Little had been accomplished in Harrisburg in the way of accommodations for the five militia companies, and the scene was utter confusion and chaos. The troops spent a very uncomfortable night, but most of the men were so filled with excitement and apprehension that it had little impact upon them.

One positive aspect was that Captain Seneca G. Simmons formally mustered the five companies into the service of the United States on Thursday, April 18. The same morning, a detachment of about fifty men from the U.S. Regular Army of Company H of the Fourth Artillery under Captain John Clifford Pemberton arrived in Harrisburg from the west on their way to Fort McHenry in Baltimore Harbor.

(AUTHOR'S NOTE: Pemberton was born in Philadelphia, Pennsylvania, into an old and influential Quaker family. He graduated from West Point in 1837 and married a Virginia belle. Pemberton had served many years in the South and had become a good friend of Jefferson Davis. On April 24, 1861, he resigned from the U.S. Army and cast his lot with the rebels. He would later become the Confederate general in command of the defense of Vicksburg which he eventually surrendered to General U. S. Grant.)

The five Pennsylvania companies boarded the train with the Fourth Artillery Company under Pemberton and departed from

Harrisburg at nine o'clock on the eighteenth. They arrived at Baltimore's Bolton station at one o'clock in the afternoon. From there they had to march two miles to Camden station where they would board another train to transport them to Washington, D.C.

As the troops disembarked from the train, they were met by an excited, howling, extremely hostile mob of thousands of men ready to launch an apparent bloody and brutal attack upon the unarmed troops. The companies promptly formed into a marching battalion with the following order: the detached unit of regulars under Pemberton on the right; Selheimer and his Logan Guards were next; then the Allen Rifles, the Washington Artillery, and the National Light Infantry. The Ringgold Artillery brought up the rear.

At the head of the column of the Logan Guards Private William Galbraith Mitchell proudly carried the Logan flag. His custodianship of this symbol was a paramount responsibility for this young soldier, one that he approached with aggressiveness and authoritativeness. (Mitchell would be rewarded for his later exploits, gentlemanly deportment, and gallantry, and would be promoted rapidly. Within two years William Mitchell would become a general.)

The companies had been promised new uniforms when they reached Harrisburg, but this did not happen. Many of the men were dressed in everyday work clothes. The mob took great delight in insulting the intimidated and overwhelmed columns. "You look like a gang of convicts!" "You call yourselves fighting men, you're nothing but rabble!" "You look like a pack of unwashed paupers!" "Looks like Pennsylvania emptied its jails and poorhouses to send their contents down here to be food for southern powder!"

Noting the aggressiveness of the intimidating mob, the captains addressed their companies. "Men, we're virtually unarmed. None of our muskets or rifles have any powder, so under no circumstances are you to lose your tempers and react aggressively. No matter how many insults or oaths they heap upon us, you have to ignore them."

A line of police under the leadership of Marshal Kane kept the belligerent throng at bay, but the numbers increased with every step of the agonizing march to the station.

Some of the men disobeyed the captains' orders and offered to fight the whole mob one by one. This seemed to amuse some of the ruffians, who taunted the Pennsylvanians ever further. "You boys don't amount to a hill of beans anyway, so it wouldn't be much of a fight. Besides, we're neighbors, and neighbors shouldn't fight each other. We're going to let you worthless play-soldiers pass on by, and we'll save ourselves for that bunch of scum from Massachusetts that are supposed to be on their way. We're going to give those Massachusetts Yankees pure hell. They're going to wish they would have stayed up North where they belong."

To add to the anxiety of the Pennsylvanians as they neared the center of the city, Pemberton and his regulars separated from the battalion and filed off towards their original objective of Fort McHenry. By this time, the mob had reached a frenetic pitch and had broken through the ranks of the police.

One of the Logan Guards had produced a box of percussion caps and distributed them to the members of his company who were carrying Springfield muskets. "Here, cap your muskets with these, and maybe these rowdies will think that our weapons are actually loaded."

The thirty-four Springfields were capped and carried half-cocked, giving the impression that the weapons were loaded and could be fired at the mass of southern sympathizers. This little ruse probably prevented a bloody confrontation between the mob and the soldiers.

The Pennsylvanians arrived at Camden Station and began to board the train. The hostile mob showered the soldiers with cobblestones, clubs, and bricks. Several members of the frenzied horde unsuccessfully attempted to uncouple the engine from the cars and to tear up the rails leading to the capital. The engineer and his firemen drew their revolvers, and shouted, "Stop right where you are, or we're going to drop you right on the tracks."

Those attempts were halted, but it did not dampen the demonic mood of the crowd. The locomotive built up steam and slowly propelled the beleaguered militia towards the nation's capital, which had become an island surrounded by the supporters of slaveocracy.

The five companies disembarked at the B & O depot at seven o'clock the evening of the eighteenth, much to the relief of the besieged presidential administration. Major, later Major General, Irwin McDowell assumed command and ordered them to quarters in the Capitol Building. The Logan Guards assumed the honor of being the first company of volunteers to enter the Capitol Building for its defense.

The Pennsylvania companies were issued arms, ammunition, and equipment in preparation for the duties they were to perform. Although they were tired, dirty, and hungry, they immediately began barricading all the open spaces and corridors in the building and fronting the Potomac River with cement barrels and large sheets of iron boiler plates, which were on hand to finish the dome of the capitol building.

After completing the task of barricading the Capitol Building and its surrounding environs, the Keystone State troops received their first taste of hard tack and bacon, which would soon become one of their main staples during their three-month-plus tenure. The Logan Guards bivouacked in the hall of the House of Representatives, which they occupied for eleven days. Some of the other companies were quartered in the Senate Chamber.

These first five companies of Pennsylvania volunteers that arrived in the capital to defend the unprotected city earned the well-deserved title of "First Defenders."

Back in Harrisburg, Governor Curtin and his executive and staff officers waited anxiously for a dispatch from the nation's capital, which would confirm that the five unarmed volunteer companies had safely maneuvered through the hostile mob during the two-mile trek between Bolten and Camden railroad stations. When the message finally arrived in Harrisburg that the volunteers had arrived at the B & O depot in Washington, the governor was quite animated. Curtin raised his right hand and pledged, "Never again will a Pennsylvania soldier leave this state unarmed, even if the capital should be razed to the ground." The governor was extremely distressed over the turn of events and became quite ill as the result of the stress of the ordeal.

Luckily, that first night in Washington passed quietly, because many of the secessionists had heard a rumor that ten thousand Yankee volunteers were marching into the capital, and they skedaddled across the Long Bridge into Alexandria, Virginia. On the rebel side of the Potomac, squads of rebel troops of an eight- thousand-man garrison had been drilling under the watchful eye of General Benjamin McCullough.

At daybreak of April 19, after spending their first uneventful night in the capital, the morning report of the Logan Guard was officially signed and handed by First Sergeant Joseph A. Mathews to Adjutant-General Thomas, who remarked, "Congratulations, Sergeant, your morning report is the first official volunteer report to be received by our department."

During this same day, the Sixth Massachusetts attempted to march the same route through Baltimore that the intimidated Pennsylvanians had trekked while under constant harassment the previous day. The Sixth Massachusetts was not as fortunate as the Pennsylvanians; besides being pummeled with stones and bricks, the southern sympathizers fired into their ranks, and the Sixth returned the fire. Twelve citizens were killed, and many were wounded; four soldiers lost their lives, while seventeen were wounded.

In retaliation for this activity and Lincoln's insistence that he have troops to defend the city and that they march through Baltimore, the Baltimore thugs cut the telegraph lines, tore up the railroad tracks, and destroyed the bridges. These actions cut Washington off from the rest of the Union.

Lincoln was harried and disillusioned. "I don't believe there is a North. The Seventh (New York) Regiment is a myth! Rhode Island is not known in our geography any longer!" As time passed and there was no additional sign of the 75,000 that the President had called for, he wondered, "Why don't they come? Why don't they come?"

All he had at his disposal were six companies of regulars, fifteen companies of volunteers, and a handful of marines stationed at the navy yard. Finally, at noon on April 25, a piercing locomotive whistle announced the arrival of New York's Seventh Regiment. The regiment had to lay rails and rebuild bridges to allow their train to arrive from Baltimore. They were the first of northern regiments to arrive; by early May, Washington's defense had swollen to 10,000 troops.

At the conclusion of their occupation and guarding of the capital, the Logan Guards and the two Pottsville companies were sent downriver fourteen miles to garrison Fort Washington, which was under the command of Brevet-Major J. A. Haskins, a one-armed veteran of the Mexican War.

The troops at Fort Washington were placed on fatigue duty and subjected to the most rigid discipline. They mounted all the guns that dominated the Potomac River for miles up and down the river. River navigation was under rigid surveillance by this garrison, and every vessel had to stop and account for its reason for traveling on the river in the vicinity of the capital. Any vessel refusing to comply with the fort's request had an eight inch shell placed across its bow, always a convincing argument for standing to and giving a valid reason for navigating the river.

Part of the Ringgold Artillerists was assigned to defend the Navy Yard, the Short Bridge, and as guards on the steamer *Powhatan*. Later they were returned to the capital, and after that, to the Washington Arsenal.

Finally, after much delay, these first five Pennsylvania companies, now known as the "First Defenders," were organized as a part of the Twenty-Fifth Regiment, the last regiment organized for the three months' service.

On the first Sunday after the fall of Fort Sumter, most people were involved in displaying their unbounded patriotism while vowing to continue their unwavering support for President Lincoln and his policies. The Evans family and a large majority of their neighbors filled the Lower Tuscarora Presbyterian Church to overflowing. The congregation was anxious to hear the reverend's reaction to the firing on Fort Sumter.

It didn't take long for Pastor Thompson to address the situation, and he delivered a blistering attack upon the secessionist government and army.

Many of you have remained reluctant abolitionists over the past five years due to your abhorrence of strife and possible loss of human life, but now it is time for you to stand up and be counted. You can no longer sit on the fence like the cartoon characters, the mugwumps; you must come around to the cause since secession and bloodshed have occurred.

The "wayward sisters," the southern states, must be compelled to return to the fold by military force if necessary; we should not allow them to go their own way in peace. President Buchanan did nothing to check the secession movement. Buchanan maintained that secession was unconstitutional, but he made it clear that the federal government should not employ force to preserve the Union. Now our new president will have to resolve the cantankerous uncertainty. Recently, the secessionists have seized post offices, customhouses, and federal forts located in the seceding states, but since the bombardment and surrender of Fort Sumter last Sunday, the twelfth, and President Lincoln's call for the militia on the fifteenth, the world has turned upside down.

The South has precipitated the war, but we cannot stand idly by while the secessionists break up our Union. The secession of the southern states is unthinkable.

I ask you good people, can this nation continue to flourish as an un-United States? If we attempt to survive as two separate nations, will we not become vulnerable to forces from other areas of the continent or the world?

Daniel Webster, the foremost senator from Massachusetts, stated back in 1832, "Liberty and Union, now and forever, one and inseparable." Later he told us, "Hold on to the Constitution, for if the American Constitution should fail, there will be anarchy throughout the world."

If the free states make no effort to vindicate their sovereign rights, if the majority of the people have moved away from the spirit of our founding fathers and yield their birthright without a struggle, then I believe that the Union of these states are stripped of all title of our willing allegiance.

Although Daniel Webster was not an abolitionist and he turned against the anti-slavery zealots in his famed Seventh of March speech on the Compromise of 1850, he was a good prophet. He saw the impracticality of peaceful secession when he stated, "There can be no such thing as a peaceable secession. Peaceful secession is an utter impossibility."

Besides the question of secession, I firmly believe that slavery is the greatest sin against God's will. Our president, our government, and our future avenging army should be God's instrument for fulfilling the meaning of Thomas Jefferson's declaration.

Daniel Webster said it best, 'If we abide by the principles taught in the Bible, our country will go on prospering; but if we and our posterity neglect its instruction and authority, no man can tell how sudden a catastrophe may overwhelm us and bury all our glory in profound obscurity.'

That sudden catastrophe that Webster alluded to is now facing this nation. Every man, woman, and child living in the North is now faced to choose between neglecting the Constitution and disunion or supporting our president's request and uniting behind him to defeat the supporters of the crime of slavery and the destruction of the union.

War is a terrible thing. It is sheer madness and a crime against humanity and civilization. This beautiful land of ours will be drenched in blood, and our losses will be excruciating and incomprehensible. Unfortunately, there are times and events which lead a people, a government, down a road when there is no turning back, and a decision to utilize war as a vehicle of preservation of a union or system of government is the only alternative.

The die is cast. The United States has been forced into the decision to employ war as a last option in resolving the differences between itself and the seceded States. We must now develop a steadfast and unfaltering resolve not to allow the wayward or erring sisters to depart in peace.

I firmly believe that God's favor will continue to rest upon the Union. Our cause is a righteous cause; therefore, it will triumph, and triumph magnificently. Under God's blessing and guidance, we will endure this calamity of war and usher in a new spirit of democracy and even higher principles of human equality.

God has a special plan for this great nation of ours, and the northern states will serve as the crucible of this new enduring hope. It has been said many times over the centuries that Christians make good soldiers because they are attentive to their responsibilities and obligations. Good Christian men, your responsibility and obligation are to actively and vigorously give your aid to the Republic and the president. For God and country, do your duty! Follow the route of your neighbors of Mifflin County, the Logan Guards, and take up arms to defend your nation in its direst time of need.

Now let us pray for guidance to allow each of us to survive in this great time of veritable crisis. Dear Almighty Father, allow each and everyone of us to rally around President Lincoln so that the power of his office will be sustained. Grant us the guidance and courage to support the government in the exercise of its necessary and just authority. Let us be uncompromising in our desire to fulfill the justification that the Union shall be preserved and the laws enacted by our legislature be enforced.

Please give us the iron determination to be unbending and inflexible in addressing the challenge of secession and the anarchy or despotism it represents. Lead our armies to victory, and in the process reunite this nation as one nation, indivisible.

We ask that you bless all these souls that are gathered here today. We ask to receive the fullness of Christ's blessing, and all these things in your Son's Holy Name. Amen.

God bless President Abraham Lincoln! God bless the United States of America!"

The congregation responded with an assuming and spontaneous AMEN!

At the conclusion of the church service, David and the young men his age collected along the fence next to the cemetery just to the west of the church, where they stood facing the almost abandoned seminary.

"It's hard to believe that it's come down to this," said a troubled Ed Green. Gesturing towards the large stone seminary mansion, he added, "We're going to end up fighting the kin of those young ladies with whom we shared our church, our school, our time, and our very lives."

Fred Gray was even more apprehensive. "Dave, how are you handling this situation? You are, or were, awfully sweet on Abbey. Will you have any consternation in taking up arms against her home state if the situation warrants it?"

"Abbey resides in Virginia, and Virginia hasn't seceded as yet, although it's probably just a matter of days or weeks until she does. My parents and I had a lengthy discussion over my desire to serve and perform my duty, but they refuse to give their approval to my enlistment. Their argument is that I'm not old enough and that I have to complete my studies at the academy first. When the time comes, I'll be ready to serve. My state and nation are foremost, and Abbey understands my convictions. She and I had concurring opinions on the slavery question. Her family doesn't own any slaves and certainly doesn't support that repugnant institution."

David soon realized that the boys his age were all in the same predicament; they weren't going to receive their parents' approval to volunteer until they were eighteen or had completed their studies at the Tuscarora Academy. Within their acquaintances, there were several young men who were or soon would be eighteen, and they were on the verge of traveling to Perrysville or Mifflintown and volunteering for the militia regiments that would soon be organizing.

At first, patriotism was running so high and the response was so great that neither the state nor federal government had sufficient arms, equipment, or training facilities to cope with the overwhelming number of recruits. Pennsylvania suspended mass recruitment for a period; therefore, many early enlistments were placed on hold until later in the summer, and some of David's friends, classmates, and neighbors, spent a few more weeks in Juniata County during the summer of anticipation.

CHAPTER 37
THOMAS J. JACKSON'S GREAT TRAIN RAID

Normally when a letter arrived from Abbey, David would not divulge much of its contents because he considered all her letters to be quite personal in nature. In early June, David received a letter, part of which amazed him, and he knew his parents would appreciate knowing about it.

I have attempted to avoid the events involving Virginia's Secession Convention and its provisional vote to secede based on the condition of ratification by a statewide referendum, and the mobilizing of the Virginia State Militia. By now, you probably have been informed that on May 23, our Commonwealth conducted its popular vote and the secession of Virginia was formally ratified. It appears that Richmond will become the new capital of the Confederacy.

On the days immediately following Virginia's secession, an extraordinary or bizarre event occurred involving my small hometown of Strasburg. Before this action, on April 27 our state governor assigned Colonel Thomas J. Jackson of the Virginia State Militia to organize the defense of Virginia at Harpers Ferry. Harpers Ferry is the site of important arms production factories and is a vital location on the B & O Railroad, the Chesapeake and Ohio Canal, and the essential telegraph lines that connect Baltimore to the Ohio Valley and the nation's interior.

On May 24, Colonel Thomas Jackson's forces implemented a raid on the B & O Railroad that cut the rail line east of Martinsburg and west of Point of Rocks, thus trapping a huge complement of locomotives and rolling stock, especially coal gondolas. At Harpers Ferry, the spur line, the Winchester and Potomac Railroad, branches off the B & O, making it possible for Jackson to transport his captured rail stock south to Winchester.

The next step is the astonishing part. If you remember, there is no railroad that connects Winchester with the rest of the Shenandoah Valley or with eastern Virginia. There is about a twenty-mile gap in the tracks between Winchester and the railhead of the Manassas Gap Railroad at Strasburg.

What happened next is something that I would find difficult to believe if I hadn't seen it with my own eyes. Our neighbor, Mr. Stouffer, rode up to our house in a cloud of dust yelling, "Hurry up and come to town. You just won't believe what that former professor at Virginia Military Institute, Thomas Jackson, is pulling off." The whole family jumped in the carriage, and we headed for town. A large crowd was forming along the Valley Pike through town and down to the train station when we arrived. Before long, we were rewarded with an astonishing sight.

Down the Valley Pike from Winchester struggled teams of forty horses rigged artillery-style, towing four disassembled locomotives on special carriages and dollies designed and constructed by Thomas R. Sharp, the chief engineer of the Winchester and Potomac Railroad; an experienced railroad engineer from Richmond, Hugh Longust; and Joseph and Charles Keeler, two wagoneers from Stephenson's Depot.

It was an incredible feat. Rumor has it that more locomotive and rail cars will be dragged down the Valley Pike from Martinsburg to Strasburg, or the 125 miles to Staunton and be used on the Virginia Central Railroad.

Mr. Evans shook his head in disbelief. "Jackson's astounding feat will only convince the South that they can really win this conflict. Successful endeavors like this train raid will only prolong this struggle and lead to much bloodshed and suffering."

CHAPTER 38
AMATEUR ARMIES COLLIDE AT BULL RUN

The reply to Lincoln's proclamation of April 15 calling for 75,000 volunteers was met with overwhelming enthusiasm, and the Union states promptly overreached their quotas. The president was compelled to request that the governors scale down the induction of men. The states' training camps could not handle the spontaneous increase in manpower.

Each state had its own militia regiments, but their combat efficiency and level of training was of uneven quality. Some militia regiments were well equipped and trained; others were drilled solely for parade-ground maneuvers. Many of these units had adopted gaudy and impractical uniforms, as well as flamboyant names.

Very few of the officers of these units had any essential qualifications for military command; the rank and file elected most of the leaders. The governors commissioned majors and colonels, while the president appointed generals. Lincoln and the governors were under constant pressure to make military appointments based on political considerations—to reward loyal party members. Some officers achieved their positions by personally recruiting, arming, and outfitting their units, and leading them into battle.

By his own authority, President Lincoln created forty regiments of U. S. Volunteers (42,034 men) to serve three years or for the duration of the war. The Regular Army was to be increased by one regiment of artillery, one regiment of cavalry, and eight of infantry (later increased to nine) and the Navy by 18,000 sailors.

These newly created regular regiments had difficulty recruiting manpower to fill their newly expanded ranks, partly because of competition from the volunteer regiments. A prospective soldier would obtain better pay, less discipline, and higher enlistment bounties by joining a volunteer regiment rather than the Regular

Army. Eventually mobilization was completed and much of the early urgency and despair was overcome.

General Ben Butler of Massachusetts opened a roundabout route to Washington via Annapolis and a feeder line of the B & O Railroad after April 25, and slowly Washington was transformed into a garrison city. Soon Brigadier General Irvin McDowell's army had burgeoned to 30,000 and became poised for an offensive against the Virginia Heights across from Washington.

On the southern side of the Potomac, another army was also building up, based on a defensive concept with an army of 12,000 in the lower Shenandoah Valley at Harpers Ferry under General Joseph E. Johnston facing a Union army of 18,000 under General Robert Patterson and Brigadier General Beauregard's 20,000 in Northern Virginia protecting the most direct overland route to Richmond.

Lincoln recognized that the South's greatest advantage was simply that if it were not attacked, it could win by doing absolutely nothing. For the Union to be restored, federal forces would have to move southward and conquer the Confederacy. Union General-in-Chief Winfield Scott objected to an early offensive; he realized that his army was essentially a group of civilians in military garb with little discipline, hopelessly disorganized and unprepared to maneuver and fight as a cohesive unit.

The Union assumed the offensive and soon Harpers Ferry was recaptured, while Alexandria and Arlington Heights were occupied by federal troops. An attack against western Virginia was launched, and Fortress Monroe at the tip of the York-James Rivers Peninsula was reinforced.

Both armies were manned by raw, underarmed and sometimes unarmed, untrained troops not fit for combat; both sides needed more time to prepare to fight. In the North, the cry went up, "On to Richmond!" Lincoln was under increased pressure to move into action. Adding to his dilemma was that the enlistment terms of the three-month militia were about to expire. The president reluctantly gave the order to McDowell on July 16 to move his troops from their camps surrounding Washington to engage Beauregard's rebel army near the town of Manassas.

The president stated, "You are all green, it is true, but they are green, also; you are all green alike." On the afternoon of the sixteenth, the Union army moved south. Contact with the enemy was made on July 18, resulting in one Union division being driven back. In the meantime, in the Shenandoah Valley, Johnston gave Patterson the slip, and the rebels moved eastward to join the main army. Thomas Jackson's Virginia brigade also arrived from the Shenandoah Valley.

Union forces scouted the Bull Run crossings on July 19 and 20, and McDowell was ready to make his move the following day. July 21 was a Sunday, and before the troops engaged, senators, congressmen and other government officials, newspapermen, and citizen sightseers arrived in their buggies and carriages from Washington, eighteen to twenty miles away, to watch the show. Many brought their picnic baskets and settled on the grassy slopes a few miles away to watch the expected route of the rebels.

In the early going, McDowell's forces drove the Confederates from their defensive positions and managed to turn the left flank of the rebels. This was greeted by loud cheers from the Washingtonian picnickers. Then the Yankees met resistance from the Virginia division commanded by General Thomas A. Jackson, and Jackson's men held their ground against the federal onslaught.

It was during this action that General Barnard Bee created the war's most renowned nickname by stating, "There is Jackson standing like a stone wall." Bee was mortally wounded within an hour after making this statement, but what he said translated into "Stonewall Jackson."

The battle descended into total confusion as troops mistakenly identified friends and foes. The Union forces appeared ready to overwhelm the Confederates until Johnston's army arrived, and McDowell failed to bring up reinforcements. The Confederates had been fighting mainly a defensive battle, but suddenly they counterattacked and by 4:00 p.m., the Union army had begun to disintegrate.

Eventually, fear and panic struck the Union army, and the retreat turned into a disorderly rout. The panic-stricken Union soldiers fled across the Stone Bridge and became entangled with hysterical civilian sightseers and picnickers along the choked roads leading back to Washington.

The first battle of amateur armies ended with the Union army in full flight, and the Confederates chose not to pursue them across the Potomac. The southerners settled into camp, assuming that the war might be over quickly. Lincoln had to rally and reorganize his shattered army, and he responded by shuffling his generals. General George B. McClellan replaced McDowell, and Patterson was mustered out of the army. In August, two new brigadier generals were appointed who had a tremendous influence in the outcome of the war: Ulysses S. Grant and William T. Sherman.

CHAPTER 39
THE LOGAN GUARDS RETURN HOME

Back in Washington on the hot Sunday of July 21, the First Defenders heard the sounds of the battle just twenty miles to the south. Major Haskins received a dispatch that the Union had been driven from the field and were now in disorderly retreat back to the city. The Pennsylvanians were ordered to be prepared for a night attack if the Confederates chose to pursue the fleeing defeated Union army.

Captain Wren's Washington Artillery reinforced the water battery, and extra heavy details were prepared for the rifle battery. While the guns were trained and loaded, the howitzers on the land side were double-slotted. Videttes were placed out on the roads leading into the city, and the men were required to stand to their arms during that long and gloomy night.

The first panic-stricken battle runaways that hastened through the defensive positions of the First Defenders were the scores of senators, congressmen, correspondents, Washington socialites and citizens. These civilians had journeyed across the Potomac for an afternoon of picnicking and frolicking while observing the "show" as the Union forces were supposed to whip the rebels and end this silly business of seceding.

Every one of the First Defenders was well aware that if the Confederate forces pushed from Centerville to the capital, the results could be disastrous. All night long and into the next day, exhausted, demoralized men stumbled across the Long Bridge and sought the safety of the city.

On Monday July 22, the day after the disaster at Bull Run, the Congress of the United States acknowledged the invaluable services rendered by the first five volunteer companies in defense of the capital during those early days of the war by proclaiming:

Resolved that the thanks of this House are due and are hereby tendered to the five hundred and thirty soldiers from Pennsylvania, who passed through the mob of Baltimore and reached Washington, on the Eighteenth of April last, for the defense of the national capital.

Galusha A. Grow,
Speaker of the House of Representatives

By this date, the time of enlistment of the First Defenders had expired, but at the request of the government, the group remained for about two weeks beyond their term of enlistment. The five companies were mustered out and received their pay in gold and returned home on the train through Harrisburg.

In Harrisburg, at the Pennsylvania Railroad Station and at Camp Curtin, the Logan Guards displayed their newly developed military skills, soldierly appearances, and exemplary conduct to the good citizens of the state capital. Then they reboarded the train that transported them westward to home in Lewistown.

Upon arrival at the Lewistown station, an appreciative and enthusiastic throng of well-wishers welcomed the Guards home. The Guards were accorded full military honors as conquering heroes for their exploits in protecting the capital, the president, the cabinet members, members of Congress, the Supreme Court, the public archives, and buildings of the national government, as well as many bureaucrats and ordinary citizens.

It seemed as if the entire population of Lewistown and the surrounding region was on hand to salute the men who had performed well beyond anyone's expectations. The mass of supporters escorted the Guards over the river and down Main Street to the courthouse. Inside the courthouse, a bountiful banquet was bestowed upon the conquering heroes.

After the generous meal had been consumed, the soldiers leaned back on their benches and chairs and listened to a deluge of tributes and acclamations that extolled the virtues and accomplishments of these splendid Mifflin County warriors. The celebration continued almost until dawn for some Guard members.

Many a demilitarized Guard greeted the new day with a sizable headache, but it was a day that each man would remember for the rest of his life.

For the majority of the Guards, the war was not over. One half of the Logan Guards would become commissioned officers in various Pennsylvania regiments; four of the company would become brevet brigadier generals; four colonels, four lieutenant colonels, six majors, eighteen captains, and thirty-two lieutenants also rose from the ranks of the Guards.

They were heroes, and a large portion of Central Pennsylvania was well aware of their exploits due to the coverage of the local newspapers. Many a young Central Pennsylvanian male read the descriptions about the Logan Guards in the local newspapers and was moved to join the flood of volunteers that arrived in Camp Curtain, Harrisburg, to train and serve their state and nation.

CHAPTER 40
THE NORTH REORGANIZES

In accordance with President Lincoln's request for 75,000 troops, Pennsylvania's governor, Andrew Curtin, issued a proclamation summoning 13,000 able-bodied Pennsylvanians to fulfill his state's quota. The response was spontaneous, and within three days, thousands of men converged on the state capital to answer the government's call. As with all the northern states, there was no formal installation to house and drill such an influx of manpower.

The Dauphin County Agricultural Society's grounds were offered to fill the state's needs for an enlistment and training facility. Initially, the camp was called Camp Union, but Major Joseph Knipe renamed it Camp Curtin in honor of the governor. The camp was officially opened on April 18, 1861.

The camp was located between Reel's Lane on the north, Fifth Street on the west, Maclay Street on the south, and the Pennsylvania Railroad tracks on the east. Camp Simmons was located out on Ridge Avenue, adjoining Camp Curtin.

At Camp Curtin, the new recruits were supplied with arms, clothing, and necessary military camp equipment. In the early days of the camp, the new soldiers were marched to the quartermaster's building and issued a cap, coat, overcoat, a pair of trousers, two shirts, two suits of underwear, and a pair of shoes. Unfortunately, the clothing was issued regardless of size, and some strange mismatches occurred. A great deal of time was wasted as the men sought someone to trade clothing with until they had a satisfactory fit. Haversacks, knapsacks, woolen blankets, and a gum blanket were also issued.

Large numbers of young men from Juniata County answered the call immediately by joining the ranks of various regiments and companies throughout the summer of 1861. The same spirit of volunteerism was manifested in every state in the North. Soon the floodtide of patriotic manpower became overwhelming; the states simply did not have the facilities to handle the masses of men.

The War Department was flooded with requests to hold the number of volunteers to manageable numbers. Ohio's quota had been thirteen regiments, but Governor Dennison related that he could hardly stop short of twenty regiments. The northern states quickly oversubscribed and oversupplied their quotas, and President Lincoln had to place a check or suspension on the recruitment efforts.

This changed after the "military picnic" at Bull Run on July 21. The concept of a short, one-punch war envisioned by many northerners was quickly dispelled, and the need for additional manpower was recognized. The day after the battle, the United States Congress authorized the enlistment of 500,000 volunteers, so the short moratorium on recruitment was lifted, and the flood of manpower resurged to the state capitals and to Washington, D.C.

CHAPTER 41
THE LAST LETTER

Shortly after learning of the Battle at Bull Run, David received a distressful letter from Abbey that turned out to be his last letter from her. She explained the situation:

As you remember, we discussed the fact that it might become impossible for us to continue to communicate using the postal system. We have been warned that our mails now face considerable delays no matter to what locale they are being sent.

The mail is evidently much deranged, and apparently all letters are examined in certain post offices near the Mason-Dixon Line, which suggests the need for great caution about what we write. My parents are urging, no, demanding, that I discontinue writing to you until a more peaceful situation develops between our states. They are afraid that I could jeopardize my family's pacifist stance concerning the war by divulging information that may aid the Union cause.

Members of our belief have promised never to own slaves or engage in war. Our lives closely align with the teachings of Jesus Christ. Christ taught in Matthew 5:43, "Ye have heard that it hath been said, Thou shalt love thy neighbor, and hate thine enemy. But I say unto you, love your enemies, bless them that curse you, do good to them that hate you, and pray for them which despitefully use you, and persecute you."

If the war continues, it will bring tremendous implications to our people. Where do you draw the line between supporting the war, or being kind by supplying food, medical supplies, and care for the wounded? The consensus is that if any of our members were to volunteer for the Confederate Army, then they were to volunteer to leave the church.

A conscription law was passed this month, subjecting young

Brethren, Mennonites, Quakers, and Dunkers to be placed in jail because they would not serve in the army. Since war and fighting is the antithesis of our beliefs, many will accept death before violating their faith; others will flee the state or hide in the mountains.

There are few people in the Shenandoah Valley outside the peace churches that display any understanding for pacifists. My problem is amplified since I have such close ties and friendships in what is now enemy territory. These bonds or relationships could lead to distrust and misunderstandings that could soon culminate in animosity and hatred.

Therefore, I began to keep a journal of my thoughts which I would normally convey to you by mail correspondence. I urge you to follow the same procedure, and then when this horrible war has ended, we can read each other's thoughts. Hopefully, this condition will only exist for a few more months, and then we can commence corresponding once again, or better yet, I can return to school and you.

All my love, Abbey

David sat in stunned silence after reading the letter. He had sent a letter to her just two days before; now he wondered if it would arrive at its destination in Strasburg. Nevertheless, he would engage in jotting down his daily thoughts of her in a journal and would be happy to exchange it with her once this conflict was terminated.

CHAPTER 42
THE FORTY-NINTH REGIMENT OF PENNSYLVANIA

One regiment of the huge 110,000-man army commanded by McClellan was the Forty-ninth Regiment of Pennsylvania. During the early days of the war when there was such a spontaneous out-pouring of patriotism, and more men than could be managed volunteered to defend the Union, Governor Curtin was asked to scale down the induction in Pennsylvania.

The enthusiastic response by volunteers had overtaxed the Commonwealth's mustering camps, such as Camp Curtin. Much of the earlier recruiting was curtailed until later in the summer; thus, the 49th wasn't mustered until September 1861.

Large numbers of Juniata County's manpower eagerly answered President Lincoln's call to arms. The ratio of volunteers in proportion to the population of the county far outnumbered most of Pennsylvania's other counties. The original Company I of the 49th was organized at Perrysville and was enrolled on August 18, 1861, and it was given orders to muster into service on September 9.

September 9 was a glorious late summer day in Juniata County, and a huge crowd gathered early in the morning at the fairgrounds in Perrysville to give the recruits of I Company a tremendous send-off.

The new recruits were dressed in a hodgepodge of their own clothing. Captain DeWitt had encouraged them not to be dressed in their "go-to -meeting" clothing, because they soon would be issued military attire, and their own clothing could be lost or stolen in the turmoil of the owners being mustered into the service of their state and nation. Although some men did not heed the captain's advice and were dressed splendidly for the occasion, many were attired in their normal work clothes.

David Evans and his family left their Half Moon farm early in the morning to join the crowd of onlookers, first at the edge of the oval in the fairgrounds and later along Market Street in the middle of town. David observed in envy and frustration—he should be marching towards the railroad tracks in preparation for boarding the train for Harrisburg. If only he were older...

At the fairgrounds, each recruit was presented with a "housewife" donated by the various women groups of the town and surrounding townships. The "housewife" consisted of a sewing kit with various-sized needles, pins, a collection of different colors of thread, and a thimble.

Captain Calvin DeWitt formed the company into a marching column near the racing oval in the center of the fairgrounds. They marched out the entrance/exit of the grounds via Sixth Street, swung left into the alley that bordered the fairgrounds, and immediately turned right onto Eighth Street. Within a few yards, they arrived opposite Airy View Academy on Middle Street and turned left on that street.

The streets were lined with flags, patriotic bunting, and signs bearing messages, such as "Good Luck 49th," "Send those Rebs to Hell," and "Remember Bull Run." Almost every spectator was waving some kind of patriotic symbol. The stirring sendoff would surely motivate the men of I Company.

The Perrysville Coronet Band, although their numbers were depleted because several of its members were marching with the company, still carried a lively tune and sparked the men into marching in unison.

The Evans family scurried from the fairgrounds through the alleys to a spot near the corner of Fourth and Market streets to enjoy the festivities. As the column of I Company paraded past their vantage point, David became even more distressed; it really galled him that he was unable to join the 49th at this time and enjoy all the glory being bestowed upon the young men of the valley who were able to take up the colors.

Several of his friends and acquaintances marched smartly past David: William Moreland and Abram Milliken from East Waterford, Josiah Barton and George Bryner from Pleasant View, John Patton of Spruce Hill with whom he played baseball, and the real kicker, Howard "Howey" McCormick, his good friend who was only sixteen. There were at least thirty recruits from the small village Perrysville alone.

The new recruits marched the length of the street until they came to Second Street where they abruptly swung left, covered a block on Second, and swung another left onto Market Street. The largest portion of the crowd now lined this street, and just as before, the new soldiers quickly marched the length of the town back to Eighth Street, where they turned right onto that street, covered a block to North Street, and swung onto North.

By now, the men were in fine marching form, and they soon arrived back on Second Street and the access to the railroad-loading platform. The throngs of onlookers that had gathered at the fairgrounds or lined the streets had now assembled around the loading platform near the Pennsylvania Railroad Station.

In the vicinity of the depot each future soldier was presented with a New Testament and a pocket booklet that contained the Ten Commandments, passages of scriptures that matched unique situations, prayers for special occasions, as well as advice on how to avoid the pitfalls of immoral activities that might otherwise tempt soldiers while serving in the army.

The Presbyterian, Methodist, and Lutheran pastors of the Perrysville congregations gave short sermons and blessed the men, asking that "each man would perform his duties as expected and they would all return in full health and vigor." Even the most optimistic members of the crowd knew that this desire was well beyond reality, but on a beautiful day such as this, a day so full of enthusiasm and anticipation, some people would be apt to believe anything.

The unattached young females of the Tuscarora Valley and surrounding areas maneuvered freely throughout the assembled I Company, placing flowers in the men's hatbands or buttonholes, or in their hands, while bestowing one last embrace upon these brave young men. David recognized many of the young maidens; several were his cousins and neighbors, and one, of course, had caused him so much turmoil about a year earlier. After performing this touching duty, every one of the young females burst into tears and most of them sought their mothers for support.

The train assigned to haul the newly formed companies to Harrisburg and Camp Curtin was delayed nearly two hours because the scene that was unfolding in Perrysville was also being enacted at Lewistown and Mifflintown as other newly organized companies joined the ranks. The 49th Regiment included three companies from Mifflin County (E, H, and K), Company I from Juniata County, and at least four other companies with recruits from Juniata, Mifflin, and Union Counties.

The telegraph operator stepped out of his tiny office and announced that he had received word that the train had finally left Lewistown. It was over an hour until he reappeared and bellowed that the train had cleared Patterson and would be on the scene within ten minutes.

Finally, the patriotically decorated engine huffed and puffed into Perrysville. New recruits from earlier depots hung out from every opening on the train and yelled at the crowd, especially at all the pretty girls. Everyone was in high spirits; an observer would never have guessed that these men would soon be involved in a violent life-and-death struggle that would determine the future of this country.

Despite all the frantic activity of the railroad employees and the men deployed by the adjutant general, it took considerable time and effort to encourage the raw recruits to tear away from their loved ones and friends and board the railroad cars.

Each recruit took a lengthy time in saying his last goodbyes, especially the younger ones, who had young women hanging on to them for just one last hug and kiss. Mothers were extremely reluctant to release their sons, but tearfully they eventually did. Fathers in most cases hung back, seemingly not knowing what to say, but most just shook hands, embraced in one last bear hug, and stepped back out of the way.

Captain DeWitt and the newly elected sergeants lost their patience and herded the throng of well-wishers away from the railroad cars and the tracks by deploying armed uniformed soldiers to keep the crowd at bay.

Finally, the men of I Company released their loved ones, picked up their meager belongings, and trudged to the steps of the cars. As each man approached the railcar steps, the young girls handed over a box lunch prepared by the three local churches. Before the day was over, I Company was very glad for these lunches, because stops were scheduled at Thompsonstown, Millerstown, Newport, Duncannon, and Marysville to load more soldiers.

The special train hauling the 49th Regiment to Harrisburg built up steam and slowly chugged out of the Perrysville station. The crowd flooded onto the railroad bed and watched it make its turn and cross the small bridge over the Tuscarora Creek. Soon the caboose was out of sight, and the crowd did not disperse until it heard the train's whistle announcing its arrival at Mexico depot.

The crowd then grew quiet; most, with heads now hanging low, walked the length of town to the fairgrounds to retrieve their horses and buggies and make the long trek homeward. Many were returning to homes where sons or husbands no longer resided, and some might never reside again.

The Evans buggy quickly left the fairgrounds, headed across the Tuscarora Creek through St. Tammany's Town, and began the journey into Groninger Valley. David sat in the back seat with his sister, silent, his thoughts with his friends, relatives, and neighbors on their way to Camp Curtin.

Finally, his mother broke the silence. "David, we know where you think you'd rather be tonight, but we believe, we *know*, that you're not quite ready for army life. In two years, when you're eighteen, you can join whatever unit you desire."

"In a little more than two weeks the school term will be over. Couldn't I join the company at the end of the month?" asked David.

Mr. Evans shook his head. "David, we had this discussion back in April when the war began. We had an agreement that you would wait until you were eighteen and had finished your studies at the academy, and then you would be free to make your own decision to join the army."

"I realize you think you know what is best for me, but it is really difficult to see your good friends, cousins, and close neighbors marching away while you're still here at home playing the role of the student. I would have given anything to be boarding that train this afternoon."

The other members of the family continued to discuss the day's events, but David withdrew and made no other comments until he told his family goodnight as they retired to their respective bedrooms. In the morning David left for school without mentioning his desire to join the company, and it was a subject that was left unmentioned for several weeks.

In the meantime, David received information about the activities of I Company, either from his good baseball friend, Howdy McCormick, or by reading the weekly newspaper, the *Juniata Sentinel,* published in Mifflintown. The news from either source was sporadic, but at least David gained considerable knowledge about the company that he considered his comrades in arms.

At first, there was little for Howdy to report; army camp life appeared to be quite dull, but finally in early October, David received his first communication from his good friend:

On Wednesday, September 19, the quartermaster department issued arms to the different companies. We drew Harpers Ferry muskets that had been changed from flint lock to percussion of .68 caliber. The cartridges are made with paper, with a round bullet and three buckshot, seemingly unserviceable, and could be dangerous to the shooter as well as the intended target.

The next day, dress parade was held, and Governor Curtin and his staff appeared and presented the regiment with its national and state flags. This was followed by a very patriotic speech by Colonel Irwin who declared that while he had an arm to wield a sword or a man to fire a gun, the colors should never drop in the face of the enemy nor be desecrated by the touch of rebel hands.

The big news is that on the twenty-first we had reveille at 4:00 a.m. We tore down our tents, broke camp, marched to the railroad station, and loaded on cars of the Northern Central Railroad Company. Two trains were needed to haul the whole regiment, and disaster struck near Mount Washington outside of Baltimore when the second train ran into the first. Two men from Company G were killed and several were injured. Eventually we got underway again, arrived at Baltimore about midnight, and then marched to the Baltimore and Ohio station. We finally arrived in Washington around 2:00 p.m. on Sunday, September 22.

Will send more news later.

David and his remaining classmates followed the campaigns and battles diligently, utilizing maps, both homemade and published, letters from the camps and battlefronts, and every newspaper story they could get their hands on. They read every geography book they could find in order to become acquainted with all the rivers, valleys, bays, cities, and mountains that would affect the terrain of the various battlefields.

Since they could not participate in the war, they became obsessed with the futility of the Union's objective to capture Richmond. Most of the students were surprised that the war was not over when they returned to school for the winter term.

David mounted a huge map of the eastern United States on his bedroom wall so that he could plot each battle and campaign. He decided when it came time for him to enlist, he would leave nothing to chance. He would be prepared to serve in whatever theater that his nation needed him.

On October 22, a seemingly overconfident South created the Department of Northern Virginia, with General Joseph Johnston as its commander. Meanwhile, in Washington, news of setbacks in Missouri, Kentucky, and Virginia flooded into the White House. In an attempt to reverse Union losses, Lincoln accepted General Winfield Scott's offer to retire as general-in-chief of the army, and on November 1, General George McClellan was appointed as general-in-chief of all United States forces.

McClellan reorganized, drilled, equipped, and trained his army, and made them feel like real soldiers. His plan was to transport his army down the Potomac into the Chesapeake Bay, then down to the mouth of the Rappahannock River, and up the Rappahannock to Urbanna, Virginia, about fifty miles from Richmond. From here, the attack would be launched upon the Confederate capital.

At first, McClellan appeared ready to set out immediately to attack Johnston and move on Richmond. He stated, "I have no intention of putting the army into winter quarters. I mean, the campaign will be short, sharp, and decisive." The press referred to the general as "the young Napoleon."

The final months of 1861 faded into memory, and another setback occurred when Lincoln fired Secretary of War Simon Cameron for speaking out publicly against emancipation and alleged corruption involving army contracts and military appointments.

McClellan built up an imposing army of 110,000 men, but due to inclement weather, the general's illness, and hesitancy to attack, Lincoln could not nudge McClellan to make his move. Meanwhile, General Ulysses S. Grant, who commanded a district in the "West" with his headquarters in Cairo, Illinois, finally received permission to attack two Tennessee forts near the Kentucky line: Fort Henry on the Tennessee River and Fort Donelson on the Cumberland River. Grant was successful, and Fort Henry surrendered on February 6 and Fort Donelson on February 16.

On February 22, President Lincoln ordered all Union troops to advance, but McClellan ignored the order. Lincoln's patience with his commander ended on March 11, when Lincoln removed him as general-in-chief but allowed him to remain as commander of the Army of the Potomac. Finally, six days later, McClellan made his move on Richmond, an amphibious movement.

Pennsylvania's 49th Regiment was encamped at Lewinsville, Virginia, during most of the winter, performing camp and picket duties until March 10, when it moved to Manassas and then back to Alexandria.

On March 13, President Davis appointed General Robert E. Lee as his military adviser, which placed him in charge of the military operations of the Confederacy, but in truth, Lee was given no real authority.

CHAPTER 44
MAJOR CAMPAIGNS OF 1862

On April 4, General McClellan began his peninsular campaign against Richmond, Virginia, and commenced the siege of Yorktown the next day. The Pennsylvania 49th held its position on the left bank of the Warwick River. In the west, the Battle of Shiloh on April 6-7 was considered a victory for Grant inasmuch as the Confederates were forced to withdraw. At the time of this battle, it was the largest and bloodiest battle ever seen in North America.

The South received another major blow in April when the city of New Orleans surrendered on the twenty-fifth of that month.

On May 4, the Confederates withdrew from Yorktown, and McClellan's forces occupied the city before throwing the weight of their attack against Williamsburg. The armies continued to face each other until May 31, when the Chickahominy River overflowed and isolated part of the Union army. The Rebels under General Joseph Johnston launched an attack known as the Battle of Seven Pines or Fair Oaks. The general was severely wounded and replaced by Robert E. Lee, who restored order to the Confederate lines. Lee's offensive strategy pushed McClellan's superior army back to the Potomac.

In the meantime, General Stonewall Jackson was conducting a month-long campaign in the Shenandoah Valley, where he won five consecutive battles, outmaneuvering three Union armies led by Nathaniel Banks, John C. Fremont, and Irvin McDowell.

During the last week of June, Lee went on the offensive in what is known as the Seven Days Campaign. On June 26, General John Pope was assigned to head the Union's new Army of Virginia. On July 11, President Lincoln appointed Henry Wager "Old Brains" Halleck as general-in-chief of the Union armies.

On July 22 President Lincoln disclosed to his cabinet the first draft of his Emancipation Proclamation. The cabinet advised him to postpone publication of the document until the Union achieved a significant victory. The president wisely decided to heed his cabinet's advice.

At the beginning of August, Halleck ordered the Army of the Potomac to march back down the peninsula and board ships to take them up the Chesapeake to join General John Pope. Halleck devised a plan to combine McClellan's and Pope's forces to march together on Richmond. General Jeb Stuart captured information regarding this offensive, and Lee reacted boldly by dividing his army and sending Stonewall Jackson to move around Pope's forces and stand between them and Washington. Pope sent his army directly after Jackson who by then had captured Manassas Junction.

Jackson confused and evaded Pope until Pope sent his men on a direct attack on August 29, bragging that he would "bag the whole crowd." Pope did seize and hold the initiative during the first day of battle, and Jackson withdrew, with Pope in hot pursuit.

Pope's arrogance led him to forget about the other half of Lee's army led by General Longstreet, who had arrived on the scene but didn't join the battle. Instead of a hot pursuit, Pope faced five rebel divisions and suffered a costly defeat. Luckily for the 49th, the regiment was held at Centerville, and did not see action in this engagement.

Three days after the Second Battle of Bull Run, John Pope was relieved of his command, and exiled to the U.S. Army's Department of the Northwest to battle the Sioux nation in Minnesota. Since McClellan had never been officially relieved of command of the Army of the Potomac, he was once more placed in charge. McClellan wrote to his wife, "Again I have been called upon to save the country."

CHAPTER 45
LEE MOVES NORTH, 1862

On September 5, 1862, Robert E. Lee led his Army of Northern Virginia containing 60,000 men across the Potomac River into Maryland. This would be Lee's first invasion of a Union state. By September 7, Lee's army had reached Frederick, and shortly afterwards he devised a rather bold plan, Special Order No. 191, to divide his army into four sections.

One of the plans was written on a paper used as a cigar wrap, later discarded by an officer and found by an Union soldier, W.B. Mitchell, who turned it over to General McClellan. McClellan was gleeful. "Here is a paper with which, if I cannot whip Bobby Lee, I will be willing to go home."

McClellan was not sure if the plans were legitimate and hesitated for sixteen hours. In the meantime, Lee had been informed about the lost order and began pulling his troops back together as McClellan's forces approached.

The two armies collided at 6:00 a.m. on September 17 on the banks of Antietam Creek near Sharpsburg. Charges and countercharges produced horrific losses on both sides. McClellan mismanaged his attacks by not committing his full force at one time, which allowed Lee to position and reposition to match each Union assault. What resulted was the "single bloodiest day of the war"; Union casualties numbered about 12,000 to Confederate losses of nearly 14,000.

Lee considered a counterattack, but heeded the advice of Jackson and Longstreet, and after waiting a day, he withdrew the night of the eighteenth and headed back to Virginia. Lee's Maryland campaign, his first invasion of the North, failed, but the Army of Northern Virginia was not destroyed and would fight again.

President Lincoln judged Antietam of Sharpsburg as enough of a victory to issue a preliminary Emancipation Proclamation on

September 22, 1862. This document freed only those slaves in parts of the nation that were still in rebellion. Slaves that resided in areas of the Confederacy living under Union control and in the border states would not be liberated until ratification of the Thirteenth Amendment in December 1865, after the war had ended.

In the meantime, McClellan did not pursue Lee and still had not done so by the beginning of October. On October 1, Lincoln ordered his commander to "cross the Potomac and give battle to the enemy." Over a week later, McClellan still had not moved, but Lee did. During October 9-12, Jeb Stuart repeated the actions that he undertook prior to the battle of Mechanicsville at the start of the Seven Days battle when Stuart rode around McClellan's army, by riding around McClellan again, and then raided Chambersburg, Pennsylvania.

Finally, on October 26 McClellan began to move south toward Warrington, Virginia, but by this time the president had decided that McClellan had a bad case of the slows, and on November 7, Halleck relieved General McClellan. McClellan's replacement was General Ambrose Burnside.

Burnside blundered immediately by reorganizing the army into three large two-corps divisions commanded by Generals Joseph Hooker, William B. Franklin, and Edwin V. Sumner. This type of restructuring made the army's movement in the field entirely too unwieldy.

On November 15, Burnside got his army of nearly 120,000 moving and reached the Rappahannock River across from Fredericksburg two days later. The river was too high to cross, and Burnside waited six days for pontoons to arrive, but once they did arrive he took no action for another three weeks. This delay allowed Lee to position his army of 75,000 on the Marye's Heights overlooking Fredericksburg.

Burnside began shelling the town on December 11 and sent his troops over the pontoons on the river to occupy the deserted town. This was followed by an attack up sloping open terrain against formidable, entrenched Confederate forces. The result was a rout as the Union soldiers were sent repeatedly against an impregnable wall. The ensuing carnage was a total disaster as the Union army suffered losses of 12,700 to the Confederates 5,700. On December 16, the 49th Regiment, as part of the Army of the Potomac, re-crossed the Rappahannock River and went into winter quarters.

CHAPTER 46
THE EMANCIPATION PROCLAMATION

After the battle of Antietam, on September 22, 1862, President Lincoln had issued a preliminary Emancipation Proclamation. The document did not free a single slave; it merely warned slaveowners living in states still in rebellion that on January 1, 1863, their living property would be declared forever free.

A complete copy of the document appeared in many newspapers throughout the North, but it was almost a week into the new year of 1863 before the young men at the Tuscarora Academy had the opportunity to examine it. David Evans and his classmates in his American history class passed the newspaper around in order to give everyone in the room the chance to read the document.

"Under what authority did the president issue such a statement?" asked Todd Stephens.

Nate Henry had a ready answer. "Lincoln utilized his powers as commander-in-chief under Article II, section 2 of the U.S. Constitution, as a necessary war measure. However, I believe that Lincoln moved cautiously to avoid alienating his soldiers and officers, many of whom are not abolitionists."

"It appears that slavery will remain alive and well in the areas where our army has been victorious," David interjected. "Under this plan, no slave will be set free in the border states of Kentucky, Missouri, Maryland, and Delaware. Tennessee is not mentioned, because most of the state is controlled by our armies. In the states where the slaves have been declared free, the law can not be enforced until the war has been won.

"It's interesting to read Secretary of State William H. Seward's reaction: 'We show our sympathy with slavery by emancipating slaves where we cannot reach them and holding them in bondage where we can set them free.'

"I can see that this proclamation gives the war a new moral

force. Some people will envision the struggle as one to make men free. I think it commits our government to end slavery, which inflames the areas of the South now under Union army control. It also will give us additional manpower because it allows for the enrollment of freed slaves into the Union army."

Meanwhile, on the battlefront, reactions were varied. Some regiments were inspired by the president, and one went as far as adopting the motto "For Union and Liberty." However, other units almost mutinied in protest, and there was an increase in desertions at this time.

On the political front, the Copperhead Democrats, who opposed the war and tolerated secession and slavery, had denounced the preliminary proclamation and made it a political issue in the 1862 congressional elections that had just been held in November. This allowed the Democrats to gain twenty-eight seats in the House of Representatives and the vital governorship of the State of New York.

CHAPTER 47
LEE MOVES NORTH IN 1863

On January 20, 1863, after a month of preparation, Burnside decided to make a circular movement, cross the Rappahannock River again, and surprise the left flank of Lee's army. Torrential rains, forceful winds, and mud bogged down the Union army in what became known as the "Mud March."

This was enough for Lincoln; General Joseph "Fighting Joe" Hooker replaced Burnside on January 26. Under Hooker's reorganization plan, the 49th was assigned to Sedgwick's Sixth Corps, First Division, Third Brigade, commanded by General Russell. Hooker waited until April to make his first major movement. Before beginning his operation, Hooker sent a message to President Lincoln: "My plans are perfect, and when I carry them out, may God have mercy on General Lee, for I shall have none."

Lee had about 60,000 troops securing the area around Fredericksburg, while Hooker had 115,000 under his command. Hooker's strategy was to leave 40,000 troops facing Fredericksburg, and deploy 75,000 to cross the Rappahannock and Rapidan rivers upstream and attack Lee from the rear and the left flank.

By April the Union army had advanced to within ten miles west of Fredericksburg at Chancellorsville. General Lee outmaneuvered Hooker and divided his troops, leaving 10,000 to guard Fredericksburg, and sending the bulk of his forces to protect his flank.

While Hooker was struggling to advance through the entangled woods known as the Wilderness, General Stonewall Jackson surprised Hooker and drove him back. Lee reacted boldly and divided his army further. Lee himself remained at Chancellorsville with only 14,000 troops facing 73,000 and sent the remainder with Jackson to attack the Union rear.

Jackson successfully hit Oliver Howard's troops on May 1 and drove them back. That evening at dusk, Jackson and his staff were out scouting when they came under friendly fire from their own troops. Two of Stonewall's aides were killed immediately, while the general was struck on the right palm, left wrist, and left arm. The bone in his left arm was splintered, and the general was transported to a field hospital where the doctors had to amputate the arm to save his life.

Lee was stunned when he was informed of the incident. "He has lost his left arm, but I have lost my right." Jackson's forces were placed under the command of General Jeb Stuart, who attacked Hooker on May 3 and drove the Union to the banks of the Rappahannock and Rapidan Rivers.

Union General John Sedgwick then attacked Lee's forces. Some of the Confederate forces protecting Fredericksburg counterattacked on May 4 and forced Sedgwick to retreat to the Rappahannock River. "Lee's Masterpiece" was one of the most humiliating defeats suffered by the Army of the Potomac, but in the end, the southern losses hurt them more than the northern losses.

After the Union calamity at Chancellorsville in early May of 1863, the morale of the Army of the Potomac lining the banks of the Rappahannock River in Virginia was at its lowest ebb. They seemingly had begun to accept the idea that they were incapable of defeating Lee's Army of Northern Virginia. The expiration of the term of service of a large number of Union infantry also required General Hooker to attempt to reinforce his crippled army.

On the other side of the river, the morale of Lee's Confederate army was flying high, and the men felt invincible. Lieutenant General James Longstreet and his two divisions returned from the Carolinas; that brought Lee's strength to nearly 70,000 tough veterans.

It appeared that the initiative was temporarily in the hands of the Confederates. Therefore, for the second time in less than a year, Robert E. Lee determined to invade the North, although Lee's commanders were at odds as to how to proceed. Lee envisioned that his campaign would force Lincoln to recall his far-flung armies from every theater to fight one great decisive battle on the quiet and fertile soil of Pennsylvania.

The excitement of invasion was suddenly tempered by the startling news that on May 10 General Thomas "Stonewall" Jackson succumbed to the pneumonia that he had contracted after being wounded by friendly fire and losing his left arm during the Battle of Chancellorsville.

The death of Stonewall Jackson left an enormous void in Lee's high command. He quickly reorganized the Army of Northern Virginia by creating a Third Corps under the command of Lieutenant General A.P. Hill and elevating Lieutenant General Richard S. Ewell as commander of Jackson's Second Corps.

Lee, slowly and with careful planning, began to shift his army from the lines along the Rappahannock River to the northwest along the Blue Ridge Mountains, commencing on June 2. By June 8 only General A. P. Hill was left to continue to man the trenches along the Rappahannock just in case "Fighting" Joe Hooker decided to make a dash toward Richmond while the main Confederate army was moving into position for the invasion.

As intelligence reports filtered into Hooker's headquarters concerning Lee's repositioning, the commander of the Army of the Potomac sought permission to cross the Rappahannock and attack Richmond while Lee was still maneuvering. His request to attack was quickly rebuked by General Henry W. Halleck. Hooker was informed that his major target was Lee's army, not the capital of the Confederacy, and above all else, his primary responsibility was the protection of Washington, D.C.

Hooker was ordered to march parallel to Lee's columns as they marched north in order to protect the national capital against any sudden attack from Lee. The Union commander was infuriated and disheartened over this turn of events, but on June 5 he ordered his troops to perform a series of forced marches northward.

Meanwhile, Halleck ordered General Schenck to abandon Winchester, Virginia, in the Shenandoah Valley and defend Harpers Ferry instead. This decision came too late, because on June 14 General Dick Ewell attacked Major General Robert Milroy's division at Winchester and captured nearly 5,000 defenders. Ewell continued to surge up the Shenandoah towards Hagerstown and into the Cumberland Valley of Pennsylvania.

While Ewell was moving toward Chambersburg, Pennsylvania, Lee and Longstreet crossed the Potomac River near Sharpsburg, Maryland. The dashing horseman, J. E. B. Stuart, in an attempt to restore his tarnished reputation, received permission from Lee to ride around Hooker's army and collect intelligence, gather supplies, and destroy Yankee supply bases.

The leadership in Washington, D. C. was in a state of panic. Two new military departments in Pennsylvania were created: the Department of the Monongahela, headquartered at Pittsburgh under Major General W. T. H. Brooks, and the Department of the Susquehanna at Harrisburg, commanded by Major General D. N. Couch.

On June 12, Governor Curtin of Pennsylvania issued a warning about the immediate invasion by Lee and called for volunteers to meet the emergency. On the fifteenth, President Lincoln asked for 120,000 volunteers from Maryland, Pennsylvania, New York, New Jersey, West Virginia, and Ohio to join the ranks to defend against this new invasion.

General A. G. Jenkins's large cavalry force led the advance of Lee's invasion by crossing the Potomac River on the evening of June 14 at Williamsport, Maryland. In front of this cavalry force fled the scattered elements of Milroy's army from Winchester, Virginia. These thoroughly demoralized and frightened men added to the terrorization of the inhabitants of the Cumberland Valley.

By the next day, June 15, a general exodus began with General Milroy's wagon train leading the way. Many of the men were without weapons, hats, or coats, and were intermingled with the people living along Pennsylvania's border. Farmers herded their livestock northward, and merchants packed up their goods and attempted to ship them across the Susquehanna or northward. The banks shipped their money, while families moved their valuables to what they hoped was a safe place.

The scene was of utter chaos, as the roads were clogged with fleeing, terrorized people, doing what they could to avoid the enemy. Everyone felt that the Rebels were just on their heels. To make matters worse, there was no organized military force in the Cumberland Valley to impede the invaders.

CHAPTER 48
EWELL'S OCCUPATION OF CHAMBERSBURG

The town of Chambersburg lay in the path of this exodus of refugees and the onslaught of the advancing Confederate army. The local militia units evacuated the town and left the town undefended. All day of the fifteenth, wagons, horses, cattle, and a flood of humanity passed through the town on their way to apparent safety.

Just before dusk, the news spread that the Rebels were in Greencastle and that the town was on fire. Later, some retreating militia reported having just had a skirmish with the Rebels and that they would be in Chambersburg within an hour. This signaled another large exodus of people as they grabbed their packable goods and left town, although most people elected to remain in the hopes that they would not be disturbed.

About eleven o'clock when most of Chambersburg's residents had retired for the night, all was quiet, until suddenly there was a clattering of horses' hoofs that announced the arrival of the first of the Greybacks.

Brigadier General Albert Gallatin Jenkins, a graduate of Harvard Law School and a former member of Congress, led the cavalry force that took possession of the town without conflict. His cavalry brigade was leading the Confederate drive from the Shenandoah Valley into the Cumberland Valley, following the Cumberland Valley Railroad from Hagerstown through Greencastle to Chambersburg. The main thrust of the southern cavalry was still located far to the south, attempting to screen Lee's invasion and scrutinizing the Union reaction to Lee's advance.

General Jenkins and his 1,300-man force moved through the main section of town, left a strong guard deployed in the center of town, and established his headquarters and camp on the farm of Alexander K. McClure. McClure was a distinguished journalist and politician who, at the time of this occupation of his estate named "Norland," was in Harrisburg serving on the governor's staff. McClure had arrived in Harrisburg on the last train through the Cumberland Valley before Lee's forces arrived, although his wife had stayed behind to watch their property.

On the morning of the sixteenth, General Jenkins returned to town and established his headquarters at the Montgomery House Hotel. Some of his men were deployed to watch for approaching enemy soldiers, while detachments fanned out on the countryside to secure food and fodder. Foraging for food proved to be a difficult task because most of the farmers had moved their livestock and disposed of their foodstuffs; there was little of value left in the region.

Jenkins ordered anyone possessing firearms to deposit them in front of city hall. Failure to comply would lead to a house-by-house search. Eventually a number of guns were delivered, but most were ancient or outdated weapons of little use to the Rebels, and a search was never carried out.

Early the next morning, General Jenkins ordered all shopkeepers to open their stores for two hours to allow his men to make purchases. All merchandise was to be paid for, but of course in Confederate money. Little had been left on the stores' shelves, but what was left soon disappeared.

On June 22, Jenkins and his men withdrew from Chambersburg, fell back to Greencastle, and spent four days in that vicinity. In the meantime, the Fourth Texas Volunteer Infantry, or the Texas Brigade, under the command of John Bell Hood, a native Kentuckian, whose colonelcy of the Fourth had officially begun on September 30, 1861, reached Williamsport, Maryland, on June 26. The brigade had waded across the Potomac next to a pontoon bridge clogged with artillery and wagons.

The Texans were in high spirits and became even more animated after the lunch break when the brigade's commander awarded each Texan a gill of whiskey. The barrels of whiskey had been confiscated near Hagerstown, and soon the order of one gill per man was ignored, and the liquid flowed by the cupful instead.

One observer said of the melee, "I don't suppose the oldest man in America ever saw so many men drunk at any one time."

Eventually, after much cursing, rolling in the mud, and the loss of the contents of hundreds of stomachs, some semblance of order was restored, and the Texas Brigade staggered and straggled across the narrow panhandle of Maryland to the vicinity of Greencastle, Pennsylvania.

The Texas Brigade's claim to fame was that they had breakfast in Virginia, lunch in Maryland, supper in Pennsylvania, and slept in a state of intoxication. Therefore, they covered four states in a twenty-four-hour period.

General Richard Ewell entered Chambersburg on June 24 to the strain of "Bonnie Blue Flag." The general took possession of Alexander K. McClure's two-hundred-acre field for his camp and utilized a nearby Dunkard church as his headquarters. Ewell's subordinate officers occupied McClure's comfortable farmhouse.

As Lee moved his army into Pennsylvania, its three corps were widely scattered. At the end of June, its advance was located near York, while its rear was at Chambersburg. Lee did not believe that Hooker had moved north of the Potomac, but actually the Army of the Potomac had crossed over on June 25 and 26.

Finally, on June 28 Lee learned that the whole enemy army was concentrated near Frederick, Maryland, and was now under the command of Major General George Gordon Meade.

ACROSS FIVE VALLEYS

(TUSCARORA, PATH, CONOCOCHEAGUE, POTOMAC AND SHENANDOAH)

JUNIATA RIVER

ACADEMIA

TUSCARORA VALLEY

CARLISLE   HARRISBURG

PATH VALLEY

SUSQUEHANNA RIVER

CONOCOCHEAGUE   YORK

CREEK   CHAMBERSBURG

CONOCOCHEAGUE VALLEY   GETTYSBURG   HANOVER

POTOMAC VALLEY

HAGERSTOWN

MARTINSBURG   BALTIMORE

HARPERS FERRY

WINCHESTER

SHENANDOAH VALLEY   WASHINGTON

STRASBURG

FRONT ROYAL

SHENANDOAH RIVER

POTOMAC RIVER

CHESAPEAKE

RAPPAHANNOCK RIVER

BAY

JAMES RIVER

RICHMOND

ACADEMIA, PENNSYLVANIA
AREA MAP

TUSCARORA ACADEMY

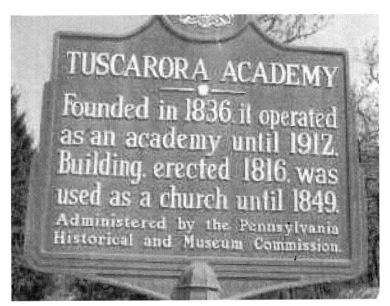

TUSCARORA ACADEMY SIGN

TUSCARORA ACADEMY

OLD STONE CHURCH - TUSCARORA ACADEMY

TUSCARORA FEMALE SEMINARY – ACADEMIA, PA.
(COURTESEY OF RICHARD BURD)

LOWER TUSCARORA PRESBYTERIAN CHURCH
ACADEMIA, PENNSYLVANIA

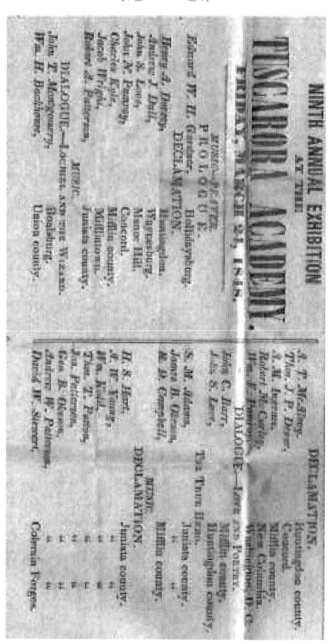

NINTH ANNUAL EXHIBITION OF THE TUSCARORA ACADEMY
MARCH 24, 1848 - PAGE ONE
(COURTESY OF DR. DARIN WHITESEL)

NINTH ANNUAL EXHIBITION OF THE TUSCARORA ACADEMY
MARCH 24, 1848 - PAGE TWO
(COURTESY OF DR. DARIN WHITESEL)

ACADEMIA-POMEROY COVERED BRIDGE

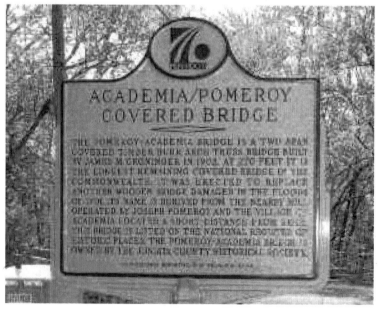

ACADEMIA-POMEROY COVERED BRIDGE SIGN

Tuscarora Academy, Pa.

October 14th, 1865

DEAR *Sir*

Your attention is respectfully invited to the following facts :

1st. The Principal expects still to devote all his time and energy to the School. He will be assisted next Session by the following teachers:

> Rev. J. A. McGINLEY, Graduate of Princeton College and Seminary.
>
> WM. G. CAIRNES, A. B., Graduate of La Fayette College.
>
> D. D. STONE, ESQ., Graduate of Dickinson College.
>
> And Messrs. E. P. FOREMAN and WILLIAM NOBLE.

2d. The increased cost of Provisions has forced us to advance our terms to $120 per Session. This, it is hoped, will enable us to meet increased expenses.

3d. As the number of applicants far exceeds our accommodations, rooms will be retained only for such applicants as *engage them positively*. Rooms cannot be retained beyond the opening of the Session, except by special agreement.

4th. Should you wish to retain the place already engaged, please inform us soon. We hope you will not be driven away by the advance in our Terms. We intend, if possible, to render full value.

Hoping to have the pleasure of seeing you   at the opening of the Session, November 1st, I have the honor, on behalf of Teachers and Trustees, to subscribe myself

> Very respectfully, yours,

> J. H. SHUMAKER, A. M., PRINCIPAL,
> *Academia, Juniata Co., Pa.*

INVITATION TO ATTEND TUSCARORA ACADEMY
OCTOBER 14, 1865 (COURTESY OF DR. DARIN WHITESEL)

STEPHEN W. POMEROY'S RIDE
JUNE 30, 1863
CHAMBERSBURG TO PERRYSVILLE

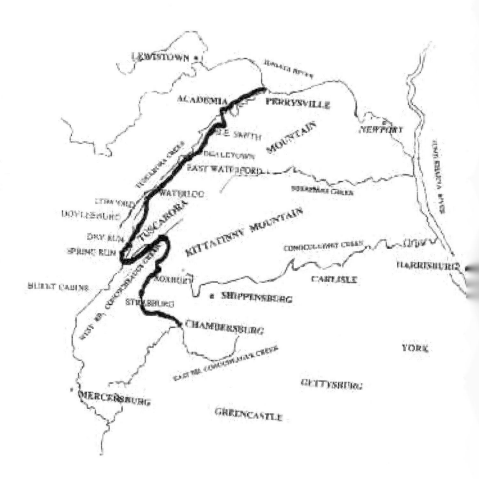

CHAPTER 49

LEE'S OCCUPATION OF CHAMBERSBURG
LATE JUNE 1863

By Monday, June 29, 1863, unbeknownst to most of the residents of Pennsylvania outside the Cumberland Valley, General Robert E. Lee had maneuvered his entire command inside the borders of Pennsylvania and established his headquarters in Chambersburg. Lee and his staff had entered the town on June 26 accompanied by General A. P. Hill.

Shortly after conferring with his staff, Lee rode eastward on the Gettysburg Pike and established his headquarters outside the borough in a little grove of trees known as Shetter's Woods. The Confederate general maintained his command there until the last day of June, when he broke camp and headed for Gettysburg.

On June 27, Lee issued General Order No. 73: "It must be remembered that we make war only against armed men. The Commanding General, therefore, earnestly exhorts the troops to abstain, with the most scrupulous care, from unnecessary or wanton injury to private property, and he enjoins upon all officers to arrest and bring to summary punishment any soldier disregarding this order."

The commanding general also ordered that all confiscated items were to be paid for in full with Confederate promissory notes or scrip. It appears that many of Hood's "Ragged Jacks" frequently ignored the order and supplemented their meager rations by taking full advantage of the choice and bountiful food to be found in the Chambersburg area.

The Texas Brigade passed through Greencastle on the morning of June 27 and entered Chambersburg that afternoon. As the Texans passed through the streets of Chambersburg, many of the townspeople displayed patriotic banners and made derisive remarks about the ill-clothed and unshod Greybacks.

One woman in particular caught the attention of the high-spirited Texans, because across her large bosom was draped a large American flag. From the center of the marching ranks a fun-filled Texan hollered, "You better take care, ma'am, because us Hoods boys are great at storming breastworks when the Yankee colors is on them."

The woman tossed her head in the air, curled her lip, and retreated into one of houses on the street, slamming the door in defiance. The marching Texans all had a good laugh at her expense.

Lee had hoped that his invasion might spark discord in Pennsylvania and throughout the whole North and lead to substantial anti-Lincoln activity. Since this section of Pennsylvania was so close to the Confederacy, had been a center of substantial political opposition, and entertained some opposition to the war itself, it was thought that Lee's invading forces might receive some cooperation from the civilian population.

This did not prove to be the case because Rebel scouts were fired upon, the civilian population attempted to hide any items and contraband they thought the Confederates might want or could use, and the townspeople had to be forced to help feed the soldiers. There also were examples of petty resistance, the withholding of supplies, and the deliberate giving of wrong directions to different towns.

During his occupation of Chambersburg, Lee showed his compassion for the civilian population of the occupied town. Chambersburg, like most towns surrounded by an agriculture-based economy, was dependent upon daily supplies of meats, vegetables, milk, and flour for its sustenance. With the advance of the Confederate forces, many of these items had been foraged by the invading army, and the teams of the farmers that normally brought these foodstuffs to market had gone into hiding.

Within a few days of occupation, the townspeople began to feel the effects of the lack of foodstuffs, especially flour. Mrs. William McLellan, the widow of a highly respected lawyer who lived in nearby Shetter's woods, took it upon herself to approach General Lee about the lack of foodstuffs. Even though he was overwhelmed with the planning and logistics of his thrust into

Pennsylvania, the benevolent southern found time to meet with Mrs. McLellan and hear her dismay and complaint.

"My dear general, I thank you for finding time in your busy schedule to meet with me and to hear my concerns."

"My dear madam, I am not completely coldhearted and immune to concerns of the good people of Chambersburg. Now, what is it you desire of me?"

"Since your occupation of Chambersburg and the surrounding countryside, it has become almost impossible for the townspeople to secure foodstuffs to sustain ourselves. All we are requesting is that you allow sufficient supplies of flour to be delivered from the gristmills outside of town to allow our people to at least have bread to eat."

"I don't find that request to be an unreasonable one. I'll instruct my aide Walter Taylor to draw up the proper papers, and we will take the necessary steps to have flour delivered to the town as soon as possible."

"General Lee, the people of Chambersburg and the Cumberland Valley thank you from the bottom of their hearts. I just wonder if I could ask one more small favor of you?"

"What is this additional favor, madam?"

"This Yankee woman would be so honored if I could have the autograph of such a famous Rebel general."

"My autograph? Are you sure you want the autograph of a Rebel?"

"General Lee, I consider myself a proud Union lady, and yet here I am asking for bread and for your autograph."

He gave her the autograph and said, "I understand why it is to your interest to be for the Union, and I hope you may be as firm in your purpose as I am in mine to the Commonwealth of Virginia and the Confederacy."

Lee's advance into the Cumberland Valley was met with only an occasional and feeble skirmish with the undermanned and undisciplined militia under the command of General Knipe of Harrisburg. Knipe and his overwhelmed militia discreetly retreated down the valley to Harrisburg.

Faced with the prospect of real fighting, Knipe's militia abandoned their positions and camp and hastily boarded the last train to Harrisburg. The militia left their tents standing with their extra clothing, many of their weapons, and all their rations on the ground. The good people of Chambersburg helped themselves to whatever items caught their fancy and quickly gathered up the vast amounts of clothing, personal items, and stores of food that the troops had foraged from the town and surrounding countryside.

These emergency troops under Knipe had been hastily thrown together, lacked a quartermaster or commissary organizations, and had to rely on foraging to meet their needs. While marching through the Cumberland Valley, the militia proved to be vastly more destructive foragers than the Confederates were.

Later, Alexander Kelly McClure would describe the destruction of his own farm outside of Chambersburg as follows: "Ewell's corps occupied the 200-acre field on my farm at the edge of Chambersburg. Military visitors had destroyed all the middle fences, and more or less of his corps remained there for a week. His 22,000 men did less injury to private property in a week's occupation than did one regiment of New York militia in a single day when it made its camp in the same field."

All communications between Chambersburg and Harrisburg were broken off as the telegraph lines were cut and all railway and highway traffic was covered by Lee's advancing troops. The entire Cumberland Valley was isolated from the state capital at Harrisburg.

Chambersburg had become an important staging area for Lee's army. A small portion of the Confederate forces continued northeast down the Cumberland Valley toward Shippensburg, Carlisle, and Harrisburg. The vast majority of Lee's forces surged eastward towards the small village of Cashtown and the town of Gettysburg.

By this time, Ewell's corps was spread over a large area. Early's division was located near York, Rhodes's had moved to Carlisle, Jenkins's cavalry had advanced down the Cumberland Valley to Mechanicsburg bearing down on the state capital, and Johnson's was in the vicinity of Shippensburg.

A. P. Hill's corps had Heth at Cashtown, and Pender's and Anderson's were located between Fayetteville and Greenwood, west of the South Mountain situated in Franklin County.

Longstreet's corps now had Pickett's division near Chambersburg to act as a rear guard; McLaws and Hood were also near Fayetteville, Imboden's cavalry was to the west at Mercersburg, and Stuart, unknown to Lee, was just a little north of Westminster, Maryland.

Stuart's cavalry had placed Lee in a dilemma. Stuart was Lee's eyes, but for almost two weeks, Lee had received no vital information concerning the Yankees' location or strength. Lee was completely frustrated by Stuart's absence. "I cannot think what has become of Stuart. In absence of his reports from him, I am ignorant as to what we have in front of us here. It may be the whole federal army; it may only be a detachment."

CHAPTER 50

GOVERNOR ANDREW CURTIN'S STAFF

The movement of Lee's forces towards the Susquehanna River created a tremendous urgency in the state capital. As early as June 16, most regular government business had been suspended and all-important documents had been removed from the capital.

On June 26, Governor Andrew Curtin announced that Pennsylvania would accept volunteers for ninety days, "but will be required to serve only so much of the period of muster as the safety of our people and the honor of the state may require."

Andrew Gregg Curtin had been born in Bellefonte, Pennsylvania, and had attended Dickinson College and its school of law. He had been a lawyer but eventually became involved in politics and joined the newly formed Republican Party. In 1861, Curtin succeeded William F. Packer as the governor of Pennsylvania and was inaugurated on January 15. In his inaugural address, he stated, "Pennsylvania would, under any circumstances, render full and determined support of the free institutions of the union."

In the early days of the war, Governor Curtin oversaw the construction of the first Union military training camp in Harrisburg, Camp Curtin, which opened on April 18, 1861. The governor was instrumental in organizing Pennsylvania's reserves into combat units.

The stresses of office involving recruitment, conscription measures, and taxation to support the war were so arduous that the governor endured a nervous breakdown. While the governor was incapacitated, Eli Slifer, the secretary of state, handled governmental affairs.

Despite poor health, Governor Curtin continued to support the Union war effort. He organized the "Loyal War Governor's Conference," held at the Logan House Hotel in Altoona, Pennsylvania, on September 24 and 25, 1862. This conference buttressed

Lincoln's administration and helped to solidify northern unity. Through the years, Andrew Curtin became a close friend and confidant of President Lincoln, and the White House always welcomed Curtin warmly.

President Lincoln offered Curtin a diplomatic position abroad, but the governor instead chose to seek reelection in 1863, which he achieved by defeating Democrat George Woodward by about fifteen thousand votes. Now, in June 1863, Governor Curtin was faced with his most challenging task, that of defending his commonwealth against Lee's invading Army of Northern Virginia.

During these dark days of late June 1863, Major General Darius Nash Couch had received the priority of protecting the state capital and the southern portions of the Commonwealth, and above all, denying the Rebel army passage over the vital Susquehanna River.

Couch's department included all troops east of Johnstown and the Laurel Highlands; its headquarters were initially at Chambersburg. General Couch was highly qualified for the position and merited the confidence placed in him. The general had graduated from the United States Military Academy in 1846. He immediately served in the Mexican War, and in the Second Seminole War, but had resigned his commission in 1855.

Darius Couch reentered the army as Colonel of the 7th Massachusetts Infantry at the outbreak of the war in April 1861, but the next month was promoted to brigadier general. For his successes during the Peninsula Campaign, Seven Days Battles, and at Antietam, he was promoted to major general in July 1862 and assumed command of the II Corps in November. After being wounded at Chancellorsville and quarreling with Major General Joseph Hooker, he was reassigned as commander of Department of the Susquehanna.

Another of the key figures within the governor's inner circle and serving under Couch was Brigadier General William "Baldy" F. Smith. Smith was the commanding officer of the First Division of the United States Army, and his major objective was to defend the state capital. General Smith had assumed command of the troops south of the Susquehanna River and in the vicinity of Harrisburg on Friday, June 26. Since then, he had been engaged in strengthening the defenses at Bridgeport, opposite the city of Harrisburg. Not only was his major objective to protect the state capital, but it was also to defend the bridges of the Pennsylvania and Northern Central Railroads at Marysville.

The prominent journalist, politician, and lawyer from Chambersburg, Alexander Kelly McClure, was in the governor's advisory group. At the outbreak of the war, McClure was the chairman of the state's Senate Committee on Military Affairs. He had assisted Governor Curtin in calling the Loyal War Governors meeting in Altoona in 1862. McClure had been commissioned by President Lincoln as an assistant adjutant general and was instrumental in raising seventeen Pennsylvania regiments for the Union army.

McClure was lucky to be in Harrisburg because he was still at his estate, Norland, in Chambersburg when Lee entered the town. He met with the general personally and then was able to flee through the Cumberland Valley and across the Susquehanna to be at Curtin's side. Alexander's wife, the former Matilda S. Gray, chose to stay behind and look after Norland during the enemy's occupation of Chambersburg.

Thomas Alexander Scott was also on hand in Harrisburg to play a key role in advising Governor Curtin in these perilous times. Thomas Scott was a native of Fort Loudoun, Franklin County, Pennsylvania. Prior to the outbreak of the Civil War, Scott had worked his way up through the ranks of the Pennsylvania Railroad to become the general superintendent of the railway. Scott had served in an advisory role to President Lincoln when he was newly elected. It was Scott who advised Lincoln not to take his published route into Washington prior to his inauguration in order to avoid potential assassination attempts, advice which Lincoln wisely followed. During the first two years of the war, Scott served as an assistant secretary of war and was charged with the supervision of all Union railways and communication lines, especially telegraph lines.

Besides initiating a new railroad to be constructed between Washington and Philadelphia, Scott organized federal river traffic on the western and northwestern rivers. He was awarded a staff commission from the War Department as a colonel. At the time of Lee's second advance into the North, Scott, although an officer in the Union army, was serving on the staff of Governor Andrew Curtin.

CHAPTER 51
THE DEFENSE OF THE STATE CAPITAL

General Couch had moved his headquarters back to Harrisburg once the Confederate army entered the Cumberland Valley. While militia units from New York and New Jersey arrived to help defend Harrisburg, the newly formed Pennsylvania emergency militia drilled and trained at Camp Curtin in preparation for their capital's defense. The commander of the Department of the Susquehanna ordered that no Confederate unit was to be allowed to cross the vital natural barrier of the Susquehanna River. Unfortunately for Couch, the War Department informed Couch that he would not receive any aid from federal units already deployed in the field.

To implement his defensive strategy, Couch assigned General Baldy Smith to provide the mainstay of the capital's defense and ordered the construction of earthworks and fortifications on the west bank of the river. Couch sent his aide-de-camp, Major Granville O. Haller, to serve as the defender of Adams and York Counties, with his headquarters in Gettysburg. Haller had three regiments of state emergency militia under his command, one each at Gettysburg, York, and the Wrightsville-Columbia Bridge.

General Couch's most pressing concern was the defense of Harrisburg, and he was extremely anxious about Hummel Heights in Lemoyne, which surveyed the west bank of the river and provided a panoramic view of the capital city and the bridges in the area. As early as June 15, a large muster of civilians, including a railroad construction gang, began scratching out the breastworks that would become known as Fort Washington.

Upon examining the remainder of the heights, it was ascertained that the higher ground located about one-half mile to the west, if under enemy control, could dominate Fort Washington. With this new knowledge, a second bastion was ordered to be constructed. Again, railroad construction crews did the bulk of the work. This second fort was named Fort Couch, even though it probably was not completed.

The forts on Hummel Heights (now Washington Heights) were armed with artillery pieces behind the hastily constructed earthworks. If enemy troops attempted to scale the heights, the cannon's barrels could be depressed to sweep the approaches to the heights.

General Lee sent his Second Corps under General Richard S. Ewell to move on Harrisburg with his two infantry divisions commanded by Major Generals Robert E. Rodes and Edward Johnson. Ewell had captured Carlisle on June 27 without a fight. On the next day, while the construction volunteers were still laboring to erect Fort Couch, General Jenkins's Confederate cavalry rode into Mechanicsburg. Jenkins divided his command; one half used the knoll occupied by Peace Church on Trindle Road, the other half moved east along Carlisle Pike to about a mile north of the church.

After some indiscriminate firing by the Rebel artillery batteries, Jenkins retreated at dusk and set up his headquarters at the John Rupp House. Rebel patrols dispersed throughout the area, investigating the Yankee defenses and network of roads. One outlying patrol explored northward as far as Sterrett's Gap, probably the farthest north that any Rebels infiltrated during the Gettysburg campaign.

While these two divisions of Ewell's infantry were advancing up the Cumberland Valley, his other division under Major General Jubal A. Early moved east through Adams County. They captured Gettysburg on June 26 by chasing away the militia detailed to defend the county seat. From there Early's Georgia Brigade under General John B. Gordon moved on York and occupied that undefended city on June 28. York gained the distinction of becoming the largest northern city to fall to Lee's forces during the Civil War.

With Rebel troops fanning out over south central Pennsylvania, thousands of farmers from Franklin, Adams, Cumberland, and York Counties fled east with their horses, livestock, valuables, and families, attempting to put the Susquehanna River between them and the rapidly advancing enemy.

The multitudes of panicked refugees became caught in a huge jam-up on the western end of 5,620-foot-long Wrightsville-Columbia Bridge, the main eastward route across the Susquehanna River. The jam-up was created by the bridge company's insistence upon extracting tolls from the throng that was desperate to cross over the bridge.

Couch realized the importance of the bridge between Wrightsville and Columbia because it was the only other crossing point of the Susquehanna between Harrisburg and Conowingo, Maryland. He had deployed Colonel Jacob G. Frick as commander of the 27th Pennsylvania Militia to defend the bridge, but that force didn't arrive on the scene until June 24.

The 27th Militia arrived in the midst of a huge traffic jam with a backlog of refugees attempting to reach the alleged safety of Lancaster County on the east bank of the river. In addition to the pedestrian traffic, the bridge was constructed to handle both railway and highway traffic. Several locomotives had smokestacks too high to allow them to use the bridge and had to have their stacks removed and taken over on rail cars, which added to the turmoil.

Major Granville Haller of the U.S. Army arrived at the approach to the bridge on June 27. The bridge was owned by the Columbia Bank, and Haller persuaded the bridge company president to allow the horde of refugees to pass over the river without their having to pay fees.

Colonel Frick realized that his untested and virtually untrained recruits and the other troops that joined him in his hastily constructed, crescent-shaped, earthwork defense would be unable to hold off the Rebel attacks for any length of time. He decided to use a delaying tactic, first allowing his troops to withdraw across the bridge, and then, under the cover of the three cannons on the east bank, destroying a span of the bridge with explosives.

The townspeople pitched in and with the aid of the militia, barricaded the side streets of the town. They also lined up rail cars on the tracks that ran parallel to the river to discourage a dash of enemy cavalry across the bridge before it could be destroyed.

About 5:30 on the afternoon of June 28, the first gray skirmishers were observed approaching the town. Shortly afterwards, Gordon's artillery batteries opened fire on the bridge's defenders, and the militia abandoned their positions and withdrew across the bridge.

Under Haller's orders, Frick attempted to blow up a span of the bridge, but the explosion failed to cleanly destroy the section of the bridge. Frick then ordered the wooden structure to be set afire to keep the Rebels on the western shore of the river. Mother Nature entered into the destruction as a prevailing wind soon spread flames across the length of the bridge, but also into the town of Wrightsville.

In a display of common concern for fellow Americans, even though they were enemies at the time, the Rebel soldiers under Gordon's command united in an effort to save as much of the town as possible. Since Gordon was unsuccessful in capturing the bridge intact, the Confederates concentrated their forces in York.

Meanwhile, the pressure continued on the defense of Harrisburg. On the morning of June 29, artillery skirmishes broke out between Jenkins's cavalry and the Union militia entrenched at Oyster Point. Later, the Rebel cavalry launched a diversionary attack on the militia that was easily repelled by the militia. Jenkins was on the high ground of Slate Hill while the alleged attack was being staged, scrutinizing the defenses surrounding Harrisburg.

Ewell received a report back in Carlisle that the defenses on Hummel's Heights posed no serious threat. Ewell then ordered General Rodes to push his mighty division forward to dispose of the Yankee militia on the western bank of the Susquehanna and to attack and capture Harrisburg.

CHAPTER 52

THE BACKGROUND OF
STEPHEN POMEROY'S RIDE

The political and economic leaders of Chambersburg realized how important it was for vital information of Lee's movements to reach Harrisburg and then be relayed to Washington, D. C., and the president, and then on to General Meade. One of the most prominent leaders in Chambersburg was Judge Francis M. Kimmel, who understood the gravity of the situation in his once sleepy little town. Kimmel was the former presiding judge of the district, and in 1862, when Chambersburg had been under martial law, he had served as provost marshal.

Governor Curtin had dictated that Judge Kimmel was to implement a general supervision of wartime activities in the Chambersburg area. In order for Kimmel and his advisors to secure intelligence concerning enemy activity, scouts were continually dispatched from the town to gain knowledge of any change in the Confederate maneuverings, and this knowledge was relayed to Harrisburg.

Many of these scouts were men who had served the Union and were home on leave or whose enlistments had expired, but intended to reenlist and rejoin their old regiments. Some of these daring young men included Benjamin S. Huber, Anthony Hollar, Sellers Montgomery, Shearer Houser, T. J. Grimeson, J. Porter Brown, and Stephen W. Pomeroy.

During the perilous journeys of these daring scouts, they were fired upon, chased by enemy cavalry, and in one instance captured by enemy forces. They had been instructed to destroy the dispatches they were carrying by chewing and swallowing them. The dispatches were hidden in articles of clothing or in boots, or in the end of a plug of tobacco.

On Sunday morning, June 28, Anthony Hollar and Mr. Kinney, the principal of the Chambersburg Academy, were posing as innocent schoolmasters transporting a bundle of dirty clothing home to be washed when they were captured by enemy forces about six or eight miles from town on their way to Strasburg. They were successful in swallowing their dispatches and feigning ignorance of any wrongdoing and were allowed to proceed towards the mountain.

After reaching Strasburg, the two parted. Principal Kinney returned to Chambersburg. Anthony crossed the Kittatinny Mountain and had arrived in Perry County on his way to Newport when Union soldiers, who refused to believe his claim that he was in fact carrying an important message to be delivered to Harrisburg, captured him. He was transported to the state capital under suspicion of being a spy, but eventually was able to establish his true identify and deliver his message.

On the night of June 29, the citizens of Chambersburg breathed a collective sigh of relief when Lee's wagon train left the encampment at Shetter's woods and headed on the pike towards Gettysburg. Judge Kimmel had awaited this decisive movement for it was concrete evidence that the center of the campaign was moving out of the Cumberland Valley to a line between South Mountain and the Potomac River.

Among the young scouts who happened to be in town that evening was Stephen W. Pomeroy. Stephen's father, Thomas Pomeroy, had been an associate judge with Francis Kimmel on the Franklin County Bench, and Judge Kimmel knew that he could trust young Pomeroy's judgment and tenacity in undertaking the task.

Stephen had proved his mettle in battle. He had recently concluded a nine-month enlistment with the 126th Pennsylvania Volunteer Infantry. He had "met the elephant," and had survived the slaughter at Fredericksburg on December 13, 1862, and most recently, the setback to Hooker at Chancellorsville on May 1-3, 1863.

Following his return to the Cumberland Valley, Stephen and several of his friends had been relaxing and enjoying their friends, families, and homes. Then Lee's advancing army appeared on the scene. The ex-soldiers were dismayed at the raiding and foraging that was taking place in their valley, especially by Jenkins's cavalry. They decided that it would be their duty and great sport to harass isolated units of the Confederate cavalry whenever the opportunity presented itself. During the morning of June 29 they sought to ambush a Confederate raiding party, but thought better of it once they realized how badly outnumbered they were. The consensus was that it would be better to wait for a better situation to present itself.

Later that day the group decided to journey to Chambersburg to see how the Johnnies were treating the townspeople. It was a walk of about fourteen miles, for the most part across open fields and roads that were patrolled by cavalry units.

The town was alive with military activity, and it was expedient for the group to split up, stick to side streets, and avoid drawing attention to themselves. Rather than return home that evening, they happily accepted the generous invitation of one of their town-dwelling friends to spend the night.

Early the next morning, a messenger arrived at the door of their friend's home with an urgent request from Judge Thomas Pomeroy's fellow jurist, Judge Kimmel, to speak to Stephen immediately. The messenger warned, "Be very discreet about your arrival at the judge's meeting place. He doesn't want anyone to have any suspicions about your presence. It is of utmost importance that he see you."

As Stephen cautiously headed for the designated meeting place, he overtook Judge Kimmel as he strolled near the Franklin Hotel on the street that leads to McConnelsburg.

The judge surveyed Stephen warily, "Are you Thomas Pomeroy's son?"

"Yes, I certainly am."

"Ah, yes, I can see the resemblance—you have his keen eyes. Follow me and, hopefully, we will be well out of view of any prying eyes."

The judge opened the door to an office building on a back alleyway, and Stephen stepped inside without a word being exchanged. The judge stood before him in the almost abandoned room, with a concerned look on his face. "No one saw you coming, did they?"

"I'm certain no one saw me. I skirted all the side streets and back alleys, and I didn't see anyone. All the locals are still holed up, and the rebs are either on the other side of town or are packing up and leaving town."

"Their leaving is what I want to talk to you about. I'm sure you're aware of our situation here. We're completely cut off from Harrisburg. The governor and his advisors have been sitting on pins and needles waiting to receive any information from us as to Lee's intentions.

"I didn't want to waste any manpower in attempting to get a message to the governor until we were absolutely positive as to Lee's movements. Lee's wagon train and the last of his infantry moved out on the pike towards Cashtown and Gettysburg. It is essential that we send a message immediately concerning Lee's concentration of troops towards Gettysburg.

"I considered attempting to send a message across the mountain into Sherman's Valley and down to Newport, but I've traveled through Perry County on several occasions, and I know that there isn't just one main valley to take to Newport. On the other hand, I know the geography of Path and the Tuscarora Valley. The Indians were wise enough to have a path through these valleys that connected the Shenandoah Valley with the Susquehanna River. It's almost a straight shot once you climb over the Kittatinny Mountain. The gap in the Tuscarora Mountain between Concord and Waterloo presents no problem whatsoever.

"I've chosen you for this undertaking for several reasons. First, I know you and your family, and I know I can trust you with any task. Secondly, you're a proven soldier who knows how to perform his duties and carry out his orders. Third, I know that you went to school in the Tuscarora Valley and that you have family living in Path Valley and the whole length of the Tuscarora Valley, and especially your aunt and uncle live in your destination, Perrysville.

You probably know the route to Perrysville like the back of your hand.

"You're undertaking one of the most important missions of the entire war. The whole future of our nation rests with you arriving at Perrysville with the dispatch that you will be secretly carrying. I'm not placing my signature or date on the message, so if it is intercepted, the enemy won't know exactly how much we know about their movements. Just remember that the governor and the president are counting on us to deliver this vital information.

"Come over here," the judge said, gesturing towards the window. "I'm going to sew this dispatch inside the lining of the buckle-strap of your pants. If you think you are going to be captured, tear the message out, roll it into a ball, and swallow it. It simply can't fall into enemy hands. Son, we're counting on you to get through and deliver the message. Do you have any questions?"

"No questions, sir. You can count on me. I'll be able to exchange horses with friends and family along the way. First, I'll have to slip out of town and find a horse. They're mighty scarce in the valley right now, but I'm sure my father's friends will help me out."

The twenty-six year old mustered-out soldier, soon to be a soldier again, straightened up and gave the judge a good, crisp military salute before leaving.

CHAPTER 53
STEPHEN POMEROY CROSSES THE MOUNTAIN AND TRAVELS THROUGH PATH VALLEY

As soon as he was outside, Stephen looked around to make sure no one saw him and headed towards the northeastern side of town in order to cover the first fourteen miles of his journey on foot across hostile territory. Several of his friends from the Roxbury area joined him as they were returning to their homes.

As they left the cover of the last houses on the outskirts of town, they crawled into an open wheat field, but some Rebel infantrymen spotted them. They yelled, "Halt! Stop right where you are!"

Stephen paid no heed to their warning and began to run in a zigzag manner. The Rebel troops never opened fire, and he knew that he could outrun these men. He figured that they had little interest in him or his small, unarmed group and would not give chase. Besides, they probably weren't frontline troops; if they were, they would be on the road and not still here occupying the town. He was lucky that these soldiers were not mounted cavalry, because they would have been able to overtake him rather easily. Then his mission would have been thwarted almost before it began.

At the forks of the Roxbury and Strasburg roads, Stephen and his group spotted both mounted and foot soldiers, so they veered into a slight hollow and from that point on, they stuck to any cover they could find, mostly making use of tree-lined fencerows and small patches of woodland. Since he was unable to follow a straight course to his home, Stephen ended up covering a greater distance, probably close to seventeen miles, and therefore taking much longer to reach his home.

When he arrived back home in Roxbury, Stephen quickly came to the point. "Judge Kimmel needs me to take an urgent message to Perrysville. In the meantime, if you haven't already done so, it might be a good idea for you to hide our valuables and livestock, and have our neighbors to do the same. The Rebs are everywhere. They chased me as I left Chambersburg. Mother, could you please make me a snack while I get Father to find me a horse?"

"Just please be careful, son. We thought for sure that we had lost you at Chancellorsville, and we certainly don't want to lose you now."

"I'll be extra careful just for you, Mother."

Meanwhile, Judge Pomeroy hurriedly explained the situation to S. L. Sentman, who had arrived in an attempt to find food for the many horses that the people of the Roxbury and Strasburg area had sequestered in valleys and hollows in the nearby mountain. Mr. Sentman's response was immediate. "Here, take my horse. He's a good strong one, and he can run like the wind. He'll get you across the mountain in no time."

Stephen immediately mounted the horse and headed north on the road across the steep Kittatinny Mountain. He knew that this would be the most challenging portion of his journey. The upper headwaters of the Conodoquinet Creek cut a slight gap in the mountain, but soon afterwards the road sloped steeply and made the going difficult for the struggling horse.

Just as Stephen began his climb up the steep slope into the gap on Timmons Road, a gruff voice rang out, "Halt right there. Don't move a muscle or we'll drop you out of that saddle in the blink of an eye. Now, just what are you doing out here on the mountain?"

"I'm Stephen Pomeroy of Roxbury and a mustered-out member of the 126th Regiment. Judge Kimmel of Chambersburg is sending me on a mission of great urgency. He wouldn't be too happy to hear that you're holding up one of his couriers."

"Just keep your hands above you head and mosey over here so we can check you out."

Stephen obeyed.

"Well, you certainly look like who you claim to be," the man declared. "We just can't be careful enough with all those Johnnies running around the area."

Then another voice rang out. "Sure enough it's Stephen.

Howdy, it's Bill Halleck, one of your neighbors. Get on your way over the mountain. We certainly don't want to upset the judge. He's been in a rather bad mood since Lee and his boys moved into the valley. Good luck to you, Stephen."

"The same to you men. I don't blame you for being cautious. A couple of Rebs tried to capture me outside of Chambersburg. Hope to see you in a few days, on my way back over the mountain."

Beyond this first precipitous incline, the road turned northeast on Cold Spring Road, and Stephen soon crossed over the South Branch of Laurel Run to the eastern reaches of Amberson Valley and the upper waters of the West Branch of the Conococheague Creek. As the road continued its descent, it made a huge bend, and he headed westward onto the Amberson Road that follows the creek on a parallel course with the mountain.

At the mouth of Dry Run Creek, Spring Run Road turns and follows this creek northwestward to the village of Spring Run. The road soon intersects the Old Tuscarora Path at Spring Run, which is known as the Path Valley Road or Pike. At this intersection, several wagons and logs barricaded the pike, as the local militia was out in force to try to delay any Rebel cavalry activity.

Stephen identified several of the men manning the barricade, and called out to them, and they in turn recognized him. John Miller appeared to be the leader, and he explained to Stephen. "Rumors abound that Confederate foraging parties, perhaps even led by the great Mosby himself, are supposed to be in Path Valley. We received word that Rebel and Union cavalry exchanged fire on June 24 near President Buchanan's birthplace in the vicinity of Mercersburg. This spurred some of the local veterans to build earthworks on the mountain passes of the valley and to barricade some of the intersections. They're just like us; all we can do is harass them and perhaps delay them for a short time, but eventually their firepower will probably overwhelm us."

After leaving the men at the intersection, Stephen realized that traversing the mountain had taken a terrible toll on his horse. The pastor of the Upper Path Valley Presbyterian Church in Spring Run was a good friend of his father, so he decided to stop at the parsonage and see if he could borrow a fresh horse. This church had been established in 1766, and a fine brick one had replaced the old log church in 1856.

Unfortunately, neither the pastor nor his wife was home, so Stephen failed to acquire a fresh horse.

Stephen figured he had covered about fifteen miles since leaving his parents' home. As he passed through the village of Dry Run, then headed towards Doylesburg, he realized that the fields were ripe with oats, wheat, and barley, ready to be harvested within the next week or two, and the corn was almost knee-high. Here and there, he observed where some farmers had just cut hay, and the smell of fresh mown hay permeated his nostrils, drowning out the smell of a sweaty horse. Nothing was out of place as far as crops were concerned, but there were no cattle, sheep, pigs, or horses to be seen in the fields or in any of the barnyards that he could observe from the road.

The word had spread like wildfire that the Rebs were on the other side of the Kittatinny Mountain and at the southern end of Path Valley. This valley was wide open all the way to the gap in the Tuscarora Mountain north of Concord. There were no physical barriers or areas of high ground that could serve to protect the valley. If the Reb cavalry swept through the valley, there wouldn't be any way to stop them.

It had been expedient for the farmers of Path Valley to herd their livestock up into the recesses of the Tuscarora, Conococheague, and Kittatinny Mountains, especially into Horse Valley near Concord.

Stephen pushed the horse at a rapid pace until it was lathered in sweat, whereupon he decided to slack off, or the horse wouldn't last very long.

When he came up the incline after Dry Run and the path leveled somewhat, he began to think of his earlier trips through this valley on his way to visit his relatives and to attend the academy at Academia.

One of his favorite stories about the early days of this valley was about the journey of the Reverend Philip Fithian, a Presbyterian minister who traveled through the region in 1775. On June 22, 1775, Fithian described Path Valley of Franklin County as follows: "This valley is in many places not more than a mile wide; it is level, and the land rich; the mountains are both high and near, that the sun is hid night and morning an hour before he rises and sets."

When he arrived at the ford of Burns Creek, Stephen allowed his horse to drink water. The poor steed was just about done in. Stephen didn't allow his horse to drink too much, because too much water consumed at once on a hot day like this could be fatal.

Stephen thought it was rather strange that no one was on the porch or even visible when he passed by the store in Concord. Then he realized that he probably would be encountering many of the men still left in the valley when he attempted to pass through the narrows or gap in the Tuscarora Mountain just northwest of the village. The narrows would be the logical location for the local militia to have erected a barricade or fortification to halt the advance of any Confederate cavalry that happened to sweep this far north.

He hoped that his Uncle William Pomeroy was at home instead of being deployed in defense of the narrows. Luckily, his uncle was in his workshop behind the house and after a series of pleasantries, the exchange of horses was made, and the young rider was on his way to the narrows.

Fithian described the narrows of the Tuscarora Mountain on Friday, June 23, 1775. "We passed from this valley by the narrows, into Tuscarora Valley, a most stony valley; two high mountains on every side. The passage so narrow, that you may take one stone in your right hand and another in your left and throw each upon a mountain, and they are so high that they obscure more than half the horizon. A rainy, dripping day, more uncomfortable for riding among the leaves. On the way all day was only a small footpath, and covered all with sharp stones."

Fithian's description of the narrows was one that Stephen would never forget. Who knows, maybe he could use them in a sermon someday when this terrible war was over and he had achieved his dream of becoming a Presbyterian minister!

CHAPTER 54
STEPHEN POMEROY IN THE TUSCARORA VALLEY

The men and boys manning the barrier at the entrance to the Tuscarora Narrows needed some lessons in camouflaging or concealing their activities and emplacements. Before Stephen had passed the last house of the village of Concord, he could smell the cooking fires and hear the bantering of the men in the barricade. If he had been part of a Reb scouting party, they would have been in for a rough go of it. They would have ended up seeing the elephant far removed from any battlefield.

Now his biggest fear was that one of the untrained militia might shoot first and ask questions later. He nudged his horse to the side of the road, picked up a three-to-four-foot-long stick, and tied his white handkerchief to the end of it. With the stick waving in the air above his head, he noisily approached the narrows, giving full notice that he was not a Rebel attempting to ride through their emplacement.

The men towards the front of the barrier yelled back into the emplacement that a rider was approaching, and they needed instructions. Apparently, Stephen was their first challenger, and they hadn't yet established any procedures for dealing with anyone wishing to travel through the narrows. He shook his head in amazement; they had better get some rules of engagement established before they were really tested. They didn't seem to realize the possibility that a Confederate force was within twenty miles of their position. It probably wasn't a sizeable Rebel force harassing the other end of Path Valley, but it could be a deadly force.

Finally, an authoritative voice bellowed out, "Just halt right there, sonny, and keep your hands where we can see them. I know you've got a white flag, but we've heard how tricky you Rebs can be."

"George Campbell, I could recognize your raspy old voice anywhere. Now, lower your guns and allow me to advance. It's Stephen Pomeroy from Roxbury on my way to Perrysville."

"Stephen Pomeroy, is it? We heard you were dead. Killed at the battle of Chancellorsville. Ride forward at a slow pace, and let us check you out."

The inspection didn't take long. "Well, I'll be darned," George said, "it *is* Stephen. I bet he's sneaking down the valley to see that Smith girl he's been sweet on ever since his days at the academy. Never did see what she saw in him."

"Yes, it's me. Never mind about the Smith girl, but that does sound like a good idea. Just who is in charge of this band of cutthroats?"

"Why, Dr. Samuel Crawford of the Uniformed Militia is in charge, of course—appointed by Governor Curtin. Dr. Crawford was directed to summon every man and boy who could fire a gun to defend and hold the Tuscarora Narrows here at Concord lest the Confederate Cavalry charge through the narrows and all the way down the Tuscarora Valley to Perrysville and cut off the Pennsylvania Railroad. From there they could converge on Harrisburg."

Just then, John Hutchinson stuck his head out from behind a boulder. "As you can see, Pomeroy, we're ready to give those Rebs a good beating if they try and come through here."

Stephen laughed, "Yes, I can see you're ready for anything. Now, could I please talk to Dr. Crawford?"

"Sure enough, he's down here by the creek. I'll take you to him."

They picked their way along the creek bed and among the white tents that had been erected on a level area of the western bank of the creek. The aroma of coffee sure smelled good to him.

"Doctor, or sir, Sergeant Pomeroy to see you."

"Why, Stephen, it's good to see you. We heard that you had met your demise down in Virginia, but I'm glad to see that those stories aren't true. Now what can I do for you?"

"I'm carrying an important message from Judge Kimmel to the telegraph office at Perrysville. I needed to get through your barricade without being shot and ride on to Bealetown, where I can exchange my Uncle William's horse for another horse from Reverend

David Beale. I'll just reverse the horses on the return trip, so I'll only have him for a day or so."

"We don't want to hold you up. Good luck to you, and plan on spending some time with us on your return trip."

"Before I go, could I please enjoy a cup of your coffee? Even though it's a warm day, it certainly would help to refresh me."

"John, get the sergeant a cup of coffee and a piece of berry pie that my wife baked yesterday."

After enjoying the hospitality, Stephen departed to the cheers of the men manning the barricade: it gave him a thrill to know that he was backed by such a fine group of men. His uncle's horse was a spirited one that wanted to run with the wind. At first, Stephen had difficulty holding him back, but eventually the stallion calmed down.

He entered Waterloo in a cloud of dust. Out of the corner of his left eye, he spotted a new, impressive, stone building on the left side of the road just at the western end of the village. Stephen remembered hearing about it. It was known as the Waterloo Seminary and had only opened its first session on April 27. He thought there wouldn't be many males over sixteen attending the new institution since most of the healthy of-age males were serving in the Army of the Potomac. A little farther to the north he saw the steeple of the Upper Tuscarora Presbyterian Church.

Waterloo was such a tiny village that if you blinked while riding through it, you would miss it. Stephen did slow down enough to nod to the woman standing on the slight porch in front of the village store, but once he was beyond the last house, he allowed the stallion to canter at its own pace.

He soon passed the road that led to the Peru Mills Post Office, and in a short time he approached the Presbyterian church on the outskirts of East Waterford. This village housed one of his favorite eating establishments, the American House. Built in 1790, it was presently owned and operated by Hugh B. McMeen. This genuine haven of rest consisted of a tavern, bedrooms, and an eating hall, and was a major stop on the stage line that Thomas Kirk operated between Perrysville and Concord.

Kirk's stage enterprise was fully equipped with several matched teams of good horses and fine coaches that he kept in excellent repair. David Van Ormer served as his main driver and was once complimented for knowing "just how to hold the ribbons and reach every station on time." Stephen had fond memories of hearing Van Ormer's horn warning of his approach to every station on the line. Before the war, the stage left Perrysville promptly after the Pennsylvania Railroad's train arrived at approximately 7:52 each morning carrying the mail.

The little village of East Waterford had sent more than its share of young men to serve in Mr. Lincoln's army since the first call for 75,000 volunteers in April of 1861. This valley had a rich tradition of having its men volunteer for the defense of this land and the cause of freedom from the time the first pioneers arrived in the middle of the previous century. For over a hundred years, beginning with the French and Indian War, through the American Revolution, the War of 1812, the Mexican War, and now this bloody conflict, which pitted Americans against each other, Tuscarora Valley males had contributed their minds and bodies to the cause.

Stephen had served in the Fredericksburg, Virginia, campaign for over five months, and in that period of time he had encountered the 49th Pennsylvania Volunteers. Company I of the 49th had been organized at Perrysville on August 18, 1861, and mustered into service at Camp Curtin on September 9. Within the membership of this company, he had counted over twenty-five members from Perrysville and nearly twenty-three from East Waterford.

He thought, "When one considers the sparse population of this region of the Tuscarora Valley, these numbers of volunteers represent a huge percentage of the young male population. It has to be highly unusual to have such a high representation from one small area."

Although he knew that he would never be able to remember the names of all those brave men from this village, some of the names did come to mind: George Diven; Bill Hurd; Jim Jacobs;

David Louden; Peter Miller; James, James G. and Abram Milliken; John McMullen; Dave Peck; Joe Richardson; Joe Rhine; Andrew N. and Andrew W. Smith; William Stitt; Robert H. Taylor; and George Wilson.

Amazingly, the only one of those brave men who had given their all was young Andrew W. Smith, who was killed at Antietam, Maryland, on September 17, 1862. Andy was only eighteen when he enlisted. Stephen chose not to dwell upon such sad memories, and he returned to the present as the Tuscarora Creek came into view.

Within about two miles, he was descending into the hamlet of Bealetown where some of his good friends resided. He knew he would receive a warm welcome and warm food at the home of David Beale, and he would be able to change horses once again. The future pastor inquired about his parents' health and about his experiences in the army. After swallowing a few morsels of food, Stephen was back in the saddle, but on David Beale's horse, after covering fourteen miles on his uncle's horse.

The road climbed an incline for less than a mile, and then it leveled off. Before he realized it, he was at a fork in the road. The main road veered slightly to the left, but straight ahead was another road, known as the Mountain Road. Also, to his left was a lane that led to Reed's farm. The Reed farmhouse stood on one of the most famous sites in the Tuscarora Valley.

Around 1749 Bigham's Fort was constructed at this location to protect the inhabitants of this part of the valley from ravaging Indians. On June 11, 1756, the fort was attacked and destroyed. The survivors were escorted to Kittaning one hundred and fifty miles to the west on the banks of the Allegheny River. A number of these unfortunate settlers survived their ordeal in captivity and returned to the valley. (Some of their descendants still resided in this area.) The fort was reconstructed in 1760. During Pontiac's Uprising in July of 1763 the fort was destroyed again, but fortunately the fort's inhabitants were forewarned of the attack and had abandoned it before the attack occurred, and no lives were lost.

Stephen urged his horse to follow the right fork and passed

the Dunkard church and cemetery. At this stage of his journey, he became anxious as he thought of George Campbell's teasing accusation that he was going to sneak down the Mountain Road and visit the alluring young Smith girl. The thought of visiting his sweetheart had formed in his mind as he urged his own horse down the steep incline of Kittatinny Mountain at the beginning of his journey.

He knew that his darling Effie would make a wonderful preacher's wife; she had all the attributes that would make them an effective pair in spreading and teaching the Lord's good word. Now he could not contain his urge to see her, to hold her in his arms, to smell her hair, and yes, to kiss and embrace her. It had been much too long since he had the pleasure of doing so. It wouldn't take that long to ride down Silas E. Smith's lane to see the love of his life if but for a few minutes. No one could blame him for extending his journey just a bit, not even the governor, although neither he nor the judge nor anyone else in authority would ever know of his short deviation from his path.

He nudged his horse into the entrance of the Smiths' lane and before he had advanced more than a hundred yards, the family dogs began to announce his intrusion into their space. As he alighted from his horse and tossed the reins over the hitching post in front of the house, he recognized the glint of a gun barrel extending from under the porch.

A booming voice demanded, "Who are you and what do you want? Whatever you do, don't take another step or I'll fill you with lead."

"Mr. Smith, it's Stephen Pomeroy."

"Stephen Pomeroy, what are you doing sneaking in here at this time of the afternoon?"

"I'm on my way to Perrysville, but I'd like to see your daughter first."

"Come on in, Stephen. I'll get Effie and my wife; we were just finishing eating. Are you hungry?"

"Somewhat, but all I really want to do is see Effie."

Stephen chatted and enjoyed a ham sandwich with Effie's parents while she made herself presentable. When at last she appeared in the parlor, Effie's parents excused themselves, ambled out to the garden, and began to weed the potato patch.

The young lovers embraced enthusiastically. She began to cry and kiss his sweaty face; then his lips found hers again and refused to disengage. The kiss lasted a long time, until both felt as though their lungs would burst, and they had to stop in order to replenish their air supply.

"Stephen, my darling Stephen, when I heard the rumor that you had been killed in action, I didn't want to go on without you. Then a week later when I received your letter, my life had meaning again. I love you so much. I can hardly wait until this horrible war is over and I can become your wife."

"And I love you, Effie, and I want to be your husband as soon as possible, but right now I've got to complete my mission. I'm sorry my visit can only be for a few minutes, but on my return trip I promise to stop here and spend ample time with you. I still have a few more days left on my leave, and I'm going to use a major portion of it with you. I have to get riding again; too many people are counting on me to deliver the message. I'll need some time to recoup at my aunt's; then I'll head back to your waiting arms."

After one last embrace, he remounted and returned to the mountain road. He soon arrived at the next road where William Taylor's blacksmith shop stood to the right of the road. The smithy was abandoned for the moment because its owner was serving in the army as a blacksmith. Stephen turned left on the crossroad that would take him across the valley to the valley road once again.

When he arrived at the valley road, he didn't turn right onto it, but instead crossed over it on the road that would take him up the ridge to Pleasant View and eventually to Academia. Near the zenith of the ridge stood the store of Laird and Barton. At this hour several farmers were still hanging out, probably discussing the war and politics.

As Stephen approached the store, the men ceased talking and called out to him, because several of the men recognized him from his days at the academy and the time he spent at his uncle's establishment in Academia.

"Howdy, Stephen, glad to see you're surviving all those bloody battles we've been hearing about. "

"I'm truly sorry I can't stop and chat awhile, but I've got some urgent business in Perrysville. Maybe I can stop on my way back home in a day or two." With that, he disappeared over the crest of the ridge and descended the other side to the ford on the Tuscarora Creek.

This was the one location of his trip that he had been dreading. About a hundred yards on the other side of the creek was the old Indian burial mound. Ever since he had been a young boy, he had nightmares and horrible visions about this final resting place of the ancient inhabitants of the valley. He believed that the farmers who had destroyed the once huge mound in an attempt to gain more agricultural acreage had vandalized and desecrated the burial ground and that an avenging spirit or spirits would seek revenge.

If he had examined his thoughts on this subject, he would have concluded that he was being superstitious and irrational. But he couldn't help himself; he remembered all too well the fate of some of those early farmers who had apparently destroyed the mound and turned the field into a productive clearing.

Also in this vicinity of the banks of the Tuscarora Creek, in 1847 Drs. J. P. Sterrett and J. L. Kelly had made the amazing discovery of a tusk and a number of teeth of a *mastodon giganteus,* a fossilized member of the elephant family. One of the teeth still had a portion of the jaw remaining. The huge tusk was nine feet long, while about two feet of it must have been in the socket. It had a diameter of eight inches at the socket end, and gradually tapered to a point. The remains of this creature were found buried six feet beneath the surface. It was estimated that the huge beast must have reached a length of twenty-five feet, allowing seven feet for its tusks, and a height of nearly twelve feet.

The knowledge of this ancient creature was of great interest to the young men who attended Tuscarora Academy. Many young men had spent hours scouring the banks of the creek, hoping that they would unearth additional bones belonging either to this particular species or to one similar to it.

He spurred his horse into a gallop and bolted past the eerie mound, and splashed through the low water of Doyles Run until he came to a crossroads. Academia and his uncle's store were located about a mile to the right, and he didn't slow down much as he made the acute right turn. Up on the ridge to his left was the female seminary whose population had greatly diminished since the outbreak of the war. About two hundred yards to the east of the school was the local Presbyterian cemetery and then the Lower Tuscarora Presbyterian Church. Farther still to the east was the boys' academy that he had attended.

Many good memories of the two schools and the church flooded his mind, but he cast them aside in order to concentrate on his mission. He wanted to make this changeover as quickly as possible, because he needed to arrive in Perrysville before the telegraph operator shut down for the night—even though telegraph operators had extended their hours to accommodate the needs of a nation at war.

It was early evening when he arrived at his Uncle Joseph's home in Academia. The few loafers who were still sitting on the porch of the store greeted him cordially, because many of them remembered Stephen when he was a student at the academy. One of the old-timers called out, "How's the war going youngster?"

"Tolerable," he answered. This had become a standard reply among members of the units of the Army of the Potomac who heard the same inquiry over and over again. "The Rebs are on their way to Gettysburg. On the other side of the Blue Mountain, the whole countryside is in a state of utter turmoil, but don't worry, Meade and his boys will stop the Rebs. They'll never get to Harrisburg or Washington."

From out of the dusk, a young voice inquired, "Would you like your horse to be unsaddled, dried off, watered, fed, and put away, Mr. Pomeroy?"

"That would be mighty kind of you. I've ridden him rather hard, and he's earned some oats, water, and a good night's rest. What's your name, young man?"

"I'm David Evans from over on Half Moon. I attend the academy just as you did. We just finished a baseball game over at Spruce Hill. It's hard to find enough players with all the men and boys in the army, but we had just enough tonight. I'd like to be in the army, but my parents want me to finish out my final term this summer. I plan to join the 49th at the end of school in September."

"The 49th is a mighty fine outfit," Stephen declared. "Several of my friends and relatives are serving in it. Fact is, when I came through East Waterford, my thoughts were about many of those men serving in that unit. You'll do well to serve with them. Thanks for taking care of my uncle's horse; I'll be picking him up on my return trip tomorrow. I'm on a mission for Judge Kimmel from Chambersburg to take a message to the telegraph office in Perrysville.

"I'll only be here for a short time. I have just enough time to say hello, grab something to eat, and change horses. David, before you attend my horse, please step inside with me, and we'll find out which horse I can borrow from my Uncle Joe to complete my journey. Then you can switch the saddle to the new mount."

With all the commotion on the porch, the Pomeroys came out to see what all the fuss was about. They were surprised and delighted to see their nephew. Like so many other people who had been incorrectly informed of his demise, they needed a moment to recover from the shock of seeing their nephew alive. And then they greeted him enthusiastically.

Stephen quickly informed his relatives of his mission, and they attended to his needs immediately. His aunt and uncle quizzed him about his exploits in the war and how his family was faring during these stressful times. They fed him an ample meal and supplied him with a new horse saddled by David Evans, all within fifteen minutes.

By the time Stephen was back in the saddle, complete darkness had settled over the Tuscarora Valley due to a heavy cloud cover. Soon he was blessed with a break in the clouds, and then he was enjoying a cloudless night that was barely illuminated by a half-moon. He headed east on the valley road that eventually would become known as the Groninger Valley Road, as more and more of the farms in this section of the valley were purchased by descendants of Leonard Groninger.

While Stephen headed east on the final leg of his journey to Perrysville, David Evans returned home, as did the other men from Pomeroy's Store. By the next morning, most of the residents of the valley, especially the students at the academy, knew about the heroic exploits of the graduate of Tuscarora Academy. It was the talk of the valley for a few days until the purpose of Stephen's mission hit home when the thunder of artillery from Gettysburg could be heard and felt in the Tuscarora Valley.

Finally, he began the slight descent that he realized was the approach to Groninger's Ford on the Tuscarora Creek. As he passed Groninger's barn, he heard the nervous snorting and movement of the barn's residents. There were no visible lights in either of the stone residences that he passed between on his final descent to the ford.

The horse accepted the challenge of wading the creek, and soon was back on solid, dry soil, climbing the slight bank away from the creek. The uneven dirt road continued on an incline for almost a half-mile before the road leveled off for a short distance. Beyond that, the road went down a slight depression and up the other side, and continued to ascend for about a quarter of a mile until it intersected with a wider, more traveled road.

The new road that he intersected wasn't really a new road. It was the same road that he had been traveling upon since Spring Run. He had left it near Fort Bigham when he took the Mountain Road to visit his sweetheart, but now he was back on the same road. To many, this road at this location was known as the Fort Granville Road, but it was still the old Tuscarora Path or the Tuscarora Valley Pike or Road.

Now he turned left or northeast and began to descend a steep hill, known to the locals as Hertzler's Hill. As he descended, he passed Hertzler's Mill and crossed a small stream known as Hunter's Run, which had been dammed to supply water for the millrace that ran the mill. The road made a left turn, and on his left was Hertzler's Store, which had been established in 1838 while the nondescript stone house beside it had been built in 1842. Like Pomeroy's store in Academia, and Laird and Barton's in Pleasant View, the store had a front porch filled with benches that probably had been occupied by loafers earlier in the evening, but now they stood empty.

Across the road from the store was the elegant brick residence of Noah Hertzler. Stephen urged his horse towards the bridge across the Tuscarora Creek that would allow him to approach Perrysville. This covered bridge's floor dated back to 1818, and the sides and roof had been added since then.

In the dim moonlight, he noticed something amiss; the entrance was blocked by a wagon. Suddenly he heard the all-too-familiar metallic clicking of guns being pulled to full cock, and a challenging voice boomed out. "Halt! Stop right where you are mister, or we'll empty your saddle with a double barrel of shot."

Four men armed to the teeth appeared out of the gloom of the bridge and inspected him thoroughly. Stephen instantly pulled back on his reins and brought the now nervous horse to an abrupt standstill. Apprehensively he responded, "Don't pull that trigger. This is no Reb in your sights. I'm Stephen Pomeroy from Roxbury in Franklin County. Judge Kimmel of Chambersburg has me carrying an urgent message to be sent to Governor Curtin in Harrisburg. Look at me closely; this is the nice, blue uniform of the 126th Regiment."

"So it is, Sergeant Pomeroy," as one of the men recognized Stephen. "Thomas Pomeroy's boy is all grown up and in a soldier's uniform. Now slow down and tell your old comrade-in-arms John Phillips what your big rush is about."

"Sergeant John Phillips of Company F of the 126th? What are you doing out here in the dark?

"Company F is back in business, doing Abe Lincoln's dirty work once again. Captain Wharton reassembled the old company to guard against any Reb attacks against the railroad here in Perrysville. He constructed a makeshift fort several hundred yards up from the mouth of the Tuscarora. Some of us are encamped next to the fairgrounds and the rest are on the other side of the creek east of St. Tammany's Town. What's this about an urgent message for the governor?"

"I thought I smelled a lot of smoke as I rode down Hertzler's hill," Stephen said, "but I just never expected to see the whole company turned out again. As to the message to Governor Curtin, I can't go into much detail because I haven't read the message myself. All I know is that Lee's army is on its way to Gettysburg, and the governor needs to inform the president that we desperately need to maneuver our troops in that direction immediately."

"If that's the case, don't dally, boy; get that horse across the bridge and down to the telegraph station. I'll ride with you. We sure don't want those Rebs taking Gettysburg and invading the rest of Pennsylvania."

Stephen spurred his horse across the bridge as soon as the wagon pulled away from the mouth of the bridge. As he galloped up the lane to Perrysville, he could vaguely make out the fence and several exhibition buildings of the Juniata County Fair Ground located to his right towards the creek. He could also make out rows of tents erected below the fairgrounds, and here and there, the embers of dying fires flared up and illuminated men sitting next to the fires.

The horse followed his lead to the left between the dormitory or boardinghouse of Airy View Academy and the three-story academy building. This institution had opened its doors in October

1852 under the direction of Professor David Wilson and David Laughlin. David Wilson had been the first principal of the Tuscarora Academy and now had created one of the best classical schools in the Commonwealth at Airy View.

They traveled one block and turned right onto Market Street. Since it was so late and no one was on the street, Stephen allowed the horse to have its head and go at full gallop. Several startled dogs barked and howled in protest, but none came out to harass them.

Halfway down the street he charged past the Lutheran parsonage and church, and before he knew it, he was bearing down on the tracks of the Pennsylvania Railroad. He guided the horse to the left, and was elated and relieved to see the dim light of an oil lamp flickering through the telegraph office's window.

Stephen quickly dismounted and tied the reins of the horse to the hitching rail and dashed across the tracks to the office. He heaved open the office door and burst into the undersized telegraph office that was part of the Pennsylvania Railroad's station at Perrysville, startling the operator out of a sleep-induced stupor.

When the operator gained his senses, he immediately challenged Stephen. "What is all the ruckus about, son? Did the Rebs chase you down the valley?" At this he chuckled, as if it were impossible that a rebel force could be in the valley.

"Well, I know you're joking about the Rebs, but they're the reason I've been in the saddle since early this morning. I'm Stephen Pomeroy from Roxbury over in Franklin County. Associate Judge Thomas Pomeroy is my father, and we have relatives, including my uncle, Major J. M. Pomeroy, living here in Perrysville and the whole way up the valley. I went to school at the academy in Academia.

"But to get to my mission at hand, Judge Kimmel of Chambersburg sent me with this urgent message for the governor. The Reb cavalry has cut off all communication between Chambersburg and Harrisburg, so the judge gave me the task of riding here to get you to send this message to Governor Curtin. Here, it's hidden in my buckle." Stephen carefully removed the folded message from its hiding place and handed it to the operator. "I'm glad that it's in your hands. I was so afraid that a Reb raiding party would apprehend me in Path Valley and spoil our chances of getting the word through about Lee's movements.

"As soon as we receive word from Harrisburg that the governor has been alerted to Lee's maneuvering, I'll be heading up the street to my aunt's for refreshments and a good night's rest. I'm plum worn out, and so is my horse or, I should say, horses. I've left a string of worn horses from Spring Run to Perrysville."

After the operator's fingers pounded out the message on the single key, they waited anxiously for the Harrisburg operator to acknowledge that the message was received and was on its way to the governor's mansion. Finally, the key came alive, and Operator Olson jotted down the acknowledgment on a pad.

George Olson turned to Stephen and smiled. "You've accomplished an amazing feat in the past eighteen or twenty hours. You'll be one of those unsung heroes we sometimes hear about. I want to shake your hand and say thank you for a job well done. We won't know for several days, but you may have helped to swing the tide of war in the Union's favor.

"You're a very plucky young man. May God bless you and keep you from harm when you return to the battlefield. When this tragedy is over, drop back into my office and we'll discuss this eventful night. Good luck to you, Stephen Pomeroy.

"Now if Governor Curtin and his aides will just act on the information they just received and warn Lincoln and his generals about what's transpiring down in Franklin and Adams County, we could see a huge turnaround in this war; maybe it will help to shorten the war and get our boys back home."

Stephen suddenly realized just how exhausted he was. He shook Mr. Olson's hand, went out the door, crossed the tracks, unhitched his horse, swung up in the saddle, and headed up the street to his aunt and uncle's house.

John Phillips, who had waited patiently while Stephen attended to his business in the telegraph office, shook hands with his former comrade in arms. "I'm right proud to know you, Stephen. Your performance speaks well of our regiment and the entire army. I know you'll be anxious to get back to Franklin County, but if you have a minute, stop by and say hello to the boys. I'll inform Captain Wharton of your exploits, and if I know him, you'll probably be requested to report to him before you return home. Good luck to you, Stephen, and when this mess is finally over, I hope we can spend some time together and reminiscence about this special day."

"Good luck to you too, John. I will make an effort to look you up after this ordeal is over. I know I'll be back in Juniata County from time to time."

At this ungodly hour, his aunt and uncle were sound asleep. It took a monumental effort to finally gain his aunt's attention, and she warily shuffled down the stairs and with a substantial effort, swung the door open. Her eyesight was not very keen in the dim light of the kerosene lamp, and at first, she had no idea who was standing in her doorway. She remained skeptical even when he spoke to her. "Hello, Auntie, it's your favorite nephew, Stephen."

"Stephen, is it? My Stephen would never allow himself to look so untidy. He's a perfect gentleman and is always dressed in perfect attire."

"Look again, Auntie. It *is* Stephen. I've been in the saddle since early this morning, riding all the way from home to Perrysville. I'm sorry I don't measure up to your image of me, but I've been through a great deal today."

With this, she finally recognized her young nephew from Franklin County. "Oh, my God, it *is* you, Stephen. Well, don't just stand there. Get inside and give your old aunt a big hug and a kiss. I'll roust your uncle out of bed; he'll want to know all the details of your activities and adventures."

Stephen sprang through the doorway and embraced his aunt. Then she began to cry with happiness. "I was so distraught when I heard you had been lost in battle down in Virginia. I prayed and prayed that it was a mistake, and now my prayers are answered. However, never in my wildest dreams did I think that you would be awakening me from my sleep, especially looking the way you do. Oh, Stephen, it's so wonderful to see you and to hug you, just as I did when you were a little boy. Now let's get you cleaned up and fed. I bet you're about starved, riding the way you must have done."

When she began to fire the stove, Stephen retired to the back porch and removed his boots, socks, and outer clothing. While food was sizzling on the stove, she began to heat water for his bath and to wash his dirty socks and uniform. By this time, his uncle was waiting for him in the kitchen.

Soon after Stephen was fed and washed, he staggered up the steps and into the front bedroom that he had slept in since he first began to visit his aunt and uncle as a baby. His head barely hit the pillow before he passed out, completely exhausted. It wouldn't be until around noon that he would stir from the bedroom, and then he began to wonder if his message had arrived in time for the Union army to react to Lee's movements towards Gettysburg. By the time Stephen Pomeroy fully roused himself from his sleeping stupor, history was being made at the crossroads of Gettysburg.

When Stephen went downstairs, he found an anxious aunt awaiting him in the foyer.

"I must say you look a little more like my favorite nephew than you did earlier this morning. You gave me quite a start; it's hard to believe that you looked so dog-tired. Now, what can I fix you for breakfast, or I guess I'd better say lunch? You can have just about anything your heart desires—just name it."

"Some coffee and ham and eggs will do just fine. I still haven't eaten my fill of those after being deprived of them during my stint in the army."

"I know you've been asked about your exploits in the army so many times, but I've never been privy to hear about them. So could you pamper your old aunt and uncle and fill us in about life in Abe Lincoln's army? Please don't spare us any details; we want to hear it all."

Just then, there was a knock at the door, and she answered it quickly. There stood three of her neighbor women and two young teenagers. "We heard the rumors about Stephen's heroic ride, and we'd like to listen to his version of the war firsthand, that is, if he doesn't mind doing so."

"Come in and say hello to the hero of the moment. I was just in the middle of attempting to persuade him to tell me about army life. It will be up to him as to how much he wants to tell you."

One of the youngsters chimed in, "We'd love to hear as much as possible. If the war lasts long enough, I'm going to join as soon as I become of age."

"I hope the war doesn't last much longer," Stephen said. "Too many good men have been foolishly sacrificed on both sides. If you will allow me to eat my breakfast, or lunch, I'll fill you in on some of my experiences."

Stephen ate the two slices of ham and three eggs quickly and began to dispose of his second cup of coffee when his uncle came in. And then he began his tale of his nine months in Uncle Sam's army.

"My unit assembled at Chambersburg on August 7 of last summer amid great celebration and anticipation. Friends, families, and well-wishers showered us with gifts, such as New Testaments, booklets containing scriptures, prayers, hymns, and moral and physical advice, sewing kits, and box lunches to be consumed during the train ride to Harrisburg and Camp Curtin.

"I was officially mustered into Company H of the 126th Regiment on August 9 at Camp Curtin. Company H was mainly composed of men from Path Valley and St. Thomas. We were supplied with uniforms and other military clothing, shoes, weapons, and camp equipment upon our arrival in camp.

"In the afternoon of August 15, we received orders to march to the railroad yards, and we boarded coal cars for the overnight trip to Washington, D. C. The regiment arrived in the capital at 4:00 a.m., and we joined the forces defending the city. Intelligence affirmed that Lee's army was marching northward in the direction of the federal capital. To counter this move, the regiment moved across the river that afternoon to reinforce a brigade commanded by General Erastus B. Tyler. Tyler's Brigade was part of the Third Division of the Fifth Corps of the Army of the Potomac.

"The rebel army continued to thrust forward, and by August 29 the fighting began that became known as the Second Battle of Bull Run, or Second Manassas. The battle raged fiercely for two days, but we never became involved. All we observed was a defeated army retreating to the outskirts of Washington, with many walking wounded and bewildered stragglers intermixed with hospital wagons filled to capacity with wounded and dying soldiers.

"After the debacle at Bull Run, President Lincoln relieved General Pope of his command on September 2, and replaced him with General George McClellan. McClellan's army was renamed the Army of the Potomac.

"Second Bull Run was a crushing blow to our army. Lee was encouraged by his success, and on September 5 he moved his army across the Potomac River for his first invasion of a Union state. The men of the 126th were greatly concerned for the safety of our friends and loved ones back in Franklin County because we were not at home to defend them if Lee continued northward."

When Stephen paused to allow his coffee cup to be refilled, his uncle John said, "Why don't we go out on the front porch? Even though it's a hot and humid day, there's a decent breeze out there."

"That sounds like a good idea to me; I'd always rather be out-doors."

When the little group had settled on the porch, Stephen continued, "Now where was I? Oh yes, we heard all kinds of rumors about farmers fleeing in front of Lee's troops, taking their livestock and belongings with them. We were constantly asking ourselves, 'What if the rebels aren't stopped in Maryland? What will happen in Waynesboro, Chambersburg, Greencastle, Mercersburg, and elsewhere in Franklin County if the Rebels keep moving north-ward?'

"A bizarre event occurred that should have given McClellan the upper hand in outmaneuvering Lee, but McClellan botched it. McClellan obtained written instructions issued by Lee to divide his small army into four sections, but he did not take advantage of his knowledge and failed to attack. Lee became aware of the situation and was pulling his troops back together when the two armies collided at Antietam Creek on September 17.

"The 126th was ordered to proceed towards Sharpsburg, Mary-land. As the brigade marched through Rockville and reached the Monocracy River, we learned that a major battle was underway on the banks of Antietam Creek.

"We marched through the night and arrived at Antietam at 6:00 a.m. the morning of September 18. Once again, we arrived too late to see any action, and we were held in reserve. Lee's bat-tered army withdrew back into Virginia, while we encamped near the scene of the war's bloodiest day.

"McClellan once again took his good time in pursuing Lee into Virginia and it cost him his job. An angry President Lincoln relieved McClellan as commander of the Army of the Potomac on November 5 because it had taken the general six weeks after Antietam to move his army over the Potomac into Virginia to face Lee. General Ambrose Burnside took command of the Army of the Potomac and moved his army of 120,000 on November 15 to the banks of the Rappahannock River across from Fredericksburg, Virginia. The river was too high to attempt a crossing at Falmouth, so we waited for six days for pontoons to arrive, and then another three weeks for the high brass to decide on a plan of attack. In the meantime, Lee positioned his 75,000 troops on Marye's Heights, which overlooked Fredericksburg from the south."

Just then several more people appeared at the steps of the porch, and John Pomeroy greeted them cordially, "Come in out of the sun, Mrs. Dunn, Mrs. McCahan, and Mr. Stoner. The young man who is the center of our attention is my nephew Stephen from Roxbury in Franklin County. He is describing his adventures in the army."

"Thank you, Major Pomeroy," said Mr. Stoner. "Your nephew is the reason we are here. The word spread rapidly about his late-night appearance, and we hoped we would not be taking advantage of his time by asking him to tell us about life in the army. The three of us have or have had relatives serving in the army, and we are always anxious to learn about the hardships, sacrifices, and exploits of our young men."

"It is nice to make your acquaintances," Stephen said. "Don't feel as though you are taking advantage of my time, but I will have to curtail my story somewhat; I need to head back up the Tuscarora Valley soon.

"I was just beginning to describe our movements against Fredericksburg in December of last year. We bombarded the town of Fredericksburg on December 11, then crossed the Rappahannock River and captured the deserted town. Two days later Burnside attempted to surprise Lee by rushing us up the sloping open field towards the Rebs' formidable position.

"I'm not going to divulge all the details, but we were untested, green troops, under fire for the first time. Three futile attacks had been attempted before we were finally ordered into action. An artillery duel provided a prelude to our attack. With daylight fading rapidly, we were ordered to fix bayonets, and not to fire and reload. It was simply a matter of employing cold steel against the enemy's musket fire.

"Men from previous attacks were lying on the ground, either too frightened to move, or waiting for nightfall to retreat back to our lines. We moved through these men, as they called for us not to attack but rather to return to the rear. This helped to break our momentum and disarranged our lines.

"Then the real nightmare began. The men lying to the rear began firing at the enemy, and we suddenly found ourselves taking bullets from both the front and the rear. The bayonet charge broke down, and the men began to fire and reload, which meant increased casualties. More and more of our officers and men fell, including General Tyler and Perrysville's own Captain Wharton.

"Darkness covered the field, and retreat was sounded, and the survivors straggled down the hill. We spent the long, cold night in the streets of the town. The next day was Sunday, and the 126th was sent out on the advanced picket line. On Monday, the Army of the Potomac began its retreat back over the Rappahannock. Our regiment was assigned to cover the humiliating retreat, and we were the last to leave Fredericksburg and return to Falmouth on the other side of the river."

Stephen paused as he noticed the tear-filled eyes of his audience. "Are you sure you want me to continue? I know that some of you are relatives or friends of the twenty-seven killed and fifty wounded in this action."

He looked around for some indication that he should continue. Finally, Mr. Stoner spoke up. "I'm here to learn what really happened. I lost my son George in this debacle. He died at Stoneman's Switch, Virginia, on January 24 of this year. We miss him terribly, but I want to be assured that his loss was not in vain, and that this horrible war will soon come to an end."

"I am sorry about your loss, Mr. Stoner. I didn't know your son, but I can tell you that the men of Company F always exhibited the brave characteristics of a true soldier, and I feel sure that your son performed his duties to the utmost."

Everyone took time to express their condolences to Mr. Stoner, then the grieving father said quietly, "Please continue, Stephen; I know your time to leave is growing near."

Stephen nodded and continued, "I don't like to speak in a derogatory manner about our army's commanding generals, but General Burnside's leadership was completely suspect. I don't think he should have been elevated to such an important position.

"Christmas was not very special to most of us who suffered through the early winter of 1862-1863 in Northern Virginia. It was the first time that most of us were away from home at Christmas, so that in itself was traumatic. Food, warm clothes, footwear, bedding, and shelter were also cause for concern. One important event that occurred while we wintered on the banks of the Rappahannock was that the Emancipation Proclamation took effect on January 1, 1863. Although I do not believe that the proclamation will bring the war to a speedier end, it should allow a more permanent peace in the years to come.

"It appears that General Burnside wanted to make amends for his blunder at Fredericksburg by planning a circular march, which entailed crossing the Rappahannock farther upriver to move our army behind Lee at Fredericksburg and attack Lee's left flank.

"We moved out on January 20, but we soon were besieged by bad luck. Sleet, snow, torrential freezing rains, and howling winds bombarded the troops, and the troops, horses, mules, wagons, and artillery became bogged down in a sea of mud. The waterlogged and mud-covered soldiers referred to this debacle as the 'Mud March.'

"President Lincoln was outraged at Burnside's ineptness, and on January 26 replaced him with General Joseph 'Fighting Joe' Hooker. Hooker spent the rest of the winter preparing his army of 115,000 men to move against Lee in the spring when the weather would allow such an undertaking.

"New recruits refilled our shattered ranks, and Fighting Joe Hooker instilled in us a new fighting spirit; this time we were sure we would whip the Rebs. General George Stoneman was given a separate command of cavalry, and a number of horsemen from our area rode with him. President Lincoln inspired us when he and his family visited our camps.

"Hooker planned for us to be on the move by April 12, but the rising rivers blocked his movements at first. Finally, at mid-day on April 27, we moved upriver, crossed the Rappahannock and Rapidan Rivers, and began marching through the tangled woods known as the Wilderness of Northern Virginia. We were to hit Lee from the rear, while Stoneman was to disrupt Lee's communications network, blocking roads and destroying railroads and canals.

"By May 1 we were ten miles west of Fredericks at Chancellorsville when Lee left a force of nearly 10,000 at Fredericksburg. Then Stonewall Jackson feinted a retreat towards Richmond but instead turned on us, and we were caught in an attack from the rear and both flanks.

"Our forces panicked and became totally confused. The 126th was caught in an exposed position, and we received the main thrust of the enemy's attack. We fought valiantly for over two hours until our ammunition was exhausted, but our gallant brigade held its position against overwhelming odds. Unfortunately, our losses were nine killed, forty-nine wounded, and eleven taken prisoners.

"Finally, all we had left were our bayonets, and we were forced to fall back. We emerged from the thick woods and re-formed in an open field in support of batteries of artillery. The guns checked the enemy's advance, allowing us to retire a short distance where we remained until we were ordered to re-cross the river and return to camp at Falmouth.

"Our term of service expired a week after this disaster at Chancellorsville, and we made final preparations to depart for home on May 12. We left camp at 6:00 a.m. by rail to Aquia's Landing, where we boarded the *Warner* which transported us up the Potomac to Washington. On May 14, we boarded a train that took us to Baltimore and then another train to Harrisburg.

"The 126ᵗʰ pulled into Harrisburg at seven o'clock, and we marched across to Camp Curtin. It took four long days to process our papers, and we were mustered out and dismissed from the service on May 20. We headed home with our discharge papers and full pay. Every hometown held a special celebration that meant so much to each of us.

"I could tell you more, but the sun is moving across the sky, and I have to head back to Franklin County. I'm terribly concerned about what's taking place in the vicinity of Gettysburg."

Mr. Stoner stood up and in a shaking voice, conveyed his appreciation to Stephen. "Words can never express what you and our boys have experienced and what we have undergone here at home. I want to thank you for your time and kind words, and may God bless you and keep you safe on your return trip."

At that moment, Sergeant John Phillips appeared at the front steps astride his horse. "Good afternoon everyone. Sergeant Pomeroy, Captain Wharton sends his compliments. If it wouldn't inconvenience you, Captain Wharton would like a word with you before you return to Franklin County."

"Thank you, Sergeant Phillips. I will be ready to travel within ten minutes, and I will call at the captain's headquarters on my way out of town."

The guests departed from the Pomeroys' front porch rather reluctantly, but they knew Stephen needed to be on his way. Stephen went to the small barn at the back of the house to saddle his Uncle Joseph's horse; when he returned, his aunt had packed him a small lunch and a container of lemonade.

"I certainly am within your debt for taking me in unannounced and feeding me," Stephen told her. "I only hope the next time I'm within your company, this dreadful war is a just a vague memory. Thank you so much for your hospitality, and I'll give your regards to the other members of the family as I make my return trip up the valley."

The next line of business was to report to Captain Wharton down near the Tuscarora Creek and the fairgrounds. He found the captain sitting under a large maple tree reading a report.

"Former Sergeant Pomeroy at your service, sir."

"Good to see you again, Stephen. We certainly do live in extraordinary times, don't we? I want to congratulate you on the tremendous feat that you performed for your state and nation. Your efforts might well have saved the Union.

"It appears that Harry Heth's boys went shopping for shoes in Gettysburg and were spotted by John Burford, and then all hell broke loose. Oops, sorry about the use of that word; I know how you feel about that kind of language. At any rate, reinforcements are pouring in from both sides and all of a sudden, it looks like we have a major battle developing.

"Thanks to your message, General Meade was able to divert our main force in the direction of Gettysburg and meet Lee head on. It will be the devil to pay if the Rebs whip us. The road to Washington from the north and northwest will be wide open. Also

Harrisburg, Lancaster, and Philadelphia will be almost defenseless as well."

"Here I am, with perhaps the most colossal battle to ever be fought in North America taking place almost in my own backyard, and I'm seventy miles away. I'm going to miss it all," Stephen said sadly.

"Relax, sergeant, what you have accomplished has given us a fighting chance. Lee could have slipped right by and moved on Washington from the north." The captain smiled. "God must be on our side."

"Sometimes I wonder whose side He really is on, or if He really favors either side," Stephen commented.

"You of all people question that concept? Aren't you the one who was schooled by the Presbyterians at Academia and at Lafayette College and headed to divinity school at Princeton?"

Stephen paused, then replied, "Yes, when this war is over, I'll return to my studies. The war has changed me drastically, but I still see the need for me to do God's work. I've seen so much needless bloodshed on both sides in such a short period. For instance, I'll never understand Stonewall Jackson's untimely death. We Yanks couldn't kill him; it took his own troops to do him in."

"I understand Stonewall was a tremendously religious person, a staunch Presbyterian just like you," said Captain Wharton.

"It would have been an honor to sit down with him and discuss the major religious issues of our time," Stephen declared. "On the other hand, he must have been a military genius the way he outmaneuvered us, time and time again, with such a small force of men.

"By the way, before I arrived here, I had a very moving experience. My aunt and uncle and several of their friends asked me to talk about some of my exploits; among the small group was a Mr. Stoner. George Stoner was his son. What can you tell me about George?"

"George's loss was a real shame. He was an outstanding young soldier, never complained, always anxious to perform his duty—he made you wish you had a whole company just like him. I wrote his father and told him that George was a son he could be very proud of. As soon as we mustered out, I went to visit the Stoners, and they seemed pleased that I made the effort to console them but more pleased about what I told them of their son's performance.

"Well, I don't want to delay you any longer; you have a long trip ahead of you and quite a few stops along the way. I would imagine one of those stops would be out along the Tuscarora Mountain at Silas and Elizabeth Smith's farm. How is Euphemia or Effie? How much longer are you going to allow her to remain single?"

Stephen grinned. "Yes, I plan on stopping at the Smiths' farm, and as far as I know, Effie is fine. We plan on getting married after I finish seminary. So I guess the date for that event will be determined somewhat by Robert E. Lee and Jefferson Davis."

"I guess you're right if you plan on waiting until this mess is over. Best you get going. Also, I want to go home to see the missus. I only have a few blocks to travel to Middle and Third Streets, but you, my friend, have about seventy miles. Godspeed on your return trip."

With that, Stephen was on his way, back over the creek, through St. Tammany's Town, up the hill to the road that took him to his first layover at Academia at his Uncle Joseph's. To his dismay, the porch of the store was filled with local people as well as several students from the academy. David Evans, the boy who had helped with his horse earlier, was one of the anxious onlookers.

David spoke excitedly, "We had lookouts watching the road all day during school, and after school we decided to wait here until you returned."

"I'm sorry I won't be here long. I just need to exchange horses, grab a drink, and move on again. All I can tell you is that the two armies have slammed into each other at the town of Gettysburg down in Adams County. If all that artillery gets into a shooting match, you should be able to hear it here if the weather is right. It could turn out to be the biggest battle of the war. You just better hope that we win; if not, you could be seeing some gray visitors in your valley."

Stephen disappeared into the store to thank his uncle for the use of his horse and then ran across the road to the big brick house to extend his regards to his aunt. By that time, David Beale's horse had been saddled, and Stephen was ready to gallop off. This time he went down the hill to the ford below Pomeroy's Dam and skirted along the creek as it formed what is known as Half Moon.

He turned onto the valley pike, the old Tuscarora Path, and headed southwest. After about three miles he turned south on a crossroad that took him towards the Tuscarora Mountain, and most important, the farmhouse of his beloved Effie.

As he reached the zenith of the slight rise above the Smith farm, he could see Effie sitting on the front porch. She must have seen him about the same time, because she threw down her book and bolted for the gate and the road. Effie had covered about twenty yards up the road when he reached her and leaped from the saddle, hitting the ground and embracing her feverishly.

"Oh, Stephen, you took so long in returning," Effie said, trying to catch her breath. "I was beginning to think they sent you to Harrisburg. You still look awfully tired; did you get any rest last night?"

"Yes, I was so exhausted that I slept until almost noon. Then I had to answer questions for some of the neighbors there for about an hour. I felt sorry for those people; some of them have suffered immensely during this terrible war. Captain Wharton requested that I join him for a few minutes as well; he has reactivated his old company, and they're defending the railroad at Perrysville."

She smiled at him understandingly. "Mother has roasted a nice big fat hen for us, and she said she had no qualms about you spending the night under our roof. In times like these no one is going to think that I've compromised my reputation."

He nodded. "That sounds like a good idea. I have a number of things to discuss with you, and it's going to take some time. So, after dinner maybe we can have some privacy on the porch."

After dinner, Mr. and Mrs. Smith excused themselves, while the young couple retired to the soft summer breezes of the porch. The first item of business was one that had been on his mind for over a year. "I'm sorry I have no token to give you because I wasn't in any way prepared for my visit to you. Nevertheless, I need to ask you the most important question of my life: Will you please do me the pleasure of spending the rest of our lives as my wife?"

"I've been hoping and waiting several years to hear you ask this question. Of course, I'll marry you. When do you think we should have the ceremony performed?"

"I know you would probably want it to occur sooner, but I want to wait until I have received my divinity degree from the seminary so that I can support you on my own. Not that we will ever be wealthy: preachers just aren't paid very much. It could be worse, I could be a teacher."

(AUTHOR'S NOTE: Reverend Stephen Wilson Pomeroy and Euphemia Knox Smith were united in holy matrimony on December 11, 1867.)

As Effie snuggled against Stephen in the moonlight, she looked into his eyes. "Is there anything you want to tell me about the war? If there's anything bothering you that you want to discuss, don't ever be afraid to approach me about it."

"The only thing that I want to tell you about is the celebration we received on our return. It was so heartwarming to have all those people turn out to welcome us back. It's something none of us will ever forget.

"Our tenure ended right after the disaster at Chancellorsville and on May 13 we left Falmouth by rail to Aquia's Landing and arrived in Washington by ship. From there we went to Baltimore by rail and then on to Harrisburg and Camp Curtin. Finally, on Wednesday, May 20 we were dismissed from active duty and freed to start homeward.

"We thought we would arrive in Chambersburg the next day, but that was not to be; we didn't see the old hometown until Saturday. Many people had arrived in town expecting the celebration on Thursday, but they stuck around until Saturday. The hotels were filled to overflowing, as the good people of Franklin County were poised for a day of rejoicing and happiness.

"Later we were told that the Court House bell announced that our train had left Harrisburg, and it was rung a third time when the train reached Shippensburg to signal for the crowd to proceed to the depot. The Catholic Church bell tolled at about 10:30 a.m. to announce that the train had attained the curve three miles outside of town.

"The train halted at the intersection east of town to allow the regiment to disembark and be joined by the official delegation and procession. The procession consisted of Mr. Kinney and his cadets from Chambersburg Academy; thirty-four young girls decked out in red, white, and blue, each representing one of the states of the Union; and carriages containing Colonel Elder, Judge Chambers, and Judge Nill.

"The 126th was under the command of Lieutenant Colonel David Watson Rowe, and we marched smartly in our best military bearing up Second Street to Market Street. From there we headed out East Market Street to the point on East Queen Street to Second Street, up Second Street to Catherine Street, down Catherine to the Diamond, out West Market to New England Hill, and then we sharply countermarched back to the Diamond.

"We all came to stiff attention when a wagon containing a number of wounded comrades from the recent battles pulled into the Diamond. Just about every man around me had tears in his eyes, for we not only felt the pain and suffering of these good men, but we were also reminded of those who were no longer within our ranks, but instead resting on the battlefields of Northern Virginia.

"On the Diamond we were addressed by the Reverend S. J. Niccolls. The good reverend referred to us as brave comrades and battle-scarred sons of whom he was very proud, and he saluted our brave deeds. He stated that the loyal citizens owed us a huge debt for being the heroic defenders of our nation and laws. It was a moving speech. I think it made us all feel better about our endeavors at Fredericksburg and Chancellorsville.

"The parade route was crowded with spectators waving flags and banners; it was very touching. The town band played some stirring martial music, and then Miss Virginia Reilly's music class from the Chambersburg Academy entertained us with some vocal and instrumental music.

"After the music presentation we were invited to the Town Hall for a buffet prepared by the patriotic ladies of the town. The walls of the Hall were adorned with flowers, evergreens, and inscriptions such as "Tyler's Brave Boys," "Welcome 126th," "Welcome to Our Brave Defenders," and "Honor to the Brave 126th."

"Seven long tables ran the length of the hall, loaded with an overabundance of local victuals, sustenance, and refreshments. The reception lasted into the late afternoon; then the men from Companies B, C, E, and K boarded railroad cars to take them to their hometowns of Mercersburg, Waynesboro, and Greencastle. In those towns, the men were treated to additional celebrations. In Perrysville and Mifflintown, and many other towns throughout South-central Pennsylvania, similar receptions were held for the other companies of the 126th Regiment."

The young lovers sat in silence and listened to the night birds and the soft breeze off the Tuscarora Mountain for a time, allowing the impact of Stephen's recounting of the celebration to sink in. Effie thought how different her life would be if the news of Stephen's death had been a reality; then she decided that she would never allow those thoughts to enter her mind again.

They sat on the porch until almost midnight discussing their plans for the future. Finally, they both realized that Stephen needed rest to be able to make his return journey tomorrow. They were apprehensive as to what conditions he would find on the other side of the mountain, but he had to go; his home and family could be in the path of destruction.

Everyone awoke at daybreak, and within an hour Stephen was in the saddle. He stopped at Bealetown and exchanged horses, briefly describing the turn of events to David Beale. He pushed his horse to East Waterford, called out to the men at the store and the American House, and then continued on to the gap in the Tuscarora Mountain.

The barricade was manned with nearly twice as many men as before, and they were all on edge. The noises of the second day of battle were accessible to their ears; even untrained ears knew that the thunder of those guns meant a terrible toll of men's lives and the destruction of vast amounts of property. They had been informed by scouts that the Union and Confederate forces were engaged in a paramount struggle the likes of which had never been observed before. If the outcome went the wrong way, they knew that they probably would be tested within the week.

Stephen didn't spend much time with the men defending the Tuscarora Gap. His horse cantered through the gap and past the entrance to Horse Valley and soon arrived at his Uncle William's in Concord. The Pomeroys and most of the citizens of Path Valley were involved in deciding what valuables should be removed to the safety of the mountains, in case Meade and his army weren't successful in halting Lee.

As at his other horse exchange points, Stephen didn't waste much time, he wanted to arrive at Roxbury well before sundown. Stephen was cautious in crossing the Kittatinny Mountain, fearing that some of Jenkins's men might have been left behind to gather any horses that had not been hidden very well.

CHAPTER 58
DECISION AT THE CAPITAL IN HARRISBURG
JULY 1, 1863

Meanwhile in Harrisburg, on Tuesday, June 30, while Stephen Pomeroy was engaged in his dangerous mission, an anxious party of Governor Curtin's advisors continued to await information, any information, as to the next movement of Lee's army. For three long days, these men had not received any concrete information on the Confederate army's maneuverings. Scouts had been sent out, but the intelligence that they gleaned was not conclusive.

Sleep was a luxury for the embattled advisors. From time to time, various members of the governor's inner circle would doze off in broken naps forced by sheer exhaustion, but no one had been in bed for three nights. The men had almost worn a path in the carpet in the executive office as they paced back and forth.

Not only Harrisburg, but the whole state also appeared to be paralyzed by the appalling lack of adequate intelligence.

Contact with rebel cavalry forces with a section of artillery was made on Sunday, and a cavalry skirmish occurred on the Carlisle pike on Monday. Thus, the threat to the capital was a major concern and needed to be addressed immediately.

Colonel Scott rarely left the room which housed the telegraph battery except when a message of utmost importance arrived. About three o'clock in the morning of July 1, Scott burst into the executive office, shouting at the top of his lungs and frantically waving a dispatch in the air. Most of the advisors were startled out of their naps by the colonel's antics.

"This is it!" he yelled. "This is the message we've been waiting for! We've got that white-bearded bastard now! He outfoxed himself this time!"

"Whoa! Whoa, slow down! Let us in on the good news also," exclaimed Alexander McClure.

Governor Curtin heard the commotion and quickly entered the room. "What's all the fuss about? Did we finally get some news about Lee's intentions?"

"We just received a telegraph message from the little village of Perrysville. It doesn't tell us much, but enough to get Meade on the move."

"Let me see that message, "McClure shouted as he snatched the message from Scott's hand. Then he read the terse and curt telegraph aloud:

MESSAGE FROM KIMMEL, VIA ROXBURY, SPRING RUN, CONCORD, AND PERRYSVILLE— LEE HAS TURNED EAST FROM CHAMBERS-BURG APPARENTLY CONCENTRATING AT GETTYSBURG

"Gettysburg!" General Darius Couch exclaimed. "That doesn't seem feasible. This could be a complete hoax."

Alexander Kelly McClure looked General Couch straight in the eyes, "No, I don't believe this is a hoax, General, but let's not jump to conclusions. If we make the wrong decision, we could invite total disaster. We could open an easy path to Harrisburg, York, Lancaster, and even Philadelphia. Then Lee could hit Washington from the north while he gained control of the railroads. We need to make sure that this is not a feint to get us to commit farther south."

"But how do we know that this message is even legitimate? There is no signature, no identity of the messenger. How do we know that some enterprising Rebel didn't concoct this whole scheme to get us to commit to the South, while Lee's army moves straight down the Cumberland Valley to the Susquehanna?"

Alexander McClure took the forefront and challenged the governor's advisors. "Gentlemen, I know that my expertise does not lie in the field of military affairs. I have spent much of my life in journalistic affairs, and in so doing I have learned to analyze and read men, as well as use hunches to my advantage. My hunch on this telegraph dispatch is that it is authentic.

"I've known Judge Kimmel for many years, and I also know the geography of the Path, Tuscarora, and Sherman's Valleys like the back of my hand. I was born in Sherman's Valley in what is now Perry County. I helped to run a newspaper in Newport, Perry County, the *Perry County Freeman*, and later I owned and operated the *Juniata Sentinel* in Mifflintown of Juniata County. Mifflintown is just four miles up the Juniata River from Perrysville.

"During those days that I lived in Perry and Juniata Counties, I traveled through the Tuscarora and Path Valleys on my way across the Kitttatinny Mountain to Chambersburg numerous times. This would have been the same route taken by the unknown messenger sent from Kimmel.

"I can assure you that no Rebel would know the geography described in this dispatch. I would not hesitate to take action on this immediately and warn President Lincoln, Secretary Stanton, and General Meade of Lee's movement towards Gettysburg.

"General Couch, as commander of the Susquehanna Division, should be sent across the Susquehanna via Bridgeport immediately to bolster the defenses there, and he and General Smith should begin to move towards Carlisle and drive the enemy's cavalry from that area."

Governor Curtin nodded. "Send telegrams immediately to Meade, Stanton, and the president regarding Lee's movement towards Gettysburg. General Couch and General Smith, I want a strong picket force to cross the river and be deployed towards Carlisle. We must know if the enemy still controls the upper Cumberland Valley and Carlisle.

"The next few hours are of utmost importance to the defense of this state and the nation. Let us hope and pray that the message from Perrysville contained the correct information concerning Lee's departure from Chambersburg. The fate of our nation rests on the contents of that message. If the information is incorrect, then Harrisburg and Philadelphia are threatened.

"On the other hand, if the information is valid, and Lee is not contained and halted, Baltimore and Washington are at risk. Hopefully, Meade, Stanton, and Lincoln recognize the merit in the message and will react accordingly.

"Now, gentlemen, I suggest we all attempt to garner a few hours of rest. When the sun comes up tomorrow, we are going to need all the strength we can muster to address the challenges of the Confederate invasion. Hopefully, we will be informed that our army has contacted the enemy and has halted their advance. Gentlemen, I thank you for your endeavors during this long and eventful night and, I guess I should add, this early morning. Now, let's get some rest."

CHAPTER 59
SOUNDS OF THE BATTLE

As Stephen Pomeroy continued his journey home, he would encounter the sounds of cannonading, whether he was on a high rise, such as the top of a ridge or the Kittatinny Mountain, or deep within a defile, escarpment, or hollow. At times, the sounds of battle would be quite distinct, with heavy and continuous discharges reminiscent of Fredericksburg. Other times the sounds were barely audible, which he attributed to the ebb and flow of battle.

He especially heard the thud of artillery as he began to ascend the Kittatinny or Blue Mountain on his way out of Amberson Valley. Once he reached the zenith of the mountain the audibility of the weaponry vastly increased. Stephen remembered all too well the destructiveness of the cannons at Fredericksburg and Chancellorsville.

Stephen knew that thousands of good men were being killed and maimed, while he rode safely about thirty-five miles as the crow flies from the scene of the battle. As he descended the mountain, the reverberation of the artillery diminished slightly.

At last he arrived home, much to the relief of his mother. His father informed him that no Rebel cavalry had been seen since yesterday morning. Stephen decided to ride into Chambersburg to deliver this information to Judge Kimmel.

Oddly, as Stephen rode across the valley from the mountain towards Chambersburg, the thundering cannonading diminished until it was barely audible by the time he entered the town. Here he was, only twenty-five miles from the scene of the largest battle ever pitched in North America, and if he didn't have foreknowledge that a battle was ensuing, he would never have been able to ascertain that indeed it was in progress.

It took Stephen nearly fifteen minutes to locate Judge Kimmel, but the moment the judge spied his young hero, he applauded his efforts to the utmost.

"There you are, Sergeant Pomeroy. I am so proud of your exploits. You, my young friend, are a national hero. I wish I had the authority to award you a medal. Alas, I am only a former judge, with little influence on military affairs, but I assure you that your name will appear in the government archives as a man who rendered a service so magnanimous that your contribution to the war effort will gain the attention of a grateful nation."

"I thank you for your compliments, but you have to remember that I was only performing my duties as a soldier, even though I wasn't officially a soldier. I love my country, and I want to see her win this tragic conflict and have our nation reunited."

"Nevertheless, you have performed a momentous task and have helped in limiting the enemy's maneuverings," the judge said.

"Sir, do you think it is strange that we here in Chambersburg can barely hear the sounds of battle? When I was descending the mountain, it sounded if the battle was in the valley below me, but now that I am much closer, it's hard to determine that a battle is even being fought only twenty-five miles away."

"It is indeed strange and unusual. Perhaps it is the location of the clouds. Someday we will have to seek the opinions of eminent scientists to see if they can explain this unusual phenomenon. I'm sorry, Stephen, but I was on my way to a very important meeting when you arrived. Could you please excuse me for now? I will need to spend several hours debriefing you on your journey. Could you please visit my office tomorrow at ten o'clock so that we may continue our discussion?"

"That will be fine with me, sir."

Throughout the entire region, people were aware of the distant sounds of battle discharging from the outskirts of Gettysburg. In Western Pennsylvania, near Mount Pleasant in Westmoreland County, Reverend George H. Johnston of Somerset and Reverend C. Cort were traveling through Ligonier Valley and stopped for a late dinner at a Mr. Hay's about two o'clock on July 3.

During the course of the meal, Mr. Hay remarked, "There must be a terrible battle taking place somewhere."

Reverend Cort responded, "When we were in Mount Pleasant, we were informed that Lee's invading forces had been met by federal forces at Gettysburg, and undoubtedly a large battle would be fought there."

"It must be going on now," replied Mr. Hay. "Come out on the porch, and you will be able to hear the cannonading. We've been able to hear the sounds of artillery for several days."

Reverend Cort shook his head in amazement. "It's hard to believe that we can hear continuous discharges at a straight-line distance of nearly one hundred and forty miles."

L.W. Stahl resided in Madison, Westmoreland County, about twenty-eight miles from Pittsburgh. He related that he was in a field harvesting wheat on July 2, and could distinctly hear the roar of cannon, at a distance of nearly one hundred and fifty air miles.

Presbyterian minister Reverend C. R. Lane, who resided in Wyoming County, Pennsylvania, stated that "the sound of artillery was heard on a mountain in the southwestern part of Wyoming County," a straight line distance of one hundred twenty miles.

If people were hearing the sounds of battle in Westmoreland and Wyoming Counties, it is little wonder that the residents of the Tuscarora Valley were also hearing the distinct thuds of artillery for three days, especially the afternoon of July 3. Because of the extraordinary exploits of Stephen Pomeroy, the people residing in Path Valley and Tuscarora Valley had been alerted that a battle was about to take place somewhere southeast of Chambersburg, probably Gettysburg.

David Evans had returned home the night of June 30, after saddling Joseph Pomeroy's horse for Stephen, as the youthful Pomeroy delivered his vital dispatch to the telegraph office in Perrysville. David was bursting with excitement over the news of Lee's invasion of Pennsylvania. Once again, he was full of envy for his friends and neighbors who would be called upon to stem the horde of gray-clad invaders. He was missing one of the greatest battles of American history.

Late in the afternoon of July 1, the first sounds of battle were heard in the Tuscarora Valley, but they dwindled by nightfall. That night on the porches of most homes and the local country stores, the subject was whether Meade's army would be successful in stemming the advance of Lee's Confederate invaders.

A special church service was held at the beginning of school on July 2 to bless the soldiers and urge them on to victory. By midmorning, the thud of artillery was felt across the Tuscarora Mountain, and uppermost in everyone's minds was that the Union forces had to drive the Rebels back over the Potomac. David Evans and his classmates found it impossible to concentrate on their studies. What was transpiring in Adams County was much more important than literature, mathematics, or ancient history; they were concerned with current history.

The professors finally relented and allowed their classes to speculate about the outcome of the battle and the consequences of one side winning versus the other. At noon on the third, a recess of school was announced, and the local boys returned to their homes.

David's father met him on the porch. "David, I know you've been itching to get into the army and fight. I hope you realize what is taking place at the origins of all that cannonading. Men are dying by the thousands. I witnessed it in Mexico, but I am quite sure that the magnitude is so much greater today.

"In the last half hour or so, the intensity of the cannonading has increased dramatically. One side or the other probably is making one last major effort to place victory within its grasp. That means that the killing is increasing at an alarming rate. Somehow, I believe that come tomorrow, we will not hear any more artillery. I know from my limited military experience, one army, or perhaps both, will be so badly spent that the battle will not continue into another day."

Just like the other two days, once the sun finished its journey across the sky, the sounds of battle diminished and the valley became tranquil once again. When a new day dawned, July 4, the natal day of our great nation, no cannonading was heard. Instead, all was quiet, and the clouds replaced the sun in the sky. Rain was imminent; maybe it was being sent to cleanse the blood-soaked battlefield.

CHAPTER 60
THE AFTERMATH OF GETTYSBURG

Lee's army was spent and incapable of any additional operations after the bloody repulse of Pickett's division made up of the three brigades of Garnett, Kemper, and Armistead. The Confederate army had approximately fifty thousand men remaining fit for duty, while the federal army numbered about seventy-two thousand available men.

Lee decided that his crippled Army of Northern Virginia must retreat because the army was far from its base of supplies in the lower Shenandoah Valley, and now low in food and ammunition. Lee's army had two major thoroughfares through the South Mountain to safety across the Potomac River: the Chambersburg Pike by way of the Cashtown Pass, and the Monterey Gap on the Hagerstown road.

At five o'clock on July 3, Lee recalled the divisions of Major General Lafayette McLaws and Brigadier General Evander Law from their positions near the Little and Big Round Tops. Lee appealed to the remnants of Pickett's and Pettigrew's division. "It was all my fault this time. Form your ranks again when you get back to cover. We want all good men to hold together now."

During the night of July 3-4, Lee continued his rearrangement of the Confederate lines by joining General A. P. Hill's and James Longstreet's corps in a defensive line on Seminary Ridge, and withdrawing Lieutenant General Richard Ewell's corps from Culp's Hill. Brigadier General John Imboden's cavalry was given the task of escorting the wagon train of wounded.

At daybreak on the morning of July 4, the two exhausted armies observed each other in stunned silence. The Rebel forces in front of Seminary Ridge began the deceptive operation of entrenching, while the rest of the forces began to prepare to move across South Mountain to Hagerstown and then on to Falling Waters on the Potomac River.

By 10 a.m., word spread throughout the Confederate lines that their forces were to begin moving in the direction of Virginia. Shortly after noon, the rain began to fall, and by 1 p.m., the rain began to descend in torrents. The wagons, mules, cattle, and horses captured in Pennsylvania had been moving slowly down the road towards Fairfield since daybreak, and the wagon train carrying the wounded began to move at 4 o'clock.

General Imboden issued orders prohibiting a halt to the march, and he stationed sentinels every third of a mile to make sure the line kept moving. The whole army marched much of the forty miles to Williamsport, Maryland, asleep while marching.

The long column of soaked wagons bearing vast numbers of wounded and dirty, barefoot, ragged soldiers clad in butternut stretched for seventeen miles. Observers reported that the "train of misery" took thirty hours to pass by their homes along the Chambersburg Pike.

The night of July 4-5 featured very bad thunder and lightning, and the roads were knee-deep in mud and water. The progress of the retreat was slow, scarcely two miles an hour, and cavalry skirmishing continued as the Union cavalrymen harassed the retreating Rebels.

Along the line of retreat, local Keystoners were taking pot shots at the passing columns of gray-clad troops, further harassing the Rebels. This type of bushwhacking soon discouraged straggling and helped to keep the retreating men in line.

About thirty to forty civilians, many of them ex-soldiers, attacked the wagon train at Greencastle at dawn on July 5 and smashed the wheels of the wagons with axes. Many townspeople liberated horses and cattle from the train as it passed through town. John Imboden's protective cavalry screen finally drove the attackers off. Hit-and-run attacks from civilians and federal cavalry continued along the line of retreat.

Numerous famished, wounded Confederates were taken into the hospital at Chambersburg, and were later interned by General Couch's troops. Captain Jones of the Fourteenth Cavalry out of

McConnellsburg met the wagon train of wounded at Cearfoss' Crossroads on July 5 and captured about one hundred wagons and a thousand wounded enemy.

In the meantime, the vanguard of the Army of Northern Virginia was struggling along the Fairfield or Hagerstown Road via Monterey Gap and was being continually harassed by Union cavalry. As the wagons were being hauled to the summit of the gap about midnight, Union cavalry under the command of General Hugh Kilpatrick struck the retreating column. In the midst of flashing gunfire and lightning, Grumble Jones's brigade arrived and aided Captain G. M. Emack's troopers to allow the Confederate column to continue towards Hagerstown.

In late afternoon of July 5, Imboden's beleaguered forces reached Williamsport, where to their dismay they found the Potomac running exceedingly high due to the recent torrential rains. Two confiscated flatboats were pressed into service to transport the wounded across the swollen river. The slow, dangerous process of crossing the river took forty hours.

About seven thousand Union cavalry arrived in front of Imboden's lines the next morning but were beaten off. When Major General Fitzhugh Lee's cavalry arrived on the scene that evening, the federal cavalry withdrew. On the morning of July 7, Longstreet's corps marched into Williamsport, and the Rebels constructed a formidable defensive position at the Potomac's important ford.

Meade, in the meantime, had issued General Order No. 68, which congratulated his men for their performance during the battle. He began his overly cautious southward pursuit after noon on July 5. The Union army did not follow the mauled Confederates directly but followed three separate routes into Maryland before sending them to face Lee at Williamsport.

President Abraham Lincoln and Major General Henry Halleck grew uneasy and frustrated at Meade's reluctance to finish Lee off. Halleck telegraphed Meade on July 7: "You have given the enemy a stunning blow at Gettysburg. Follow and give him another one before he can cross the Potomac...."

Lee utilized the time that Meade whiled away by moving his army into position to cross over into Virginia and constructing formidable defensive entrenchments. Meade finally made his decision to attack a day too late.

The Potomac River had fallen considerably by July 13, and Major John Harman constructed a rickety pontoon bridge from dismembered houses and warehouses. Longstreet began the crossing early in the morning, and the rest of the army soon followed.

When the Union cavalry struck, only the rear guard under Major General Henry Heth was still on the Maryland side of the Potomac. Heth lost several hundred prisoners, but the mission was accomplished. Lee's army was back in Virginia, and Meade had lost a golden opportunity to cut Lee off and perhaps end the war.

On July 14, President Lincoln penned a letter to General Meade. At the beginning of the second paragraph of this letter, Lincoln took Meade to task:

Again, my dear general, I do not believe you appreciate the magnitude of the misfortune involved in Lee's escape. He was within your easy grasp, and to have closed upon him would, in connection with our other late successes, have ended the war. As it is, the war will be prolonged indefinitely. If you could not safely attack Lee last Monday, how can you possibly do so south of the river, when you can take with you very few more than two thirds of the force you then had in hand? It would be unreasonable to expect, and I do not expect you can now affect much. Your golden opportunity is gone, and I am distressed immeasurably because of it.

CHAPTER 61
HORRIFIC CONDITIONS AT GETTYSBURG

The United States of America should have been celebrating the eighty-seventh anniversary of its independence from Great Britain on July 4, 1863 as a united nation. Instead, the states that remained within the Union were celebrating General Grant's victory at Vicksburg as the news broke concerning Meade's victory at Gettysburg. At the same time, the Confederate states were lamenting over what could have been.

Back in Gettysburg, the retreating Confederate army and the victorious Union army left a horrific scene of death and suffering. In the outskirts of the sleepy little town of 2,400, the Union army suffered 3,155 dead, 14,529 wounded, and 5,365 missing in action, while the Confederate losses were 3,903 killed, 18,735 wounded, and 5,425 missing in action.

With the withdrawal of Lee's forces on July 4, the great battle had ended, but for many the misery was just beginning. When the victorious Union soldiers realized that the battlefield was becoming quiet and Lee's forces were abandoning their positions, they began celebrating victory. A joyous sound reverberated from Little Round Top, Big Round Top, Culps Hill, Devils Den, and into the valleys, as the entire line of blue-clad soldiers took up the cheer of victory.

July 4 began hot and humid, with thunderstorms hanging on the horizon. Sulphurous clouds hovered over the mournful battlefield; then the rain began to fall steadily, and eventually it fell in torrents. Now thunder and lightning replaced the crashing and flashing of artillery that for three long days had made it seem as though heaven and earth had collided with each together. The scorched battlefield and roads were gone, and instead the torrential rains transformed them into quagmires.

The rains washed out many unsightly locations and smoothed

over some traces of the physical evidence of the horrific struggle of three days, but in most instances the evidence remained, and would for a lengthy time to come.

Most townspeople dared not to go out of their hiding places or even to chance looking out their windows. Vigilant sharpshooters remained at their tasks, and they appeared to fire at any moving objects, although the Rebels continued their retreat towards the Potomac. For most civilians, July 4 was a dreadfully long day, but when it ended, all appeared quiet, and for the first time that month, the townspeople were able to go to bed feeling safe.

The second day after the battle, Sunday July 5, dawned bright and beautiful but promised another hot and sultry day. Townspeople who had fled Gettysburg at the first sound of fighting began to return to their homes and businesses. Exhausted folks who had refused to abandon their hometown emerged from their havens of safety. Everywhere people looked, appalling scenes met their gaze. Most shrank back aghast at the horrific sights that remained in the streets of the town and the surrounding fields.

The task of clearing the streets of the litter of the two armies such as dead horses, canteens, torn clothing, empty cartridge belts, and knapsacks was begun in earnest. Those people who journeyed just outside of town were presented with horrible sights and misery on both sides of the roads. The roads and fields were strewn with the carcasses of numerous mules and hundreds of dead horses, and a few dead men, although with almost around-the-clock efforts, most had been removed or buried.

Once the scorching sun reappeared, the stench intensified tremendously. Woe to those unfortunate individuals involved in the disposal of the animal carcasses and the deceased soldiers.

CHAPTER 62
REVEREND THOMPSON'S CALLING
TO GETTYSBURG

On Sunday morning, July 5, Reverend Thompson of the Lower Tuscarora Presbyterian Church of Academia announced to his congregation at the end of his service:

I feel that God wants me to travel to Adams County and Gettysburg to aid in the cleanup in the aftermath of the horrific battle that ensued in that small town this past week. The need is so tremendous to administer to the huge numbers of wounded of both armies and to bury the dead.

Once the firing stopped on Friday night, fires were built all over the battlefield to begin the mountainous task of burying the dead of both the Blue and the Gray. The burying details worked throughout the night and continued through the morning and into the afternoon until the torrential rain struck. It rained so hard that the burying operation had to be discontinued.

All night long we were pummeled by torrents of rain and very severe thunder and lightning. As we came to church this morning, the rains continued to besiege South Central Pennsylvania. As you experienced traveling here, our roads throughout the region are knee-deep in mud and water, which adds to the woes of those unfortunate people surrounded by the misfortunes of war in Adams County.

I have been informed that the wounded are packed into churches, barns, and private homes, basically anything that has a roof, to give those poor wretched souls some protection from the elements. They have a near-calamity on their hands in Gettysburg. The surgeons and their support staff are so overtaxed that they are on the verge of collapsing. Thousands of men were wounded during the three days of fighting, and as of yesterday, most still had not received proper medical attention.

The odor of death is permeating the entire region, and with the inclement weather, burial details are having a difficult time in reaching some areas and removing the bodies. Once the sun reappears over the battlefield, the stench will become unbearable.

As soon as I partake of my noon meal after this service, I will be departing to render what aid I can. I urge those of you who are free of obligations to journey with me on this mission of mercy. Those of you that cannot travel with me, please return home quickly and return with cloth for bandages, blankets, food, or any medical supplies at your disposal.

God bless you all for any materials and food that you can donate.

I also thank you for your prayers and support for my attempt to carry God's message and aid to these unfortunate people.

By a quarter past one Reverend Thompson and his small delegation had headed across the valley to the Tuscarora Valley Pike and turned southwest. Their pace was slowed by the muddy condition of the roads. Soon they passed through the gap in the Tuscarora Mountain that was still being defended by the home guard, and then rode into Path Valley. At Spring Run, they turned south to meet the challenge of traversing the Kitttatinny or Blue Mountain.

By dusk, they arrived amidst the turmoil in Chambersburg, where the townspeople were assisting wounded rebels and rounding up a few stragglers. Reverend Thompson and his small party spent the night in the Presbyterian manse. After a hearty breakfast the next morning, they continued their trek to Gettysburg.

The pike to Gettysburg was impossible to travel upon because of the deep ruts, mud, and debris left by the retreating Rebel army, so they took to the fields, which also were quite muddy. As the sun climbed into the morning sky, the stench began to rise from the scattered dead horses that were beginning to swell to twice their size. About five or six miles from Gettysburg, the stench and the presence of clouds of flies gained their attention.

As the delegation approached the outskirts of Gettysburg, they observed the carnage of the battle everywhere. Fences had disappeared; buildings were either completely gone or ruined. Trees and bushes were stripped of branches and leaves, and the fields that had held wheat, hay, corn, or other crops were devastated. In any direction they looked, dead horses or mules littered the landscape; army accoutrements and disabled artillery pieces covered the ground.

Reverend Thompson sighed with relief that from his perch on the horse he didn't observe any human bodies still littering the landscape. It appeared that all the dead and wounded of both sides had been removed from the field of battle. "But," he asked himself, "where did they take all the dead and wounded? I guess I'll find out soon enough." Then he urged his horse towards the center of town.

The streets appeared snow-covered due to the disinfectant powder that was being spread over the muddy streets to fight the odor of death and to control disease. Around the outskirts of town, in most of the muddy fields and on the hillsides, huge bonfires emitted smoke, flame, and the smell of burning flesh as the victorious Union army began the slow process of pouring kerosene on the bodies of three to five thousand horses and mules to dispose of them in an attempt to eliminate the smell of rotting carcasses.

The square of the town was in an utter state of confusion and turmoil. After questioning several officers, Reverend Thompson was directed to a large building just a block away. As he entered the building, he found it to be filled with the wounded, who were moaning, groaning, and crying out for help and mercy. Everywhere they looked, they observed wounded, dying, and dead men.

Tables had been erected, and men, one after another, were lifted upon them for the surgeons to perform their grizzly work. Reverend Thompson was aghast at the carnage being performed by the utterly exhausted surgeons. As soon as a man was cast upon the table, the surgeon immediately placed a cattle horn over the wounded man's mouth and administered chloroform to render him unconscious or thereabouts. Then the doctor began probing and picking lead balls from the man's flesh, or in most cases, he began sawing and cutting off arms or legs.

Many of these doctors had been engaged in their bloody trade since the first day of battle, July 1, which was last Tuesday. While one of the surgeons washed his hands and waited for the table to be washed down and another wounded placed upon it, Reverend Thompson introduced himself. "How can we make ourselves useful by rendering assistance in the most meaningful way?"

The doctor looked over his shoulder and shouted, "Temple, put these good men to work tearing cloth into bandages and helping the doctors place them on the wounded once we finish with them."

Then the doctor addressed Reverend Thompson. "You said you are a Presbyterian minister. At this stage it doesn't really matter the faith of these men. Many of them just need a man of the cloth to bless them and administer their last rites."

Reverend Thompson nodded and began to go about God's work immediately, while the others worked with the bandages. They continued their bloody work until about midnight, when they were relieved and directed to a house down the street for some much needed food and rest.

When they awoke the next morning, a young lieutenant by the name of Fisher interrupted the Reverend's meager breakfast. "Reverend Thompson, you have been selected to accompany a detachment of infantry to help mark hastily dug graves so that those men who fell on the battlefield can be properly buried later." The pastor wasn't pleased with his new assignment, but he followed the young officer down the street to find the detachment of men that he was to accompany.

Before the detachment moved out, Lieutenant Fisher explained further to Reverend Thompson. "The reason you were selected for this task is that our commander is a devout Christian, and he wanted a minister or priest to read passages or to bless the temporary resting places of these gallant fallen soldiers. In addition, I must warn you that you may discover some bodies that have not been buried. In instances like that, the odor of death will be horrific; therefore, I am giving you handkerchiefs dipped in vanilla and peppermint oil to cover your faces so that you will be able to breathe without gagging. We have been using this method of masking the odor the last three days; although it is not perfect, it certainly helps.

"Pardon me for being so bold, sir, but what you are about to do is not for the weak of heart or stomach. I admire your courage. To me you and the others like you who have journeyed here to aid in this horrific cleanup are genuine heroes and as courageous as the dead you will be burying.

"If you had arrived here on Friday or yesterday, you would have viewed a scene straight from Hades. Everywhere you looked there would have been dead bodies. Under the torrid sun prior to the rain, bodies became oily, blackened, and swollen by their internal gases to the point of bursting the remnants of their uniforms.

"The flies are the most despicable of our afflictions. They came in droves immediately as soon as excrement and wounds appeared. The men would turn black as the flies covered the wounded and laid their eggs in the open sores and body openings of the men. The eggs would quickly turn into maggots by the millions or billions and then eventually become flies. The town and hospitals are overwhelmed with the loathsome vermin. I'm sorry, if this is repulsive, I will halt my description. "

Reverend Thompson looked the young officer straight in the eyes. "No, Lieutenant, I want to know every aspect of this task that lies before me. Please continue."

"As you wish, sir. The deceased men's eyes were bulging out, and their bloated tongues were protruding from their filthy mouths. To make matters even worse, the battlefield had been turned into a vast outdoor toilet. The dying evacuated their bowels and bladders involuntarily. The wounded that could not move did it on purpose, and the living fighters did it out of necessity or, fear, or because they had diarrhea. Thus, you had about 170,000 daily excretions of the men. To add to the putrid air, there were probably about 90,000 horses and mules on the battlefield, each producing about ten pounds of manure a day.

"Even without the deplorable stench of dead bodies and amputated limbs, we would still be detecting a relentless abomination of our nostrils. Now all about us we see the plumes of smoke spiraling skyward as crews attempt to eliminate the masses of rotting horseflesh and horsehair by drenching the carcasses with kerosene and incinerating them.

"All I can say is thank you for coming, and good luck, sir."

CHAPTER 63
REVEREND THOMPSON'S DEPLORABLE DUTIES

As Reverend Thompson traveled over the battleground, he found evidence of recent, temporary graves by observing little patches of freshly upturned earth raised a foot or so above the ground. In one little patch of trees he observed several trees where the bark had been removed by an axe or knife, and written in red chalk appeared the message "75 Rebs burried here" or an arrow pointing to another trench "54 Rebs, there." At any of these locations, he would read passages from his worn Bible and bless those fallen men with a prayer of absolution.

Here and there among the boulders and chasms, the unmistakable stench of death penetrated the air, forcing the men to don their treated handkerchiefs to mask the sickening smell. Most of the time it was the swollen carcass of a horse, but on at least a dozen incidents, it was the body of a dead soldier wedged among the rocks, lying where he had fallen or been thrown by his comrades as a means of cleaning out their gun position during the bloody encounter. One of the burial crews discovered the body of a young woman dressed in the uniform of a Confederate private.

Removing these decaying bodies was a ghastly endeavor, and even with the treated handkerchiefs, the men would react violently, retching and heaving the contents of their stomachs. Reverend Thompson couldn't believe he was involved in this sickening detail; it was too terrible to contemplate. He was attempting to perform God's work by giving these men a final blessing, but he knew he would never be the same and undoubtedly would suffer from horrible nightmares the rest of his days.

On several occasions, shots rang out across the battlefield, and the men would react by leaping for cover, but they soon realized that the shots were from their own detail or another detail nearby. The source of the disturbance was that during the course of the battle, dogs, cats, and especially pigs escaped from their pens and were now marauding the countryside in search of food. In addition, the crows and vultures or buzzards that had fled the deafening sounds of battle had returned.

Repugnantly, these starving birds and animals were turning to an almost unhindered source of foods, not only the dead animals, but worse yet, the unburied or poorly buried fallen soldiers. The men became so incensed over this desecration of their fallen comrades and enemies that they irately vented their exasperation on the perpetrators by firing volleys into the violators until they no longer moved a muscle, and then finishing them by severing their heads with bayonets.

Reverend Thompson was appalled at the number of civilians, including boys and girls, who scoured the battlefield in search of gold or silver valuables, serviceable weapons, unsoiled knapsacks, blankets, articles of clothing, canteens, and personal items such as letters, dairies, and Bibles. Anything of value was fair game to these scavengers. What disturbed him was that their faces indicated no sadness, humanity, or horror.

Brigadier General Marsena Randolph Patrick, Provost Marshal of the Army of the Potomac since the Battle of Antietam, arrived on the scene to bring control to Gettysburg. He had to deal with the human scavengers who plundered the dead and wounded, the curious civilians who came to gawk, unscrupulous speculators who hoped to make a fortune at the expense of the wounded (some charged the exorbitant price of 6 cents for a glass of water), and the displaced townfolks.

General Patrick organized two provost units to control all the deserters and stragglers. Some of the stragglers were organized to escort over two thousand Confederate prisoners to aid in the cleanup of the battlefield. Patrick contracted local citizens to bring in the dead and secure their personal belongings.

Vast numbers of plunderers overwhelmed the original forces and the 36th Pennsylvania Militia, which had been ordered to police the battlefield. They were headquartered at Camp Harper, which was constructed outside of town along the Baltimore Pike.

Eventually, the Patapsco Guard Infantry of Maryland Volunteers were deployed to aid in controlling the battlefield, and they camped southeast of the town until Christmas.

Later, in a move that would swell the number of civilians engaged in plundering, the federal government offered a payment of 13 cents a pound for lead taken from the battlefield.

Another group of civilians that challenged Patrick's control was the huge number of relatives, mostly women, who descended upon Gettysburg in search of information concerning their loved ones. Many hoped to find their wounded husbands, fathers, and sons, and take them home. Local residents were often requested to guide these visitors from one hospital to another to find their convalescing kin.

This was heart-wrenching enough, but others arrived searching for the resting place of their fallen loved ones in order to return their kinsmen home for burial. Many of the skeletal remains were exposed in partially eroded graves and needed a better resting location. Because of the high death toll, the use of mass burials, and the lack of markers or clearly marked shallow graves, this became an almost impossible task. Many relatives returned empty-handed, knowing that their loved ones rested in unmarked graves far from home.

Something had to be done immediately with the partly covered bodies that were scattered in makeshift graves for several square miles over the vast battlefield. If the bodies were not buried deeply enough, they would soon fall prey to the various scavengers, as Reverend Thompson's detail had experienced.

When the pastor returned to the town square that evening, he voiced his concerns, and followed up with a letter to Governor Curtin in Harrisburg describing the desecration of these gallant men. He requested that action be taken immediately to purchase a suitable section of land to inter the men of both armies. In the letter, he stated, "I realize that it might be years before we discover all those who gave their all on this battlefield, but we must try and find as many as possible and re-inter them in a proper burial site."

Later, when bids were taken for the transfer of Union soldiers' bodies from their temporary graves to the National Cemetery at Gettysburg, some relatives became even more confused about the location of their kin. Frank Biesecker oversaw the re-interment of bodies, having placed the highest of thirty-four bids at $1.59 a body for the transfer of the bodies to the National Cemetery.

(AUTHOR'S NOTE: The initial concept of a cemetery was spearheaded by lawyer David McConaughy, although another local attorney, David Wills, was primarily responsible for the project. Governor Andrew Curtin enthusiastically supported the creation of the cemetery. Landscape architect William Saunders designed the cemetery that originally was known as the Soldier's National Cemetery at Gettysburg. The dedication of the cemetery occurred on November 19, 1863, when President Lincoln delivered his famous Gettysburg Address.)

One heroine whom Reverend Thompson encountered who did more than her share in solving the burial problem was six-months-pregnant Elizabeth Thorn. Normally, Elizabeth's husband Peter was the caretaker for Evergreen Cemetery, and the couple lived in the cemetery's gatehouse. However, in July 1863, Peter was serving in the Union army, and Elizabeth and her three sons were living with her father. During the course of the battle, Elizabeth baked bread, and she and her boys distributed the bread and water to hungry and thirsty soldiers. The soldiers used her gatehouse home as a refuge.

When Reverend Thompson met Elizabeth and her father, they were engaged in burying dead soldiers in Evergreen Cemetery. The six-months-pregnant mother of three had attempted to hire men to dig graves, but the two hired hands could not tolerate the hard labor and the repugnant odor. Elizabeth, along with her father, rose to the challenge by burying 105 soldiers. Her endeavors took a terrible toll on her own body as well as the unborn baby, as the baby was sickly for most of her life.

A volunteer nurse from Philadelphia, Eliza Farnham, reported, "The whole town is one vast hospital." Dwellings housing the wounded were identified by red-and-green flags.

The task of treating the wounded left on the battlefield fell upon the capable shoulders of Dr. Jonathan Letterman, Medical Director of the Army of the Potomac. Drawing from his previous experience in earlier campaigns, he had ordered tents, medical supplies, medical personnel, and provisions to be channeled to Gettysburg on the first evening of the encounter.

During the engagement, Dr. Letterman gave the regimental surgeons full rein to perform their missions of mercy in temporary field hospitals erected near a source of water and shelter. Sometimes the field hospital was located only under a tent or in an open yard. As the battle continued, medical supplies began to run low, and doctors and their attendants became overworked and exhausted.

The United States Christian Commission and the United States Sanitary Commission provided personnel and medical supplies to assist with staffing and running the temporary field hospitals and transporting the wounded. Dr. Gordon Winslow, Superintendent of the U.S. Sanitary Commission, established his headquarters at Camp Letterman.

On Sunday, July 5, Dr. Letterman issued orders to establish a general hospital in the Gettysburg area where the wounded would be transported from the temporary field hospitals as soon as they were capable of being moved. The site for this general hospital was the George Wolf Farm on the York Pike about one and a half miles east of Gettysburg.

The hospital, which was named Camp Letterman in honor of the doctor, was in an advantageous location, near the main road and the railroad, which would connect the hospital with Philadelphia, Baltimore, and Washington. Also, it had a good wood supply and water supply.

A temporary morgue and cemetery were also established near Camp Letterman. The dead received a Christian burial in the presence of an Army chaplain.

Throughout the Civil War, tools were washed in cold water, and were not properly sterilized, which led to catastrophic cases of gangrene, tetanus, and infection. In addition to these abysmal conditions, the patients at Camp Letterman and elsewhere were subjected to the wrath of diarrhea and dysentery.

During the stifling, hot days and nights of July, the townspeople kept their windows closed in order to keep the stench out of their homes. Displaced folks who lived out in the open or in tents like the hospitals received little relief from the odors as the task of removing animal carcasses and burying the dead extended deep into July.

Everyone feared that the town would be visited with an outbreak of pestilence. There never was an epidemic, although there were isolated instances where attendants, soldiers, townspeople, or workers fell ill.

One such incident involved the Reverend Thompson, who had devoted so much time, energy, and effort into bringing relief to the wounded of Gettysburg, the families of those who lost loved ones on this vast battlefield, and the townspeople of the little town. He never complained about the stench, the long hours of painstaking labor, the scantiness of food, the lack of sleep, or the lack of supplies. As a minister of God, he knew back in Academia that the commitment that he decided to undertake would probably change his life forever.

Unfortunately, he never envisioned that his journey to Adams County would be his final journey out of Juniata County. Reverend Thompson was one of those few ill-fated souls who became a casualty of war without losing his life as a combatant on the battlefield. He succumbed to an infection or disease that in a very short time eroded his hardy body and left him in a deteriorating physical condition.

Sadly, the Reverend G. W. Thompson, who had arrived in Academia in the spring of 1847 and had served his church, the Tuscarora Female Seminary, and the Tuscarora Academy for seventeen years, succumbed to the consequences of performing the duties of the good Samaritan at the age of forty-five, on January 28, 1864.

David Evans was in winter quarters in Virginia when he learned of his pastor's untimely death. Reverend Thompson was the only pastor to serve the Lower Tuscarora Presbyterian Church during David's short life. Pastor Thompson had baptized David and confirmed him as a member of the church. He had a tremendous influence on David, and David would sorely miss him.

The devastating news of the death and wounding of local men filtered back into the valley. Special services honoring the casualties of the battle were held in almost every church throughout the county. In addition, thanks were offered to those soldiers who had been spared.

One local hero was Sergeant James B. Thompson of Company G of the First Pennsylvania Rifles, who had been inducted at Perrysville. On Thursday, July 3, the final day of the battle, Sergeant Thompson displayed courage beyond the call of duty and captured the flag of the Fifteenth Georgia Infantry, Confederate States of America. For Thompson's stupendous achievement, he was awarded the Medal of Honor. The Medal of Honor is the highest award for valor bestowed by the United States and it is presented to a member of the United States armed forces who distinguishes himself "conspicuously by gallantry and intrepidity at the risk of his life above and beyond the call of duty while engaged in an action against an enemy of the United States." Thompson was one of fifty-eight Union soldiers who were awarded the medal for their actions on the Battlefield of Gettysburg.

CHAPTER 64
DAVID JOINS THE FORTY-NINTH REGIMENT

By the time that David finished his studies at the end of September 1863, the war had changed significantly since its first major encounter at Manassas in 1861, and it would change even more by the war's end. During the winters of 1861-62, 1862-63, and the oncoming winter of 1863-64, very little fighting took place. That would not be the case in the final winter of the war in 1864-65. The fighting would be continuous on every front, every day, and it would be a different type of warfare.

Gone were the straight lines of stout-hearted infantry advancing across an open battlefield, stopping to fire one volley from an antiquated muzzle-loading smooth-bored rifle and then carrying the field with a bayonet attached to the end of the rifle. The new type of warfare did not require an army to march across a field with its banners flying to meet the enemy head on. Instead the foes would fight while seeking shelter from behind rocks, trees, trenches, man-made wooden obstructions, wire entanglements, and elaborate breastworks.

Soldiers were now equipped with rifles that spiraled a soft lead Minie bullet, an elongated, hollow-based cone capable of inflicting terrible damage to a body hit from a considerable distance. Most of these rifles were either Springfield .58 caliber or Enfield .577 caliber. Even with a muzzleloader, a skilled soldier could fire at least an average of three shots per minute and could hit whatever he was aiming at.

Breechloaders and repeaters were introduced but were not widely used by foot soldiers; their usage was largely restricted to cavalrymen. The most popular of the repeaters was the Henry lever-action repeater that could hold sixteen shots. Also quite popular was the Spencer seven- shot rifle. Of the carbines, the most widely used was the single-shot Sharps. As it seems true of all wars, both sides were guilty of not supplying their soldiers with more effective weapons that were available.

Artillery gunners had at their disposal a huge assortment of weapons from light field pieces to enormous siege cannons. Hollow shells filled with explosives that could be lobbed on opposing troops could now replace solid iron cannonballs. The artillery pieces could also be converted into huge shotguns by loading the guns with canister, grape, and shrapnel, making them capable of killing and maiming dozens with one blast.

In the autumn of 1863, as David Evans arrived at the recruitment staging area at Camp Curtin, his fellow recruits were men like him who were leaving a safe civilian life behind to join the Union army, and who were taking this step for several reasons.

Some had the purest patriotic motives in supporting their nation and flag in a war that had split the union of the nation. Some joined for financial reasons. The state and federal governments were dangling bounties in front of young men to entice them to join up. These payments amounted to hundreds of dollars to a young volunteer. Many young men were avoiding the stigma of the draft, which implied to some that they were avoiding service until their nation required it. Other motivating factors were strong curiosity, guilt, envy, or adventure. Some simply didn't want the war to pass them by, when it appeared by the fall of 1863 that the war would soon be over.

New recruit David Evans finally caught up with Company A of the Pennsylvania 49th Volunteers on Sunday, October 26, while the regiment was encamped near Warrenton, Virginia. His assimilation into army camp life began immediately, and he was placed under the guidance or supervision of Corporal Matthew McFarland.

Corporal McFarland matched David with Abram Milliken who had enlisted on August 28, 1862, in Old Company I at the age of nineteen. Abram was from East Waterford, and David had known him since he was twelve. The young soldiers greeted each other heartily. Abram laughed, "When I think of you, I remember the disaster of the race at the county fair. You would have won that race easily if it hadn't been for that gust of wind and that girl's fancy hat."

"That is a day I don't allow myself to think about. It's still a painful memory when I do."

"The last time I saw you, we were playing ball against each other in June of '62, just before I enlisted. Do you still like to play ball?"

"I'd love to play again. Do the men in our company play?"

"Yes, we have a pretty good team that plays against the other companies. If things calm down, we'll get to play some. Right now, I'd better get you squared away and set up our dog tent before retreat. After supper, I'll introduce you to the men in our squad. The bugler will be playing taps sooner than we want."

David's first full day in Company A began with reveille being sounded, the signal for morning roll call. Normally, reveille was sounded about five o'clock, but as winter approached, reveille was sounded an hour later. Failure to answer roll call would mean extra duty or a stint in the guardhouse. The sleepy soldiers of Company A stood in their places while First Sergeant Stewart of Perrysville called the roll, and then the men completed their toilet duties.

About thirty minutes later the call was sounded for breakfast, which David soon learned was commonly known as "peas on a trencher." Shortly afterwards, sick call was sounded, and men who were ill were marched to the regimental surgeon to be examined and to receive prescriptions.

The policing of company grounds, digging drainage ditches, cleaning up the quarters, cutting wood, and related activities known as fatigue duty were carried out before the musicians sounded the call for guard mounting. Guard detail was arranged so that each man stood guard two hours out of six.

Drill call was next on the schedule, and it lasted until the call for dinner (known as "roast beef") was sounded. After the noon meal, the men enjoyed a short free period followed by another period of drilling.

During the free period, Abram introduced David to as many members of the company as possible. Many of them remembered

David well. One said, "Sure, I remember you. You're the poor horseman who lost the race at the fair because one of your lady friends lost her bonnet, and it frightened your ride. You're famous throughout the Tuscarora Valley for that ride. It's no wonder that you're in the infantry instead of the cavalry."

Then the men prepared for retreat exercises by brushing their uniforms, blackening their leather, and polishing their brass. Retreat consisted of roll call, inspection, and dress parade.

Dress parades were dignified affairs during which orders were read to the men. Shortly after retreat, supper call was sounded, with tattoo following right after dusk, which brought a final roll call and an ordering of the men to their quarters. The final official action of the day was the sounding of taps, which signified that all noise must cease. The men had to be in their quarters, and all lights had to be out.

The routine for Sundays was different from that of other days; for the most part, it was a day of inspection. The feature that the men enjoyed least was "knapsack drill" when their knapsacks were opened for inspection. Sunday afternoons after retreat usually was free time, but Company A was required to attend religious services, which David thoroughly enjoyed.

Although the company was not engaged in any action during David's first few days in camp, the harsh realities of army life were thrust upon him on Wednesday, October 28. Sam Wellers of the 49th and two men of the 119th Pennsylvania had their heads shaved, and they were drummed up and down in front of the brigade, having been charged with desertion.

This shocking event was followed by a similar situation on Friday, when Private Joseph Richardson of Company A and David Meghan were court-martialed for desertion. They were found guilty and sentenced to be executed on November 4. Sam Weller's execution date was set for the same day.

On Wednesday, November 4, a heavy detail of the 49th, including David and Abram, relieved the 95th Pennsylvania at the Warrenton rail depot where they unloaded two trains. Later in the day, the men of the 49th were extremely relieved when the execution of Sam Wellers was postponed. The men drew rations for five days and were ordered to be ready to march in the morning.

On Friday, November 6, the Sixth Corps moved out at daybreak, marching towards Rappahannock Station, and by noon they were about two miles from their objective. David was terrified; he found it difficult to breathe. He kept repeating to himself, "Please don't let me be a coward. Please give me the strength to fire my weapon in the direction of the enemy." It had never entered his mind just how difficult it would be to shoot at another human being, even if he was the despised enemy. Abram marched beside David and offered encouragement.

David began to concentrate on the steps he needed to execute in order to fire and reload his rifle. This helped to lessen the tension somewhat, but he still was concerned about what his reaction would be when they encountered the enemy face to face.

When the company came in contact with Rebel pickets, they formed a line of battle, and the 6th Maine relieved the Keystone state's skirmishers. The 5th Wisconsin was on the left, David and the 49th in the center, and the 119th Pennsylvania on the right.

The moment of truth came for David and the other raw recruits when the Maine skirmishers were pushed back a little, and General Russell ordered the battle line to move forward, followed by a command to "charge on the run."

The battle line advanced on the run and eventually gained the enemy's battle works with the use of bayonets and gun butts. Some of the enemy attempted to escape across the pontoon bridge, but were mowed down by volleys of hot lead from fifty yards away. Any wounded Reb who fell into that deep, swift-moving water was a dead Reb. The surviving enemy soldiers threw down their weapons and surrendered, giving the victorious Yankees four pieces of artillery, four caissons filled with ammunition, an intact pontoon bridge, seven stands of rebel colors, one flagstaff, and between 1,800 and 2,000 prisoners.

The men were ecstatic about their victory, and General Sedgwick was quick in sending his congratulatory orders. David dropped to his knees and gave thanks to God not only for allowing him to survive his first encounter with the enemy, but also for giving him the courage not to falter while under enemy fire.

CHAPTER 65
LINCOLN'S GETTYSBURG ADDRESS

On November 24, Sergeant Sam Steiner of F Company was reading a copy of the *Philadelphia Inquirer* of November 20, which he had bought in camp for four cents. "Hey, men, the president delivered a speech at Gettysburg on the nineteenth dedicating the Soldiers National Cemetery at Gettysburg."

"What did our commander-in-chief have to say?" David inquired.

"Yes, Sam, fill us in on what the president said about that bloody mess," demanded Clint Ross.

"Just bear with me for a minute, and I'll give you a quick summary. On last Thursday, November 19, a parade and dedication were held in the small community commemorating a burial ground for our brave soldiers who fell on that gigantic, gory battleground back in early July. David Wills, a prominent Gettysburg attorney, helped to create the cemetery and organized the event. A crowd of nearly 15,000 witnessed the parade and dedicatory speeches.

"The president wasn't the main speaker; Edward Everett, the eminent Unitarian clergyman who is thought to be our nation's leading orator, presented the main address. Everett delivered a speech that evidently rambled on for an hour and fifty-seven minutes.

"President Lincoln was invited to speak only at the last minute. Apparently, his appearance was an afterthought. The president's address lasted only two minutes. Those of you who can read ought to take the time to read his speech. You men who can't read, I'm sure someone will be kind enough to read it to you.

"The opening sentence is unique in the way he refers to time in our country's history. At least, I find it exceptional and distinctive. Fact is, I feel that way about the whole address. But not everyone was impressed with the president's oration. Some people are criticizing Lincoln's economy of language. There is a quote from the *Chicago Times* that described the address as "silly, flat, and dishwater utterances."

"The President tries hard, but he just can't seem to please everyone, no matter what he does. It's going to be interesting when the presidential election occurs next November. For the president's sake, I sure hope this war will be over or nearly over by that time."

David interjected, "We will all say 'Amen' to that."

The regiment moved to Hazel River near Brandy Station and encamped until November 26, and then crossed the Rapidan River where they were placed on the front to support the Third Corps at Locust Grove. The 49th marched and skirmished against the Rebels until they arrived at Mine Run, where they were placed on the skirmish line. General Meade decided to withdraw from the enemy's front, and on December 2 the Pennsylvanians re-crossed the Rapidan River at Germania Ford and returned to their original camp at Hazel Run.

CHAPTER 66
THE WINTER OF 1863-64

The 49ᵗʰ Regiment wintered at Hazel Run. After returning from the front, the men began to build substantial shelters. The normal summer home for a Yankee soldier was a two-man tent known as a dog tent made by buttoning together two half shelters. Now that winter was at hand, some men built log huts much like frontier cabins, with the cracks filled with mud. Most winter quarters were a combination of materials with a log base, and shelter tents, ponchos, or rubber blankets for roofs.

The shelters were most often heated by fireplaces made out of wood covered with clay. Most huts contained two bunks, one above the other, extending across the end of the shelter. Floors, shelves, stools, tables, and other furnishings were added according to the bunkmates' tastes.

David and Abram decided to dig down about three feet to get below the frost line to embed their logs. This, they reasoned, would provide more warmth and stability. They confiscated a local farmer's shed and tore it down to provide a board floor, a framework for their bunks, and a framework for their roof, over which they stretched canvas and rubber blankets.

They found several barrels in the farmer's shed, and used some of the staves for the bottom of their bunks. The barrels were also used as a table and storage locker. From a partially destroyed barn, they removed some straw and feed bags, which they converted into mattresses.

At first they figured to use one of the barrels as a chimney for their fireplace or furnace, but after witnessing several barrels catching on fire, they abandoned that idea. Instead, they gathered stones and built a small fireplace at the closed end of the cabin.

As time went on, Abram and David placed pegs into the log walls and erected several shelves to hang and store their few personal items. They also built two crude stools. The open fireplace provided ample lighting, but they also fashioned several holders for candles. Their little hut provided them with warmth and comfort from early December until March 1864.

Christmas Day 1863 arrived frosty and overcast, with clouds clearing late afternoon into the evening. For many of the veterans, this was their third Christmas away from home, but it didn't matter whether you were an old vet or a raw recruit—being away from home at Christmas was a somber experience.

Many of the men sat around singing Christmas carols and sharing memories of their favorite Christmas experience. Some read from their Bibles and held Christmas services; others sought out the chaplains and attended real Christmas services. Even though turkeys were scarce, those who were lucky enough to secure one of the birds shared as best as they could.

Every man was thinking about the same things on this day: home and the loved ones they left behind. The most sobering event on this Holy Day was the pealing of the church bells, as the local people attempted to forget about the war and attend church as if it were just a normal Christmas Day.

Company A greeted the New Year of 1864 by firing their weapons into the air, each man hoping that before this new year ended, the war would also end and they would all be home to welcome in 1865.

Throughout January, replacements continued to join the 49th Regiment. Earlier in the war, recruits had been drilled in the fundamentals at a special camp of instruction near Annapolis. Now new troops were sent directly to their units almost on a daily basis, because it was believed that a new recruit could learn more in one day in camp than what he could be taught in a month at a special venue.

Just as David had experienced when he arrived at the end of October, the replacements were placed under the tutelage of a veteran noncommissioned officer and were given intensive drilling in squad and company movements. The replacements faced long hours on the drill field until they were sick of soldiering. They would drill, drill, drill, and then drill some more. Soon these new men became proficient in saluting, marching, shifting arms, loading their weapons, and parrying and thrusting with their bayonets.

Once they learned the fundamentals, they were introduced to skirmish drill and maneuvers by brigades or larger military units. Many soldiers regarded the skirmish drill as a mock fight, especially when the activity was enlivened with the use of blank cartridges.

Winter quarters normally meant that drilling for veterans would be greatly curtailed because most regimental commanders did not want their men getting burned out by six or eight hours of drill each day. Most of the men agreed that as long as they weren't shoeless or wanting for warm clothing and food, they would perform whatever duties they were ordered to perform.

January and February were times between campaigns filled with dullness, despondency, and homesickness, which could have made life intolerable and destroyed the army's will to fight. Therefore, the men relied upon their own ingenuity to devise methods of relaxation and recreation that would lift their spirits and make camp life tolerable.

Probably the most common diversion was reading. Newspapers, usually local weeklies sent by homefolk, as well as metropolitan dailies, were extremely popular. David received the *Juniata Sentinel* published in Mifflintown and shared this county paper with anyone who wanted to read it. Normally, once he loaned an issue out, he never saw it again.

David was extremely upset when he read of Reverend Thompson's untimely death in the *Juniata Sentinel* of February 5. He had known that the pastor was never the same after returning from his endeavors in the aftermath of the Battle of Gettysburg. David never imagined that the sickness contracted by the minister at Gettysburg would lead to his death.

Literary periodicals like *Harper's* and *Atlantic* were read by the wealthier soldiers. Classic novels, dime novels, the Bible, and religious periodicals were popular reading also.

Music ranked close to reading as a camp diversion. No matter where the troops were situated, other than the firing line, the strains of popular songs would be sung. Brigade bands gave twilight concerts on holidays, and on special occasions the bands serenaded the men and officers.

Many men carried small instruments to entertain themselves and their comrades. David was amazed at the variety of small musical instruments that the men had collected, such as harmonicas, tin whistles, fifes, fiddles, dulcimers, jew harps, bones, spoons, banjos, guitars, mandolins, and concertinas. David drew great pleasure from listening to the wide range of music that permeated the camp.

Sports were a major diversion. Boxing, cricket, foot races, wrestling, broadjumping, horse racing, leapfrog, snowball fights, boating, fishing, hunting, swimming, tug of war, pitching horseshoes, and football were just some of the sports that the soldiers enjoyed. The most popular competitive sport was baseball, which had begun to sweep the nation just prior to the outbreak of the war.

Football was a rough, soccer-like game, a kicking game, rather than a running game in the style of rugby. Actually, it was a huge brawl; some referred to it as mob soccer. The game was responsible for many injuries; most common were broken noses and fingers.

Less strenuous, but just as relaxing, were chess, checkers, dominoes, and cards. Teasing and pulling pranks were great ways of seeking fun, as were take-offs on army procedures and institutions, such as dress parades and court-martials.

Soldiers competed for money prizes in shooting matches, sack races, and wheelbarrow races. Chasing greased pigs or climbing a greased pole to retrieve paper money nailed to the top usually ended in free-for-alls. Whiskey flowed freely during some of these activities, adding to the festivity.

In some locations where women were found in sufficient numbers, dances were held. Although there were occasions when dances were held without the benefit of female participation, usually such activities were stimulated by generous swigs of alcohol. Cotillions, jigs, and polkas were types of lively dances performed at these affairs.

Some more enterprising soldiers relied upon their own handicrafts to amuse themselves. Painting, drawing, carving of pipes or rings, publishing of a camp newspaper, or even debating and spelling bees found their way into camps.

Overall, the men themselves made an alien and unpleasant atmosphere bearable by finding ways to have fun and to combat boredom.

Baseball and football (soccer) served as the biggest avenues of amusement throughout January and February. The men especially enjoyed the football matches when the officers joined in. The officers would always return to their quarters with bloody shins and bodies, as the men took the opportunity to rough up their officers.

Baseball was still David's game of choice, and every chance he got he would arrange games between his company and the others. Soon A Company had the reputation as the best team in the regiment.

Baseball games were played every day that the weather permitted. Soon baseball fever swept through all the Union camps, and many officers encouraged and often participated in the games. Sometimes the enemy sat on the opposite bank of the river to observe the games in progress, and at other times the enemy could be seen playing games of their own.

Finally it happened; one afternoon while a game was in progress, one of the Rebs yelled across the river, "Would you Yanks be interested in playing a game of ball against us?"

The Yankees yelled in unison, "Sure enough, Johnny. Just let us get it cleared by our officers, and we'll be more than glad to beat up on you. Are you coming across the river?"

"Sure, Yank, but let's make this interesting. For what kind of stakes are you willing to play?"

David yelled, "Most of us would be interested in some good rich Virginia tobacco."

The Rebel leader responded, "We sure would like to take some of your coffee and sugar off your hands. What say you to that, Yank?"

"You've got a deal. Just let me talk to the captain and get his permission."

David returned in about ten minutes with permission. "See you over here tomorrow at two o'clock, just as long as no weapons are brought across the river. This is to be a game between gentlemen, not soldiers."

"See you tomorrow afternoon, Yank. Just make sure you have that coffee and sugar on hand. We can taste them already."

During the next two weeks baseball games between the blue- and gray-clad soldiers became a common occurrence, although all the players realized that once the roads dried up, the games would come to an end, and the fighting and dying would resume. The games alternated from one side of the river to the other, with no problems ever erupting; the games indeed were played between gentlemen. For a short time, the war was forgotten, and the men, including the spectators, were more concerned with winning a simple ball game than attempting to kill their opponents on the other side of the river.

CHAPTER 67
AN INTRODUCTION TO THE GRAY GHOST

On occasions, there would be grim reminders that there was still a war to be fought. Tuesday, January 26 was one of those eventful days that the men of the 49th would have liked to avoid. During a routine picket-line duty, Rebel guerrillas struck with lightning-like penetration and captured Jacob G. Fink and James Leach of Company E and Nelson Shepard of New Company F.

One of the veterans shook his head. "We'll never see those boys again. They'll be sent to Libby Prison near Richmond, or worse, sent farther south to Andersonville. Either way, it will be a miracle if they survive. You fresh fish, you raw recruits, better take heed and not be daydreaming of that young thing back home while you are on picket duty, or you'll find yourselves in the same predicament."

"Yep, probably the work of the Gray Ghost. His irregulars constantly operate in our rear and flanks. They're known for destroying supplies, cutting telegraph wires, capturing or killing pickets, blocking railroads or destroying rails, raiding wagon trains, storming isolated outposts, and capturing couriers."

Another vet quipped, "If you youngsters know what is good for you, you'll keep your files closed up while you're on night guard or picket duty, and you won't straggle, unless you want to end up like Fink, Leach, and Shepard."

"It seems to me that Mosby is more trouble than a full brigade of Rebs. He attacks without warning and then disappears into thin air, back into Mosby's Confederacy."

"Mosby's Confederacy? Where's that located?"

"Here, take look at this map. Mosby's base of operations is in an area that basically includes Prince William, Fairfax, Loudoun and Fauquier Counties. As you can see, it's really a large triangle. We're located somewhat south of the triangle, but if we look north of here towards Warrenton, you find the Plains just a little west of Thoroughfare Gap; that's probably the southeastern angle of the triangle. Then follow a side of the triangle northwest to Snickersville and Snickers Gap; that would be the northern angle. Turn southwest along the mountains until you arrive near Linden and Manassas Gap and you have the final angle; then turn east to the Plains and you complete the triangle.

"Now that doesn't mean he won't leave his Confederacy and strike elsewhere, but normally this is his base. But you have to realize that other irregular groups often get the credit or the blame for Mosby's partisan activities."

"What do we really know about this Gray Ghost?" inquired one of the new recruits.

"Not to belittle you, but I can't believe you haven't heard of this legendary rebel leader," declared John Pollock. "Since last summer he's been in many newspaper and magazine articles in both the North and the South. The *Washington Star* has been carrying stories about him for the past year. The Gray Ghost is John Singleton Mosby of the 43rd Battalion of the Virginia Cavalry.

"I've become fascinated by this man so I read everything I can about him. John Mosby was born in Edgemont in Powhatan County, Virginia, on December 6, 1833. Later his family moved near Charlottesville, so it was only natural for him to enroll at the University of Virginia, which he did in 1850. Mosby ran afoul of the law while a student and was charged with "malicious shooting" and "unlawful shooting" of George Turpin, the alleged town bully.

"He was found not guilty of the first charge, but guilty of the second and spent seven months of a one-year sentence in the Charlottesville jail. While in jail, he began a study of law and soon was admitted to the bar. John married Pauline Clarke and they relocated to Bristol, Virginia.

"Prior to Virginia's secession, John opposed the secession of the lower southern states. He joined the Confederate forces as a private in Company D of the First Virginia Cavalry where he met Jeb Stuart. Mosby became Stuart's regimental adjutant as a first lieutenant and quickly gained a reputation as an outstanding scout.

"From what I gather, Mosby looks like anything but a warrior. He is supposed to be slight in build, about five feet seven or eight inches tall, and weighs about 130 pounds. He is fair-complexioned with sandy-colored hair and he has a slight stoop in his posture. One trait that stands out is his blue, piercing eyes. He is described as a restless man with a very keen intellect and a bad temper.

"Mosby began his mission of raids, attacks, and ambushes in January 1863 after apparently telling Stuart, 'I could make things lively during the winter months.' We just witnessed how lively the Gray Ghost can make things for us. If you survive, you will learn that he strikes during inclement weather, at dawn when you are the sleepiest during picket duty, while you are escorting a wagon train (because he regards wagon trains and sutler wagons as traveling retail general stores), or at any opportunity where he believes he can profit from hit-and-run tactics."

CHAPTER 68
AN INTERESTING CONVERSATION

On Tuesday, February 2, Company A received about twenty conscripts, and David overheard Third Sergeant Ritner and Fourth Sergeant Thompson discussing the arrival of the new men.

Ritner observed, "It's a shame, but the Army of the Potomac is really not a volunteer army anymore. The twenty we got today are men who were made to come; if they had any money, they wouldn't be here. If their old man had money, he would have paid a substitute to gain permanent exemption."

Sergeant Thompson snorted, "We might complain about the conscripts, but I'll take them over a bounty collector any day. Most of those collectors are nothing but out-and-out criminals; they are of no use whatsoever to our army. Many of them enlist to collect their bounty and quickly desert so that they can enlist at another location and collect more money there.

"The word from army command is that we are no longer to place bounty men on picket or outpost duty. You just can't trust those types of men anywhere in camp, on picket duty or on the firing line. They're utterly unreliable."

"You're absolutely right," agreed Ritner. "The substitutes and bounty collectors or jumpers are undermining the relationship between our officers and the men, especially the veterans. Some units have over 50 percent of their recruits deserting within two weeks after they arrive. The situation better improve before warm weather arrives and dries up the muddy roads so that we can maneuver, or we are going to face a bloody spring.

"The Rebs have been using those who voluntarily deserted us as workers in their war plants, but some of our informants say that is about to change. Since we have had this influx of riff-raff who are of no use to our army, the Confederacy is finding that they are of no use in their factories either. Therefore the Rebs' new policy will be to simply place these undesirables in prison camps just as if they had been captured in combat.

"Another thing we need to rectify is the large number of men pretending to be sick or disabled so they can avoid drill and picket duty."

Thompson nodded. "I understand that some doctors have found a cure for all those who claim to have rheumatism so bad they can't bend their joints. They simply chloroform the claimers and render them unconscious, and while they are under, they manipulate the men's legs. If nothing is found amiss, the soldier is escorted back to his unit for regular duty once he recovers from the anesthetic.

"All we need to do is resort to Regular Army discipline even if it means employing brutal punishments. I've never enjoyed the prospect of tying a man to the rack, the "buck and gag," or tying a man up by his thumbs, but this army is going to have to fight when April or May arrives and we need discipline desperately."

Thompson added, "The other major crisis I see developing is the loss of men like you and me, the original veterans of our three-year enlistment regiments. Our enlistments are going to start to expire in May and through the summer and into fall. There is no way under our law of enlistment that the federal authorities can force us to remain in our nation's service beyond our enlistment period if we choose not to remain in the army."

Ritner agreed once again. "The only way they can keep us here is to beg us to reenlist. I don't think they can bribe us with bounties; we've seen how money corrupts men. If they would just allow us to go home as a unit for about a month, they might get a majority of the regiments to accept that as a motivation for reenlistment."

"Yes, what a furlough could do for a man's spirits! That reminds me of a story I was told about an Irish private who attempted to wrangle a furlough from his regimental commander by giving the officer the old story that his wife and kids were all sick and the private needed to return home to care for his family. The officer then showed the private a letter that he had received from the private's wife begging the colonel to deny the private permission to return home because he had raised the devil the last time. The private then stated that there were two splendid liars present, for he had never been married."

Both men laughed heartily at the story, for they had heard similar stories over the years as some men under their command attempted to gain permission to speak to their commanding officer about the possibility of receiving a furlough.

David Evans was deeply moved by the conversation he had just heard. Many of the issues that Ritner and Thompson had discussed were ones that David Evans had not previously considered. He had so much to learn about army life. David hoped he would live long enough to become a veteran and have the ability to understand what the three-year enlistees had endured since 1861.

On Friday, February 12, the president's birthday, the company celebrated by playing ball all day, but at brigade dress parade the mood grew somber. Private O'Donnell of A Company and George W. Chandlier of Company I of the 5th Wisconsin had their heads shaved; then they were drummed up and down in front of the brigade and dishonorably discharged. The newer men were immensely impressed with this action.

CHAPTER 69
PREPARING FOR THE 1864 SPRING OFFENSIVE

On the evening of March 9 Abram, David, and the rest of their squad were finishing their supper, when John Porter of Company B arrived with the latest news from Corps headquarters. Porter was excited as he sat down. "Men, we have just experienced a reshuffling of our army's high command. General Halleck is being replaced but will remain as chief of staff in Washington. For the second time since George Washington, we have a lieutenant general as commander of all the armies of the United States— Ulysses S. Grant. William Tecumseh Sherman has been elevated to the command of the Military Division of the Mississippi, the post that Grant formerly held."

"Ulysses S. Grant—who's he?" inquired Private Thomas.

"You mean to tell me you never heard of Grant? Have you been living in a cave the last year or so? Grant's a West Pointer, class of 1843. He served in Mexico, where he was twice cited for gallantry, and he rose to the rank of captain of infantry. After the war, he resigned from the army and fell into financial difficulties, along with some alleged drinking problems.

"When the current war broke out, he received a commission as colonel of volunteers of Illinois. For the last two years Sam Grant— that's what his army friends call him—has molded the course of the war in the West and has delivered a succession of victories for Lincoln. His greatest victory came at Vicksburg last July."

"What about Meade? Did they fire him too?" chimed in James Riden.

"Nope, Meade offered to resign, but Grant kept him in command of the Army of the Potomac."

"What about Sheridan? I've heard he's a no-nonsense fighter and leader."

"Another West Pointer, class of 1853. He's not a westerner; he was born in Albany, New York, but grew up in Ohio. His men affectionately call him 'Little Phil,' since he's only five feet five inches tall. The word is that he's a scrappy, resourceful, and courageous infantry commander."

"Sounds like a good man to me."

"Let's wait until we get back in action before we judge him,"

The new commander of the Army of the Potomac soon enacted changes. On April 17, Grant ordered a halt to all prisoner exchanges. This change in policy was a grim decision in response to several incidents. After Grant's victory at Vicksburg, he chose to parole about 31,000 captured Rebel soldiers, but during the Chattanooga Campaign, it was discovered that many of the prisoners then being captured were men he had paroled after Vicksburg. The Confederacy also refused to exchange black prisoners of war or the white officers who commanded the black regiments. Grant's major consideration was that the prisoner exchange greatly benefited the manpower-poor South; furthermore, Union prisoners added to the burden the South faced in feeding and clothing its own army.

The next day, Monday, April 18, the whole Sixth Corps turned out in all its spit and polish to be reviewed by General Grant. The review occurred at noon, and afterwards the men had the rest of the afternoon to themselves. Many of the men became involved in ball games that lasted until time for dress parade. It was a tremendous thrill and honor for the men of the Sixth.

In implementing his strategy, the new commander immediately decided that the capture of Southern cities and the South's strategic points, and the occupation of Southern territory were less important than destroying the Confederate armies that continued to fight.

There were two Confederate armies that concerned Grant: the Army of Northern Virginia commanded by Robert E. Lee and the Army of Tennessee commanded by Joseph E. Johnston; each of these armies contained about 60,000 men. Since the Union armies now controlled the Mississippi River, the forces west of that river were of little importance.

Grant had turned control of the West over to General William

Tecumseh Sherman, who was given the position of an army group commander. Sherman's own Army of Tennessee was located in and around Chattanooga, with Major General James Birdseye McPherson in command. Sherman's command also included the Army of the Cumberland under Major General George Henry Thomas, known as "The Rock of Chickamauga," and the smaller Army of the Ohio commanded by Major General John M. Schofield.

Sherman had upwards of 100,000 men in his command. Grant's instructions to Sherman were straightforward: "to move against Johnston's army, to break it up, and to get into the interior of the enemy's country as far as you can, inflicting all the damage you can against their war resources."

Sherman's main objective was the city of Atlanta. Until 1845, the city had been known as Terminus, as it was the gateway of overland traffic from the coast of Georgia to the West. To implement Grant's instructions, Sherman would have to wage war against the civilian population and their property as well as against Confederate military targets in order to destroy the enemy's capacity and will to fight. In other words, Sherman was to wage Total War. Sherman stated simply, "I will make Georgia howl."

Grant's mission with the Army of the Potomac was as uncomplicated as Sherman's farther south: it was simply to head straight for the Confederate Army of Northern Virginia under Lee and fight until it broke. The Army of the Potomac was to head for Richmond, but its real objective was to destroy Lee's army rather than capturing the Confederate capital.

Besides the main thrust from the north, Grant was sending the Army of the James under General Benjamin Butler from the Fort Monroe area up the James River towards Richmond. Butler's army would occupy part of Lee's defensive forces, and Lee would not be able to divert those defensive forces to the North to reinforce the Army of Northern Virginia.

In addition, German-born Major General Franz Sigel was in command of the Union army in the Shenandoah Valley. Sigel's army was to move up the valley to Staunton and then head east through the Blue Ridge in the direction of Richmond.

This marked the first time that the Union army would move in a coordinated campaign under central control. All the Union armies would move as a team; Sherman, Grant, Meade, Sigel, and Butler would march at the same time. Grant's timetable set the beginning of May as the kick-off for the coordinated war machine to advance to victory.

As the men of the Sixth Corps enjoyed the warm, pleasant days of late April on the banks of the Rapidan River, one of the changes in their daily schedule was a new emphasis on target practice. To entice the recruits to concentrate on their shooting skills, it was announced that any private who made the best score would be excused from picket duty, although noncommissioned officers were not included in this exercise.

This prize created great excitement throughout the companies. Abram confided in David, "I'm really going to concentrate on my target. It would be a blessing not to have to worry about going out on picket at night."

David laughed, "Just look around you; who doesn't want to shoot the best score? I know I do."

When the results were in, David had missed winning by three points, and Abram five. Both were deeply disappointed because they considered themselves excellent rifle shots, but evidently they weren't the best.

Then amidst all the excitement of the shooting contest, tragedy struck on Thursday, April 28. After the men came back to camp from target practice and were following standard procedure by cleaning their guns, Sergeant Transne placed a cap on his gun, believing it was unloaded. Transne stepped back out of his tent to snap the cap to blow any dirt left in his barrel, when the unknown load discharged.

The ball entered one of Company B's tents and struck James Ewing of Company H, who was visiting members of the company. The ball slammed into Ewing's left arm. He was immediately transported to the hospital where the surgeons had to amputate the unfortunate man's shattered arm.

That evening the whole regiment felt the impact of the accident, as sympathy went out to both James Ewing and Sergeant Transne. The mood of the camp had shifted swiftly from one of merriment to one of sorrow.

Sometimes punishment that didn't make much sense was administered. What occurred on Monday, May 2, involving John N. Patterson, was a classic example. While Colonel Duffy was inspecting the brigade, he found two extra shirts in Patterson's knapsack and threw them out, stating, "Private, you are only allowed to carry two shirts."

Patterson, who had just received these shirts from home, stepped out of the ranks and retrieved his shirts, remarking, "I will carry what I please."

This infuriated the colonel, who exclaimed to Captain Robert Barr, "Is that the way you allow your men to speak to their officers? Punish him immediately."

Captain Barr bellowed, "Sergeant, place this man on three extra days of picket duty."

The next day, when the men were leaving for picket duty, the inspecting officer appeared and ordered Patterson out of the ranks, exclaiming, "That is no punishment: make this man carry sixty pounds of stone for four hours, with one hour's rest." Sergeant Samuel H. Irvin weighed the stones and Patterson marched with the weight instead of manning picket duty.

The rest of the men practiced target shooting, and when the company returned to camp, they noticed that the hospital had been sent away. They were issued six days of rations, and told to prepare to march at four o'clock the next morning.

The camp was alive at three o'clock, and the company moved out an hour later. Men left behind their winter's accumulation of books, magazines, letters, and other personal items. Good old Patterson had a smile on his face as he carried the four shirts in his knapsack out of camp, although his back might have been a little sore at the end of the march.

This was Wednesday, May 4, and the Army of the Potomac was on the move south. The 49th marched rapidly through Brandy

Station and Stephenson and crossed the Rapidan River at Germania Ford on pontoon bridges.

David looked around at his mates as they stepped onto the bridge. He was experiencing a weird sensation because the bridge was anything but stable as it bobbed up and down on the current. The current was swift; if any man lost his footing and tumbled into the water, or if the bridge failed, there would be no chance of surviving. David was elated when his feet touched firm, though muddy, ground on the southern bank of the river.

Along the way, the recruits began to unload items they found too heavy to carry during this warm springtime march. Everywhere overcoats, extra blankets, the contents of overloaded knapsacks, and extra gear littered the countryside, to be looted by the troops and artillerists following behind.

After marching about sixteen miles, the company halted at 5:00 p.m. about two miles south of the ford along the plank road. In the distance David was relieved to see other blue troops out in front of his own company.

That night some of the veterans were discussing what lay ahead. "Grant's intentions are to go straight at Lee, cling to him and batter him all the way back to Richmond," one said.

"Gentlemen, straight ahead of us are the tangled thickets of the Wilderness," said another. "It's as forbidding a place as you will ever see. It's filled with nothing but saplings, vines, creepers, stunted pines, and dense underbrush. This isn't any place that two armies should be meeting; it spells disaster for both. We clashed with Lee's army here last year in what is called the Battle of Chancellorsville. It was a calamity; just pray that history doesn't repeat itself tomorrow."

Company A resumed its march Thursday, May 5, on the plank road, with Company C deployed as flankers. Just west of the Wilderness Tavern, the skirmishers made contact with the enemy; the flankers were withdrawn, and they rejoined the regiment. David could hear the musket fire off in the distance, and his uneasiness grew.

In the confusion of this opening sparring, Company A advanced about a mile through the entangled forest on the north side of the turnpike, in what amounted to a slight charge. They ran straight into the enemy, whom they drove forward like a flock of sheep.

The moving line of battle soon lost its formation because the men were unable to maintain elbow-to-elbow contact. Colonel Hulings ordered them back to re-form; then they advanced and the firing grew stronger.

Here and there, the dry underbrush caught fire, adding more smoke to the confusion. The battle line could not advance in formation, and the separate regiments or companies blindly attempted to move forward.

Corporal Reynolds complained, "It's like fighting blindfolded. You can't see anything distinctly. I guess we just move towards the heaviest firing and shoot at anything that moves."

David agreed, "It's difficult to distinguish us from the enemy; our blue uniforms have developed a gray cast from the smoke and ashes of smoldering forest fires."

Suddenly, some companies of the 49th found this to be true when soldiers of the 119th Pennsylvania mistakenly opened fire on David and his company. All along the line, members of the 49th began to swear and holler at the 119th. "You stupid Dutchmen, you're shooting at the 49th Pennsylvania. Can't you tell blue from gray?" Finally, after some loss of blood, the firing ceased, and the two Keystone State regiments got their lines straightened out and re-formed.

As the fighting during the day progressed, a high wind developed, whipping the flames in the underbrush into bigger flames that spread into the treetops. The unwounded fighting men of both sides forgot about fighting the enemy and attempted to drag their wounded comrades from the path of the flames to safety. Some of the wounded, rather than face an agonizing death by being roasted alive, capped their rifles and ended their own lives.

As the flames increased, more and more wounded were consumed by the conflagration. Even more horrible was the plight of those wounded whose paper cartridges ignited and exploded in boxes around their waists. Unfortunately, the pop-pop-pop of these cartridges could be heard throughout the day and night. These exploding cartridges produced terrible wounds that probably ended the men's lives before the flames consumed them.

In most situations, the men could not see what they were shooting at. Instead, they were forced to point their weapon into the brush, smoke, and flames and shoot away, hoping to hit the enemy. Officers attempted with little success to utilize compasses to lead their men through the dense forest to reach the enemy's positions.

When darkness descended on the battlefield, the armies did not pull apart as they had done in most battles; rather, they simply halted where they were and attempted to rest. The two armies were intermingled, and all night long men blundered into the wrong camp and were either shot or taken prisoner.

Any sound or movement would be the recipient of rifle fire, and in some areas there was heavy firing along the line at intervals all night long. Company A sustained three killed, thirty-four wounded, and two taken prisoner.

Besides the firing and the crackling of smoldering flames, the night was full of horrible, inhuman sounds, as wounded men cried out in pain and in need of water. Worst of all was when the blazes engulfed an immobile, wounded man, who was unable to drag himself away from the path of the encroaching flames.

It was the worst night of David's young life. Before bedding down for the night, David and his squad brushed and scraped away the dry pine needles, leaves, and underbrush within about a twenty-foot radius, hoping that this would protect them from any fires. They did allow three large logs to remain within that radius. They pushed and shoved the logs into a triangular formation, leaving an open space at the north end of the triangle for an escape route. They chose to sleep behind the logs, so that they would have something to hide behind if a Rebel force stumbled upon them during the night.

The wind continued to blow throughout the night, lifting cinders and sparks to other locations and igniting more fires in the entangled woodlands. Besides the worry of the wind-dispersed flames, the cries of the wounded permeated the night air, making it almost impossible to sleep.

David could no longer stand to listen to the screaming, wailing, whimpering, and blubbering of the wounded. He and his squad mates stuffed strips of clothing in their ears and wrapped their heads to keep the strips in place. Even with these efforts, the sounds were not completely drowned out, and the men knew that they would have nightmares about those sounds the rest of their lives.

General Grant planned for the attack to get underway at 4:00 a.m., but the corps commanders found their lines in such disarray that Meade was successful in persuading the commander to postpone the attack until 5:00.

Friday morning the fighting along the five-mile front resumed with sharp skirmishing in front of David's company. From the right of the line an order was barked, "Let's move out, men. We're going to advance across the ravine in front of us." Against heavy musket fire, the company advanced in a jagged line out of the murky woods across the swampy ravine overgrown with scrub pine. They were hit by occasional attacks, which were thrown back.

At noon, another order was passed down the line. "Halt where you are and start digging and building breastworks. We can expect a major engagement any time."

A stout log breastwork was constructed along the western edge of Brock Road, but in the confusion, a two-mile gap had emerged in the Union line, which Longstreet exploited with a flank attack. Longstreet's counteroffensive drove the Union flank back towards Brock Road, but Lady Luck smiled on Grant shortly after the attack began.

In the confusion of battle, Longstreet was severely wounded by friendly fire, with a ball passing through his throat and into his shoulder. General Longstreet was removed to the rear while coughing blood. This was a crippling loss to Lee, reminiscent of General Thomas "Stonewall" Jackson's death under similar circumstances on May 10 the year before. Another blow inflicted by friendly Confederate fire killed General Micah Jenkins.

A lull developed in the fighting as Longstreet's men were left without direction and leadership, allowing the Union to halt its retreat and reorganize behind the log breastworks.

David and his regiment waited and waited until about 4:00 p.m., when heavy firing broke out to their right. Later, a green New Jersey regiment allowed the Rebs to break through on the right and hit the rear of the brigade, forcing Company A from their breastworks.

The enemy then advanced on their front, and the brigade faced about and repulsed the attack, allowing the company to straighten out its line and retake the breastworks. Periodic firing continued throughout the evening, with David and his comrades popping away. About midnight the word was whispered down the line, "Slip out of your rifle pits without making a sound. Pickets, hold your positions until the whole column has passed."

This procedure was carried out by three o'clock, and it was determined that the regiment had sustained eight wounded and one man was taken prisoner.

The regiment was on the move along the Brock Road on Saturday morning before the sun rose, and it stopped for a short rest just as the sun came up. One of the veterans grumbled, "We're probably going to do exactly what Burnside and Hooker had us do after a fight like the one we encountered the last two days, head back north, while admitting to an ignominious retreat."

Oliver Zell added, "It just doesn't seem right to lose that many good men and then retreat. It's like we bled and died for nothing."

David made an interesting observation as they came to a fork in the road. "Men, look where the sun is located. If we were headed north, the sun would be on our right shoulders, but it's on our left. We're marching south, not north."

Immediately the mood of the marching column was transformed. Instead of slogging along in a gloomy manner, the men began to banter and chatter among themselves; some units began to sing, 'Ain't I glad to get out of the Wilderness.' They were leaving the Wilderness behind and plodding south towards Richmond.

Throughout the day the regiment repulsed several attacks, but by midnight they had arrived near Chancellorsville completely worn out and sleepy.

CHAPTER 71
SPOTSYLVANIA

Lee had been surprised by Grant's decision to send Meade's army south past his own right side to an area located between his army and Richmond, towards the small crossroads town of Spotsylvania Courthouse, just twelve miles from where the previous battle had ensued.

General Richard H. Anderson replaced the wounded Longstreet and preempted Lee's orders by racing to the crossroads four hours before Lee had specified, thus arriving just ahead of General Gouverneur K. Warren's dog-tired Yankees.

On Sunday, a hot engagement broke out near the crossroads, and the Iron Brigade was outflanked. David's brigade received the order, "Quick march, men, we need to support the Iron Brigade by forming the second line of battle." The front line held, but the enemy shelled the woods behind them, while harassing the front line with constant musket fire.

Then, at 6:00 p.m. came the dreaded order, "Men, pile up your knapsacks, we're going to charge the enemy's works. The left of the line will lead the way, and we will follow if necessary."

David and his comrades looked at each other; in everyone's eyes you could read, "Please, let the left take the works and save us from charging. Please, don't make it necessary for us to charge."

David's silent pleas were answered when the left flank was successful in carrying the front, and the charge of David's brigade was not needed. At eight o'clock the order was made, "Men, stack your arms and fall out for the night for a much deserved rest."

Lee began to entrench his army and foiled Grant's plan to position his army between Richmond and the Army of Northern Virginia. The Confederate lines resembled an enormous inverted V, with the tangents running generally southwesterly and almost due south from the apex. The two lines did not intersect but formed a stopgap center over a mile long and a half-mile wide, which bulged out towards the north, thus earning the name "Mule Shoe." When the sun rose on Monday, May 9, it was hot already, and General John Robinson's men were given the task of driving the Rebels from a wooded knoll where they were working feverishly to construct a low breastwork. The woods were not as dense as those back at the Wilderness, but repeated Rebel volleys devastated Robinson's exhausted men.

David's company, as part of General Sedgwick's corps, was pushed along the Brock Road to enforce Warren's corps. They soon were involved in a confused fight that began as a small scrap for possession of a small wooded ridge, but spread into the valley and onto ridges on both sides. Most of the woods were tall oaks and pines with little underbrush, unlike the terrain at the Wilderness.

Company A was moved off to the left on higher ground in support of the Second Division. Private William Farris yelled, "Hey, isn't that General Sedgwick's aide following the ambulance that is coming this way?"

"Yes, it is," answered David. "That doesn't look good; let's hope he's only wounded."

Doctor Wilson had also noticed the ambulance, and quickly rode down the road to inquire if he could be of any assistance. The doctor was gone less than an hour when he returned with a solemn expression on his face.

"I'm sorry, men, but the general is gone. It appears that the general was inspecting some artillery emplacements and was giving the battery commander some directions while some Reb sharpshooters were pinging shots towards the gunners. The gunners were ducking to avoid the shots and the general allegedly joked, 'Those Reb sharpshooters are so far away they couldn't hit an elephant at this distance.'

"About a minute later, there was another shot, and a sharp, painful cry erupted from the gun pit. Someone screamed, 'The general's been hit!' The headquarters personnel ran over to the pit, and the general was lying on the ground with a bullet hole under the left eye.

"They loaded him on the ambulance which passed by our position on the way to army headquarters. At the headquarters, the general was wrapped in a flag and placed in an evergreen bower."

The men appeared stunned by the news of the death of the corps commander, and for several minutes, no one spoke a word. Finally, the comments began to flow. "He certainly was a good leader." "The corps will never be the same without him to lead us." "Old Pap really knew how to motivate us." "I wonder who will replace him." "Grant will give us a good leader; we're a good outfit."

The melancholy mood was broken by a command from the captain, "Pack up, men. We've moving off to the left about a half-mile from here. Once we get there we're to dig rifle pits and prepare to hold the woods."

Skirmishing erupted throughout the day, and then about 6:00 p.m., the Rebs made a charge that carried into the pine timber defended by Company A, which they repulsed after sustaining several casualties. The company spent the night in the pits, hoping they would be able to catch some sleep.

Much to the relief of the men, the word spread that General Horatio G. Wright would assume command of the Sixth Corps. Wright had graduated from West Point in 1841, ranking second in a class of fifty-two. He had joined the VI Corps in May 1863 as commander of the First Division, and would now be promoted to major general to replace the fallen John Sedgwick.

Unbeknownst to David and his company mates, a new method of attack had been formulated by Colonel Emory Upton, a Regular Army officer, who had become the colonel of the 121st New York in the Sixth Corps. Upton was given command of twelve regiments of the Sixth Corps, of which David's regiment was included.

Tuesday, May 10 began like many other days, with artillery and musketry firing commencing at 8:00 a.m. and continued throughout the day. At 4:00 p.m., the order was given to the men to pile their knapsacks and move out through the heavy timber in front of them to within 100 to 125 yards of the Rebels' breastworks at the border of the heavy timber.

Colonel Upton spoke to the men reassuringly. "Men, our formation is three regiments front and four regiments deep, with our four lines of battle located at intervals of four feet. Now listen carefully. Every man is to have his musket loaded and his bayonet fixed, but only the men in the three leading regiments are to cap their weapons.

"The reason for this is that with your musket uncapped, you cannot fire while charging. Therefore, you will have a loaded gun when you reach the trench, and you will be able to cap it quickly and fire. The first three regiments will fan out to the right and the left and drive the defenders off down the line, until they reach the trench. Meanwhile, the second wave will swarm in behind the first wave and open fire on any reinforcements that might come up from the Rebels' second line.

"You men in the remaining two lines will lie down just short of the trench and will be utilized in any manner that you are needed. I think every man knows his duty, but just in case, are there any questions?" No questions were forthcoming. Colonel Upton gave one last order, "Now, men, just lie low for a few moments while the officers and I take a final look at the approaches. See you in the trenches."

David and the men did as ordered and lay down in the woods until the officers returned. Some of the men spoke in low whispers, but they all knew what was expected of them. Soon the order was whispered down the line, "Cap your muskets and fix your bayonets." Then a loud bellow sounded, "Forward, charge!"

Every man in all twelve regiments sprang to his feet and ran as a solid column through the abates and into the trench screaming at the top of his lungs. Frantic, reckless, hand-to-hand fighting broke out on the parapet, as the Rebels refused to budge and the Yankees would not be repulsed. There was no time to reload once a weapon was fired, so the men had to resort to stabbing with bayonets, or clubbing with gun butts, fists, and rocks.

Upton's strategy worked to perfection as the leading regiments swept down the line to the right or left, and the second wave seized the second trench. The Rebel line had been broken where it was supposed to be the strongest.

David observed Corporal Riden hitting a big Rebel with his fist. Lieutenant Howell was overwhelmed by three Rebs before he cut one over the head with his trusty cavalry saber. The lieutenant knocked the second rebel aside with his left hand and was saved by Miles Wakefield, as Wakefield bayoneted the third rebel just as the Rebel's bayonet was about to enter the lieutenant's stomach.

Lieutenant G. E. Hackenberg of Company I did the honors of grabbing a stand of Rebel colors from a big Rebel, and he quickly tore the colors from its staff and stuffed them inside his shirt. Bob Davison captured a piece of artillery to gain further glory for the company.

Once the regiment entered the second trench, disaster was avoided by Sergeant Sam Steiner's quick reaction. Steiner overheard a Rebel officer ordering his men to pick up the guns left behind on the field by the dead and wounded and fire on the company from the rear. Steiner's lightning-fast reaction placed a ball into the Rebel's back and dropped him dead. The rest of the Rebels abandoned the idea of picking up the guns after that.

Some of the men reached the third line of works, and made a dash for three pieces of artillery, one of which they fired into the enemy's lines. Suddenly, the Rebels regained the guns, and began to bring up reinforcements. The plan was for the twelve regiments to hold on to the emplacements until Mott's division from the II Corps advanced to reinforce them. This never materialized, and Upton's twelve regiments were left out on a limb.

The survivors of the twelve regiments left the Rebel works and formed in the direction over the ground they had just charged. They fought back into the heavy timber, then fell back to where they had dropped their knapsacks, and spent the night in that area.

CHAPTER 72
DAVID IS WOUNDED

Just as David and his confused squad entered the woods, several artillery shots detonated over their heads and into the ground around them. The men never knew what hit them. Some screamed in terror and pain as they were struck by shrapnel, flying debris, or tree limbs.

David felt an incredible wallop to the right side of his head and body. For an instant the woods spun out of control, while he observed a kaleidoscope of colors and bright lights gyrating in front of his eyes. He fell face down, and lapsed into unconsciousness.

When David became cognizant, it was dark and a heavy rain was falling, adding to his bewilderment. He had no clue as to where he was or what he was doing in a rainstorm in the middle of the night. He slowly used his fingers to ascertain whether he had any injuries, and to what extent they might be.

To his immediate relief, he found no wounds on his torso or extremities. But he did discover a gaping laceration on the right side of his skull. The battered right side of his head was drenched in blood, indicating that the gash must have spurted or gushed at impact, but now it was just oozing. He attempted to rise to his knees but immediately felt nauseous and collapsed again into a comatose state.

Sometime later David regained consciousness, and immediately his fingers sought out the wound that continued to seep blood. He hurriedly searched through his pockets until he discovered a dressing. He located his battered canteen and poured the precious liquid onto the dressing and deftly cleansed the wound before covering it with a clean bandage. Finally, he tore a piece of material from his shredded shirt, and tied it tightly around his head to hold the dressing in place, hoping this would stem the blood.

For a while, he was disoriented, almost in a stupor, but that finally passed. As his mind began to clear, he became mindful that all around him men lay moaning, groaning, and crying out for help, food, and water. He was shivering with cold and felt clammy. He so much wanted to help his wounded comrades, but he was not well enough himself to render aid to them.

Flashes from artillery and muskets lighted the woods, allowing him to locate a ravine about one hundred yards to his right, where he might find protection if he could only maneuver himself in that direction. As his head cleared and his vision improved, he recognized several men leaning with their backs against the trunks of trees.

David called out, "How badly are you hit?" Some didn't respond; others stated that they were hit bad and wouldn't survive, but five or six felt that their wounds weren't fatal. Fighting an acid taste in his mouth, along with a violent headache, he appealed to those with nonfatal wounds, "Come on, let's drag ourselves into the safety of the ravine. Perhaps it's callous not to aid the others, but let's relocate before the sun rises and see how we fare."

The rain continued to fall, and David and the others could hear water surging in the ravine. Seven men dragged themselves over the lip of the ravine and down into the wooded gully. In the murky light, David detected a small grove of scrubby pines that would offer some relief from the steady rain and might shield them from enemy eyes.

There was no fear of the woods and underbrush catching fire due to the downpour, so the men tugged additional pine bows into the grove of pines with the idea of hiding under them during daylight hours. The pines protected them from the drenching rains, but their comrades who were still at the mercy of the elements in the woods or on the approaches to the rebel breastworks presented a heart-rending spectacle. Many of them would certainly die from exposure.

The seven men checked their food supply and saw that all they had was enough hardtack to see them through the coming day. But since it was May, and they were in a wooded ravine where there should be wild plants and roots, food should not be a problem.

Once David regained his stability and was able to move about, he began looking around for edible plants.

The men slept sporadically throughout the day, as firing continued in the woods to their left, and a little farther to the south. They attempted to attend to each other's wounds, hoping to ward off gangrene or other infections. They also inventoried their weapons: they had five muskets, three bayonets, and one pistol in their arsenal.

Three of the men could walk without any impairment, and once David's head cleared, he was able to move about also. Therefore, it was decided that when night arrived this foursome would sneak back into the tall woods area to search for more food and also to recover weaponry from the dead soldiers lying on the ground.

No sooner had the men left their concealed location than they heard whispered voices with a deep southern drawl, and the movement of several dozen men. The four Yankees scrambled back to the hiding place, returning in the nick of time. To make things even worse for the seven, the Rebel patrol was only about fifty yards to their left between the woods and the gully.

The men attempted to sleep during the night, but all of them suffered deep anxiety and throbbing pain. By daybreak, the enemy patrol had moved on, but it was too late to retrieve any food or weapons. The rain had let up during the night, but early in the morning, it started up again in torrents.

David decided to look for edible wild plants near the source of the stream. It was considered too dangerous to return to the woods where the wounded and dead were located; besides, the odor was horrific. David's plan was a huge gamble, because he could stumble into a Rebel patrol at any moment. But he determined it was worth the risk. He hoped his thumping headache would not impair his judgment, and he would be able to return with some foodstuffs.

The rain intensified and several claps of thunder joined the occasional artillery barrages; this aided David because it muffled the sound of his movements. Shortly after he left their haven, David suffered an attack of vertigo. He rested for about fifteen minutes and then continued his quest. He was searching for an area that even in drier periods would sustain ferns and other edible plants that appear in May.

He found a spot where the stream split and created a small island that was conducive to the growth of ferns. Luck was with David, for he quickly was able to harvest an armload of arrowhead roots, wild cucumbers, dandelion, and fiddleheads, along with some early June berries.

When he dumped his larder on the ground in front of the others, David simply instructed, "Don't smell them, don't look at them, just eat them. They're actually good for you." He suddenly felt nauseous, and he emptied the meager contents of his stomach; then the vertigo returned and he fell forward and lost consciousness.

The seven men were almost discovered later that afternoon, but fortunately the Rebel skirmishers moved off to the left as the previous group had done. Private Albert Logan from New York announced as he displayed his pistol, "I was going to take five of those Rebs out of action."

George Auker asked him, "Why only five? The gun holds six bullets."

"The sixth one was for me. There's no way they were going to take me prisoner and I'd end up in Libby Prison or Andersonville."

George agreed. "You've got something there, and I don't want to be taken either."

That night, five other Union soldiers were observed moving into the ravine whose stream had now overflowed its banks and spread over a wider segment of the gully. George Auker whistled to the men and then yelled, "Hey, Yanks, we're from the 49th Pennsylvania. What outfit are you from?"

"We're from Russell's First Division. Can we come on in?"

"Sure enough, just don't make too much noise."

The new men were carrying some hardtack, which they shared with the others, but they realized that if they hoped to survive another day or two, they all would have to rely upon David's skill in identifying edible wild plants.

Some of the men began to grow weaker, and finally on Friday,

May 13, four of the lesser wounded decided to move down the ravine to see if they could contact their own forces. Luck was with them as they stumbled into the picket lines of Wheaton's brigade of the Second Division.

Additional men with litters were sent back up the ravine to remove the wounded and carry them to the hospital located in the rear. All the men who endured those anxious four days in the ravine attributed their survival to Private David Evans of Company A.

David remained in the hospital until Monday, May 16, and then returned to the breastworks, where Company A maintained its vigil against enemy infiltration through the morass of mud and slime as the torrential rains continued to fall. David's company mates were elated to see him, and even more impressed when they learned of his heroism in the chaotic aftermath of Upton's charge.

Some observers concluded that the only battle that could compare with Upton's charge by those twelve regiments on May 10, 1864, was Pickett's charge at Gettysburg on July 3, 1863.

The 49th Regiment had more than half of its men killed and wounded. Colonel Thomas Hulings and Lieutenant Colonel John B. Miles were killed, while fifteen line officers and 230 enlisted men were killed and wounded. General Wright was incensed over Mott's failure to support his Sixth Corps, and he informed General Meade, "General, I don't want Mott's troops on my left; they are not a support; I would rather have no troops there."

To make matters worse, the federals wounded from this charge were left on the field of battle for eleven days without having their wounds treated. The wounded had only three days' rations to eat and no water except what they could gather when it rained.

Upton's initial success impressed Grant, who decided to employ the strategy on a grander scale with a massive assault on the apex of the salient or Mule Shoe. Wednesday, May 11, passed without any major incident, with some heavy skirmishing and some artillery firing. During David's absence, his company constructed a rifle pit to the left of the previous day's battlefield. Again, the weather was warm, with rain falling in the afternoon and into the evening.

During this same day, another devastating blow was delivered to Lee's officers corps. In an encounter between Phil Sheridan's 10,000-man cavalry and Jeb Stuart's 4,500 troopers at Yellow Tavern, Stuart was shot in the abdomen and died the following day in Richmond.

On Thursday, May 12, Hancock's corps was to go into action at daybreak about three quarters of a mile north of the salient. Burnside's corps was on the left and Wright's corps on the right. Hancock's men smashed into the Confederate lines led by General Ewell and successfully captured three or four thousand Confederate infantrymen. Wright's corps moved in at 6:00 a.m., and Burnsides later; the firing lines were just a few yards apart. Neither of these two corps had much success. The Second corps penetrated the Mule Shoe, wherein the thrust lost its momentum and became disorganized and confused.

Hancock's men became engaged in a titanic struggle on the northwest face of the salient with Rodes's division and part of Early's corps, which lasted from 10:00 a.m. on May 12 until 4:00 a.m. on May 13. The rains continued as devastating hand-to-hand combat occurred in the cramped quarters of the northwest section, later called the "Bloody Angle."

Most consider this struggle in the Bloody Angle the fiercest and deadliest struggle of the war. The attack of May 12 was the bloodiest single day in the war; nearly 12,000 men fell in the battle for one square mile of ground.

Torrential downpours turned the terrain into a sea of mud and prevented much combat until May 18, although Grant attempted to flank the enemy without success. On the eighteenth, Grant again utilized the frontal attack strategy as he sent Hancock's depleted corps against Lee's new line at the base of the salient. This frontal attack caused immense casualties for both armies, and finally Grant gave up against a strongly entrenched enemy.

The final day of this engagement saw Lee taking the offensive by sending Ewell's crippled corps out of their positions and around Grant's right. Ewell was forced back in confusion by some heavy artillerists called up from some Washington forts.

Both armies suffered severely at Spotsylvania, but Grant's tactics of hanging on and battering Lee relentlessly had transformed the struggle into a war of attrition, designed to wear down Lee. Grant once again maneuvered his army south towards Richmond. Every day witnessed a skirmish or minor battle, with Grant attempting to get around Lee's army. Grant, while under duress from Lee, crossed the North Anna River, Pamunkey River, and Totopotomoy River.

As the Army of the Potomac advanced, the movements of the regiments and brigades were too continuous and complicated to prevent them from intermingling. The army moved in a series of zigzags in order to ford the rivers. In some cases, the roads became overcrowded and the troops piled up.

During one of the pile-ups, Company A fell out by the side of the road to eat a noontime meal. A detachment of cavalry trotted along the road, stirring up huge clouds of dust. The contingent's young captain inquired of David, "What regiment are you men?"

David jumped to his feet and saluted smartly, "We're A Company of the 49th Pennsylvania, sir."

The cavalry unit's commanding officer, a colonel, overheard the answer and pulled his horse to a halt beside the captain's horse. David quickly saluted the colonel, who scrutinized David closely.

"Company A of the 49th? That's made up of boys from the Tuscarora Valley of Juniata County, isn't it?

"Yes, sir. I'm David Evans from Academia."

"Academia? That certainly brings back many fond memories. I attended the Tuscarora Academy in that quaint little village back in the late forties. I remember I wanted to leave school and fight in the war against Mexico, but my parents wouldn't hear of it."

"That's ironic, sir, because I wanted to join the army when the war broke out, but my parents insisted I finish school first. I just finished my studies at the academy last September and mustered in at the beginning of October."

"Well, son, keep your head down and stay safe. Maybe when this horrible mess is over you and I can sit down and compare notes about school and the war."

"Yes, sir, I would like to do that. It would be an honor. My father attended the academy also. Maybe you remember George Evans."

"That I do. Tell him that John P. Taylor of Reedsville sends his regards."

With that, Colonel John P. Taylor, soon to be Brigadier General Taylor of the First Pennsylvania Cavalry, wheeled his horse and spurred it down the road, with his officer corps in close pursuit, leaving David and his comrades choking in his dust.

CHAPTER 73
SIGEL'S FAILURE IN THE SHENANDOAH

While Grant led the Army of the Potomac across the Rapidan River on May 4, the other phases of Grant's strategy—Ben Butler's Army of the James and Franz Sigel's Shenandoah Valley forces—moved into action. Butler was unsuccessful in his campaign and became bottled up on the Bermuda Hundred peninsula. However, even worse, Major General Sigel met disaster in the Shenandoah Valley.

Grant ordered Major General Franz Sigel (who had graduated from Karlsruhe Academy in 1843 before he immigrated to the United States in 1852) to cooperate with the Army of the Potomac in pressuring Richmond. Sigel advanced up the Shenandoah Valley with 6,500 infantry and cavalry and instructions to disrupt Confederate communications, destroy the railroad at Staunton, demolish the major rail complex at Lynchburg, and then move on to Charlottesville. In addition, he was to destroy the granary of the valley and control the Valley Pike.

Sigel's advance was delayed by the Confederate cavalry under the command of General John Imboden. On May 15, while Lee and Grant were engaged in desperate combat at Spotsylvania Courthouse, Sigel made contact with Imboden and forces under the former vice-president of the United States, General John C. Breckinridge, at New Market.

Among the southern forces were 247 cadets from the Virginia Military Institute at Lexington, eighty miles south of New Market. The corps of cadets had quickly marched north to defend their valley against the advancing Union army.

Breckinridge attacked early in the morning, and skirmishing and actions continued until the Confederates launched an all-out assault at about 2:00 p.m. When the assault stalled, the VMI cadets, who were organized into a battalion of four companies of infantry and one section of artillery, were ordered into the fray. About 3:00 p.m., Sigel directed a confused counterattack, which was soon repulsed, with the cadets capturing a gun and many men of the 34th Massachusetts.

By late afternoon, Sigel began to rapidly retreat down the Valley Pike during a heavy rain. He left his badly wounded at Mt. Jackson, and arrived in Strasburg on May 16. Union losses were set at 831 men, while the Confederates' losses were 577, including 10 dead and 45 wounded cadets from VMI. The youngest of the participating cadets was fifteen years of age and the oldest, twenty-five.

Four days later, General Sigel was relieved of his command and replaced by Major General David Hunter, an intimate friend of Secretary of War Stanton. General Hunter renewed the Union offensive on May 26 with a force of 8,500 men.

Lee had Breckinridge rejoin Lee's Army of Northern Virginia, leaving only General W. E. "Grumble" Jones's and General Imboden's cavalry to oppose Hunter. Hunter quickly marched up the valley, captured Staunton, and prepared to cross the Blue Ridge.

On June 12, General Jubal Early was summoned to Lee's headquarters. Lee informed Early that he was to take his Second Corps on an independent mission in which he was to quickly move to the defense of Lynchburg, defeat Hunter in the Shenandoah Valley, then move down the Shenandoah, cross the Potomac, and threaten Washington.

All this activity in the Shenandoah Valley would eventually affect Private David Evans, the 49th Regiment of Pennsylvania Volunteers, and General Wright's VI Corps, but for the moment, the Sixth Corps was deployed near Cold Harbor on the outskirts of Richmond.

CHAPTER 74

COLD HARBOR AND THE MOVE TO PETERSBURG

By June 1, the two weary armies in eastern Virginia began a race for another barren, dusty crossroads known as Cold Harbor, which was located about a mile from the Chickahominy River and six miles northeast of Richmond. Lee dug in when he arrived at Cold Harbor, while Sheridan took two mounted divisions into a line of battle. Sheridan told Wright to take his VI Corps to the right end of the Yankee Line as fast as possible.

Wright's VI Corps raised a choking dust as it raced to the aid of Sheridan, and arrived completely worn out in mid-morning of June 1. General Baldy Smith transported his 16,000 men from south of the James River and filed into line to the right of Wright's Corps. A furious firefight erupted among the fields and plots of woodland along the road to Richmond where the Rebels were waiting, and by the time darkness fell, the Confederates had been driven out of Cold Harbor.

A massive federal attack was set for dawn the next day, but Hancock's II Corps had only just arrived at Cold Harbor at 7:00 a.m. Therefore, the attack was postponed until 4:00 p.m. By the assigned time, the Union army was still not prepared to attack, and the attack was postponed again until 4:30 a.m., June 3.

Lee had enough time to design an elaborate and cunning line of breastworks. He combined every swamp, stream, ravine, hill, and plot of trees and brambles, into a zigzag configuration which utilized effective crossfires. Just before dawn, the rain ended and heat became a factor.

There was little room to maneuver, and what had been planned as a massed assault broke into a conglomeration of assaults with no one line of battle. Each unit was isolated from the others, and charging into an incredibly strong defensive line. Hancock's two attacking divisions became separated, and when the support division moved forward, they were broken and driven back.

Wright's Corps, including David's 49th Regiment, advanced into a semicircle of enemy trenches, which benefited from dense thickets, swamps, and impassable briar patches. Within ten minutes, the men began to dig for shelter, as they faced firing from three sides at once. Some of the men never saw their enemy through the smoke and dust.

It took Lee's men less than a quarter of an hour to break the assault and devastate the attacking Union forces. Although the attack was over rather quickly, the fighting continued, as many of the attackers did not retreat, but stayed where they were halted. In desperation they dug shallow trenches or pits and continued to fire. Orders came from the rear for the men to charge, but there was no way they could stand up and charge.

When night arrived, the digging continued utilizing cups and bayonets, as men on both sides dug their trenches deep and strong. They used logs to solidify their breastworks and constructed zigzag alleyways to connect trenches that would enable them to move to the rear for supplies and ammunition. Grant finally called off the disastrous nine-hour attack, with estimates of Union casualties between 3,000 and 7,000 and the Confederates about 1,500.

Too stunned, exhausted, and paralyzed to move forward, the two armies stayed in position, producing a stalemate, though the shooting continued. In some places the opposing armies were only yards apart. Most faced relentless terror, with sharpshooters firing whenever a head appeared above the trench. The Union artillery bombarded the lines with mortars, while the Confederates responded with howitzers arching their death and destruction.

There were some moments of civility. Pickets met between the lines and traded items and exchanged news. At one point, the 118th Pennsylvania and the 35th North Carolina faced each other across the Chickahominy River. The two opposing units whiled a day away sitting on opposite banks of the narrow river, swapping stories, trading items, and fishing. These were not normal events, but nevertheless, they showed that the combatants had not lost their humanity entirely.

The men in the trenches endured unbearable conditions, but those who fell between the two lines suffered tremendously without medical attention, food, and water. It took until June 7 for a truce to be arranged so that unarmed stretcher-bearers could remove the dead and wounded from the battlefield. By then it was too late; only two of the Union wounded remained alive, the rest were bloated corpses.

Many of the Northern newspapers criticized Grant for his poor decisions at Cold Harbor and called him "Butcher Grant" or the "Fumbling Butcher." The losses caused a rise in antiwar sentiment during the crucial summer prior to the presidential election in November and lowered morale among the troops.

Shortly after the failed June 3 assault, Grant put in motion his next maneuver by sending Sheridan's cavalry to destroy the Virginia Central Railroad near Charlottesville, a move that was to coincide with General David Hunter's progress in the Shenandoah Valley. Grant was hoping these operations would force Lee to send reinforcements to the Shenandoah Valley and to oppose Sheridan's movements.

To augment Grant's skillful sideslip to the left with a risky flanking march, Meade's engineers built an inner line behind the frontlines at Cold Harbor. This was in preparation for a stealthy operation to withdraw the Union troops from in front of Lee's entrenched troops and across the James River. A large number of pontoons, as well as warships, transports, and barges were moved up the James River to move 100,000 Union troops across the half-mile-wide and fifteen-fathoms-deep James.

Late in the afternoon of June 12, the Union army began a march of fifty miles that would take them directly away from Lee's army towards Petersburg. When the sun rose the next morning, the Union army was gone from Cold Harbor, including David Evans whose regiment had been deployed to protect the withdrawal of the rest of the army.

Grant's objective was Petersburg, a vital transportation junction, where five railroads, two planked roads, and countless thoroughfares intersected to transform the city into an essential supply base. Lee miscalculated, believing that Grant was headed for Richmond instead of Petersburg and left General Pierre G. T. Beauregard, the commander of the city of 18,000, with only 2,500 to 3,000 Confederate troops to defend it, most of whom were reservists and home guards.

A ten-mile stretch of trenches, studded at intervals with fifty-five redoubts, protected the city of Petersburg. The trenches were connected by unwieldy breastworks that were twenty feet thick at the base and at least six feet high. These breastworks were protected by thick lines of abates and *chevaux-de-frise* that were interlaced with deep rifle pits. This deadly looking stronghold was known as the "Dimmock Line." Its only weakness was that there weren't enough soldiers to defend the city, with an average of only one man per four and a half yards.

Major General William F. "Baldy" Smith and his XVIII Corps of the Army of the James was chosen to lead the advance on Petersburg. To compensate for Smith's losses at Cold Harbor and bring him up to strength, a raw division of black troops under Brigadier General Edward W. Hinks was allotted to him.

Smith's advance elements arrived at Petersburg at 7:00 a.m. on June 15, but due to miscommunications the attack was delayed until late in the day. The Union army quickly broke through and overran the Dimmock Line. Smith ordered a halt rather than continuing his advance into the city and allowed the enemy to reorganize.

In the meantime, reinforcements for both armies arrived on the scene, with Union forces growing to 38,000 and the Confederates to 10,000 by nightfall. Fighting continued the next day, and once again the federal forces were successful in capturing another section of the enemy's line. On June 17, the Union army gained more ground, but Beauregard stripped the defenses at Bermuda Hundred, while Lee rushed reinforcements from the Army of Northern Virginia.

On the morning of June 18, the whole Union army charged with fixed bayonets, had initial success, and then to Meade's consternation, halted. In the meantime, Lee's veterans from the Army of Northern Virginia poured into the line, so when the attack was renewed late in the afternoon, it was repulsed.

Grant then settled down for a long siege, just as he had done at Vicksburg a year earlier. A five-mile-long line parallel to Lee's line was dug, with ditches, abatix, trenches, and forts to strengthen it. The great opportunity to capture Petersburg easily was bungled and a drawn-out siege materialized.

CHAPTER 75
EARLY'S MOVE NORTH

Lieutenant General Jubal Early had been given command of the Second Corps of the Army of Northern Virginia on June 12, 1864. At 2:00 a.m. the next morning, the Second Corps began its march towards Lynchburg, Virginia, to confront General Hunter and eventually relieve pressure off the Confederates at Petersburg.

On June 11, Hunter had burned the buildings of Virginia Military Institute in Stanton in retaliation for the role of the corps of cadets at New Market in defeating Sigel's army on May 15. He also had his men incinerate the residence of Governor Letcher and the homes of many other prominent citizens. Washington College was spared the torch, although it was plundered and the statute of George Washington was removed.

General Hunter was to proceed from Stanton to Charlottesville, where his forces were to join with Sheridan to destroy the railroad and canal between Charlottesville and Gordonville.

Early's and Hunter's forces met at Lynchburg on June 17 and 18, with Hunter absorbing a defeat and deciding to run for the safety of West Virginia. Hunter's exhausted troops arrived at Charleston, West Virginia, on July 29, well out of Early's way.

With the clearing of the valley of federal troops, Early's first objective was achieved, although the Confederates were more than irate as they viewed the level of destruction inflicted upon the residents of the upper Shenandoah. This would motivate the Confederate forces to retaliate later.

Early was facing a daunting task in attempting to undertake the second phase of his mission, that is, to put pressure on the federal capital. From Buchanan to the crossing of the Potomac River was a journey of two hundred miles. Once Early's forces crossed the Potomac, they would be operating in enemy territory with no hope of reinforcement or relief from Lee.

Staunton was reached on June 26, and after a short rest, Imboden's cavalry was sent ahead to destroy bridges on the B & O Railroad, with the main body moving north to Winchester by July 2. Sigel retired from Martinsburg on the third, and the federals withdrew from Harpers Ferry the next day. Next, Confederate forces occupied Shepherdstown and the fords over the Potomac River.

It wasn't until July 5 that General Grant received reliable intelligence that Early's army was closing in on Washington. Washington's defenses were considered extremely strong, but without enough men to man them. Major General Lew Wallace scrambled together a contingent of assorted troops along with General Ricketts's division of the VI Corps from Petersburg to halt Early's advance at Monocracy forty miles northwest of the capital.

During the Confederate advance of early morning July 9, the Rebels levied a ransom on the city of Frederick, Maryland, of $200,000 to be paid in gold or medical supplies. If not paid, the city would be put to the torch. The good citizens of the city met the demands and the city was saved. The Confederates attacked the troops under General Wallace, and after providing stiff resistance, the makeshift Union forces were defeated.

Early continued onward and by the morning of July 11, the exhausted Rebels reached the outskirts of Washington near Silver Spring. Every available federal man was sent into the fortifications: home guards, convalescent troops, clerks, anyone who could fire a gun. Wallace's defeat had bought time, because Grant had sent orders to Wright to load his corps on fast steamers that would carry them from the trenches of Petersburg to save the capital.

David Evans and the rest of Company A and all of the Sixth Corps were relieved on July 11 when they were given the order to pack and march to the wharfs along the James River for embarkation down the river to Norfolk. Then they would be transported up the Chesapeake Bay and into the Potomac River. It was a rough overnight voyage, and many of the veterans fought a losing battle with seasickness.

The hard-boiled cadre of veterans of the Sixth Corps, wearing their caps with the Greek Cross, were unloaded at the Seventh Street wharfs in Washington, D.C. By mid-afternoon they reached Fort Stevens, just in the nick of time. President and Mrs. Lincoln were visiting the fort against the advice of his military advisors. When General Wright arrived in the fort, he greeted his commander-in-chief, and without imagining his invitation would be taken seriously, he inquired, "Would the president desire to stand on the parapet and watch the battle?"

President Lincoln immediately accepted the suggestion and clambered up to get a good view of the action. As the president peered over the parapet, a young officer by the name of Oliver Wendell Holmes, not recognizing his commander-in-chief, shouted, "Get down, you damn fool!"

Bullets were flickering all around the president, and General Wright begged him to get down. Wright positioned his body to act as a shield for the president and finally threatened to have a squad of soldiers to remove him. Lincoln then realized the folly of his position and stepped down from the parapet.

After a brief fight, Early decided to withdraw to a location outside the lines of the fortifications and during the night of July 12-13 began a general withdrawal towards the Shenandoah Valley. His brief encounter on the outskirts of the capital had accomplished the objective of forcing Grant to send the Sixth Corps as reinforcements to defend the beleaguered city, thereby lessening the number of troops facing Lee.

As Early began his timely withdrawal, it was the task of Wright's Corps to shadow the retreating enemy. David and his fellow soldiers endured a dreadful first day and night of march because the weather was hot and the roads were dusty and congested with stragglers and discarded equipment and wagons.

The uncomfortable marching conditions continued for the next two weeks as the Sixth doggedly pursued Early. They trailed the enemy across the Potomac, through Leesburg and Snickers Gap to the banks of the Shenandoah River, finally arriving at Berrysville. General Grant determined that the threat to the capital had passed and sent orders for the Sixth to turn about and return to the trenches at Petersburg.

The infantrymen grumbled and growled as they did an about-face and headed back in the direction they had just marched, once again coping with the same forced march conditions that they had endured tailing Early into the lower Shenandoah Valley.

Just as the Sixth arrived in the vicinity of the Seventh Street wharfs to load upon the steamers again, Wright had his orders countermanded. He was to return to the Shenandoah Valley via Harpers Ferry. Early was at it again: he had sent his cavalry back across the Potomac and into Pennsylvania.

On July 28, General John McCausland received orders from General Early to cross the Potomac and proceed to the city of Chambersburg, the seat of government of Franklin County in the Cumberland Valley of Pennsylvania. On the morning of July 31, McCausland captured the city and delivered to the city's authorities a proclamation from General Early that called for the citizens of the city to furnish the Confederates with $100,000 in gold or $500,000 in greenbacks. If the demands were not met, the city was to be destroyed.

Early proclaimed that he was adopting his course of action in retaliation for the destruction of property in Virginia ordered by General Hunter, especially the homes of Andrew Hunter, A. R. Hoteler, E. J. Lee, Governor Letcher, J. T. Anderson, the Virginia Military Institute, and others. The money that was being demanded was compensation for the loss of these properties in Virginia.

McCausland met with citizens of the community, and after the grace period of six hours went by without the demand being met, the firing of the most central blocks began after the inhabitants had been removed, and the town was destroyed. About noon the troops re-formed on the high ground overlooking the town, and then re-crossed the Potomac River.

CHAPTER 76
THE HORRID BATTLE OF THE CRATER

As of June 25, the 49th's sister regiment, the 48th Pennsylvania, had been involved in a bizarre assignment as part of the siege of Petersburg. The commanding officer of the 48th was Lt. Colonel Henry Pleasants, a mining engineer from Pennsylvania. Pleasants proposed a plan to General Burnside to dig a long mineshaft underneath the enemy's First Corps line in Elliott's Salient and plant enough explosives to open a huge hole in the enemy's defenses.

Burnside gave his approval to the extraordinary scheme, and the digging of the T-shaped mineshaft commenced on June 25. The approach shaft was 511 feet in length and more than 50 feet below the Confederate battery in order to avoid detection.

Eight thousand pounds of explosives were packed into the shaft, which was then closed with eleven feet of earth. At 4:44 a.m. on the morning of July 30, the charges exploded in an incredible cascade of men, animals, guns, equipment, and earth.

When the news of the disaster at the Crater reached the 49th Regiment late in the first week of August, they were appalled at the large number of losses in just one more debacle involving Grant's overland campaign.

Sergeant Billlings of C Company had just returned to duty and had received what he described as firsthand knowledge of the disaster at the crater. "From what we were told it must have been one of the cruelest missions of the entire siege, maybe the whole war. Meade apparently screwed up the whole scheme by making a major change in plans at the last moment. Originally, Brigadier General Edward Ferrero's division of United States Colored Troops had been trained to lead the assault after the explosion, but Meade ordered Burnside not to use Ferrero's troops out of political considerations.

"Instead, Brigadier General James H. Ledlie's First Division was chosen to lead the assault without being trained or briefed as to what to expect. When the explosion occurred, Ledlie's men moved into the crater that was created, and instead of moving around the huge hole, plunged into it to use it as a huge rifle pit.

"Once the Confederates under Major General William Mahone recovered from the initial shock and slaughter, they lined up around the edge of the crater and began to fire rifles and artillery down into the hole. Our men were trapped and couldn't climb up the sides of the hole. The outcome was described as a 'turkey shoot.'

"To make matters even worse, Burnside then sent Ferrero's troops into the fray, and they also clambered down into the crater. The slaughter that ensued was unbelievable. Some of our troops eventually outflanked the crater, but what land they captured was lost when a new Reb charge drove our forces back."

The men within earshot of Sergeant Billings listened in complete disbelief. Corporal Henry inquired, "Just how bad were our losses?"

"It's been estimated that our losses were about 5,300, while the Rebs lost 1,032."

"Same old story," muttered Bill Reese. "Our losses are always much larger than theirs. Did anything happen to Meade or Burnside for the great wisdom they exhibited?"

Billings answered quickly, "For once a general was held responsible for his poor judgment. Burnside was relieved of his command, but Meade went unscathed; he wasn't even censured for his responsibility in the debacle. Pleasants had no role in the actual battle, although when you think of the plan, it certainly had some merit."

"Just another good example of why this war is taking so long to win. You wonder what kind of strategy these generals are taught as cadets at West Point. I just hope they don't come up with any wild schemes for us."

CHAPTER 77

THE SHENANDOAH VALLEY—FALL 1864

The new orders for the Sixth Corps called for it to return to Harpers Ferry as quickly as possible to meet the new threat from Early. Once again, they were to cross the Potomac and march back up the Shenandoah Valley. The heat and dust were oppressive, and many stragglers lined the course of the march.

The corps had just begun its movement up the valley when new orders arrived, directing them to return quickly to Maryland. The early days of August found David and the Sixth bivouacked on the banks of the Monocacy River not too many miles from Frederick, Maryland.

David remarked to David Bossert, "I was so happy to get out of the situation at Petersburg, but now I wonder if they know what they are doing in Washington. It's no surprise that this war has been going on for over three years; leadership seems to be completely inept."

One of the older veterans, Joseph Rose, interjected, "If you think this is bad, you should have been around when McClellan was in charge. I never saw anything so messed up. Now the Democrats are going to run him for the presidency because they think he can find a way to end the war. There is no way that man can lead us to victory and peace—I'm sticking with Lincoln and Grant."

Many of the others joined in, "Yep, we're better off with Grant; he's going to get the job done and then we can go home. I just wish someone would decide which direction we're going to go. I'm tired of marching over the same old roads and crossing the Potomac."

As the days passed, more stragglers arrived in camp, and for a few days the men spent a pleasant time on the banks of the river. They were joined by General Emory's XIX Corps, which had been conveyed on transports from Louisiana for the defense of Washington against Early, and therefore had seen action against Early's troops.

One of the reasons that the VI and XIX Corps were given time to recover from their aimless marches and countermarches was that Grant was attempting to sort out why the pursuit of Early had been ineffective. He finally decided to place one competent general in command of the whole operation in the Shenandoah Valley. Grant's first choice was Major General William B. Franklin, but Franklin was not appointed because of political reasons.

On August 1, Grant ordered General Phillip Sheridan to travel to Monocacy and take command of the troops in that area. Sheridan was instructed to "put himself south of the enemy and follow him to the death."

After receiving telegraph communications from the president, Grant boarded a fast steamer that docked at Washington, but the general didn't stop in the city. Instead, he took a special train to Monocacy Junction to confer with General Hunter. Grant swiftly removed Hunter from command and ordered the troops to begin to march to Halltown at the lower end of the Shenandoah Valley where Sheridan would join them.

Sheridan reported to Grant on August 6 at Monocacy where they met for about two hours. Grant asserted that it was imperative that Sheridan remove the threat of Early's army from the war and destroy the Shenandoah Valley as an incomparable granary and source of supply for the Army of Northern Virginia.

Grant was explicit about what he desired Sheridan to perform: "eat out Virginia clear and clean as far as they go, so that crows flying over it for the balance of the season will have to carry their provender with them."

To execute these orders Sheridan had an army of nearly 36,000 men. General George Crook commanded the VIII Corps, which were described as "ragged, famished, discouraged, sulky, and half of them in ambulances." General Emory commanded the two divisions of the XIX Corps. Both men were accustomed to victory. The nucleus was General Wright's VI Corps, which many felt was the best fighting corps in the Army of the Potomac, even if it was worn out.

Sheridan's opposition was not only Jubal Early's Second Corps but also a number of guerrilla bands, the most famous of which was led by John S. Mosby, the "Gray Ghost." Early's objectives were to "keep up a threatening attitude toward Maryland and Pennsylvania and prevent the use of the Baltimore and Ohio Railroad and the Chesapeake and Ohio Canal, as well as to keep as large a force as possible from Grant's army to defend the federal capital."

Early was concerned whether the farmers of the valley would have sufficient time to harvest their crops to help feed the southern forces. Therefore, Early needed to employ defensive tactics, as the Confederates were outnumbered by about 2 to 1. The Confederate general withdrew his forces into the Martinsburg area, while Sheridan settled into the vicinity of Harpers Ferry. Sheridan's new federal command eventually became known as the Army of the Shenandoah.

On August 15 the Army of the Shenandoah moved about a third of the way up the valley via Winchester, south of a line from Millwood to Winchester and Petticoat Gap. The Army of the Shenandoah immediately began destroying the valley's wheat and hay, while seizing all the mules, cattle, and horses. Barns, corncribs, gristmills, stacks of hay and straw, and bridges were burned and all crops were destroyed. To many men this was an unpleasant duty, but by August 22, Sheridan's forces had returned to Halltown.

One of the major challenges facing Union forces in this vicinity was the constant threat of guerrilla tactics employed by John S. Mosby and his Confederate Rangers. Mosby's hit-and-run schemes were real irritants to Sheridan's command; therefore, Sheridan organized a battalion of military scouts under the leadership of Major H. K. Young of the First Rhode Island Infantry to adopt tactics similar to those of Mosby and the other guerrilla leaders.

At the beginning of September, David Evans and his company were on the outskirts of Harpers Ferry. On Sunday, September 3, they crossed the Potomac River on a pontoon bridge into Virginia and camped near Boliver Heights. They moved on to Charlestown later in the week and then on to the outskirts of Winchester.

David was excited about being back in Winchester and remarked to his company mates, "Back in October of 1860 I visited my aunt and uncle here in Winchester. I also spent some time in Strasburg visiting my sweetheart, Abbey. Those were some of the best days of my life. It's hard to believe that over three years of war have consumed this area since my visit."

"Humph! Your sweetheart, Abbey!" snarled William Stone. "She's probably taken up with some Reb by now. She's forgotten the likes of you a long time ago. You'd just be another bluebelly to her. You better get her out of your mind and concentrate on killing her neighbors and kinfolk."

"You're just jealous because you never had a sweetheart and probably never will have, as mean and contemptible as you are," retorted David.

"That's enough. Save your fighting for the Rebs. I have a feeling that before this fall is over you will have had your fill of fighting," barked Corporal John Lepley. "Do your kin still live in Winchester?"

"No," said David. "Soon after Virginia voted to secede and join the Confederacy, they moved back north to Carlisle. I guess they had quite a scare thrown into them in late June of '63 when Carlisle was occupied for a short time. I haven't heard anything from Abbey since right before the first Battle of Bull Run. It became difficult to get letters through, so we decided to keep diaries, which we will exchange when this whole mess has ended."

Skirmishes broke out from time to time, but for the most part it was quiet on the front, and regular camp life ensued. Unbeknownst to the members of the Sixth and the Army of the Shenandoah, the politicians and newspapermen were growing impatient with Sheridan's inactivity and his lack of progress in burning out the valley.

General Grant decided to travel from City Point to visit Sheridan at Charlestown on September 17 and lay the plans to move against Early. Grant found that Little Phil was prepared to set his plans in motion upon Grant's approval, which Grant gave immediately. Grant returned to his own command, and Sheridan readied his army to move towards Winchester.

Sheridan moved his headquarters to Berryville. Six miles west of Berryville the Opequon Creek flowed northward. This creek served as the boundary between the two armies.

David and his company received the orders at 1:00 a.m. on Monday, September 19, to begin marching towards Winchester at 4:00 a.m. The company splashed over the Opequon Creek and met the enemy in force on the outskirts of the town. By 11:00, a general engagement was underway, and the Sixth Corps was successful in pushing the enemy through the fields and down a steep bluff, then across the main road into the open fields.

The Union cavalry charged the star-shaped Fort Collier from the rear, enabling the Sixth to make a left oblique move to allow other units in on the right, and then they maneuvered a left turn, which faced them towards the town. The Sixth swept the fields between the town and the Rebel fort, and drove the Rebels from the principal streets of the town. When the Sixth's skirmish line reached the outskirts of the town, other troops arrived, relieved Company A, and allowed them to take a well-deserved rest for the remainder of the night.

The next morning David's company marched back through town and set up camp at the edge of town. The rest of Sheridan's army continued the pursuit of the Rebels up the valley. Later in the week, the corps received congratulations from General Grant and the war department, even though the victory was incomplete because Early's army had not been eliminated.

Early retreated up the valley about twenty miles to his entrenchments at Fisher's Hill, while Sheridan's forces followed the Rebels, but these forces did not include the 49th Regiment.

Union forces skirmished with Early's rear guard near Middletown, Strasburg, and Cedarville on September 20 and near Fisher's Hill the next day. On the the twenty-second, Sheridan allowed Crook to launch a surprise attack at dusk on the Rebel left flank, which scattered them into a retreat or rout.

The disorganized Confederate army stampeded from Fisher's Hill, abandoning most of their artillery, with Wright and Emory in hot pursuit. The retreat continued up the valley through Woodstock, Mount Jackson, New Market, and on to Harrisonburg with the federals on their heels. The Union cavalry went all the way to Staunton and Waynesboro.

David's regiment missed all this fine activity, having been assigned to guard the prisoners returning from Fisher's Hill and other engagements along the way. They also were involved in guarding ammunition trains and a supply train laying at Martinsburg. Foraging was one of the more undesirable duties assigned to companies of the 49th.

On September 21, 1864, the *New York Times* published an article entitled "The Strategy of the Battle" as a special dispatch to the paper datelined Washington, Tuesday, September 20:

General Sheridan's grand success near Winchester is noted as the first victory achieved by the national army in the Shenandoah Valley. But it is so magnificent in its proportions as completely to wipe out the long series of reverses which have given to that region the designation of "The Valley of Humiliation." The loss to the enemy in killed, wounded and prisoners, while the circumstances of the enemy's defeat leave Early's army in a condition little short of absolute rout and demoralization.

On September 25, a reporter for the *New York Times* wrote:

It is pleasant to be able to record the fact that while there are many secessionists in this valley, occasionally good Union people are found—men and women both—who from the first have been true to the stars and stripes. These persons are more frequently seen in Winchester than in any other place in the valley—outside of Harpers Ferry—I have visited. Physicians and hospital attendants who have been compelled to remain in Winchester with the sick and wounded, when not occupied by our troops, are loved in their praises of many ladies who, despite the gibes and jeers of their Rebel sisters, and at the risk of persecution, have come forward freely in aid of Union sufferers in hospitals, furnishing all the little delicacies and attentions so agreeable and useful in the sick room. Long and happy life to the patriotic women of Winchester is the prayer of every Union soldier in this valley.

The war intensified between guerrilla forces and the Union cavalry. Lieutenant Colonel John S. Mosby led his 43rd Virginia Cavalry Battalion into the lower valley, employing hit-and-run nighttime or guerrilla tactics on raids against federal communications and installations there.

These attacks infuriated Grant, who in turn commanded Sheridan to "hang without trial" any of Mosby's men who fell into Union hands. In a clash in late September near Front Royal, irate Union cavalrymen captured six of Mosby's men, and dragged them into the town. Two were shot behind a Methodist church, two were shot later, and the last two were strangled. One of the dead men was found with a placard on his chest that read, "Such is the fate of Mosby's Men."

Mosby's men returned the favor on October 3 when they killed Lt. John R. Meigs, the son of the Union Quartermaster, General Montgomery C. Meigs, as he returned to his camp at Harrisonburg, Virginia. When Sheridan learned of the incident, he ordered the village of Dayton, near where the murder occurred, to be burned. The village was destroyed and all the cattle, sheep, horses, and other animals were confiscated from all the houses within five miles of the village.

The Gray Ghost struck again on October 14 when he derailed a B & O train about eight miles from Harpers Ferry and discovered Union paymasters carrying $173,000 in greenbacks. This action became known as the "Greenback Raid."

Shortly afterwards, the Confederate secretary of war concurred with Mosby's concept to "hang an equal number of General Custer's men in retaliation for those of his command executed by the general."

Early withdrew to Rockfish Gap near Waynesboro, a move

which left the Shenandoah Valley in Sheridan's possession. Believing that he had destroyed Early's army, Sheridan began a systematic withdrawal down the valley on October 6. As Sheridan withdrew, he sought to make sure that the abundance of the late summer's and autumn's harvest would not feed the Confederacy. Barns, stables, shocks of corn and wheat were torched; cattle, sheep, and horses were driven north, while most of the hogs were slaughtered. Gardens were ruined, although Sheridan had ordered that each family should be left enough to avoid starvation.

The systematic destruction of the valley became known as "The Burning" or "Red October." The smoke was so thick that it almost blacked out the sun during the daytime, and at night, the red glare of conflagrations was observed from horizon to horizon throughout the valley. Sheridan's operation transformed the valley from the Blue Ridge to the Alleghenies into a barren wasteland.

When the word of the burning of the valley arrived at Winchester and the camp of Company A, David could only shake his head in disbelief. "I just can't believe that we have resorted to this level of barbarity. Surely, General Sheridan must know that large numbers of Quakers, Brethren, Dunkers, and Mennonites, who are ardent pacifists, populate this valley. These people have not taken up arms against the Union; they are good people who don't believe in slavery."

"Don't fool yourself, Evans," snarled George Newton. "Those Bible thumpers, those good peace-loving folks, as you describe them, are interested in making money during this war just like anyone else not serving in the army. All those crops that they have been raising these past three years have been making their way to Lee's army, and they've been paid good money for them."

"Yep, remember, an army travels on its stomach," added Harry Stack. "This valley is the breadbasket of the Confederacy. Without all the foodstuffs raised in this valley, this war will be over soon. I'm just glad that we have some generals with the guts to do what it takes to win this war."

George sighed. "I don't know about you gents, but I've had enough of this fouled-up war. Anything that shortens it and gets me back home to my old lady is just fine and dandy with me."

"But many of these people are going to starve this winter," argued David. "Already we're seeing streams of refugees headed north to rejoin their relatives in Pennsylvania and Maryland. I just hope this is the last winter of this war. I haven't been here as long as some of you, but I've had enough."

Harry Stack quipped, "We haven't seen the last of this war. As soon as Sheridan returns, the Sixth Corps is going to be shipped back to Petersburg and Grant. We've had it easy the last few months, but harder days are just over the horizon."

CHAPTER 79
BATTLE OF CEDAR CREEK

As the Union forces moved back down the valley, Early initiated a counteroffensive and continued harassing Sheridan's rear guard. Sheridan finally ordered the cavalry to end the nuisance, and Custer and Merritt met the southern horsemen at Tom's Brook on October 9. The Confederate mounted line broke, and the Yankees pursued the enemy up the Valley Pike for over twenty miles in what became known as the "Woodstock Races."

Believing that he had cleared the valley of Early's forces, Sheridan decided to send Wright's Sixth Corps, including the Pennsylvania 49th Regiment, back to rejoin Grant at Petersburg via Culpepper. The Union army continued its burning policy and encamped near Cedar Creek just north of Strasburg.

Contact was made with Early once again; therefore, Sheridan suspended the transfer of the Sixth Corps, and decided to go to Washington to confer with Lincoln and Secretary Stanton while placing Wright in command of the army during his absence.

Sheridan arrived at Washington about 8:00 a.m. on October 17, and received approval to establish a defensive line in the valley and reduce his forces. By noon, he was on a special train headed for Martinsburg where he spent the night. The next morning he started for Winchester, arrived there in the afternoon, and spent the night at the Logan House.

The word from Cedar Creek was reassuring; it was all quiet. Unbeknownst to Wright and Sheridan, Early's forces were on the move. Early was faced with withdrawing from the valley, thereby giving complete control to the Union, or attacking in an attempt to drive Sheridan from the valley.

Early conducted a night march and a simultaneous attack on the rear, flanks, and front of the Union army at daybreak. The attack surprised and easily overwhelmed Crook's corps in their camp at Cedar Creek. The Nineteenth Corps suffered a similar fate. Only Wright's Sixth Corps maintained their composure and withdrew systematically beyond Middletown. The Sixth provided an effective screen behind which the other corps were able to regroup.

Sheridan's party, escorted by the 17th Pennsylvania Cavalry, left Winchester between 8:30 and 9:00 a.m. without any knowledge of the debacle unfolding to the south of them. Suddenly, they came upon the appalling scene of a panic-stricken army, whereupon Sheridan began to organize a counterattack. He urged his men, "Turn back! Face the other way! If I had been with you this morning, boys, this would not have happened!" He rode his black horse, Rienzi, among the men and turned the tide, shouting, "Boys, we'll get the tightest twist on them they ever saw. We'll get those camps back."

In late afternoon the Union counterattack successfully drove the Confederates back across Cedar Creek, transforming the stunning morning's defeat into a spectacular Union victory. The Union army regained their camps and drove the enemy southward to Fisher's Hill and then to New Market.

The Confederate threat to the valley was virtually eliminated with Cedar Creek, but the major outcome of the campaign was the loss of the food supply from the breadbasket of the Confederacy, the Shenandoah Valley.

All the glory and excitement of the Battle of Cedar Creek bypassed David Evans and Company A of the 49th Pennsylvania. They were still encamped on the outskirts of Winchester and had heard the heavy cannonading up the valley. All the troops had been ordered out under arms at noon and had formed a battle line south of town on both sides of the Valley Pike. Shortly afterwards, wounded soldiers and stragglers arrived from the battle, but by sundown the firing had ceased and normal camp life resumed.

Poet Thomas Buchanan immortalized Sheridan's ride from his headquarters at the Logan House in Winchester to the battlefield at Cedar Creek:

Up from the South at the break of day,
Bringing to Winchester fresh dismay,
The affrighted air with a shudder bore,
Like a herald in haste, to the chieftain's door,
The terrible grumble, rumble, and roar,
Telling the battle was on once more,
And Sheridan twenty miles away.

CHAPTER 80
FORAGING DUTIES

After the Battle of Cedar Creek, camp life settled into normalcy with pickets being posted daily. On several days the company was sent out as guards for wagon trains arriving from Martinsburg because of the constant threat of guerrilla activity.

On Wednesday, October 26, Colonel Edwards of the Thirty-seventh Massachusetts Volunteers presented a new flag to the regiment. Color Sergeant Henry Entriken received the new colors while Color Corporal T. H. McFarland took the old stand. Colonel Edwards spoke on behalf of Colonel Hickman. He began in a dry, dignified manner, "I have the honor to present to you this emblem of our nation's glory, its strength and its pride." The colonel ended his short speech by stating, "I do it (presenting the flag), knowing that as long as life lasts no man of your regiment will allow them to be dishonored; that so long as breath animates your bodies, so long will you rally around the flag."

The moving ceremony made David and the men proud of their accomplishments so far in the war. Three days later the company and regiment marched south to the outskirts of Middletown.

The next day Sergeant Entriken approached David and his small squad. "Evans, you and your squad are drawing forage guard duty today. There really shouldn't be much to it; just keep your eyes and ears open for bushwhackers. Be careful, because you'll be getting close to Strasburg, which has seen some guerrilla activity the last few days. Our company will have three wagons, and you will be joined by two other wagons. I want one guard on the seat with the driver and two others in the rear of the wagon.

"You'll head down the Valley Pike past the Cedar Creek Battlefield area. Shortly after that, you'll pick up what the locals call Long Meadows Road, which heads southeast at first, then turns west along the river. You'll continue up the river until you intersect another road, Bowman Mills Road, head right or north, and eventually you'll intersect Long Meadows Road again.

"Our informants tell us that there is a good supply of hay along this route, as well as abundant apple orchards. Don't be afraid to grab any chickens or turkeys you find on those farms, as well as anything else edible. I fancy a good chicken dinner, so make your sergeant happy by bringing me a nice plump one. Any questions?"

"No, sergeant. We understand the drill."

"Here come the wagons. Hop on, and good hunting."

There was no grumbling about the assignment; it was good to be getting out of camp and all its boring duties. George Harter and David sat in the back of the second wagon, enjoying the autumn foliage and watching the wagons and horses kick up a cloud of dust as they headed down the pike. Everyone was in good spirits with constant bantering between the wagons.

Once they left the Valley Pike and headed onto Long Meadows Road, the terrain changed, with more wooden plots intermingled with the open fields. The wooden areas worried the men. "Men, keep your eyes open. There are too many good ambush sites along this road," warned Corporal McFarland.

No one seemed to take the corporal's concern seriously; it was just too nice a day for an ambush, and the war seemed miles and miles away. As the detail progressed toward the river, they spotted several large stacks of hay on three farms, and loaded them into the wagons. The women they encountered were extremely hostile, and shouted obscenities at the soldiers. Beyond one ridge, the men moved into a large apple orchard and began picking the ripened fruit as rapidly as possible while two men stood guard.

Henry White began to complain about his hands becoming sore from plucking the apples. "You'd think we would have been able to locate a farm where the fruit had already been harvested, and all we would have to do is load it on the wagons. We just have no luck at all."

David was more upbeat. "Just think about all the good apple cobbler and pies the cooks will be able to bake from all these—although most of these apples will probably never make it that far.

Heck, there's nothing like good, fresh fruit."

David was able to observe the North Fork of the Shenandoah River as they rode along Long Meadows Road. He thought to himself, "I'm within a few miles of Abbey's home. If we were to continue up the river, we would soon arrive at the Sandy Hook Road crossing which would take me right to her front door. I've wanted to send her a message that I was near Winchester, but I didn't want to draw attention to their plantation. It's quite possible that her family's farm has survived the war with little damage."

Once they left the river they rattled through some open fields, intersected a road they assumed was Bowmans Mill Road, and turned right onto it. Then they entered a forested area where their anxiety increased immediately. "Keep alert, men," barked the corporal. "This would be an ideal location for a waylay. Make sure your weapons are capped and ready."

The drivers cracked their whips over the horses' heads and urged them to increase their pace just as the road dropped into a steep ravine. Suddenly a Rebel yell pierced the afternoon air, followed by a chorus of more yells and yelps and the thunder of weapons being discharged.

The startled federals quickly returned fire, but now they were holding useless weapons unless they could reload quickly or use them as clubs. The shocked drivers brought their whips into play, no longer cracking their whips over the heads of their teams, but instead onto their backs and hindquarters.

The wagons lurched forward at an increased speed, but the Rebels were soon beside them, creating bedlam. One wagon went out of control and spilled its driver, guards, and hay; and the soldiers were quickly made prisoners. David frantically attempted to reload his rifle, but before he could reload, a horseman with a pistol in his right hand and a saber in his left confronted him.

A shot roared from the pistol, striking David on the left side of his head, at the same instance that the sword flashed downward towards his chest. In a way, luck was with David, for the bullet only grazed the side of his head, and the slight impact twisted his torso sideways so that the saber did not strike a fatal blow to his chest.

David lost consciousness, tumbled from the wagon, and rolled down a steep embankment, coming to rest against the trunk of a large sycamore tree.

The first sound to pierce his consciousness was the crashing of thunder. Even though it was well into late fall, Northern Virginia still experienced thunderstorms at this time of year. His first words were, "Get down! Take cover! They're firing down on us again!"

Abbey, who was seated beside David in a makeshift bed, took his thin, muscular hand in hers. "It's only thunder. There are no guns firing today. Please relax and realize that you are in a safe place far from the warfront."

He did not speak for some time. His deeply sunken eyes surveyed the small room. "I have no strength," he whispered hoarsely. What is wrong with me?" Tears formed in his eyes and rolled down his cheeks.

She drew a deep breath, relieved that he could speak. "You have been wounded, my sweet, do not exert yourself."

It was then that he recognized her voice. "Abbey, how did you get here? You're not supposed to be near the fighting."

"I'll explain everything to you when you're feeling better. Just try to rest and regain your strength."

He examined himself to make sure that his arms and legs were intact. Satisfied that they were, he closed his eyes and a moment later drifted back to sleep, breathing easily now.

Abbey laid her head on the bed and prayed silently, thanking God for the blessing that David had regained consciousness. It had been four long days and nights of little sleep and anxious moments until this moment.

"Was he rational?" her mother asked as she entered the room and learned of his brief return to reality.

"Perfectly! Evidently, he heard the thunder and assumed it was the guns firing again. I assured him that it was only thunder and there were no guns nearby. He hasn't much strength yet, but he's improving by the hour. We just have to watch that the fever does-n't return, but now that it's broken I don't think it will return."

"Are you really certain he's out of danger?" her mother asked.

"The greatest danger he faces is if some loose lips reveal his presence and the guerrillas find him here; if that happens all of us on the plantation will be in dire danger. They would kill us and burn all our buildings if they knew we were harboring a Yankee. We must be very careful about who we get to help us care for him."

Another day passed before David opened his eyes again, this time to the glare of sunlight shining through the lone window in the room. He realized he was in a bed in a very small room. Pain permeated his head, and he shut his eyes again, hoping that the pain would subside. Darkness was better than the abruptness of sunlight.

A small, delicate hand took his wrist, and a voice, a sweet, loving voice, spoke. "His pulse is better." Then another voice: "The color has returned to his cheeks. I believe you're right; he is beginning to recover from the head wound."

The room swam dizzily, and then was still. He thought he was dreaming again. The angelic face of his beloved Abbey was bending over him, and he struggled to sit up.

"It's Abbey," she said softly. "You're on my family's farm. You're going to be fine, but you must not move."

He attempted to speak but his voice cracked, and he realized he had an overpowering thirst. Abbey was prepared for this and produced a cup of water, holding his head up while he drank.

"How did I get here? What's wrong with me? What are you doing here? I'm supposed to be fighting, not lying here in a bed."

"Just sit back and relax, my love. You've been seriously wounded by some bushwhackers. Your shoulder and chest muscles are badly lacerated. My cousin Rachel found you. She saved your life by binding your shirt around your chest tight enough to prevent you from bleeding to death. You also received a serious blow to your head and you've been unconscious for five days.

"We rigged a litter between two horses to bring you to our farm. We've hidden you in one of the old shacks that used to house our hired hands because we're afraid that the bushwhackers might reappear and find you. You're safe for now.

"When you're well enough, someone will ride to your army's headquarters and inform them of your whereabouts, and then eventually we'll move you to the hospital in Winchester. I'd love to keep you here, but it might prove to be dangerous. Hopefully, your army will allow me to visit you and help care for you."

David appeared to relax. "It's very reassuring that I have an angel for a nurse. I know I'm in the best hands possible. Now, could I please have a taste of those luscious lips that I've missed so much over these many months?"

She complied immediately. "You didn't realize it, but while you were unconscious I tasted your lips many, many times. I love you so much, my darling Yankee. I've prayed and prayed that you would recover."

Then he shut his eyes and plunged back into sleep in spite of the throbbing pain in his chest, shoulder, and head. He awoke several hours later to find her still sitting beside his bed.

"Are you hungry?" she asked.

"I certainly am."

"Well, you can't eat too much at first. Here is a nice big bowl of broth that should satisfy you somewhat. As you improve, I'll make sure you get something more substantial."

Abbey began to explain the situation her family faced on the banks of the North Fork of the Shenandoah River. "The members of our church and others like us have suffered tremendously because of our pacifist beliefs. We have been tormented by both sides; the South because our members did not voluntarily go to war and the North because we felt that denying food, supplies, and medical care would be unchristian.

"Many of our men were placed in jail because of the Conscription Acts. Others fled the state across the Mason-Dixon or hid in the mountains to avoid military service. As our nonpacifist neighbors sent their sons and fathers off to war, they reacted with hate and resentment as we strove to continue to live normal lives.

"For three years we suffered indignities, abuses, the theft of our livestock, grain, hay, foodstuff, money, and even what few weapons we possessed, at the hands of southerners, either bushwhackers or soldiers. They made no distinction between us pacifists and Union sympathizers.

"The most devastating events began in late September and into early October with Sheridan's burning or scorched earth policy. If you look around, you will observe that just about every barn, mill, corn crib, haystack, food crop, farm implement, and living animal has been destroyed in some sections of this once fertile valley.

"Somehow our buildings have been spared thus far, although most of our animals are gone. Maybe it's because we're off the main road, or someone is looking after us. Most of our neighbors are no more than refugees, thrown out of their comfortable homes and facing starvation. Your General Sheridan has offered to 'furnish one team and wagon to each Union sympathizer to transport his belongings and family beyond the boundaries of the Confederacy.' Hopefully, we won't be faced with that type of decision, but many of the people of the valley are, and have taken Sheridan's offer."

Abbey broke down in tears and David attempted to comfort her. Finally, she recovered and apologized for her outburst. "It's almost too much to bear," she sniffled.

Over the next few days David's expression, attitude, and overall disposition brightened and the healing process commenced. A message was sent to his regiment's headquarters that he was alive and being cared for in the best possible manner, but there was concern that the bushwhackers could find out about his location and take action to capture or eliminate him. Because of this concern, every effort would be made to conceal his recuperation site and restrict the number of people who knew of his existence.

For many of the people in this section of Northern Virginia, this war was all but over. The onslaught of General Sheridan's 1864 Second Valley campaign had resulted in a termination of formal activity around Winchester, which was known as "the gateway to the Shenandoah Valley." During the course of the war, four major engagements were fought in and around Winchester: the battle of Kernstown on March 23, 1862; the First Winchester on May 25,

1862; the battle of Stephenson's Depot or the Second Winchester, on June 14-15, 1863; and the Third Winchester or the Battle of Opequon Creek on September 19, 1864.

During these battles, the town of Winchester changed hands at least seventy-two times. Because of the vast destruction, Winchester was virtually in ruins by the late fall of 1864. In this final quest for conquest of the Shenandoah Valley, General Philip Sheridan established his headquarters at the imposing Logan home located at Braddock and Piccadilly Streets. It was here that General Sheridan spent the night when General Jubal Early surprised two Union corps on October 19, 1864, at a site that became known as Cedar Creek Battlefield, about one-half mile south of Middletown, Virginia.

On November 12 David was well enough to make the trip from Abbey's family farm to Winchester, a distance of about twenty-five miles. Abbey and Jacob, her twelve-year-old brother, would accompany him.

The entire Old Valley Pike was heavily maintained and guarded by federal troops. The Volkners would stay with a cousin whose small home on the northwestern outskirts of the town had not been destroyed in the struggle to control the Gateway to the Valley.

On the outskirts of Strasburg, or Pot Town, the wagon carrying the recuperating Yankee was challenged by a small detachment of troops under the command of a gruff Irish sergeant. David was able to quickly identify himself as a member of Company A of the Pennsylvania 49th Regiment of the Sixth Corps which until lately was bivouacked near Middletown.

The Irish sergeant was only too happy to inform the wounded private, "Sorry, son, but your boys are no longer at Middletown. They're moved to right outside Kernstown, Virginia. I don't make judgments about the wounded, but I would venture a guess that they'll allow you to continue your recuperation for a few more weeks, and then you'll be rejoining the Forty-Ninth down the road.

"Now get this broken-down nag and wagon out of here and headed north to headquarters at Winchester." He added with a sly grin, "If I'd been you I would have spent the rest of the war under the care of this fine, young nurse. Now, the best of luck to you, sonny, and Godspeed."

Once they turned onto the Valley Pike, no one challenged them for several miles. After about five miles, they were amazed to see that the fine limestone mansion known as Belle Grove was still standing and in apparently good condition. David remembered that this magnificent mansion had served as Union headquarters during the Battle of Cedar Creek and still seemed to be used for housing officers, owing to all the flags on display and the fine horses hitched in front.

All along the pike were signs of bitter fighting. Most of the dwellings that could be observed from the road were no longer intact; some had burned to the ground. The fields and once abundant orchards were in the same condition, destroyed beyond any productive use. The concept of total war had certainly been carried out in this section of the Shenandoah Valley. Abbey fought back tears for the land and the survivors who no longer inhabited a productive agricultural valley.

Once they entered the town of Winchester, David sat propped up because he wanted everyone to recognize that his beautiful nurse and her brother were transporting a wounded Union soldier and were not just a ruse to enter the army's center of activity.

The wagon was stopped and its occupants questioned on three occasions until finally the trio arrived at the location where David had been ordered to report. They were originally instructed to drive the wagon to the regimental hospital near the center of the town and not far from the railroad yard. Instead, he was assigned a bed in the Shawnee Springs Hospital just off Pleasant Valley Road. This was the largest temporary hospital of the war and had been established following the last battle for Winchester in September 19, 1864.

The Shawnee Springs Hospital was designated Sheridan Field Hospital and had been laid out by Surgeon John H. Brinton. The facility extended from Shawnee Springs northward to Jacob Senseny's house on Church Ridge. On September 28, Surgeon V.

Z. Blaney assumed command of the hospital, which was designed to accommodate four thousand patients.

At this stage of the war, Sheridan Field Hospital was a clearing and evacuation center. Patients had been brought here from engagements fought farther up the Shenandoah Valley. Once the patients had been processed, they were transferred to medical facilities in the North. Since the fighting in the Valley had diminished, the population of the hospital had dwindled.

Upon arrival at the tents comprising the Sheridan Field Hospital, David was quickly transferred from the wagon to a litter, which to him was a waste of effort because he felt well enough to walk to his new lodgings. Abbey showed the doctor the letter she had received when she first contacted the army about nursing a wounded Union soldier. The letter entitled her to visit David daily and assist in changing his wounds and bathing his body. She also arranged to accompany him on daily strolls that would enable him to recuperate sooner.

Even though the weather became much colder in the latter days of November, the young couple paid it no heed, as they were able to spend much of the days together. From the moment David regained consciousness, the young couple had become even more deeply in love. Neither of them had any doubts about being meant for each other.

Even with all these arrangements going in their favor, the young couple found the transfer to the military hospital to be emotionally draining. Abbey hugged David and looked him straight in the eyes. "You have been restored to me when I thought I would lose you forever. God has begun the healing process that will make you well enough to return to duty. I feel somewhat guilty, because I know that soon you will be reassigned to active duty and face the prospects of being wounded again or killed. If I hadn't done such a good job of nursing you, you might still be with me back on the banks of the river."

"You can't think that way, and don't worry, I'll be much more careful this time. Besides, all indications are that the war will be over shortly, and we can get married as soon as I get discharged."

After a week he was no longer confined to the hospital and was assigned to light duties that aided in returning his body to marching and fighting condition. With this reassignment, David and Abbey could no longer take the long walks to which they had become accustomed. Instead, they had to shift their time together to the short period after the evening meal and taps.

As David returned to normalcy, it became apparent that Abbey could no longer stay in Winchester. There were rumors that the Corps would soon be leaving the Shenandoah and returning to the trenches of Petersburg.

This parting was even more emotional than the one of April 1861, because they and the nation had been through so much since then. "When this war ends, I will be back in your waiting arms as soon as possible. Lee simply cannot resist much longer, especially since Sheridan has eliminated your valley as the Confederacy's food source. It's just a matter of time. Our corps's return to Petersburg will only hasten the end."

She smiled meekly. "I hope you are correct. The people of this valley cannot handle much more. Many of our neighbors will find it difficult to survive this winter. All I can say is, please hurry back to me. I want our life together to begin as soon as possible. I'm tired of being alone."

He looked into her face, such a beautiful face with almost flawless skin. She moved swiftly against him, lifted her face, and pressed her lips against his. She kissed him hungrily and he responded with a deep intensity.

"I refuse to say good-bye to you. Instead, I'll simply say, I'll see you soon," she whispered.

"Yes, it will be soon," he said, and kissed her one more time. "I love you. "

He helped her up in the buggy and kissed her hand in farewell. Tears streamed down her cheeks, and she turned away and took out a handkerchief to wipe them away. She turned to face him, "I love you, David. Please stay safe."

Then Jacob slapped the reins over the horse's back and they headed south. She turned one more time and waved to him. Then she was gone, and David headed towards his tent and the duties he had to perform.

CHAPTER 82

ELECTION CAMPAIGN OF 1864

One major event that was shaped by events in the war, but not a part of Grant's victory strategy, was the presidential election of 1864. The majority of the men serving in the United States Army in 1864 were little aware of the opposition to Lincoln's administration and its methods of conducting the war. Quietly, while conducting military operations, Lincoln went about the business of securing the Republican Party's nomination.

There was much war weariness in the North, and the military results during the early part of 1864 did not encourage confidence in the administration. The campaign really began in February when Kansas Senator Samuel C. Pomeroy issued a letter designed to prevent Lincoln's renomination and promoted the presidential candidacy of Secretary of the Treasury Salmon P. Chase. Lincoln sidestepped this potential hurdle by easing Chase out of the cabinet during the summer.

On May 31, a group of Radical Republicans nominated John C. Fremont as their presidential standard-bearer, although he withdrew from the campaign in September. The Radical Republicans wanted to free all the slaves at once, hang Jefferson Davis (and as many other Rebels as could be caught), seize all rebel property, and bring the war to a short and successful end by placing Butler and Fremont in command,

On June 8, 1864, Lincoln was unanimously renominated on the first ballot by a coalition of Republicans and War Democrats in Baltimore. This coalition called themselves the National Union Party, and they selected Andrew Johnson, Tennessee's loyal Democratic governor, as Lincoln's running mate.

The Democrats delayed their convention until late August and met in Chicago hoping to gain an advantage from the Union military reverses during the summer. They demanded peace on the "basis of the Federal Union of the states" and nominated General George B. McClellan for president and George II. Pendleton of Ohio as his vice-president.

The presidential campaign was noisy and heated. The Democrats exclaimed, "Mac Will Win the Union Back," and "Old Abe removed McClellan—We'll now remove Old Abe." The Republicans countered with, "Vote as you shot," and "Don't swap horses in the middle of the stream."

What was about to transpire on the first Tuesday after the first Monday in November of 1864 was unique; never before had a democratic nation attempted to hold free elections while in the midst of a bloody civil war. On Election Day, it appeared that the nation's voters would be deciding whether to drop out of the war or to carry on the war at any cost.

Many people in the North were disillusioned about the war, and the riots over the draft act had shown just how deep the underlying unrest and discontent had grown. The military campaigns initiated in early May were not the successes that had been sought. Neither Atlanta nor Richmond had been captured, and neither Lee nor Johnston been defeated. To make matters worse, casualty lists were higher than ever, Early's army had threatened Washington itself, and the system of prisoner exchanges had broken down.

A succession of Union victories changed the gloomy atmosphere of the war for the Republicans. As David and Abbey witnessed, Phil Sheridan laid waste to the Shenandoah Valley and removed the valley as the major breadbasket of the Confederacy. Admiral David G. Farragut exclaimed, "Damn the torpedoes! Full speed ahead!" while capturing Mobile, Alabama, on August 5. General William T. Sherman seized Atlanta, Georgia, on September 2 and began his famous "March to the Sea."

Tuesday, November 8, 1864, was Presidential Election Day, and the members of the Union army performed their civic duty by turning out to vote. Many northern soldiers were furloughed home in order to support Lincoln at the ballot box. It was reported that one Pennsylvania veteran voted forty-nine times—once for himself and once each for his company members who remained at the front. Most soldiers cast their ballots at the front, as did the members of the 49th. The result of David's regimental vote was 180 votes for Lincoln and 68 for General McClellan.

On the national level Lincoln won 55 percent of the popular vote, taking 2,213,665 votes to McClellan's 1,805,237. The electoral vote was another story, as Lincoln gained 212 electoral votes to McClellan's 21. Only Kentucky, New Jersey, and Delaware went to the Democrats.

The Republican Party also gained huge majorities in both houses of Congress, overturning the Democrats' majority after sixty years of rule. Lincoln declared, "The election has demonstrated that a people's government can sustain a national election in the midst of a great civil war. Until now, it has not been known to the world that this was a possibility. It shows, also, how sound and how strong we are."

The reelection of Lincoln was a crushing blow to the South. The removal of Lincoln as president was the last major hope of victory for the Confederacy. Desertions increased dramatically, and the "Lost Cause" of the South became more of a reality in late 1864.

CHAPTER 88

THE LAST WINTER OF THE WAR

On Thursday, December 1, the regiment was called up at two o'clock in the morning with orders that they should be ready to march at six o'clock. They left camp and marched up the pike to Winchester, arriving at Stephenson Station at eleven o'clock and embarking on the train via Harpers Ferry. The troops traveled all night and, at seven o'clock in the morning, arrived at Annapolis where the train took on water and wood, and then continued on to Washington, arriving in the capital about noon. Two days' rations were drawn, and the regiment then marched down to the steamboat landing where they and the 119th Pennsylvania Regiment boarded the steamboat, the *John A. Warner*. The steamboat carried them down to Alexandria, Virginia, where it cast anchor and the soldiers remained on board for the night.

On Saturday, the *John A. Warner* weighed anchor at daybreak and sailed down the Potomac River, crossing the bay and arriving at Fortress Monroe at eleven o'clock at night. Due to a windy night which resulted in a rough bay, the troops suffered seasickness.

The following day the ship weighed anchor at daybreak, headed up the James River, and arrived at City Point, Virginia, at 2:00 p.m. The troops unloaded and marched towards the front to await a train that would take them farther inland. They bivouacked near the rail station and boarded the train the next morning.

On December 5, the VI corps along with the 49th Regiment returned to the same general area they had left in early July when they were sent to bolster the defense of Washington and then were sent to the Shenandoah Valley to remove Early. Now they were back in the trenches at Fort Wadsworth near the crossing of the Weldon railroad where they went into winter quarters. They constructed winter quarters similar to those they had lived in during the previous winter.

The men of the 49th fell into a daily routine of army life—picket duty, repairing roads, drills, inspections, and cleaning guns, equipment, and clothing. On Christmas Day, most of the Union army enjoyed a fine Christmas dinner, as boxes and barrels of turkeys, chickens, mince pies, and cakes were off-loaded at City Point and sent into the trenches.

As 1864 passed into 1865, the men were of one accord: this simply had to be the last year of the war. The men of the Union Army hoped that spring would bring the last campaign. On Thursday, January 4, 1865, David and the men received a belated Christmas gift; they turned in their old Austrian rifles and were issued Springfield rifles manufactured in 1861.

The winter of 1864-65 was a severe one, and it took its toll on both armies, especially the Confederates. Just about every night deserters would appear in the lines, many of whom were willing to enlist in the Union army. A new order came down that these deserters would be sent west to fight the Indians instead of facing their former countrymen.

In mid-January when there was a break in the snowy weather, David and several of his company visited other Pennsylvania units. As they walked through the mud, they began to realize just how large this army was and how many Pennsylvanians had answered the call. They observed the flags of the 205th, 200th, 210th, and the 162nd as they slogged along. When they entered the encampment area of the 161st Regiment Company F, a familiar voice called out to David, "David Evans, is that you?"

David turned towards the tent from where the question originated, and there stood his cousin Thomas W. Evans. "Cousin Tom, when did you enlist?"

"It will be a year on the fourteenth of next month. Look around and you'll see several other Juniata County men you know from baseball, or maybe you went to school together."

Within a few minutes, David was overwhelmed with men from the Tuscarora Valley that he knew so well. The reunion was brought to an abrupt halt when the company first sergeant called his men for drill, so David said his farewells and promised to return for another visit in the near future.

On the return trip, they were circumventing the encampment of Company F and the 208th Regiment when David almost tripped over a man who was deeply involved in writing a letter. David pardoned himself, as the men recognized each other. "You're David Evans of Half Moon, aren't you?" inquired the letter writer.

"Yes, I am, and you're Jonathan Packard the teamster. You've delivered farm equipment, seed, and fertilizer to our farm several times. How long have you been in the 208th?"

"I mustered in back in September. I know you're a little surprised to see a man my age and with my family responsibilities serving as a volunteer, but I just felt I needed to do my duty. Ellen was a little put out; she didn't want me to join, but I couldn't stay out of the fight any longer."

David nodded. "I see you're writing a letter. I assume it's to Ellen and the kids?"

"It's to Ellen and the kids, like you guessed, but it isn't a letter. It's a poem I've been working on for several days. I have it down pretty much the way I want it, but it's my first attempt at this type of thing and I'm somewhat unsure of its impact on them. You're an educated man. Would you please take a look at it, and tell me what you think?"

David took the two papers in his hands and began to read, and soon a smile came to his face. He thought the poem was wonderful.

Today while on the picket line,
With Rebel foes in view,
I thought to pass away the time
Composing lines to you.

On you, dear one, my choicest thoughts
Continually are stayed,
And hope you will forget me not,
If in the dust I'm laid.

Oft' in my dreams, I see your form,

With smiles upon your face,
But when I waken in the morn,
You are some other place.

Dear Ellen, 'tis not home for me,
So far away from you,
But still I hope to see your face,
When I'm done wearing blue.

On soldiers' rations I am fed,
'Tis not such dainty food,
But still I eat and go to bed,
Just as a soldier should.

THIS IS FOR MY THREE OLDER CHILDREN: JACOB, RACHEL AND GEORGE

Now children, this is for you,
Your mother dear, obey,
For I do often think of you
While I am far away.

Next comes my little Jake,
With sparkling eyes of blue,
And still before you go to bed,
Think of your papa, too.

Dear Rachel, your verse now comes in,
You are the next in size,
I long to kiss your dimpled chin
And see your sparkling eyes.

Now, George, you come last of all,
But you will not forget,
Although you are the least of all,
You are my little pet.

(AUTHOR'S NOTE: These poems were passed down to Joshua Taylor Packard through the Taylor-Packard families. Jonathan Packard was the author's great-great-grandfather.)

Tears filled David's eyes as he finished reading. "They're beautiful. Your wife and children will be very touched by your words and will love you even more once they have read what you have written from deep within your heart. They can be very proud of you. I know that I am very proud to have known a loving and caring man such as you."

David talked with Jonathan for about another fifteen minutes; before realizing he was due back at camp for drill. "I hope to see you in camp again, but if not, I'll see you back in Juniata County." The men shook hands and wished each other good luck, and then David and his friends returned to camp.

When February arrived, little changed on the line for the 49th. David read anything he could get his hands on and was constantly organizing baseball games. On any day that was not extremely cold or raining and snowing, a game was soon in progress.

The men's spirits were lifted on several occasions. On Tuesday, February 21, a salute of one hundred guns was fired at noon in honor of the fall of Charleston and Columbia, South Carolina to the Union army. The next day was Washington's Birthday and the guns of Fort Howard fired a salute. That week veterans like David received a $50 veteran bounty and $100 for four months' pay. On Friday, another salute was fired in honor of the fall of Wilmington, North Carolina.

Encouraged by the news of the veterans' pay, the sutlers (civilian provisioners) appeared in the trenches and camps offering all types of goods to the soldiers.

CHAPTER 84
LINCOLN'S SECOND INAUGURATION

At noon on Sunday, March 4, 1865, Abraham Lincoln, the sixteenth president of the United States, official Washington, and a converging crowd braved heavy clouds, blasts of rain, and a sea of mud to celebrate Lincoln's second inauguration as our nation's leader. Just as the president stood on the platform at the podium and began his eloquent, 703-word speech, a blazing sun broke through the clouds.

Lincoln's brief address was filled with extraordinary words of compassion, forgiveness, and justice, rather than vengeance. The conclusion was a dramatic testament to the spirit and temperament of the president's oration:

> With malice toward none, with charity for all, with firmness in the right as God gives us to see the right, let us strive to finish the work we are in, to bind up the nation's wounds, to care for him who shall have borne the battle and for his widow and his orphan, to do all which may achieve and cherish a just and lasting peace among ourselves and with all nations.

After he finished reading those words, Lincoln was administered the oath of office by Chief Justice Salmon Chase. To the south of this inaugural site, the war continued. General Grant's Army of the Potomac, about 125,000 strong, had been entrenched around Petersburg for nine months; this included the 49th Pennsylvania of which David Evans was a member.

To the northwest of Petersburg, the Shenandoah Valley—the breadbasket of the Confederacy—lay in scorched ruins. General Phillip Sheridan had taken the Shenandoah Valley out of the war the previous fall, and it could no longer provide foodstuff to feed

Lee's diminishing forces.

Farther south, on May 6, 1864, General William Tecumseh Sherman had begun his assault on the people he believed had created the war in the first place, by moving from Chattanooga, Tennessee, into Georgia. Sherman's swath of destruction reached Atlanta and left it in a smoldering ruin on November 15. He then advanced southeast to Savannah in a fiery march to the sea. Then Sherman turned his wrath on South Carolina and occupied its capital of Columbia on February 16-17, 1865. On Inauguration Day, Sherman's army was driving northward toward the rear of Lee's army.

CHAPTER 85
THE FINAL CAMPAIGN

Finally, on Tuesday, March 14, David and his regiment received orders to send all their surplus baggage away and prepare to move. Then they marched to Hatcher's Run.

As the month of March neared its end, David and his comrades sensed that something different was about to occur. About 4:00 a.m. on March 25, the enemy attacked Fort Steadman in an attempt to force Grant to contract his lines and create a breach for the Confederate army to escape to North Carolina. The Confederates overran Steadman, along with several other forts. Federal forces then launched a strong counterattack that forced the Rebels to retreat, with the loss of 1,900 captured and 4,000 casualties. However, Lee remained bottled up at Petersburg.

Three days of pelting rain soaked everything including rations and blankets, and then Grant attempted a thrust around Lee's right that was repulsed. Finally on March 31, with rain still falling, Sheridan, who had just returned from the Shenandoah Valley, headed for the junction of Five Forks. Five Forks was vital for Lee's line of supply and the route he intended to take to join Johnston in North Carolina. Sheridan outnumbered and outgeneraled George Picket, the rebels were routed, and the survivors fled for their lives and freedom. Picket's disaster at Five Forks is often referred to as "the Waterloo of the Confederacy."

During this rainy period, David and his regiment were under arms at Fort Steadman. They had packed up with filled canteens and fixed bayonets, ready to move out in silence on several occasions, only to have their orders counteracted. The men were disappointed and frustrated, because they knew the Johnnies were in poor fighting condition after spending a horrible winter in the trenches with very little to eat.

On April 1, at about nine o'clock the regiment began to march outside the breastworks at Fort Fisher. The orders specified that all canteens and tin cups were to be stored inside haversacks; the soldiers were to fix their bayonets and move noiselessly. The Rebels discovered their movement anyway and opened fire, which the Pennsylvanians answered the whole way along the line.

The brigade formed at midnight, and the troops rested the best they could until 2:00 a.m. when they marched a little to the left between their own works and the picket line in front of Fort Fisher. At 4:30, the brigade formed into three lines of battle and began the charge into the enemy's works.

The federals' grand assault drove the enemy backwards all morning long, pushed them into Petersburg, and subsequently forced them to evacuate the city. David and the other men were dog-tired, and they were glad when they were told to dig rifle pits and bivouac on the outskirts of the city. It had been an outstanding day because the brigade had captured the works and three lines of forts. In addition, they had driven the Rebels three miles and had taken a large number of prisoners. Their brigade was actually the first to take Petersburg.

When the company was called up at 4:00 a.m., they were delighted to find no Rebels in their front; Petersburg was now under federal control. They received orders to march, and march they did; they covered fifteen miles, almost to Sutherland Station. Along the way, they picked up numerous Rebel prisoners and stragglers. The word among the men was that Lee was attempting to join Johnston in North Carolina.

It was now Tuesday, April 4, and it was a repeat of the previous day, with the company marching on some very bad roads, although they laid over for a few hours while the Second and Fifth Corps trains passed them. On Wednesday, the march resumed, but on this day they covered twenty-two grueling miles, and didn't halt until 11:00 p.m.; then they pitched camp in the rain.

Pack-up was sounded at daylight on Thursday, April 6. The men realized the urgency of their movement because there was no time for breakfast, and later they weren't given any time for dinner. The Sixth Corps formed into three lines of battle that marched in parallel columns by the flank. They configured on the right and left of the road and pushed through the woods and fields, and after covering about eight miles, they arrived at the location they had started from in the morning.

They halted for a few minutes, but not long enough for the men to even make coffee. First Sergeant William Mauger explained the situation to his men. "Lee attempted to flee to Amelia Court House to find supplies and gain access to the Danville and Richmond Railroad, but Sheridan blocked that move yesterday. Now Lee has apparently turned to the southwest towards Rice Station for supplies, hoping to move south to link up with Johnston, but we've put them in a bind again.

"Up ahead you can hear what's going on. Humphrey's men slammed into Gordon's forces at 8:30 this morning. We're going to be facing Ewell's corps and a portion of Anderson's, who counterpunched and drove back our center. Our job is to halt this penetration, but we're going to have it rough because there is a deep swamp that we have to cross along Sayler's Creek .

"We're going to counterattack and effect a double envelopment of Ewell's command and trap them. I expect you to be unflinching in taking it to the enemy. The end is near, but they are still a very dangerous foe, especially since they are virtually trapped."

Mauger's prophecy proved correct. The badly outnumbered and nearly exhausted Confederates fought valiantly and with tremendous stoutheartedness in fierce hand-to-hand fighting. This action resulted in heavy casualties, although most of the enemy were engulfed and surrendered.

The enemy who surrendered included six generals: Richard S. Ewell, Joseph Kershaw, Custis Lee, Dudley Du Bose, Montgomery Corse, and Eppa Hunton, and one naval officer, Commander John Randolph Tucker. Richard H. Anderson, George Pickett, and Bushrod Johnson were able to escape.

Lee's losses were catastrophic: about one-third of the men who marched from Amelia Court House, or between 7,000 to 8,000 men, were captured, killed, or wounded. As Lee observed the survivors straggling down the road, he asked General William Mahone, "My God, has the army dissolved?"

The 49th Regiment losses were about 67 men; company A had ten wounded and one captured. Among the wounded were Lieutenant John B. Rodgers and popular First Sergeant William Mauger. The regiment was given the responsibility of guarding the large number of enemy prisoners during the night.

At about ten o'clock the next morning, they began to herd the prisoners down to Burkville Junction. A head count gave the regiment a total of 5,012 prisoners. With the captured generals leading the column down the road, the fifteen miles were covered in five hours. The prisoners were turned over to General Curtin who commanded the First Brigade, Second Division, Ninth Corps.

Once the company had been relieved of its prisoner guard duties, it camped in the rain. They could hear that fighting was still in progress; heavy artillery firing had been going on all day.

On the morning of Saturday, April 8, the company packed up and began marching to rejoin the Sixth Corps on the frontlines. They marched about eighteen miles and then halted at Farmville, a little town on the Lynchburg railroad. Throughout the day, they met large numbers of prisoners being escorted to the rear.

The company resumed its march the next morning, Palm Sunday, and marched about twenty miles to New Store where it set up camp for the night. Since they were out of rations, a squad from B Company went foraging and soon returned with ten head of cattle. A rumor spread through the camp that Grant and Lee had met in Wilmer McLean's house at Appomattox Court House, and that Lee had unconditionally surrendered the Army of Northern Virginia. It made sense to the men, because the front had gone quiet; the big guns were now silenced.

Later in the evening, enemy prisoners moving to the rear confirmed the rumor that Lee had surrendered. The boys from Pennsylvania spent a festive night in camp, barely able to comprehend that Lee had surrendered his army. One of the first actions they performed was to stand in unison and fire the loads out of their weapons.

Captain Wix called the company to order. "At ease, men. I just want to warn you that the war is still not over. Lee surrendered his Army of Northern Virginia, but not the whole Confederacy. There are still some dangerous Confederate armies in the field throughout the South. It looks like we're going to be heading south to help entrap Joe Johnston who is being harassed by Sherman in North Carolina.

"The Confederate cabinet, congress, president, and vice-president are still in existence. While the remnants of the Confederacy are fleeing for their lives and freedom, we must remain vigilant and continue to perform our duties until we are mustered out of the army.

"Relax and celebrate tonight, but remember, we are back to normal tasks and responsibilities tomorrow. In the morning, we will be marching to rejoin our brigade near Appomattox Court House and from there back to Burkville Junction."

During their short stay at Appomattox, the men were privileged to converse with members of the brigade who had been eyewitnesses to the surrender ceremony. Unfortunately, David and his company missed out in observing one of history's highlights.

The days immediately following Lee's surrender were filled with guarding and escorting prisoners and long days of marching in preparation for the move to head off Joe Johnston.

Good Friday, April 14, was a pleasant day for the 49th Regiment, but it began to rain that evening and continued into the next day. The rain dampened the camp and the spirits of the men who were looking forward to the next day, Easter Sunday. On Sunday morning, as most of the men prepared for the spiritual uplifting of an Easter Sunday church service, Captain Wix suddenly appeared in the center of camp, and A Company was called to attention and the captain somberly announced:

Men, I have the most horrible news to break to you. We just received dispatches from the War Department that the actor John Wilkes Booth slipped into the presidential box at Ford's Theater on Friday evening and fired a bullet into the back of the president's head. An attack was also carried out against Secretary of State Seward and his sons, Frederick and Augustus, by Lewis Powell.

The first dispatch stated that the president cannot live, and later we received a second message stating that the president expired at 7:22 a.m. yesterday, April 15. Secretary Seward's life probably was saved by the jaw splint that he was wearing as the result of a carriage accident. Augustus was injured and will recover, while Frederick is in critical condition.

Disbelief and outrage jolted the men of the 49th and the whole Union Army as they absorbed the shocking news. The president's death increased the bitterness that the soldiers already felt against the southerners.

George Diven reacted immediately. "I've seen men executed by firing squads and hanging, I've seen men torn apart by artillery fire, and I've read in detail about the hanging of John Brown, but I don't think any of those methods are gruesome enough for what should be done to the president's assassins. Something unique should be done to those fiends; they are no more than vandals or goons."

"The people involved in this dastardly deed have to be rounded up and executed. If Jeff Davis has had a hand in this, he should suffer the same fate. The South should pay dearly for these actions, no matter how desperate or insane these conspirators might be," echoed several of the men.

The entire company, the regiment, the corps, the whole Union army demanded revenge. It was good that the fighting had ended, because for a short period of time, the men just sat paralyzed, and then their anger and resentment began to build. If the army had been facing an enemy on this day, a bloodbath would have ensued.

Eventually, the mood changed, and the majority of the men attended church services. Although some of the preachers addressing the Union army spoke of revenge, most of them attempted to soothe the men, and were successful in doing so. It was a somber camp that night and for several days to come.

The next day the armies of the United States received General Orders No. 66, from Secretary of War Edwin Stanton, which officially announced the untimely and lamentable death of President Lincoln. The order also commanded that all military headquarters at all levels were to be draped in mourning for thirty days.

On Monday, maybe in retribution for the assassination, six Rebels were hung and ten shot for breaking their parole and tearing up the railroad between Petersburg and Burkville Station.

Back in Washington, President Lincoln's coffin lay in state in the East Room of the White House, and on Wednesday, April 19, his body was carried down Pennsylvania Avenue to the capitol. David Evans and A Company were reminded of the president's funeral by observing that all flags were at half-mast and all business was suspended throughout the army.

After several days of relative inactivity involving drills and dress parade, on Saturday, April 23, the Sixth Corps began marching in the direction of Danville, Virginia, to aid in heading off Johnston. Along the route, they encountered many deserters from Johnston's Rebel army who were on their way back home. About sunset on April 27, the corps marched through Danville and camped about one mile southeast of the town, where they heard the rumor that Johnston had surrendered.

While the Sixth was on the march, the new president, Andrew Johnson, and his cabinet rejected Sherman's original agreement with Johnston of April 17. Sherman then had to offer the Confederate general the same terms given to General Lee, and Johnston finally surrendered to Sherman at Bennett Place on April 26, the day before the Sixth arrived at Danville.

General Wright ordered the firing of a one-hundred-gun salute in honor of the surrender of the Rebel general and his army. The next day, the official communiqué announcing the terms of Johnston's surrender to Sherman arrived at Sixth Corps headquarters. Some of the boys toured Danville, but as usual, when time allowed, David soon organized a baseball game.

On Tuesday, May 2, the 119th Pennsylvania, the Second Rhode Island, and the 49th received orders to begin traveling towards Petersburg by train. They arrived at Burkville Junction once again, where they encamped for several days before moving on to Wellsville Station. Wellsville Station was home until May 17, and then the regiment marched through Petersburg and finally boarded a train for Richmond.

By Saturday, May 20, the 49th Regiment had marched in the rain to within three and one-half miles of Richmond where they set up camp. The next day was the day that David had envisioned for a lengthy period, the day that he would receive a pass to visit the Confederate Capitol.

Eight members of the company got passes at the same time and set off to visit historic sites of the embattled city or to attend church services in the city. David had written an agenda of the sites that he wanted to visit; some he had studied about as a student at the academy, and others he had read about in newspaper accounts during the war.

David was more knowledgeable about history than some of the boys, so he acted as a guide for the group. The city was alive with Union soldiers, especially provost soldiers who constantly demanded that passes be shown.

The beleaguered city showed the effects of four years of warfare; of course, it wasn't until the final days of the war that the majority of the damage occurred. On April 2, General Lee had advised Jefferson Davis that the Confederate government should evacuate the city, which was carried out quickly.

After evacuating the city, the Confederate government ordered the burning of warehouses and supplies in the area of Rocketts Landing, but the fires raged out of control. The demolition of Confederate gunboats on the James River further spread the inferno. Pandemonium ensued, a mob scene resulted, and a large portion of the city was burned. The next day federal troops under Major General Godfrey Weitzel entered the ruins of the city, and the mayor of Richmond, Joseph Mayo, delivered a message to the general: "The Army of the Confederate government having abandoned the city of Richmond, I respectfully request that you will take possession of it with organized force, to preserve order and protect women and children and property." The mayor surrendered the city at 8:15 a.m. on April 3.

The Union army occupied Petersburg and Richmond quickly, extinguished the fires, and restored order. On the morning of April 4, President Lincoln set off for Richmond where he certainly risked assassination. He mentioned to Admiral David Porter, "Thank God I have lived to see this. It seems to me that I have been dreaming a horrid dream for four years; now the nightmare is gone." As

Lincoln walked the streets of the city, he drew thousands of watchers. While the white members of the crowd remained silent, the black women, men, and children greeted him enthusiastically.

The first place David and his companions headed for was Tobacco Row. Tobacco Row was a collection of brick tobacco warehouses and cigarette factories adjacent to the James River and the Kanawha Canal. Many tobacco growers and shippers maintained facilities in this area. It wasn't that David and his group wanted to observe factories or warehouses; this was the site of the infamous Libby Prison and Castle Thunder.

As the most famous prison of the war, Libby Prison had been a source of repeated horrible nightmares for many of the men of the Union Army. Now here David and company were observing it.

The prison consisted of three tenement buildings located on the western half of a block bounded by Cary and Dock Streets at 20th Street.

It was estimated that more than 50,000 federal prisoners passed through these three buildings during the war. The cellars had been used as cells for spies, slaves under the sentence of death, and the most dangerous prisoners. Since April 3, the prison was being used to incarcerate former Confederates. As the boys peered through some cracks in the walls, doors, and windows, they could see the all-too-familiar Rebel uniforms on the men inside the cells.

Also on Carey Street was Thunder Castle, another infamous prison that gained notoriety for its brutal treatment of prisoners. It was reported that in 1863, the commandant of Thunder Castle, Captain George W. Alexander, underwent an investigation on charges of inhumanity, tyranny, harshness, and dishonesty, although the charges were later dropped.

The United States Army was now using Castle Thunder to incarcerate any of the enemy charged with war crimes. Even though David and the boys were attracted to these two prisons out of curiosity, they didn't spend much time there. They were more interested in viewing Capitol Square, located between Ninth and Governor Streets and Broad and Bank Streets, which surround the Virginia State Capitol. The Virginia State Capitol served as the seat of government of the Commonwealth of Virginia, and houses the oldest legislative body in the United States, the Virginia General Assembly, which has been convening there since October 1792.

Thomas Jefferson is credited with the architectural design of the capitol, which was modeled after the Maison Carrée at Nimes in southern France, an ancient Roman temple; thus, it is referred to as 'Jefferson's Temple of Democracy.' The capitol is situated on Shockoe Hill overlooking the falls of the James River. On May 21, 1861, Richmond was chosen as the permanent capital of the Confederacy, and the Virginia State Capitol then also served as the Capitol of the Confederacy.

At the center of Capitol Square is the bronze George Washington Equestrian Monument that was cast in Germany. This statue and the three lower-tier statues of Thomas Jefferson, George Mason, Patrick Henry, John Marshall, Andrew Lewis, and Thomas Nelson were unveiled on February 22, 1858.

Just two blocks north of the Virginia State Capitol at 1201 East Clay Street is the official residence of Virginia's governors, the Executive Mansion, occupied since 1813. This elegant, gray-stuccoed neoclassical mansion was constructed by John Brockenbrough, who was the president of the Bank of Virginia.

In August 1861, Jefferson Davis, along with his wife, Varina, and their children, moved into the house, which became known as the White House of the Confederacy until the Davis family fled Richmond in April. One major tragedy occurred while the Davis family occupied the White House. In April 1864, while five-year-old Joseph was playing on the porch, he fell fifteen feet to his death.

One site the men were somewhat apprehensive about visiting was Chimborazo Hospital, named for the hill on which it stands, while the hill itself was named after Mount Chimborazo in Ecuador. This was an extremely large medical facility, which opened on October 17, 1861, and eventually consisted of 120 buildings. Its normal occupancy was about 3,000.

This medical institution was almost self-sufficient because it contained its own soup house, bakery, soap factory, icehouse, farms, beef and goat herds, natural springs, and canal trading boat. At the beginning of the war, the patients were assigned to divisions that were named after the states of Virginia, Missouri, Tennessee, Maryland, and Kentucky, but later different names were used.

The hospital staff consisted of about forty-five medical personnel with Dr. James B. McCaw as surgeon-in-chief. It was estimated that the facility treated about 76,000 wounded during the war. When the city surrendered, General Weitzel issued a general permit for Dr. McCaw and his entire medical corps to be placed under federal protection. Dr. McCaw was enlisted in the general service of the United States Army so that he might order needed requisitions and medical supplies. It also was ordered that all wounded Confederate soldiers would continue to receive medical care in the hospital.

The Yankee visitors found it hard to comprehend the size and scope of this medical marvel. They felt somewhat guilty knowing that their actions on the battlefield created some of the misery and suffering which was being treated within the walls of Chimborazo Hospital.

Time was running out for the eight tourists, but David wanted to visit one last building, St. Paul's Episcopal Church, at 815 East Grace and Ninth Streets. "I realize it's Sunday, but why do you want to visit this particular church?" inquired Dave Peck.

"Interestingly, both Robert E. Lee and Jefferson Davis worshiped in this church," David replied without hesitation. "This church was the choice of the elite of Richmond before the war. But even more significant to me is that Davis was in the pews of this church at 11:00 a.m. on April 2 when he received Lee's urgent telegraph message about Petersburg and Richmond that stated, 'I think it is absolutely necessary that we should abandon our position tonight.'"

Dave Peck shook his head in agreement, "Yes, I think that's good enough reason for us to view this church."

After taking a quick look at St. Paul's, the eight weary, but better informed, Yankees returned to camp and one more night of sleeping in a tent.

CHAPTER 88
THE FIGHTING SIXTH CORPS IS REVIEWED IN RICHMOND

At five o'clock on the morning of Wednesday, May 24, 1865, the Sixth Corps broke camp beyond Manchester and marched across the pontoon bridge to Seventeenth Street in Richmond, where the corps formed in column by company. Following close order drill, they marched up Seventeenth Street to Broad Street and turned up Broad Street past the reviewing officer, General Henry W. Halleck. Halleck had served as general-in-chief from 1862 until he was replaced by Grant in March1864, but since then was the chief of staff serving as facilitator between Grant and the president. Commandant of the Sixth Corps Major General Wright and his staff also were part of the reviewing officers.

After passing General Halleck and his staff on the portico of the courthouse, the corps wheeled into Ninth Street, then up Cary Street onto Brook Avenue, whereupon they filed up the avenue utilizing route step with arms at will.

Along these streets, the Twentieth Corps was in line with the right, resting in front of the reviewing officer, and the left, reaching to Brook Avenue, a distance of nearly three miles. Along the parade route, the men of the Sixth recognized shattered flags of familiar commands, cheering furloughed and detached soldiers, and some favorite generals and other officers. The last company swept past the reviewing stand at 10:45 a.m.; it took two hours and fifty minutes to accomplish this grand review.

The curbs were lined with spectators made up of former Confederate soldiers, women of the city, and throngs of children. The men of the Sixth perceived no demonstrations of welcome from the former foes, who appeared sullen and probably attended only out of curiosity.

Sadly, the Sixth Corps only numbered about 19,000 rifles, with the normal strength being about 34,000 men. This corps had proven to be one of the best in the army; General Sheridan had described this unit to General Grant as "that noble legion of men who never yet failed their cause or leader in the hour of trial or danger."

Still ringing in their ears was the congratulatory order of General Meade in regards to the Sixth Corps: "I do not wish to make any invidious comparison between it and other commands of this army; they carried out with vigor and courage the parts assigned to them, but candor compels me to state that, in my opinion, the decisive movement of this campaign, which resulted in the capture of the army of Lee and the evacuation of Petersburg and Richmond, was the gallant and successful charge of the Sixth corps on the morning of April 2."

CHAPTER 89
DAVID AND HIS COMPANY RETURN HOME

The day after the grand review in Richmond, the 49th began marching north towards Pennsylvania and home. Most of the men were in a bad humor because of the hard marching; the air was full of oaths and swearing, although most of the men marched in silence. They could not believe that they were not returning north the same way they were brought south to Petersburg late last fall— by ship, or by train.

By Friday, June 2, they made camp on the banks of the Potomac at Hall's Hill, opposite Washington, where they engaged in normal camp duties. On June 6 the brigade escorted the 119th Pennsylvania to the Aqueduct Bridge on the Potomac River because they were being mustered out. The 119th gave three cheers for the 49th.

Thursday, June 8, was another big day for the 49th, for the division was to be reviewed by the president. At four o'clock in the morning, the division took position in column, according to number, and crossed the Long Bridge on the Potomac. The head of the column arrived at Capitol Hill at eight o'clock and moved forward an hour later.

At ten o'clock, the head of the column passed the reviewing stand with the new president, Andrew Johnson, and General Meade as the main reviewers. It was a sad note that the man who had led the nation and the army through four horrific years of war was absent from the viewing stand, but the nation, like the marching Forty-ninth, was moving on.

The day was stifling and as the division marched through Pennsylvania Avenue via Georgetown and back across the Potomac on the Aqueduct Bridge to camp, several of the exhausted men had to fall out of the ranks due to sunstroke.

Just about every day, a new regiment was mustered out and

sent home; it was just a matter of time until it was the 49th's turn. The military regimen continued with roll call, drills, dress parades, inspections, guard duty, fatigue parties, and mustering. The men spent their free time reading, writing, pitching quoits, playing baseball, swimming, fishing, picking huckleberries, and visiting other units. Some of the original members of the regiment visited the camping grounds they used back in 1861.

Finally, on the afternoon of Saturday, July 15, the regiment was mustered out of the service at four o'clock (although their muster-out rolls are dated July 21), and dress parade was held at sundown. At 4:00 a.m. the next morning, reveille was beaten, and the regiment formed into columns and began marching for the Long Bridge and the railroad station in Washington where the train pulled out at eleven o'clock.

The train arrived at Baltimore at five o'clock and remained in the station until ten o'clock, when they boarded another train for Harrisburg. The trip to Bridgeport across the Susquehanna River from Harrisburg took all night, and they arrived at 5:00 a.m. when they quickly marched across the bridge. The regiment smartly maneuvered down North Street and out to Camp Curtin. This was where it all started for the 49th back on September 21, 1861.

George Diven mused, "It's hard to believe our marches, trials, and tribulations are coming to an end. It gives us all great pleasure to return to the scene of our mustering-in, but I feel a great sadness for all the brave boys who marched with us who are now lying in southern battlefields."

"I was just reflecting on the same subject," said David Evans. "Those heroic men made a willing sacrifice, and their deaths were noble ones, making it possible that 'Old Glory' will once again wave over an undivided nation."

From Tuesday, July 18 through Thursday, July 20, the men were supposed to be in Camp Curtin but most visited the state capital. As usual, some ended up finding something to drink and wound up in trouble with the provost marshal. Late Thursday afternoon the men signed the payrolls in anticipation of receiving their pay the next day.

Friday was the final day that the young men from Juniata County would be members of the Army of the Potomac as elements of the Forty-Ninth Pennsylvania Volunteers. Their pay was allotted in the morning, and by noon they were marching to the train station for their final leg of the journey home. The locomotive was decked out in red-white-and-blue bunting, and the members of the regimental band who were headed for Altoona and westward played patriotic songs during the trip.

David Evans's excitement and anticipation increased as the train chugged across the Susquehanna River on the Rockville Bridge. Just about every town and whistle stop along the route had men who had served in different regiments of the Army of the Potomac. The train slowed and stopped to return them safely to their loved ones, who had been lining the track awaiting their arrival.

All the stop-and-go traffic slowed the train's progress tremendously, causing apprehension and fretfulness among the keyed-up returning heroes. When they began to pull out of the stop at the village of Tuscarora, the boys from the Tuscarora Valley were fixated on the small station at Mexico and the familiar sights of the Juniata River.

As the train approached the small bridge across the Tuscarora Creek, the men of Company A either went out on the landings between the cars or hung out the windows in their attempt to see the first signs of Perrysville. Quick, sincere goodbyes were conveyed to Martin Rowe and Anthony Rodgers of Reedsville, Henry Laub of Lewistown, and John Ferguson, Emanuel Culpetzer, and John Lepley of Milroy, who continued on the train to Lewistown. The men were astounded at the large crowd that awaited them on both sides of the tracks. Bedlam ensued as the train hissed and screeched to a halt. The soldiers leaped to the ground and ran pell-mell towards their friends and loved ones.

David Evans had no difficulty finding his family, and they hugged and kissed each other in a frenzy of emotion once they reached each other's arms. After about fifteen minutes of joyous welcome, the drums rolled for roll call and the men of Company A configured up into their routine formation.

James A. Wix, a hometown Perrysville boy, called the company to attention. Then former Corporal Joseph Rhine of East Waterford, who had been mustered out on May 17, appeared in front of the ranks. "Sir, request permission for myself and Andrew N. Smith, John A. Patterson, Robert H. Taylor, David Louden, George Bryner, James Bryner, and David Delany, all mustered-out members of the company, to rejoin the ranks and march with the company."

Captain Wix broke into a huge grin, and bellowed, "Request approved, Corporal. You and the men fall in." All members of the company cheered as the little group stood at attention.

First Sergeant William Mauger barked orders setting the company in motion across the tracks and onto North Street. A makeshift local band, the remnants of the Perrysville Coronet Band, wheeled into line in front of the company and led the way up the patriotically decorated street, which was lined with flag-waving, cheering spectators. When the procession arrived at Eighth Street, it executed a sharp left turn onto Market Street. Market Street was profusely decorated and crowded with enthusiastic on-lookers. The same was true of Main Street once the troops turned right onto Second Street for a block and then another right onto Main Street. The applause reached a crescendo when the marching columns passed through the entrance to the fairgrounds.

Most of the people lining the streets quickly strode to the fairgrounds for the grand finale to welcome home the heroes of A Company. The fairgrounds were gaily decorated, and row after row of tables and benches had been moved from private homes, schools, and churches to hold the abundance of all the foods in season for the banquet honoring the Tuscarora Valley's finest young men.

It took about ten minutes to seat everyone at the tables, and then County Commissioner Matthew Clark opened the ceremony with a few words of gratitude to the company members. He was followed by Reverend Samuel Milliken of the Lower Tuscarora Presbyterian Church, who blessed the food and praised the Lord for allowing these stalwart men to return home after fulfilling their duty of preserving the Union.

The banquet progressed amid a loud commotion of conversation and merriment. The war that these people had just experienced either on the home front or on the battlefield was pushed aside for about an hour. All they were concerned with was the present; the future could wait until tomorrow, and the past would be explored when the time was right.

In due time most of the food and drink was consumed, and the conversation died out as Captain Wharton stood and asked for the crowd's attention. "My friends, neighbors, and relatives, it is with joyous hearts that we have welcomed these young heroes back into our beautiful valley. No one needs to ask them what it means for them to come back home; just look at their faces, and after that scrumptious meal, look at their stomachs. I know only too well that most of them have not had a meal like this since they left home in the summer of 1861, or whenever their enlistment date might have been.

"It is now my pleasure to introduce to you one of our own hometown heroes, the leader of this band of conquerors, Captain James A. Wix, who joined the Forty-ninth Regiment on September 3, 1861, as a member of old I Company."

Captain Wix rose to his feet and paused briefly in front of the crowd before he began, "It is unnecessary for me to enumerate all the battles and campaigns that these stalwart men have participated in since we enlisted in September of 1861. This conquering contingent has accomplished the work set before them, having vindicated the integrity and honor of this nation's government and flag. I believe that history will do them the justice they deserve, because a grateful country will honor the living, appreciate and support the wounded and disabled, and sincerely mourn the dead. At this moment I would like to pay tribute to those comrades in arms who made the supreme sacrifice for this nation, especially those men from our company, Consolidated Company A."

Captain Wix nodded to the awaiting honor guard armed with rifles, and they quickly stepped to the front of the crowd in preparation for firing a salute to their fallen comrades.

"Unfortunately, I do not have a complete list of all those who fell on southern battlefields or were wounded and later fell victim to their wounds in hospitals. So please pardon me and correct me by adding their names once I have completed naming those that I am aware of. Most of my information comes from our muster-out roll of July 15, and it is not a complete record of all the men that served in our company."

Captain Wix produced a handwritten list from his jacket pocket and proceeded to read the names of those special heroes. "John H. Kreider, James Riden, Charles Rumbaugh, George W. Beaty, Jacob Kepperling, William Farris, Peter Miller, John Pollock, Samuel J. Weirick, George W. Wilson, Thomas McClelland, James G. Hurrell, Ben Engle, Franklin Peters, John Radican, Thomas Benjamin, Alfred Thompson, Andrew W. Smith, and John H. Enslow."

From out of the crowd a choked voice gasped, "Please add Oliver P. Zell, he died at Lancaster while on furlough."

Someone else yelled, "Gilbert McClain died in a hospital in Harrisburg."

Another man asked, "What about those that died while serving in Old Company I?"

Captain Wharton rose to aid Captain Wix. "Captain Wix does not have those names available, but we will endeavor to have a complete list compiled and published in the *Juniata Sentinel* as soon as possible."

Captain Wix continued, "We would be remiss if we did not mention the death of our Sixth Corps commandant, General Sedgwick and our commander-in-chief, President Abraham Lincoln." He then turned to the honor guard, whereupon Sergeant Mauger barked the orders for the guard to execute their firing duties, which they performed with utmost precision, and the shots reverberated throughout the valley.

Then Captain Wix delivered his closing remarks. "I want to thank you for the pleasure of serving with such patriotic, courageous, magnificent fighting men, who left your homes and families in the defense of our nation. You will be in my thoughts and memories forever as to your noble devotion to your country, and for all your patience and cheerfulness during all the privations and sacrifices you had to endure." With that, he turned and saluted the company, and the men smartly returned his salute.

Abram Milliken, from East Waterford, who had been discharged a month earlier but rejoined the company for today's celebration, yelled, "Three cheers for Captain Wix!" The company followed Milliken's suggestion with tremendous enthusiasm, and the cheers echoed through the valley just as the volleys had done a few minutes before.

Reverend David J. Beale of the Middle Tuscarora Presbyterian Church of East Waterford stepped to the podium for the final blessing. "Thanks be to the Almighty God for his blessing in granting us victory and peace. Let us earnestly pray for the strength and enlightenment to discharge our duties as citizens of this once again united country, as we have endeavored to discharge our duties as soldiers. May we enjoy peace on a permanent and enduring basis and never have to take up arms against our fellow countrymen again. Thanks be to God. Amen."

The crowd followed with an impassioned "Amen."

The celebration continued until after the sun went down behind the Herringbone Ridge and Shade Mountain. A huge bonfire erected in the center of the racetrack drew the crowd's attention. It appeared that no one wanted this day of commemoration and thanksgiving to end, but eventually the festive and celebratory throng began to break up and headed to their homes. Tentmates and good friends sought out each other for one last farewell, although most promised that once they had made the adjustment back to civilian life they wanted to have a reunion.

George Diven, Dave Peck, Abram Milliken, and David Evans decided to have a fishing expedition at Devil's Kitchen on the Tuscarora Creek two Fridays hence.

On the way up the valley, David was silent; he appeared to be enjoying seeing the valley in the moonlight. Finally, his father broke the silence. "David, we know you have been through a terrible time and have witnessed scenes from hell. We are never going to probe into your private thoughts about the war, but if you ever need to discuss anything, we will always be here for you."

"Thank you, Father, I don't know if I will ever be able to talk about what took place on those battlefields or what I observed in the hospitals, but I thank you for the kind offer."

CHAPTER 90
DAVID'S RETURN TO POST-WAR SHENANDOAH VALLEY

When David returned to the farm at Half Moon, he sent a message to Abbey that as soon as he could make arrangements he would come to see her. He wasn't sure that she would receive the letter because of the chaotic situation south of the Mason-Dixon, but it didn't matter, he was going to follow the letter in a few days.

At first, he planned to ride Tuscarora Chief southward, until he realized he would save time by traveling by rail, and it would be safer too, because the roads were filled with robbers, bushwhackers, and highwaymen. He decided to travel as lightly as possible, with very little baggage and money because he didn't want to become an easy robbery victim. On his way home from Washington, he had wisely invested in a brace of Navy Colt revolvers and two good holsters. He strapped them on his hips, feeling more like a gunfighter than a lovesick ex-soldier. The guns were well hidden by his jacket, so it wouldn't look as if he were advertising for a fight.

This trip was almost a reenactment of the trip that he and his cousin George Patterson had taken in October 1860. He left early Wednesday morning and at 2:00 a.m. the next morning, his train chugged into what was left of Winchester. Five years ago, he would have had a good soft bed in his Aunt Sarah's fine home, but she and her husband had moved to Carlisle soon after the first Battle of Bull Run and were reluctant to return.

Most of his fellow passengers looked like adventurers or businessmen, soon to be called carpetbaggers as they sought to take advantage of the plight of the vanquished and devastated inhabitants of the former Confederacy. Almost all of the passengers strolled en masse to the friendly confines of the Logan House for a late meal, drink, and a bed. Their movements were under military surveillance, because Winchester and the entire South was under an army of occupation.

David awakened at dawn, washed, dressed, and went downstairs for a hearty breakfast, but at a rather steep price because food was scarce in the valley and would be for quite some time. There were no horses or mules for hire; therefore, David began to hike the twenty-plus miles to the Volkner farm on the outlying area of Strasburg.

About a mile out of town, several military wagons overtook him. He must have had a Yankee look to him, because as the first wagon slid to a stop, a stout Irish first sergeant shouted at him. "Hop in, son, we're headed for Mt. Jackson."

"Thanks for the ride, sergeant. I'm headed for Strasburg," offered David.

"Hopefully you're not headed home to your Rebel folks," joked the sergeant.

"Nope, I'm headed to see my sweetheart on the banks of the Shenandoah. I'm going to ask her to marry me."

"You're not a Reb, are you?

"No indeed. I fought under Wright and Grant in the 49th Pennsylvania Volunteers."

"Good outfit, son, I fought beside you in the 5th Wisconsin. But why are you marrying a Rebel gal? Did you meet her when you were fighting in the valley?"

"No again. She was a student in central Pennsylvania before the war and is still waiting for me. Her family are Dunkards, complete pacifists. They don't believe in slavery or war, so they were nonparticipants."

The sergeant swept his hand in front of him, indicating the valley from horizon to horizon. "The people in this valley had it rough last winter, and for many it's not going to be much better this winter. Yep, from Winchester to Harrisonburg there isn't much left. It's hard to find a piece of fence, a crop, mule, horse, cow, pig, or chicken in the whole valley."

David shook his head in awe. "I know things were bleak when we pulled out of here at the beginning of last December. I haven't been in communication with Abbey since. I sure hope nothing happened to her or her family since then. From what I've seen so far there's nothing but extreme destitution in the whole valley."

When they reached Strasburg, David hopped off the wagon and thanked the sergeant for the ride. He walked down North Street until he came to the intersection of Sandy Hook Road and headed south. David smiled at what he observed; these good German farmers had somehow found seeds to plant crops this spring, and many of the farms were springing back to life. The road curved to the east, and it wasn't long until he could see the outer fields of the Volkner farm; they, too, were exhibiting an abundance of new crops.

David began to run once he came within a half-mile of the farmhouse. To his relief, all the buildings appeared unscathed, he hoped that was true of the residents as well. He noticed two males working in a field without the benefit of a horse or mule. Then on the porch, he recognized a familiar figure, and he called out her name.

The males in the field and the women on the porch all stopped and watched as David ran down their lane. Abbey dropped the pan she was holding and began running towards David, screaming his name as she ran. About twenty yards from the house, the two lovers leapt into each other's arms. Tears streamed down their cheeks, and they kissed each other almost violently. Abbey ended up on top of David, smothering him with succulent kisses, which David returned. They appeared to be suspended in time. Minutes passed before they realized they had an audience. Embarrassed, they composed themselves and allowed the rest of the family to join their jubilation.

After the evening meal, the Volkner family disappeared and allowed the lovers to occupy the formal sitting room by themselves. They spent the night in each other's arms, while they planned their future. He decided to stay for the next two weeks; during that period they hoped to have made all the plans for their fast-approaching wedding.

The two weeks flew by, with David helping in the fields part of the day, but mostly happily enveloped in Abbey's arms. Parting was difficult, but David knew he had to return to Juniata County to help prepare the livestock and gather the foodstuff for the wedding feast.

CHAPTER 91
THE WEDDING

Due to the scarcity of food in the former Confederacy in the fall of 1865, especially in Northern Virginia after Sheridan's handiwork the year before, the groom's family arranged for two wagonloads of food to be shipped to the Volkner farm from Juniata County in preparation for the fall wedding.

There were major fears and concerns about bushwhackers or highwaymen waylaying the over-laden wagons. The poverty-stricken sections of Maryland and Virginia just below the Potomac River were ripe for unlawful activities, and the wagons were full of food worth their weight in gold.

It was decided that a gun-toting guard would sit beside the driver in each wagon, with both a scattergun and a Henry lever action rifle at his disposal. David and six of his cousins and friends would ride along as escorts, each armed with a Henry rifle and a sidearm. It was thought that the firepower they possessed would serve as a major deterrent to any attempts to overtake the wagons and remove the foodstuff.

The wagons were filled with flour, salt, sides of bacon, cured hams, carrots, turnips, potatoes, canned peaches, canned pears, baskets of apples, several baskets of lettuce and cabbage, and several cages of turkeys and chickens. Four beef cattle and two milk cows were tethered to the wagons. Three huge hogs were butchered and their meat and by-products were sealed in barrels filled with a salt solution. Six piglets were caged and placed in one wagon. The piglets were not to be used as food but as breeding stock, just like several of the cattle and fowls.

The trip got underway on the first Monday of October, with the wagons plodding up the Tuscarora Valley via the Valley Road through the gap in the Tuscarora Mountain and into Path Valley. Path Valley led them into the valley drained by the Conococheague

Creek, which they basically followed to its mouth at the Potomac River. They crossed the Potomac at Williamsport, Maryland, and followed the river to Falling Waters where they picked up the road known earlier as the Great Wagon Road, but now the Valley Pike. Upon leaving the Potomac Valley, they were now in the lower Shenandoah Valley. They had crossed through the five valleys that had separated the young lovers since the outbreak of the war.

It took them six long days of hard travel to reach Strasburg, where they stayed for two days before returning to Juniata County to rest up for the wedding.

Having experienced this lengthy trip of nearly 150 miles, the young men decided to travel to Winchester by train instead when they returned to Virginia for the wedding. When they were returning through Winchester they made arrangements to rent what few horses and buggies were available for the trip from Winchester to Strasburg for the wedding.

David and Abbey decided to exchange the journals that they had kept during the war after the wedding. Then they could elaborate on their thoughts and perhaps read portions to each other. It was quite difficult for David to leave Abbey's arms, but she insisted that he return and spend his last several weeks on the Evans farm as a single man.

She encouraged him. "We spent almost four years apart; this will only be for about two weeks. Then we will be together for the rest of our lives. Please make your parents happy and spend these days with them."

"Of course, you're right; it seems that you are always right. I'll miss you terribly, but I guess both of us will be so busy the time will fly by. However, I will leave for Virginia the week before the wedding; there's much to be done here and I certainly can help.

"I'm really concerned that some bushwhackers will come along and try to relieve you of our food. I know that your family doesn't condone violence, but I hope they'll place a guard on the food at all times and will resist any attempts to take it away."

"Don't worry, some of Mother's relatives are arriving tomorrow, and they know how to handle guns. Some of them probably shot at you at one time or another. Come to think of it, several of my cousins from Berryville and Woodstock served under Mosby, so our defense will be in good hands."

Mrs. Volkner persuaded her husband to have Abbey and David married by the Presbyterian minister rather than in a Dunker ceremony. Abbey's parents had been married this way nearly twenty-four years earlier. Her thinking was that the young couple would undoubtedly follow in David's Presbyterian heritage, so they might as well begin life together as Presbyterians. Some members of the Volkner family would boycott the wedding. However, the majority of the family had undergone so many trials and tribulations the last four years and their faith had been tested so many times that they could tolerate one last breach of their doctrine and beliefs to see Abbey happy.

The circumstances would have been different if Abbey had chosen to be wed in the Dunker church, but since the ceremony was being performed at her parents' home, she could choose to have the Presbyterian minister perform the wedding. She knew that the Dunker leaders would disapprove of the marriage, and she would be shunned from future church activities.

At two o'clock on the twenty-ninth of October, the wedding took place with great beauty, grace, and elation on the porch of the Volkner farmhouse or mansion and its large front lawn. Luckily, the temperature hovered in the high sixties; therefore, there was no need for any fires in the farmhouse, and the large audience would not be burdened with heavy coats.

The porch was decorated beautifully. The window boxes were filled with ferns and clusters of magnificent chrysanthemums. Trailing over the porch's railings were streamers of ground pine interspersed with white mums. Bows of white satin ribbon caught with a knot of mums marked the sections of the lawn that were allotted for the seating of the couple's families.

The occasion was a memorable one, and an historical one as well. It assembled a contingency of men who at this time last year, and up until April of this year, were facing each other over the sights of gun barrel. Although David's friends and family had not been directly affected by the war, Abbey's circle of friends, family, and neighbors had felt the ravages of war firsthand. Many of them lost their businesses, barns, sheds, warehouses, and crops in the wake of Sheridan's scorched-earth campaign. In many cases, the Virginians had had their homes pillaged and robbed by both bush-whackers and the Union army.

Therefore, this wedding would be dramatically different from others that were performed since April 1861, for it marked a return to the hearty good fellowship of the days prior to the firing on Fort Sumter.

David McKisson, Abbey's piano teacher prior to her leaving for school in the Tuscarora Valley, began playing the piano in fine fashion about a quarter of an hour before the time set for the ceremony.

The four remarkably pretty bridesmaids, Abbey's two first cousins, and two neighbor girls whom she had known from child-hood, entered the porch from the left attired in matching violet dresses. At the same time, the same number of ushers, all from the Tuscarora Valley, entered from the left after performing their duties of seating all the guests. The bride, on the arm of her father, followed the bridesmaids. The groom and the best man, Julie's husband, Jonathan, followed the ushers from the left.

Abbey's fair, youthful beauty set off a chorus of murmurs of admiration and awe from the assemblage. Abbey had chosen to wear the dress her mother had worn for her own wedding nearly twenty-four years earlier. The dress had been altered slightly to accentuate Abbey's stunning figure. The dress embodied a three-tiered skirt of elegant soft white satin. It had a ruffled off-the-shoulder neckline, while the waist was accented with a bored waist cincher. The boned bodice closed with a center back lacing. She was breathtaking

Abbey carried an exquisite shower bouquet of roses and ferns, with the long beautiful strands caught with tiny bows of baby ribbon.

David and the rest of the males in the wedding party were dressed in black coats and pants, although they were not all of the same style and fashion. Most of them were of traditional pre-war vintage.

The wedding ceremony was conducted by Reverend Bruner, who acknowledged the impact of this ceremony:

As we are gathered here today in God's presence in this once again peaceful valley to celebrate the union in marriage of these fine young people, let us hope that this ceremony serves as an inauguration in the path towards reunification of our embattled nation as well.

This union should signify a new beginning, a sign that the strife that ended in April will soon be pushed into the dark pages of history and forgotten. The future of this nation rests on the shoulders, hopes, and dreams of outstanding young couples like those standing in front of us today.

Now let us bow our heads in prayer. We pray that the relationship of this young couple will embody love and integrity, shown through the relationship that Jesus has with God and human beings. Perhaps most of all, we affirm the forgiveness and grace offered by God which empowers us to love one another despite our imperfections and fallibility.

We hope and pray that this marriage may have the great blessing of God's grace and may reflect and connect this young couple with the beauty and love that is the essential core of life here on earth. Amen.

Remember that marriage is a gift that God has given to us for the well-being of the family, and it is also a civil contract between a couple.

When I think of love, I always reflect upon the thirteenth chapter of Corinthians, verses 4 to 8, which states:

Love is patient and kind,
Love is not jealous or boastful:
It is not arrogant or rude.
Love does not insist on its own way;
It is not irritable or resentful;

It does not rejoice at wrong,
But rejoices in the right.
Love bears all things,
Believes all things,
Hopes all things,
Endures all things.
Love never ends…

This reading was followed by the traditional Presbyterian wedding ceremony. When Pastor Bruner proclaimed Abbey and David man and wife, the couple engaged in a passionate kiss.

Midway through their embrace, a shrill, piercing Rebel yell shattered the peaceful stillness of the wedding. The ear-splitting shriek was followed by two more. The former Union soldiers in attendance reacted as though they were prepared to repulse an attack. The ex-Yankees had heard this Rebel battle yell too many times, and it was a sound that would create terror for the rest of their lives.

The three former Confederate soldiers responsible for the prank had a hearty laugh over the Yankees' reactions and gave the ex-bluebellies a full military salute. Joseph Stouffer, a former Mosby's Ranger and Abbey's cousin, said, "Sorry, Reverend, we just got carried away with the excitement of the moment and expressed our sentiments in the manner we had become used to the last four years."

Reverend Bruner smiled and waved to the three young men. "I agree with you, it is an exciting moment. Now if you don't mind, I'll conclude the ceremony with the final blessing.

The pastor blessed the couple and those in attendance, thus ending the impressive ceremony. The bride and groom exited down the aisle between the chairs on the lawn, and the wedding party followed them and enjoyed a plentiful meal on the southwest end of the lawn.

CHAPTER 92
PLANS OF THE NEWLYWEDS

At the end of the wedding dinner, David, with Abbey holding onto his left arm, addressed their assemblage. "Abbey and I have a rather special message for you; perhaps for some of you it will come as quite a shock. The new Mrs. Evans and I would like to make an announcement ending the speculation regarding our plans.

"Ever since I was wounded just a short distance from where I now stand, and Abbey and her friends and family sheltered me and nursed me back to health so that I could be transported to the hospital in Winchester, we began to plan for our future.

"While spending several weeks at the Sheridan Military Hospital at Shawnee Springs in Winchester, in final recuperation of my wounds, it became abundantly clear to me that God was calling me to enter a field of endeavor not to heal souls, but to heal bodies. I was appalled at the type of treatment, or in many cases the lack of treatment, of the wounded of both armies that surrounded me in Winchester. There is no need for me to go into detail about the horrible scenes I witnessed at the hospital, but it was then and there that I decided that if I survived the carnage of war, I would devote my life to aiding the sick and wounded.

"I decided to embark upon the long journey to become a physician. While in the hospital I became acquainted with a young man from Ohio, and after talking with him several times, we realized that we both entertained the same dream, that of becoming a doctor. My new friend from Ohio and I decided to attend the same medical school.

"Since I am from Pennsylvania, the logical choice would have been one of the outstanding medical schools in Philadelphia. That would mean that Abbey would be transferred to the North where the wounds and prejudice of the recently ended conflict would undoubtedly be held against her, and no matter what she would do or say, a minority would probably still consider her a Rebel.

"On the other hand, if I were to attend medical school at the University of Virginia or some other fine southern school, I would probably face similar prejudice as a "damn Yankee." Therefore, we have decided to move West in the spring to Keokuk, Iowa, where I will enroll in the College of Physicians and Surgeons of the University of Iowa located there. The school is located in a seven-story building at the corner of Third and Palaen Streets in Keokuk.

"My Ohio friend and I have thoroughly investigated this medical institution, and it appears to have a fine reputation for training medical personal to serve in the rural communities of the Midwest. The school was originally known as the Medical School of the Upper Mississippi and it was located in Davenport, Iowa, but it relocated to Keokuk in 1850.

"So in the spring, Abbey and I will be loading up our few belongings and heading west to the western shore of the Mississippi River at the mouth of the Des Moines River. We will be spending three or four years in that vicinity until I receive my medical training; then I'll probably practice medicine in one of the frontier towns that desperately need a doctor."

Most of the audience members looked at each other in disbelief; no one had been informed of these plans prior to this announcement. It took several moments until people finally reacted. Both sets of parents appeared in shock at first, but they soon recovered, and everyone began to congratulate the newlyweds on their bold plans.

David once more stood in front of the audience. "Abbey and I didn't mean to damper the spirits of this party. Please refrain from questioning us about our plans, and let's just have fun. Tomorrow, before we leave for a few days of solitude, we will sit in the parlor and outline our plans in more detail and answer any questions you might have."

"What's all this about you moving to Iowa and going to medical school?" inquired David's father the morning after the wedding, while members of both families listened in great anticipation.

"Abbey and I knew that most of you would not be happy with

our plans. Please allow us to give you some information about our plans. Keokuk, Iowa, is located at the confluence of Des Moines and Mississippi Rivers. The small city received its name from a distinguished chief of the Sacs and Foxes, Keokuk. Since steamboats could not travel beyond the Des Moines rapids on the Mississippi River, Keokuk served as a gateway for nineteenth- century travels heading north and west, and thus gained some prominence at first."

Abbey's mother interrupted, "But what kind of credentials does this school have? Wouldn't you receive a better education at one of the schools in Philadelphia or some other eastern school? I just don't know about you investing your time and money in something that won't offer anything for your future."

"I've investigated the background of the school, and I'm satisfied I will receive a solid medical education that will enable me to practice medicine on the frontier, just as Abbey and I plan," replied David. "One of the school's most prominent surgeons is Dr. John F. Sanford. He's a graduate of the University of Pennsylvania, and it was due to his efforts that the Iowa State Medical Society was organized in June of 1850.

"Another key physician is Dr. Justin F. Simonds, who graduated from Albany Medical School in New York. Dr. Simonds gained an outstanding reputation for his success in treating smallpox on the Iowa frontier prior to this disastrous war. When smallpox broke out in Memphis, Tennessee, during the war, Dr. Simonds successfully combatted the outbreak of this plague and returned to Iowa when hostilities ceased.

"The admission requirements aren't as demanding as they would be for the more established eastern schools. Tuscarora Academy has given me an outstanding academic background so that I would expect to maintain a good academic standing at the school.

"I have to complete three years of medical education, with at least one year of practical instruction by an active practitioner and two years of academic courses. The school's standard curriculum consists of lectures on the theory and practice of medicine, midwifery, surgery, and the diseases of children and women, anatomy, chemistry, and physiology.

"In addition I'll be required to take courses on medical jurisprudence, and dentistry and receive hands-on experience on chemical analysis, human dissection, use of microscopes, and clinical experience in a hospital or outpatient clinic.

"The yearly session of school lasts four months, from late October to early March, at a cost of $80. During my second year, I will be required to write a thesis, and at the end of the third year, I will take an oral examination administered by my professors. The fee for the exam is either one-quarter or one-third of the annual tuition.

"Since the school term doesn't last the full calendar year, I hope to find a job either teaching or helping a local physician. If that doesn't materialize, I can always work as a farm laborer or as a laborer down on the docks. Abbey can always tutor young girls or give music lessons. Somehow, we will survive the next three years until I finish medical school; then we plan to practice in some small frontier town."

"Your mother and I are disappointed that you won't be living in the vicinity of the Tuscarora Valley, but we realize that you have to live your own life," said Mr. Evans. "If you feel that practicing medicine on the frontier is your calling, then all I can say is 'go do it.'"

"You have our blessing as well," added Mr. Volkner. "I always wanted to see what was on the other side of the Alleghenies, so I'll be one of your first visitors."

Abbey then spoke up. "Between now and the spring, we will alternate between living in the Shenandoah and the Tuscarora Valleys, thus traveling across five valleys: the Shenandoah, Potomac, Conococheague, Path, and Tuscarora. These valleys have separated us long enough, and will no longer do so. We want to spend as much time as possible with each family before we travel westward."

Abbey and David smiled at each other, and David quietly said, "In April we will board the train in Perrysville and head west through Pittsburgh and Chicago to Iowa to start our lives together. We hope both sets of parents will come to visit us often while I'm in school and after I complete my studies. Once I finish school and establish a practice somewhere on the frontier, we promise to make annual railroad trips back east."

BIBLIOGRAPHY

Bates, Samuel P. *History of Pennsylvania Volunteers, 1861-1865; Prepared In Compliance With Acts Of The Legislature. Vol. 1.* Harrisburg: B. Singerly, State Printer. 1869.

Brown, Kent Masterson. "Trains of Misery: Lee's Retreat From Gettysburg," *Virginia Country's Civil War,* 1:40-42, 1983.

Catton, Bruce. *The Army of the Potomac: A Stillness At Appomattox.* Garden City, New York: Doubleday & Company, 1953.

History of Port Royal and Vicinity and Sesqui-Centennial Celebration July 24-29, 1962. Port Royal, PA.: Times Print, 1962.

History of That Part of the Susquehanna and Juniata Valleys Embraced in the Counties of Mifflin, Juniata, Perry, Union, and Snyder in the Commonwealth of Pennsylvania, Vol. I. Philadelphia: Everts, Peck and Richards, 1886; reprint, Mt. Vernon, IN, Windmill Publications, Inc. 1996.

Hoke, Joseph. *The Great Invasion or General Lee in Pennsylvania.* Dayton, OH: W .J. Shuey Publisher, 1887.

Hower, Jane Short. "A Ride That Turned the Tide of the Civil War." *Pennsylvania,* Vol. 19, No. 2, 26-27.

Kirsch, George B. *Baseball In Blue and Gray.* Princeton, NJ: Princeton University Press, 2003.

Stackpole, Edward J. *Sheridan In The Shenandoah: Jubal Early's Nemesis.* New York: Bonanza Books, 1961.

Switala, William J. *Underground Railroad in Pennsylvania*. Mechanicsburg, PA: Stackpole Books, 2001.

Taylor, Wayne E. *Hope Rekindled*. Tarentum, PA: Word Association Publishers, 2007.

Westbrook, Robert S. *History Of The 49th Pennsylvania Volunteers*. Altoona, PA: 1898.

Wert, Jeffery D. *Mosby's Rangers*. New York: A Touchstone Book by Simon and Schuster, 1990.

Wert, Miriam Taylor. *People, Places & Passages of Tuscarora Valley and Other Parts of Juniata County*. Port Royal, PA: 1994.

Winik, Jan. *April 1865: The Month That Saved America*. New York: Harper Collins Publishers, 2001.

HERTZLER'S STORE - ST. TAMMANY'S TOWN
(OLD PORT) ESTABLISHED 1838

PERRYSVILLE
NOW PORT ROYAL

JUNIATA COUNTY FAIR GROUND

PERRYSVILLE PENNSYLVANIA RAILROAD STATION
(COURTESY OF DR. TODD TAYLOR)

JUNIATA COUNTY COURTHOUSE
1833-1873

TRAIN STATION AT STRASBURG, VA

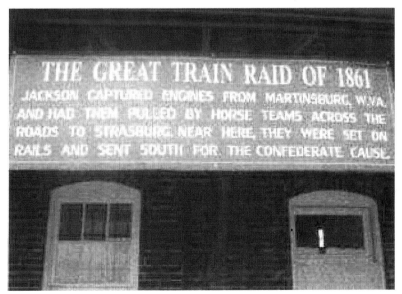

THE GREAT TRAIN RAID OF 1861
JACKSON CAPTURED ENGINES FROM MARTINSBURG, W.VA.
AND HAD THEM PULLED BY HORSE TEAMS ACROSS THE
ROADS TO STRASBURG NEAR HERE, THEY WERE SET ON
RAILS AND SENT SOUTH FOR THE CONFEDERATE CAUSE.

SIGN OF THE GREAT TRAIN RAID OF 1861

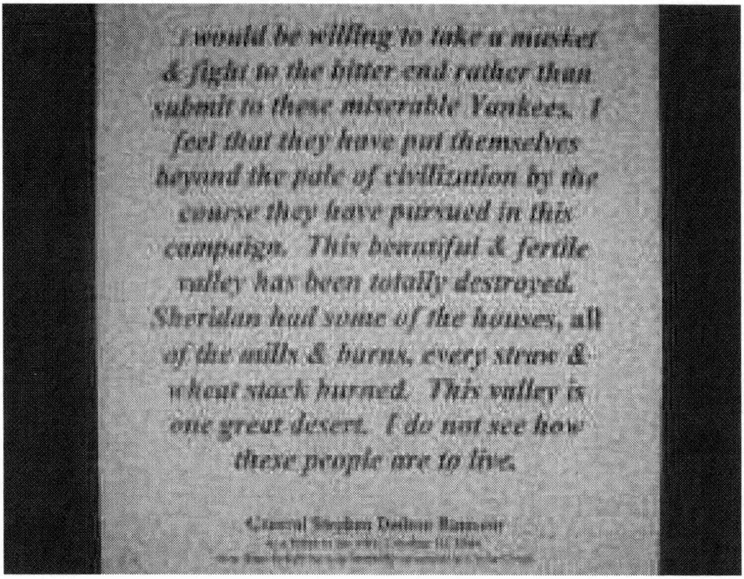

GENERAL RAMSEUR'S STATEMENT

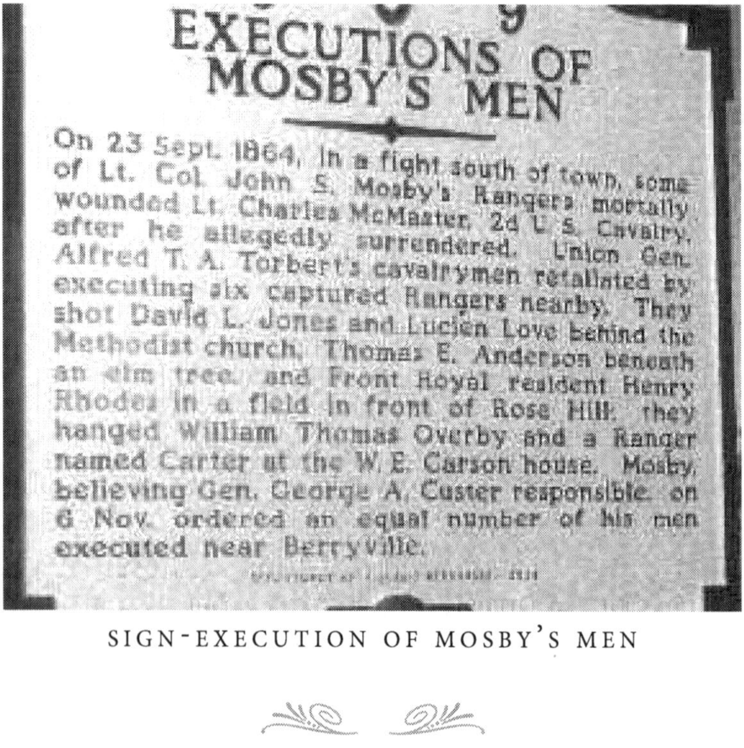

SIGN-EXECUTION OF MOSBY'S MEN

VOLUNTEER ENLISTMENT PAPERS OF JONATHAN (PECKARD)
PACKARD (COURTESY OF JOSHUAL TAYLOR PACKARD

MUSTER PAPERS OF JONATHAN (PECKARD) PACKARD
(COURTESY OF JOSHUA TAYLOR PACKARD)

WA